PRAISE FOR
FOOTSTEPS TO FOREVER

"This is a tough, suspenseful story set in the behind-the-scenes arena of covert operations as the U.S. prepares to enter WW2. Full of thrills and tight situations, Baty writes with skill and expert knowledge about two young American officers, a man and woman, who are sent to rescue an ailing physicist trapped in occupied Norway, where heavy water, an essential ingredient for the atomic bomb, is being secretly prepared. The two fall in love, and their hair-raising exploits keep the final outcome in doubt to the end. Baty brings in real characters, such as Winston Churchill, Roosevelt, and George Marshall, adding further authenticity to the tale. A must-read for WW2 buffs and all those who love a gripping story."

--Francis Roe, MD
author of Doctors and
Doctors' Wives and other novels

"If you are interested in tragedy, love, and personal bravery, spread across historically accurate events of World War II, this is your book. The author has woven the lives of victors and vanquished into a complex story of conflicted emotions, duty, and reconciliation. The breadth and depth of Sam Baty's Air Force career make him a well qualified and capable story teller. His plot involves Presidents, Prime Ministers, Nobel Prize physicists, back room handshakes, and unparalleled bravery in carrying out those agreements. From the 1941 raid on a German heavy water plant in Norway to the final battles in the Pacific, this story rings with human truth and individual struggles. FOOTSTEPS TO FOREVER is a compelling tale and a wonderful reading experience for students of history and human relationships."

--Donn A. Byrnes
author of
BLACKBIRD RISING –
Birth of an Aviation Legend,
IR SUPERIORITY
BLUE – The F-15 Story

"In "Footsteps," Sam Baty has meticulously crafted a taut and suspenseful thriller. Amid the churning maelstrom of global conflict, his finely-honed characters struggle through war, love and betrayal to ultimately find salvation and heroism."

--Robert Woltman
poet, non-fiction writer and critic

"Baty's thriller is as expansive as the global war that it takes as its subject. It reminds us that the Second World War was an immense political and personal drama. *Footsteps to Forever* is a story of courage and loss. The author's attention to detail and passion for the era comes through on every page."

--Scott C. Zeman
Associate Professor of
History at New Mexico Tech

"Through varied military assignments, Baty's intriguing characters in the romantic adventure Footsteps to Forever cleverly intertwine the European and Pacific theaters of World War II. His American heroine, through courage and intelligence, successfully obtains vital information behind enemy lines. The dangerous undertakings in the novel will trigger nostalgia in those who lived during this period, or excite curiosity in those who were born later."

-- Nancy R. Bartlit
author of Silent Voices of WWII

"Exciting World War II reading that addresses Norway and its strategic role to full effect."

--Martha Otte
Festival Director, Tromsø International Film Festival

FOOTSTEPS TO FOREVER

by
R. Samuel Baty

iUniverse, Inc.
New York   Bloomington

Footsteps to Forever

iUniverse books may be ordered through booksellers or by contacting:

iUniverse
1663 Liberty Drive
Bloomington, IN 47403
www.iuniverse.com
1-800-Authors (1-800-288-4677)

ISBN: 978-0-595-49640-2 (pbk)
ISBN: 978-0-595-49376-0 (cloth)
ISBN: 978-0-595-61188-1 (ebk)

Printed in the United States of America

Dedicated to my wonderful wife, Linda
(My Jennifer)

We come into this world without knowledge and without expectations. Soon, we begin to change. The human experience fills us with needs, desires, and passions. The most fortunate among us find great adventure and great love, while the less fortunate do not. Regardless of the path we take through life, we are all headed to the inevitable *forever*.

Prologue

Lieutenants Jonathon "Dude" Partude and Jennifer Haraldsson must make the decision of a lifetime. Germany has declared war on the United States, and President Roosevelt's prized physicist—who was sent to Norway to spy on the Germans' progress in developing atomic weapons—is now behind enemy lines.

Army Chief of Staff George Marshall selects Dude and Jennifer as the potential rescuers of the physicist. The two are excellent skiers and fluent in Norwegian. *If anyone can get into Norway in clandestine fashion and rescue the scientist,* General Marshall surmises, *it is these two.* The physicist, Professor James Flannigan, is elderly, so Jennifer's nursing background is an added benefit.

Marshall tells the young lieutenants that the mission is voluntary, since it is fraught with danger. He gives them one emotionally charged night to decide. Their decision is monumental, and its impact stretches to the end of World War II and beyond.

Part I

1

The Beginning

IT WAS A crisp October afternoon in 1941, and President Franklin Delano Roosevelt peered out an Oval Office window at the vivid red, orange, and yellow leaves dropping onto the White House lawn. *How nice it would be if the whole world could stop for a moment and simply admire the beauty that is all around,* he thought. Sighing, the president realized that this would be impossible. War was raging in just about every corner of the world. While the United States was not in the war—at least not yet—1941, he feared, would be remembered as history's bloodiest year.

For relaxation, the president was listening to the Sunday football game between the Washington Redskins and the New York Giants. It was halftime, and the Redskins were winning. The president, a New Yorker, was rooting for the Giants. But he'd become acquainted with Sammy Baugh, the Redskin quarterback. Baugh, a tall, lanky Texan, could throw the football with amazing speed and uncanny accuracy. The president respected Baugh's mastery of modern football and thought it wouldn't be so bad if the Redskins won.

As the third quarter was about to start, Harry Hopkins, the president's closest adviser, entered the room. Hopkins, tall and rather frail-looking, had a history of digestive ailments, but his stamina was second to none.

Hopkins stood in front of the president's desk. "You wanted to see me, Mr. President?"

Turning around in his wheelchair, the president smiled warmly at the man who would do almost anything for him. "Harry, always a pleasure to see you! Please have a seat." Hopkins sank into one of the two chairs facing FDR's big mahogany desk.

The president turned down the radio and maneuvered his wheelchair around the desk to get closer. Putting a Camel in his cigarette holder, the president lamented, "Harry, how did the world get in such a mess? You'd think that the human race would move forward. Instead, we seem determined to kill everybody off."

"I know, Mr. President. Part of the problem, I believe, is that very poor decisions were made after World War I. Representatives of powerful countries made self-serving decisions that allowed people like Hitler to come into power. Now we all have to pay for it."

"Well said, as always. However, it's Sunday afternoon. You have other things to do, so I'll get right to the point."

The president took a moment to light his cigarette. "I wanted to talk to you about this business of the Germans developing atomic weapons. That letter from Albert Einstein that came in a while back, saying a single bomb might be able to destroy a whole city, also said that the Germans are actively working on such a device."

"I remember the letter."

"As you know, I have decided that *we* should make some of those terrible things. But we must keep track of German progress as well. We can't allow them to develop such a weapon first!"

"I couldn't agree more, Mr. President."

"Any ideas on how we can find out what they're up to?"

"Yes, sir. Based on a briefing I recently heard, success for the Germans depends on how much 'heavy water'—deuterium replacing normal hydrogen—they can import from Norway. My recommendation is that we send someone to Norway who can secretly monitor their heavy water production. If they seem to be making enough of the stuff for an atomic weapon, the plant should be destroyed. Of course, it would have to be destroyed by the Norwegians, or perhaps the British, since we are not at war with Germany—at least not yet."

After thinking for a moment, the president replied, "Your input is right on the nose, Harry. I'll get Vannevar Bush up here. He'll know whom to send." Smiling, the president added, "Enjoy the rest of the day, whatever is left of it." He then wheeled himself back to the radio and turned up the volume, just as Sammy Baugh was completing his third touchdown pass of the game. The pass went to Dick Todd, the Redskins' star halfback.

Hopkins stood and left the office.

The next day, FDR met Vannevar Bush, his director of the Office of Scientific Research and Development. When Bush arrived, the president was just finishing a lobster lunch. There were lobster shells all over his desk, as well as on the floor, and a spatter of butter on some papers spread out on his desktop.

The president smiled and said, "Hello, Vannie. So good to see you. Please have a seat." He swept the lobster shells to the side and readjusted some of the many trinkets on his desk, including several of the large number of donkeys and—*no show of favoritism here!*—an approximately equal number of elephants.

"Vannie, you and I haven't spoken about the possibility of someone other than our own people making an atomic bomb, but I guess it is high time that we did."

"Yes, sir, we have good people such as Fermi and Szilárd working on it, but Germany has good people, too. Heisenberg, for example, is top-notch."

The president nodded. "Hopefully, we or the British can develop it first. I'm sure you know the British have started a classified project, called 'tube alloys,' to create an atomic bomb. Eventually, I suppose, we and the Brits will pool our efforts. But for now, they have their hands full with more immediate problems."

The president puffed on a cigarette and continued, "Hopkins thinks we should send someone to Norway who is highly qualified to spy on the Germans' production of heavy water. My understanding is that their success will depend on getting adequate supplies of it. What I need from you, Vannie, is to tell me who we need to send to Norway to monitor their heavy water production. I believe that a competent scientist would be best."

"Mr. President, I would like to ponder this matter for a little while. I think I know the man for you, but I want to make absolutely sure. Would it be all right if I got back to you tomorrow morning?"

"That would be fine, but time is of the essence. We don't want the Nazis to be able to blow us to smithereens."

Professor Bush bade the president farewell and hurried out of the White House. He had several candidates in mind for the Norway task, but first he wanted to call his good friend, James B. Conant, president of Harvard University.

When he reached Conant, he got right to the point. "Jim, I can only talk to you in general terms, but I think you are aware of certain Norwegian activities these days."

"Yes, I certainly am."

"Do you think James Flannigan would be the right man to make an assessment?"

"Yes, I do. I can't think of anyone who would be as good."

"Thank you very much, Jim. You've been a big help. Please give my love to your family."

"And mine to yours."

Bush smiled and felt very much relieved. In his own mind he'd kept coming back to Flannigan, an outstanding physicist at Princeton who had won the Nobel Prize for his research on subatomic particles. Flannigan had done some of that research in Norway. Perhaps most importantly, he was a man of impeccable character.

The next morning when Bush was again ushered into the Oval Office, the president was studying a document marked "Top Secret." When he finally looked up, he asked, "You have a name for me?"

"Sir, I think that we should send James Flannigan to Norway. James has spent time there, working with a Professor Jungstad. James is an outstanding physicist. Plus, he speaks Norwegian and knows the country."

"Is that Flannigan, the Nobel Laureate?"

"Yes."

The president broke into a broad smile. "Vannie, I think you have selected the perfect man for the job. Congratulations."

"Thank you, Mr. President. I appreciate your very kind words."

"Ordinarily, I would let you make the contact. However, I want to make sure that he goes, so I will invite him to the White House."

The president paused. "Besides," he added with a wink and a wicked little grin, "I've always wanted to match wits with a Nobel Laureate."

The president rang for his aide, Pa Watson. "Pa, get this fellow Flannigan up here. We have an interesting journey to propose to him. Vannie can give you all the information you need to contact him."

"I'll get right on it, sir."

As Bush and Watson exited the Oval Office, FDR turned his attention back to the top secret document he still held in his hand.

2

The President and the Professor

A T 5 P.M. on October 21, Professor James Flannigan was escorted into the president's favorite room, his private study on the second floor of the White House. Here, FDR conducted a great deal of the business of the presidency. He also used the cozy little room to rest and relax—reading, playing poker with some of his close friends, and working on his beloved stamp collection.

Flannigan felt himself honored to be asked to meet with one of the most powerful men in the world. The professor was a very unassuming man, known for his modesty. In technical circles, he was noted for sharing the philosophy of Sir Isaac Newton, "If I have seen farther than others, it is because I have stood on the shoulders of giants." Flannigan was certainly not hesitant to give credit where credit was due.

While he waited for the president to arrive, he glanced at the titles of the books lining the shelves and piled on the corner of the president's small desk. Remembering that FDR had been Assistant Secretary of the Navy during World War I, Flannigan was not surprised to see a book titled *The Old Navy and the New*. He also saw one with dog-eared pages titled *The Papers of John David Long*. Obviously, the president had referred to it often. But who was Long? *Ah, yes!* He'd been Secretary of the Navy at the end of the nineteenth century. No wonder the president had referred to it often.

The books looked very interesting, and the professor wished he had time to read some of them. "Hello, James," the president said, wheeling briskly into the room with an aide at his side. "It's all right if I call you James, isn't it?"

"Why certainly, Mr. President."

"Would you like one of my famous martinis, James?"

"Mr. President, that's the best offer I've had all day!"

FDR motioned for the aide to bring in his martini fixings. Soon, the president was putting the drinks together: a hint of vermouth, a fine grade of gin, and two chilled, plump green olives on a toothpick.

"James, I propose a toast to the United States."

"Hear! Hear!" They each took a sip. "Mr. President, this is the best martini that I've ever had!"

The famous smile spread over the president's face.

It didn't take them long to discover they had a common interest in stamp collecting. The president pulled out his albums, and Flannigan noted FDR had some very rare stamps. The professor was amazed at how much time and care Roosevelt must have put into assembling the albums and the stamp displays.

"You're obviously devoted to this hobby," he said.

"It's my favorite pastime," the president replied. "But let me tell you about some of my other off-duty interests."

The books in his study, he said, were only a small part of his 14,000-volume library, which included many rare bibliographic treasures. He'd amassed a vast coin collection and accumulated thousands of naval paintings. The mounted birds evident in substantial numbers around the room had been collected over a lifetime. Especially pleasing to the president were his splendid models of sailing ships—they gave the small room a nautical flavor. FDR related to Flannigan the detailed histories of each of these ships.

"Mr. President, you are truly amazing. I had no idea of the breadth and depth of your interests."

"James," the president said. "I find that I like your company! Would you like another martini?" After mixing two more, the president got down to business.

"I need you to take on a very important mission," he said. "Vannevar Bush tells me you already know of the Germans' interest in heavy water. You know that if they produce enough of it, they might be able to develop an atomic weapon. We believe it may become necessary to disrupt that production."

"I completely agree," Flannigan said. "I will help in any way I can. I have a wife and children and grandchildren to protect."

"James, I want you to go to Norway on some scientific pretext that will allow you to monitor heavy water production there. The Germans must not know you are there for that purpose. They must not know that you are there at all."

"Mr. President, when do you want me to leave?"

The famous smile once again crossed the president's face. "James, you are a true American, and I want to share one more secret with you: how to carve roast beef! Let's go to dinner."

On their way to the executive dining room, the president stopped at Mrs. Roosevelt's sitting room and asked her to join them. Mrs. Roosevelt was sitting at her desk answering letters from the voluminous pile of daily mail. She stood and shook Flannigan's hand. "I'm so happy to meet you, Professor Flannigan. I've heard so much about you."

"The pleasure is all mine, Mrs. Roosevelt, but please call me James."

Mrs. Roosevelt laughed. "James, you have saved me from writer's cramp. I shall forever be grateful."

When they reached the dining room, Flannigan met the evening's other guests in what FDR described as "a small, intimate group" he'd invited. "I hope you'll feel right at home with my selection," the president said.

The other guests were Crown Princess Märtha of Norway, Harry Hopkins, and Harry's eight-year-old daughter, Diana. Märtha and members of her royal family had fled Norway when Germany invaded in April 1940. The king and crown prince went to London, but Märtha and her three children came to America at the invitation of President Roosevelt, so they would not be subject to the nightly bombings. Märtha rented an estate in Maryland, but she was a regular guest at the White House.

After introductions were completed, the six sat down at the table. *An impressive group*, Flannigan thought.

"I invited James here tonight," the president said, "because I heard that he was in town, and I had never met a Nobel Laureate in physics. So I jumped at the opportunity!" The slight smirk on Hopkins' face revealed that he knew otherwise.

"Professor," Märtha added, "You probably don't remember me, but I was at the Oslo ceremony when you received your Nobel Prize."

"I most certainly do remember the beautiful teenage girl with the blonde hair. I feared just the opposite—that you wouldn't remember me!" The president beamed, as his guests were hitting it off well.

Turning to Hopkins, the professor said, "Harry, there is something awfully familiar about you. But I can't put my finger on it."

"You do have a good memory, Professor. I took your freshmen physics class back when we both had full heads of hair!"

"Now I remember! You were the one who was always interrupting me with questions."

"And he hasn't quit asking questions since," FDR said. "That's why he is so valuable to me."

Food was brought in, and dinner was served. Roast beef, mashed potatoes and gravy, peas, and piping hot biscuits. Suddenly, out of the corner of his eye, Flannigan saw a pea landing on the president's vest. He heard Diana, the young guest, giggle. She had used her knife to flip a pea at the president!

"Why, Diana," the president said. "How rude of me! I have ignored you. And now you have been kind enough to pass me some food." He picked up the pea and ate it. "Very tasty," he said. The little girl giggled again

During dinner, the president and Mrs. Roosevelt were the perfect host and hostess. The conversation was light; however, it eventually got around to the world situation.

"I am, of course, very concerned, since we have four sons." Mrs. Roosevelt said, "And all are of military age."

Hopkins said that his two sons were also likely to be in uniform.

"My son, James Jr., has registered for the draft, but I hope that he won't have to go," Flannigan said. "Here's an idea, Mr. President. Why don't we old men fight the wars so that the young ones can stay at home?"

Smiling broadly, the president responded, "That is an excellent suggestion, James. However, I would have to clear it with General Marshall first!" Everyone laughed, and the mood lightened again. But not for long.

"I told Congress I expect it to appropriate enough money to add a half million more men to the army, build many more tanks and ships, and quickly convert or expand the nation's industrial capacity to the point where we can produce fifty thousand planes a year," the president said as apple pie and ice cream was served. "By God, for the first time, I believe they actually listened!"

How fortunate the country is, Flannigan thought, *to have a man of Roosevelt's capability at the helm, with Harry Hopkins as an adviser.* But Hopkins looked pale and exhausted. *Could he hold up through a long and difficult war?*

After Mrs. Roosevelt and the others left the table, FDR asked Flannigan to remain for a moment.

"James, if our country goes to war with Germany, we will pull you out of Norway," he said. "My Army chief of staff, General Marshall, will personally see to it. I understand that you know George, so you also know that he will select the right people to go get you. After all, we can't let the Nazis acquire one of the great minds of the twentieth century."

"I have the utmost confidence in George Marshall, Mr. President, and I greatly appreciate your kind words. I will do everything in my power to accomplish this mission successfully."

"I know you will."

An aide drove Flannigan back to the hotel. He would be taking the train to Princeton early the next morning. If all went well, he would arrive just in time to teach his afternoon class.

Before leaving for Norway, he needed to arrange for his physics classes to be taught by alternate instructors and insure that his graduate assistants would keep his research projects steadily moving forward.

He needed to talk with his wife. Although he could not tell her much about where he was going or why, he knew she would—as always—support him however she could.

Finally, he needed to buy more life insurance.

3

The Professor Goes to Work

FLANNIGAN ARRIVED SECRETLY in Norway in early November 1941 using an assumed name. He was brought to Narvik on the northwestern shore by an American submarine that had been granted safe passage by the British fleet. There, he was met by members of the Norwegian Underground, assigned to protect him during his stay.

The country had a mystical beauty that was almost indescribable. No words could do justice to the landscape: steep, jagged, snow-covered mountains wreathed by wispy clouds and blue lakes glimmering in deep valleys. It was scenery that could be found nowhere else in the world.

Flannigan had all the necessary paperwork for travel in occupied Norway, courtesy of Norwegian government officials now exiled in London. He showed his papers to German soldiers when challenged, and there were no unpleasant incidents as he and his companions moved through the town. Obviously, Flannigan was not considered a threat by anyone.

After resting in Narvik for a day, Flannigan and one member of the Underground boarded a bus heading south. Their destination was Professor Knut Jungstad's house. Jungstad and his wife lived in

Vemork, a little village with colorfully painted houses and cobblestone streets. The center of town was built around a square that contained a marketplace. The square was a hub of activity where people conducted both business and social activities.

As Flannigan and his escort neared Vemork, he spotted the mighty Hardangervidda River flowing down into the Vestfjord valley. The river provided the vast amount of power that was required to separate the heavy water out of normal water. Soon, he saw the Norsk Hydro electric plant with its array of huge inflow and outflow tubes protruding from one side. This innocent-looking facility was where the Nazis hoped to gather the substance they believed might be the key to world domination.

Flannigan had stayed with the Jungstads before and was very familiar with their town. Vemork was only a couple of miles from the heavy water facility. The Jungstads' house would provide a perfect base of operations.

After his guide left him in front of the house, Flannigan rang the doorbell. The door opened almost immediately, but only slightly. Jungstad peered out warily, then broke into a huge grin as soon as he recognized Flannigan. "Welcome!" he roared in Norwegian, stepping out and wrapping his arms around Flannigan. "Helga will be so happy to see you!"

To anyone watching, the two eminent professors would have looked comically mismatched. Jungstad was tall and thin; Flannigan, portly and peaceful-looking, was rather short. Some American scientists had compared them to the comedy team of Abbott and Costello. The two joked often about that.

"How is my good friend Abbott?" Flannigan asked.

"I am fine, and how are you, Costello?"

"Actually, I'm rather hungry."

Flannigan knocked the snow from his shoes before Jungstad led him into the house.

"Please take off your coat, and I will move your bags into the guest bedroom."

"Thank you, Knut."

Looking around, Flannigan saw that the small bungalow was just as he had remembered it. *What a warm and pleasant home*, he thought. Mrs. Jungstad had adorned the living room with pretty, though inexpensive, knick-knacks. The walls were nearly covered with paintings and family photographs. The furniture was well-worn but far from threadbare. It was a room that recalled many good and memorable times, some of which he had shared on earlier visits.

Hearing a shriek, James turned to see Helga Jungstad coming towards him with her arms wide open and a big smile on her face.

"James, it has been too long!"

"Helga, my dear, you are a beautiful sight for these tired, old eyes."

Flannigan wasn't sure that the Jungstads knew exactly why he was here. He was soon given a clue. "James," Helga whispered in his ear, "I pray you won't get Knut in trouble. Whatever it is you need to do, please be careful."

Flannigan had never seen her look so anguished. "I assure you that I will," James whispered back. "The last thing I want to do is cause either of you any problems."

As Jungstad returned to the living room, Helga changed the subject. "Knut, we must feed James immediately. I will not send him back to his wife as skinny as St. Olaf's horse!"

Jungstad laughed. "Helga, I don't think we will ever have to worry about Costello being as skinny as St. Olaf's horse."

Helga had made a lamb stew, and James attacked it voraciously at their dining room table. "James, you always do wonders for my ego," she said as he finished a second helping. "Let's have coffee and dessert in the living room."

With Knut and James settled in easy chairs, Helga brought out ample pieces of cherry cobbler. Between bites of cobbler and sips of coffee, they were able to catch up on each others' lives.

But finally James asked, "How have things been under German occupation?"

"Terrible!" Jungstad replied. "We are prisoners in our own country. We have to show papers to travel anywhere outside our own township. Perhaps the worst thing is that the Germans simply take anything they want and ship it back to their homeland."

"Times are very bad here," Helga said, heading back to the kitchen, "but now I better let the two of you talk. James, don't forget what I said."

"I won't, my dear."

"She worries too much," Jungstad said as he trailed Helga with his eyes.

"I can't say that I blame her," Flannigan replied. Helga looked back triumphantly. Jungstad sighed.

After she was out of sight, Flannigan said, "Knut, I don't know if you are aware of this, but I'm here to monitor the heavy water production."

"Nobody told me, but I suspected it."

"I'm to give my government an estimate of when they're producing enough that the facility must be destroyed. Have you been inside the plant?"

"Yes, a long time ago," Jungstad replied. "But they've made significant changes since then, so I don't know for sure what process they're using today. You'd have to know that to make a reasonable estimate."

"But why would they change from electrolysis?" Flannigan asked. "The plant has used it successfully since 1933 to produce ammonia fertilizer. Heavy water just happens to be a desirable byproduct of the electrolysis——to the Germans, anyway."

Realizing that Jungstad was just being judiciously cautious, James quickly added, "I agree, though, that nothing should be assumed. A guess won't be good enough for a firm recommendation."

The two professors considered other options, such as distillation or a chemical exchange process, with the latter using a readily available gas such as carbon dioxide. Flannigan lit his pipe, and the two sat quietly thinking for a while. Finally, Flannigan said, "Knut, I'm afraid we can't be sure yet what process they're using. My only option is to get inside the plant and see for myself."

"The plant is heavily guarded," Jungstad said. "If we're to get in, we'll have to use the Underground."

"We?"

"Yes, James. I can't permit you to have all of the fun! Did you think I wouldn't be part of the resistance?"

Flannigan recalled the anguished look on Helga's face, and questions that he had suppressed began to surface. *Why does the government need to find out the status of the facility? Is it worth risking our lives? Why not destroy the plant now and get it over with? Surely, though, the president of the United States must have good reasons. Maybe there are more pressing issues, since heavy-water production is not yet thought to be critical. Perhaps FDR doesn't want to alert the Germans that people are worried about their progress. After all, that could make them even more determined.* In any event, the professor had made a promise to the president of the United States and was determined that he would keep it.

"Knut, I hate to drag you into this, but it appears you give me no choice."

"You are absolutely correct, Costello."

The next day shortly after dark, a tall, thin man arrived at the Jungstad residence. He was Alf Haldor, head of the local Underground organization. After introductions were made, Jungstad said, "Alf, James has to report to his government how much heavy water is being produced—and when it will be necessary to put the plant out of operation. To make the estimates, we need your help getting inside."

Haldor shook his head. "The Germans refuse entrance to anyone not on the access list."

"Are you saying that it can't be done?" Flannigan asked.

"No, but it will require patience. It can't be done quickly."

"How long will we have to wait?" Flannigan asked.

"A week. Maybe several weeks."

"In the meantime, Alf, James and I will monitor the plant from the outside," Jungstad said. "We may get some clues."

"Any plan to come up with a way to get you inside will have to be one that won't result in massive reprisals," Haldor cautioned.

"Of course," Flannigan agreed. "And if we get into trouble, even without going inside, we may need your help."

"I'll be nearby," Haldor said. Then he departed into the cold evening air.

The professors decided that monitoring the heavy water plant during daylight hours would be sufficient. Jungstad said activity there seemed to decrease significantly as evening approached. They would find a vantage point and take turns watching.

"The only thing I'm still wondering," Flannigan said, "is how much heavy water the Germans have gotten already?"

"Not much," Jungstad replied. "The people at the Norsk facility became suspicious of the Germans' activities and alerted the French. Shortly before Norway was attacked by the Germans, French agents got all of the heavy water out of here and took it to safety."

"Good for them," Flannigan replied. "But I'm surprised that the French recognized the implications of heavy water production."

"They didn't," Jungstad said. "They incorrectly suspected that heavy water might be used in chemical warfare."

The following day, James and Knut strolled together at a leisurely pace toward the plant, which was actually a complex of buildings. They tried to be as inconspicuous as possible. Men in trench coats, potentially German agents, seemed to be everywhere.

Flannigan could not help but be impressed by the beauty of the plant's surroundings. He particularly enjoyed looking at the colorful houses clustered among the trees on both sides of the deep gorge below the dam. Pointing to the water cascading down the face of the dam, which was wedged into the steep mountainside, he said, "Knut, I don't think there is a scene to match this anywhere in the world. I wish I could paint so I could capture it on canvas."

"It is beautiful despite what is happening here."

Flannigan looked around to make sure no one was eavesdropping. "But that isn't your fault," he replied. "People in Norway wanted this hydroelectric facility for power generation only, not for building new and more powerful weapons."

Jungstad nodded, and both went back to taking in the scenery.

During the next several weeks, the professors took turns watching the plant from a scenic overlook at the edge of a small park. They had selected the overlook because of its clear view to the generating station. It also had a few benches, which allowed the professors to observe in relative comfort.

Their main problems were boredom and not attracting the attention of anyone else. Bringing a book solved the first problem, but all they could do about the second was to be as careful as possible.

As Flannigan finished the morning shift of what had been a routine watch, two uniformed German guards with an attack dog walked up the incline to the scenic overlook.

The lead guard said in a menacing tone, "I have seen you here before. Why do you come here?" Flannigan shrugged and pretended that he did not understand the German's heavily accented Norwegian. Infuriated, the guard grabbed him by his coat lapels and shook him hard. "If I ever see you here again, you will be in serious trouble." By now, the dog was snarling and straining at its leash to get at Flannigan. Holding the beast, the second guard had his work cut out for him just trying to keep the dog under control.

The lead guard shoved Flannigan to the ground. In shock, the professor lay there for a few moments, trying to regain his composure. As they strolled off, the guards looked back and laughed. Perhaps this was good, James thought. If they were joking about his predicament, they certainly didn't consider him a threat.

As he lay on the ground, Flannigan tried to regain his composure. *Better keep my guard up,* he thought, recognizing that the commotion might have brought some unwanted attention. Looking around, he saw two men in civilian clothes keeping a close eye on him. "That can't be good," he muttered.

Flannigan was right. The men were Carl Jergens and Erwin Kaufmeir, members of the dreaded Gestapo, or German Secret State Police. "Who is that small fellow who got knocked over?" Jergens wondered aloud. "I've seen him here before at the overlook."

"I don't know," Kaufmeir said. "But one of us should follow him."

"I'll do that," Jergens said. "You contact headquarters to see if we have any information on a man fitting his description. Who knows? If he turns out to be important, I may get a promotion."

"Humph!" Kaufmeir replied.

Flannigan picked himself up. Although still shocked by the assault, he had the presence of mind to check to make sure he wasn't being followed. Looking back, he saw one of the two sinister-looking civilians he had seen moments ago following him. As he approached the center of town, Flannigan ducked into an open doorway and found that it led to an area lined with garbage cans. Crouching behind one, he waited. Soon, the man passed by the doorway. After a minute or so, Flannigan carefully peered out on the street. There was no sign of the man, so he quickly resumed his journey.

Flannigan was still trembling when he reached the Jungstad residence. "James, you are white as a sheet!" Helga exclaimed. "What happened?" Jungstad asked.

"A guard became suspicious of me, grabbed me by my lapels, and threw me to the ground. He told me to never come around again. His dog wanted to kill me."

"How awful! Would you like something to drink, a glass of wine perhaps?" Helga asked.

"I would like something stronger. Vodka, if you have it."

"Certainly. I will bring it right away." She headed to the kitchen.

"Knut, we have to find a different place," Flannigan said.

"Yes. Of course. I know of a cabin on top of a ridge. It's farther away, but the Germans have not yet discovered it. We can take some supplies and camp there. With binoculars, we can see anyone or anything entering or leaving the facility."

"We will have to go at night, so we can carry knapsacks without making ourselves conspicuous. Can we see well enough to travel after dark?"

"I think so. But I have a couple of small flashlights that should provide adequate light just in case."

Helga came back with a tumbler of vodka for each of the professors. "Salut!" They each gulped a large swig. Soon, Flannigan began to relax. "Helga, my dear, you are an absolute lifesaver," he said.

"Don't you sweet-talk me, James Flannigan!" Helga snapped. "I told you to be careful, and look what you've done! You've alerted the whole German Army!"

"Don't be too hard on him, Helga," Jungstad murmured. "It could just as easily have happened to me."

"Oh, all right," Helga replied. "But I wish just once that you two would take my advice!"

"Oh, we intend to, my dear," Flannigan said playfully. "What do you suggest we take to the cabin?" Helga picked up a pillow and hurled it at his head as Flannigan ducked. She stomped out of the room as both men chuckled.

"We don't want to carry too much," Knut said, turning serious.

"How about some sausages, potatoes, bread, and jam for our food supply?"

"You ask for the heavy items and not any vegetables," Knut said. "No wonder you are Costello!"

"I admit it. My tastes aren't conducive to a sleek profile."

Helga returned, and Flannigan was relieved to see that she had regained her composure. "You can melt snow up there for water," she said, "so you don't have to carry any."

"My dear, as always, you have made an excellent observation," Flannigan replied.

Flannigan and Jungstad reached the cabin that night after a two-mile hike. It turned out to be a sparsely furnished one-room affair with a fireplace on one side and a cooking stove on the other. A big pot hung over the fireplace, and a counter and pantry area stood to one side.

A small table and four wooden chairs were positioned in the center of the room. Two bearskin rugs were on the floor and would have to serve as mattresses, as there were no other furnishings in the dwelling. Flannigan hoped his sixty-nine-year-old body would hold up to the abuse.

The cabin had a wraparound porch with two wooden chairs on it. From the porch, the heavy water plant could be seen with the aid of binoculars.

"Under different circumstances," Flannigan said, "this cabin would provide a very enjoyable getaway spot."

"It's done just that many times," Jungstad replied. "Helga and I have spent vacations here with our children. I can still picture them stretched out in their bedrolls."

It was a while before anything exciting happened. On the fifth day, as dusk approached, they heard a loud knock at the door. Cautiously,

Jungstad opened it and peered out. It was Alf Haldor. "Helga told me where you were, and I have some interesting news for you," he said.

Jungstad pulled Haldor inside. "James, I have a feeling that this is the break we've been waiting for," he said. "Alf, please continue."

"We have finally succeeded in getting three of our people into the Norsk facility as employees. They report that a series of fifteen electrolysis cells have been installed to produce high-purity heavy water."

"That is exactly what we need to know!" Flannigan said. Based on what they knew of state-of-the-art electrolytic equipment, the professors calculated how much heavy water could be produced per day.

"Knut, I hope we're erring on the side of safety."

"Oh, I wouldn't worry about that," Haldor said, smiling wickedly. "My men added castor oil to the electrolyte. The Germans are now getting more foam than heavy water!"

Knut and James roared. They hugged Haldor as he departed. Then they memorized the results of their calculations and threw the paperwork into the fire. After quickly gathering their gear, they put on their snowshoes and headed back down to Jungstad's house. As they hiked, snow began to fall.

"I know you're anxious to get home," Flannigan called to Jungstad. "But don't go so fast. I can't keep up."

"I'll wait for you at that clearing," Jungstad shouted, pointing to a substantial widening in the trail.

Flannigan hurried. Reaching the opening, he looked around. There was no sign of Jungstad. *Had something happened to him? Had the Germans—or perhaps traitors—gotten hold of him?* Somewhat panicked, Flannigan moved quickly around the periphery of the opening. Finally, much to his relief, he spotted his host. Over to the side and tucked among some conifers, Jungstad sat on a big rock, grinning.

"Did you think I had gone on without you?" Jungstad asked.

"The thought crossed my mind," Flannigan replied a little testily.

"I apologize," Jungstad said. "Here. Sit on this rock. It's nice and warm for you."

Jungstad stood up and motioned his friend over.

"Thank you," James said gratefully. "I do need a little rest."

After a few minutes, Flannigan felt better. "We should go," he said. "The weather isn't getting any better."

As the snow intensified, both men had trouble remaining upright. "How much further?" Flannigan asked.

"About a half mile," Jungstad said. *Thank goodness*, James thought. He knew he could make it that far.

The next morning at breakfast, Jungstad said, "My friend, this means that you can get ready to go home."

"The only sad part is the thought of leaving you and Helga."

"Don't worry about us. We'll remain here in our beloved Norway, and we will be thinking of how America will help destroy the Nazis."

Just then, there was an urgent knock at the front door. Helga opened it, and a Norwegian in his early twenties hurriedly entered. "Germany has declared war on the United States," he said. "Your American guest is now behind enemy lines! A German detachment is headed this way! We have to get him out immediately."

With time only to throw on a coat and hat, Flannigan followed the man out the back door. As they fled, he heard men approaching the front of the house and dogs barking.

With his adrenaline flowing, James struggled to keep up with his young guide. Soon, they came upon two men rapidly attaching a team of dogs to a sled. The men motioned for Flannigan to hop on. As he did, one of the men who'd been handling the dogs took the lines and urged the dogs into motion.

Flannigan asked the sled driver in Norwegian, "Where are you taking me?"

"Telemark, southeast of here."

"Why?"

"It is bigger, and there are lots of resistance fighters there."

"Why," Flannigan asked, "did Germany declare war on America?"

"Because its new ally, Japan, attacked America at a place called Pearl Harbor. Thousands of Americans were killed."

My God, James thought, *all those big ships. Aircraft carriers, battleships, cruisers...*

Right now, though, he couldn't worry about the Pacific or what might happen to the Jungstads. He had a sizeable problem of his own: how to avoid capture while waiting for whomever General Marshall would send to get him out of Norway. Surely, it would be a large and well-experienced special operations team.

Part II

4

A Mission to Remember

THE DATE WAS December 18, 1941, and Lieutenant Jonathon Partude sat waiting to see Army Chief of Staff General George Catlett Marshall. Dude, as Jonathon was called by his friends, had no idea why the general wanted to see a lowly Army second lieutenant. All he knew was that the world was in chaos. Most of America's vaunted Pacific Fleet was at the bottom of Pearl Harbor after a surprise attack by the Japanese. The other two Axis powers, Germany and Italy, had come to Japan's aid by declaring war on the United States. It was hard to fathom how the situation could be any worse.

The morning so far was a blur to Dude. He had been whisked down Constitution Avenue by a military driver to the old Munitions Building, where Marshall's office was located. The building, to Dude's way of thinking, was not one of the prettiest in the city. It was a rather plain-looking, albeit huge, chunk of glass and concrete. The location, however, couldn't be better. The White House was a few blocks to the northeast, and the National Mall was a stone's throw to the south. *Marshall must like working here*, Dude thought. But it wouldn't be for long. Once the five-sided Pentagon was completed in just a few months, the general would be moving to Arlington, Virginia.

General Marshall's outer office was spacious but not luxurious. The walls were painted a dull green, and the leather-upholstered furniture had been selected for durability rather than looks. The big chairs were comfortable, though, and the big desks—one for the secretary and one for the general's aide—were made of impressive mahogany. Somehow the office had a quiet elegance that let people know they were waiting to see someone important.

Thoughts raced through Dude's mind. He wondered whether he had done something so terrible that it had come to the attention of the Army chief of staff. Probably not, but the uncertainty was killing him. He wanted to just go over, open the general's door, walk in, and find out, but he knew better. The Army was steeped in protocol, tradition, and RHIP—rank had its privileges.

As he agonized, a young lady joined him in the waiting area. She was in an Army nurse's uniform, and her insignia was that of a second lieutenant. She was exceptionally pretty, with blonde hair and pale blue eyes.

After checking in with the secretary, she walked to an overstuffed chair across from Dude, sank down into it, and carefully removed her cap. She smiled at Dude and said, "Hi, my name is Jennifer Haraldsson."

"I'm Jonathon Partude, but you can call me Dude," he said, struggling out of his chair and extending a hand that she grasped lightly and quickly released.

He'd noticed that Jennifer had a slight accent. Taking a chance, he offered a compliment in Norwegian: "*Du ha en god smil.*"

"I'm glad you like my smile," she replied somewhat amused. "But how did you guess that I could speak Norwegian?"

"I had a roommate in college from Norway. He had an accent that sounded like yours, but stronger."

Before they could talk further, the buzzer on the secretary's desk beeped, and she announced that the general was ready to see them.

"Both of us at once?" Dude blurted out.

"Yes, sir."

Now he was really curious.

Ushered into the general's office by the secretary, Dude and Jennifer saluted crisply. General Marshall returned their salutes.

Marshall had what could only be described as a commanding presence. It was no wonder President Roosevelt had passed over other senior officers to select George Marshall as his Army chief of staff.

The general's massive desk and the long conference table in the center of the room were both made out of mahogany. There were also a leather couch and a scattering of cushioned chairs. "Sit down," the general said, motioning Dude and Jennifer toward two chairs facing his desk, pulled close enough that when they sat their knees almost rubbed against the wood.

As the secretary was leaving the room, General Marshall called after her, "Let me know immediately if there is any progress in getting the trapped sailors out of the *West Virginia*." "Yes, sir!" she responded.

The *West Virginia* was a great battleship that had been sunk by the Japanese and was now lying at the bottom of Pearl Harbor. Eleven days after the sinking, clanking noises still sounded from inside, indicating some sailors were still alive. But would-be rescuers were running out of time. Unlike the *Oklahoma*, which had capsized during the attack, the *West Virginia* remained upright, which meant that rescuers had farther to go to reach the bottom of the ship where the men were stranded.

Marshall studied Dude and Jennifer for a while, saying nothing. After what seemed like an eternity to the young officers, he finally spoke, "You are being considered for a very important and very dangerous mission, one that has special significance to the president. I want to make sure you understand what you will be getting into if you accept the assignment."

General Marshall paused briefly. "If you decide not to volunteer for this assignment, your military careers will not be negatively impacted. However, if you do accept, there will be no backing out. Either way, you cannot discuss this top-secret mission with anyone outside of an extremely small group of people who will help you get ready. The penalty for any violation of this secrecy could be death by firing squad."

As the general let his words sink in, Dude and Jennifer shot glances at each other. After getting a nod from her, Dude answered for both of them, "Sir, Lieutenant Haraldsson and I are eager to help in any way. Please continue."

"Good. Have either of you heard of Professor James Flannigan?"

"Didn't he win the Nobel Prize in physics?" Jennifer asked. "Something to do with how atoms work?"

"Yes, he discovered new subatomic particles," Marshall said. "Unfortunately, the professor is now in Norway. He was sent there by President Roosevelt to consult with the Norwegians on their heavy water supply and to secretly monitor any German activity related to it."

"Heavy water?" Jonathon asked.

"You'll learn more about that," Marshall replied. "The current thinking is that heavy water might hold the key to unlocking nuclear energy and allowing scientists to construct weapons that are far more deadly than any presently available to us."

The general paused for a moment, stood up to stretch, and then sat back down. "When Germany declared war on the United States, it meant that Professor Flannigan was officially behind enemy lines. The Germans may discover at any moment that he is in Norway. We cannot take the chance that the Germans might capture him. By all measures, he is one of the top ten nuclear physicists in the world. If tortured, he might—however unwillingly and even unwittingly—help the Germans build horrible new weapons. We can't allow that to happen."

Jennifer frowned, but Dude felt himself smiling. *At last, adventure!* Trying to control his eagerness, he asked, "How will we find the professor?"

"First, you will fly to England. From there you will be taken by submarine to the coast of Norway, where members of the Norwegian Underground will meet you and take you to him. You will pose as man and wife—a Norwegian couple, actually. The fact that you are both excellent skiers and fluent in the language will be extremely useful. Lieutenant Haraldsson, you have a question?"

"Yes, sir. I was wondering if my being a nurse had anything to do with my selection."

"Good question, and yes, it did. While the professor is very healthy as far as we know, he is in his late sixties. We decided at least one of the people we send to retrieve him should be a nurse or doctor, in case medical assistance becomes necessary."

"I understand."

"How about you, Partude?"

"What do we do once we reach the professor?"

"Your task then will be to bring the professor out of Norway. You may have to cross some treacherous mountain ranges. The Germans have imposed such tight security that it could be impossible to get him out by going over easier routes. Therefore, your exit strategy will rely greatly on assistance from the resistance group."

Jennifer asked, "What if we find the professor can't make it over the mountains?"

"The Germans must not be allowed to capture him alive."

"Oh, my!" Jennifer replied with some bewilderment.

After another short pause, Marshall continued. "I have every confidence in both of you," he said. "If you accept this mission, you will be doing your country a great service. You will return here tomorrow at 0800 hours to give me your answer."

He told them they had been given accommodations at the Mayflower Hotel in downtown Washington and that his aide would arrange for a car to take them there. He bade them farewell.

Dude and Jennifer rode mainly in silence, glancing occasionally at each other. As he looked at her, Dude couldn't help but wonder if both of them would make it out alive. And what if they did? What would their fates be for the rest of the war?

The staff car headed east on Constitution Avenue, turning north on 17th Street. "Oh, look!" Jennifer exclaimed. "The White House!" They both craned their necks to get as good a view of the building as possible. The South Portico, with its rounded porch and massive columns, was now in full view as they proceeded due west of the Ellipse.

"What a beautiful sight," Jennifer said. "It looks just like the pictures I've seen of it."

"That fountain's a dandy, too," Dude replied. He pointed toward the South Lawn, where streams of water arched toward the sky. Jennifer nodded.

Suddenly, Dude was aware that he had scrunched Jennifer into the corner of the backseat as he gawked at the magnificent scenery. "Oops, sorry!" He blurted out. "I was so busy looking out that I didn't realize I had you squeezed in so tightly."

"That's quite all right," Jennifer replied with a mischievous little smile. "If the situation had been reversed, I would have been on top of you."

Good sign, Dude thought. *She certainly isn't a straight-laced prude!* He moved back over to his side.

They got a final look at the White House as the car crossed Pennsylvania Avenue. "Just as pretty from the north," Dude said.

"Sure is," Jennifer agreed.

The car continued northward on 17th Street, past Lafayette Square and Farragut Square. It turned northwest onto Connecticut Avenue, and the beautiful Mayflower Hotel appeared almost instantly. *Wow*, Dude thought, *our mission must be important for them to put us up here.*

5

To Go or Not to Go

THE TWO HAD agreed to meet for dinner. In the Mayflower lobby, Dude located a sign pointing the way to the dining room, but when he got there, he saw that Jennifer had not yet arrived.

As he waited for her, the maitre d' approached. "May I help you, sir?"

"Yes. I would like a table near the fireplace."

"Right this way, sir."

The maitre d' led him to a table directly in front of the hearth. Dude plopped into a chair facing the entrance so he would be sure to see Jennifer the instant she appeared.

"Can I ask you a question?" Dude called out as the maitre d' began walking to the front.

"Yes, sir."

"Doesn't this dining room also serve as a ballroom?"

"Yes, sir. It does. We remove the tables, and people dance to the big bands on the hardwood floor." The maitre d' swept his hand in an arc to indicate where the band sat and where the people danced.

"Thank you," Dude said. The maitre d' nodded.

As he sat there, Dude recalled hearing a speech that President Franklin D. Roosevelt had broadcast from this very room. The announcer had noted that Roosevelt was speaking from the balcony. Looking around, Dude spotted it. He'd have to remember to point it out to Jennifer.

As he sat enjoying the warmth of the fire and the hum of conversation, a waiter approached with a cart holding silverware, glasses, and a pitcher of water.

"How many for dinner, sir?"

"There will be one more." The waiter nodded, then set out the silverware arrangements and poured the water.

At 1800 sharp, Jennifer entered the dining room. She wore a light pink dress that enhanced her fair complexion. She sparkled as if she had just stepped out of the bathtub. Jumping up, Dude waved to get her attention.

The sight of Jennifer walking toward him took Dude's breath away. He couldn't help but think it would be worth accepting the Norway assignment just to stay near her. If she said yes to the general, Dude would have no choice but to go along, if only to stay by her side.

Dude gazed steadily at her, admiring her long, graceful strides. She was probably five foot seven, he estimated, with ample supplies of athleticism and confidence. Soon, she was at the table, smiling and looking at him expectantly.

Her eye contact pulled him out of his trance. He moved quickly to pull out the chair on his right. "Please sit here," he said. "This will give you a good view of the whole room." She smiled and nodded, and he nudged her chair toward the table once she was seated. He leaned over and sat back down.

"Did you notice how beautiful this hotel is?" Jennifer said excitedly. "I can't get over all of the gold leaf and that huge skylight. No wonder they call this hotel the 'Grand Dame.'"

"Unfortunately," Dude replied. "That skylight will have to be covered over. I understand that blackout orders are going into effect as we speak."

"Oh, no!" Jennifer said dejectedly.

"But just think," Dude said, trying to make amends for his blunder. "We may get to see some famous people while we're here. I understand

J. Edgar Hoover eats lunch here almost every day when he's in town. And Franklin Roosevelt actually holed up here to work on his 1933 inaugural address."

"Really?" Jennifer responded enthusiastically.

"Yes. And before I forget it, that balcony is where FDR gave an important speech a while back." He pointed to a platform overlooking the dining room.

"I remember," Jennifer replied. "Wasn't that when he said 'We have nothing to fear but fear itself'?"

"I think so." *Actually, those words probably came from one of FDR's fireside chats*, he thought. But he wasn't about to contradict her.

"I have an idea," Jennifer said. "Let's play a little game while we wait to place our orders. Let's tell each other about ourselves but in the fewest possible words."

"Great idea!" Dude replied. "I'll start. Kansas farm boy. Two younger brothers. University of Colorado ski team. Norwegian roommate. Majored in languages. Your turn."

"Two younger brothers and two younger sisters. Idaho dairy farm. Grandparents from Norway. University of Idaho nursing degree. Skiing at Sun Valley. Over and out."

Laughing, they clinked water glasses. "Now we can relax and enjoy the evening," Dude said.

"Oh, you won't get off that easy," Jennifer replied. "I have some questions."

"Such as?"

"Why the University of Colorado, and where is your Norwegian roommate now?"

"Well, my parents, of course, wanted me to stay on the farm. But when I was ten, we made a family trip to the Colorado Rockies. From that time on, I was hooked. I knew I would never want to be far from the mountains. Finally, I was able to convince my parents to let me go to college in Boulder."

"And your Norwegian roommate?"

"His name is Lars Nefsteinn. He taught me how to ski well enough to make the team and even think about trying out for the Olympics. He also helped me with Norwegian. Without him, I doubt that I would have passed my language exams."

"Where is he now?"

"Back in Norway. And probably a member of the Norwegian Underground. He isn't the type to sit idly by while the Nazis occupy his country."

The waiter approached. "I have some questions for you, too," Dude said to Jennifer. "But I'll ask them after we place our orders."

"May I bring you something to drink?" the waiter asked.

"I'll have the house chardonnay," Jennifer replied.

"I'll have a Jack Daniels straight up with one cube of ice," Dude said.

They each ordered a rib-eye steak, medium, a baked potato with butter, and the house salad. *A good sign*, Dude thought. *We like the same things.*

"Are you sad that the 1940 Olympics were cancelled?" Jennifer asked.

"Now wait a minute," Dude said. "It's my turn to ask you some questions!"

"You'll have plenty of time before the evening's over."

"Well, all right," Dude replied. "I'll answer this one, but that's it!"

Jennifer laughed.

"I'm young enough to try out for future Olympics if the war doesn't last too long," he said. "So I'm not devastated about it, although some of the older skiers are just plain out of luck."

"Do you really think you're good enough to make the Olympics squad?"

Dude laughed. "You don't give up, do you?" Jennifer grinned and shook her head.

"Well, I don't know. Lars was in the 1936 Olympics and won a bronze medal for Norway in the slalom. He said he thought I was good enough. Was he just being polite? I hope to find out some day."

Before long, the food arrived. As they ate, the two laughed easily. Their possible mission to Norway seemed far from their minds.

"Why did you become a nurse?" Dude asked.

"I like helping others. Back in Idaho, some of my friends resented having to care for their younger brothers and sisters, but I found that I enjoyed it. I also liked helping my elderly grandparents. So when it came time to think about my future, I decided that nursing—helping people—would be very fulfilling."

"Very commendable," Dude said. "Unfortunately, I share your friends' feelings. I thought my younger brothers could be a real pain."

"I'll bet you're a wonderful big brother," Jennifer said. "But I want to hear more about you. Tell me a funny story about yourself."

"I will if you will," Dude replied.

"Agreed."

"After I made the ski team," Dude started, "I was pretty well-known around campus. One day, I decided to go to the Student Union Building and play some ping-pong. Unbeknownst to me, I had a loose sole on my left shoe. As I lunged for the ball, I tripped and broke my nose on the edge of the table."

"Ooh. I'll bet that hurt."

"It did, but not half as much as having to tell people that I had broken my nose playing ping-pong!"

"I'll never top that," Jennifer said chuckling, "except for my talent in breaking up with boys."

"This one boy I dated had a cute convertible. After going to a movie one night with another couple, he started showing off by driving around in circles in a field at the edge of town, seeing how much he could skid on the turns. The girl in the back seat got scared and started screaming, so I decided I had to do something. I reached over, turned off the ignition, pulled out the keys, and threw them as far as I could. Naturally, the boy was furious. He never spoke to me again. And it was a long walk home for all of us!"

"That story tells me you haven't met the right boy yet!"

"I guess you're right," Jennifer replied, "but enough about that. You said you had some questions for me."

"I did, but now they seem insignificant. I'm finding out everything I need to know by just being with you."

"Good! I hate to answer questions about myself."

They finished eating, and the waiter brought the check. "It's too bad," Dude sighed, "that all good things must come to an end."

"It certainly is," Jennifer replied.

Jennifer reached for her purse, but Dude insisted on paying for both of their dinners.

"Okay, but don't plan on making it a habit."

"Agreed," Dude responded.

Dude walked Jennifer upstairs, and when they reached her door, she gazed up at him with a deep, searching look before inviting him in.

Dude sat in the room's easy chair and Jennifer sat on the bed. Each looked quietly at the other, waiting. Finally, Jennifer began. "The general said we can't let that physicist be captured, no matter what. That really bothers me. I'm used to saving lives, not taking them."

"I can see how that would be repulsive to you," Dude said. "But I also understand why we wouldn't have a choice."

"I agree," Jennifer replied. "There might be no alternative. But I wouldn't want to point a gun at him and pull the trigger."

"I could do that," Dude said. "But it would be a lot easier if we could just give him a pill."

"That's a thought," Jennifer said after a moment. "Some poisons are painless."

Dude nodded. "Any other issues?"

"Well, we could get killed," she replied. "But I suppose that's not a legitimate reason to say no when we're at war. Many other Americans are facing the same risk."

Dude didn't say anything for a moment. Then he surprised himself by blurting out, "I'll go if you'll go." *Whoops. Maybe I shouldn't have said that*, he thought. He knew impulsiveness was one of his weaknesses, and he feared it would cost him now. However, it didn't seem to faze Jennifer, much to his relief. She nodded and let out a sigh as she flopped back onto the bed.

"We both know our country needs us," she said, staring at the ceiling.

Dude took the opportunity to admire her figure, the rounded breasts and full hips and thighs. After a minute, she sat back up and gave Dude a big smile.

"Well, I guess we've decided," Dude said. The relationship was going fine, he thought, so why push it? He stood up. "I'll see you in the morning."

Jennifer followed Dude to the door. As he turned to say good night, she gave him a soft kiss on the lips.

6

Final Preparations

AT PRECISELY 0800, they were ushered into General Marshall's office. He gazed at them for a few moments before asking, "Well, what's your decision?"

"We'll go, sir," they answered simultaneously, almost as if they'd rehearsed.

The general smiled slightly. "I thought you would. I've arranged for Lieutenant Haraldsson to get some training with a handgun before you leave. Partude, you've just completed Officer Training School. I see by your record that you're already proficient with firearms."

"My staff," Marshall continued, "has set up a number of briefings and other activities to prepare you for your mission. One of those briefings will cover heavy water. The president and I have decided that you should know why it is so important."

"Thank you, sir," Dude replied. "We're both curious."

The general stood and walked them to the door. "I'm sure you'll like old Professor Flannigan," he said. "He's a real down-to-earth type. He'll be very appreciative of what you're doing for him." At the door, he gave each of them a firm handshake. "Good luck and Godspeed."

The general's secretary arranged transportation back to the Mayflower so they could change into less formal military attire. When they arrived, they checked for messages at the front desk. A telegram awaited Dude from his brother Jacob, who was one year younger. The telegram read: "Arriving tonight for short visit. Stop. Leaving tomorrow morning for Air Cadet training. Stop."

Dude read the telegram aloud to Jennifer.

"What's Jacob like?" she asked.

"Just an ordinary guy," Dude said with a shrug. "He's a lot like me."

"If he's like you, he can't be ordinary," she said. "Now I am really anxious to meet him."

Oh, great, Dude thought.

But there was much work to be done before Jacob arrived. Sergeant Melvin Johnson, an aide to Marshall, soon arrived in a staff car. By then, Dude and Jennifer had changed into crisp-looking military fatigues and were back in the lobby waiting for him.

Johnson took them to a supply warehouse where they were fitted for clothing appropriate for mountain travel and other clothes that someone at the warehouse had decided would be typical of Norwegian town wear. They were also issued other provisions they would need for their mission including simple medical instruments such as a blood pressure device. Jennifer asked for and received capsules of a medication that could bring death quickly and painlessly if taken in sufficient quantity.

As they were leaving the warehouse, Johnson turned to Dude. "Lieutenant Partude, I can drop you off at the hotel, if you like, before taking Lieutenant Haraldsson to the firing range."

"Thank you Sergeant, but I'd better come along with the lieutenant. I may be able to give her some helpful pointers."

"Your call, sir."

Jennifer looked at Dude and smiled. "Thank you," she said. "I'll probably need all of the help that I can get."

At the firing range, the instructor gave Jennifer a lecture on the use of a handgun, stressing safety concerns. He then took her to a shooting station that faced a paper bull's-eye target about twenty-five feet away.

A .38-caliber revolver awaited her, along with a box of bullets. The gun's cylinder was empty and in the open position. "Lieutenant, you may load your weapon and commence firing when ready," the instructor said.

After the first few shots, Jennifer got the hang of it and began hitting the target regularly. Finally, she looked at Dude and asked if he had any suggestions. Now was his chance, and he wasn't about to waste it. He moved forward quickly, putting his arms around her as he helped her hold her right arm straighter. Everything about her aroused him—the feel of her soft but firm body, the delicate scent of her skin, the feel of her hair gently touching his cheek, the way she seemed to lean back into him. He wished this instant could be frozen in time.

But too soon, the firearms instructor came over and said, "Lieutenant Haraldsson, your session is over for today. Come back tomorrow afternoon at 1400. I'll teach you how to field strip your weapon and put it back together."

"I'll be here," Jennifer said. "By the way, how'd I do today?"

"You did very well, particularly after Lieutenant Partude helped you hold your arm out straighter. I think we'll have a little time tomorrow for you to get more shooting practice in."

"Thank you very much."

"I'm proud of you," Dude told her as they walked to the car. "I could tell by the look in your eye that you were going to master it, and you did! I'll bet you succeed at most everything you do."

"Thank you, kind sir," Jennifer said appreciatively. "You deserve some credit, too. Your advice was very helpful."

Soon they were back at the hotel, and there was little time to spare before Jacob's arrival. They agreed to meet back at the check-in desk after going up to their rooms to shower and change.

"Well, I'll be," Dude said, feigning amazement as Jennifer arrived. "I didn't know young ladies could get ready in less than thirty minutes."

"You'd be surprised," Jennifer said with a giggle. "Miracles do happen when you have two brothers and two sisters."

A little after six, Jacob entered the hotel lobby. Dude hugged his brother and introduced him to Jennifer. She smiled and stuck out her hand. "I'm very pleased to meet you," she said. "You look a lot like

Dude." Pausing, she added that she could have picked him out of a crowd as being Dude's brother.

Jacob nodded. "How did this big lug meet someone as beautiful as you?" he asked, pointing his thumb at Dude.

As if by reflex, Dude thumped the back of his brother's head. Jacob winced.

"Now," Dude said, "you see why I told you he was a pain in the neck."

"I'm just an innocent bystander," Jennifer replied. "I'm not going to say anything." Obviously, being from a big family had taught her diplomacy.

The question now was where they should go to eat. "We like the dining room here," Dude said, "but maybe we should go somewhere else. After all, this is the nation's capital. Let's be adventurous."

They asked the hotel concierge for recommendations. "Why don't you try the Willard Hotel?" the concierge suggested. "That's where Abe Lincoln used to stay. It's on Pennsylvania Avenue and not far away. There's no need to take a cab."

Dude thanked the concierge, and the three went over to a sitting area to discuss the situation.

"I'm not thrilled about the idea of walking," Jennifer said. "It's dark, and it's freezing out there." She pulled a map out of her purse and ran her finger to where the Mayflower was positioned. "Here we are," she said. "And here is the Willard." She moved her finger to 14th and Pennsylvania. "It's a good six or seven blocks."

"Don't worry," Dude said soothingly. "Jacob and I will put you between us and keep you warm and toasty."

Jennifer gave a laugh that was nearly a snort. "How could I possibly say no to that? Let's go!"

The streets had an eerie feeling. Blackout rules were in force so windows were covered and street lighting was reduced to a minimum. "I wonder if all of this is really necessary," Jacob said.

"German submarines up and down the east coast are playing havoc with our shipping," Dude said, "And the Germans could well have moved bombers somewhere within range of Washington. God only knows how many uninhabited islands are located in the North Atlantic."

"I agree that the blackouts are necessary," Jennifer said, "However, I've read that the president still plans to light the Christmas tree on December 24. I think he's right to do it. Children deserve to have some enjoyment at Christmas, even if the world is in a terrible state."

They arrived at the Willard Hotel and went into its dining room. During the short wait before they were seated, Jennifer asked Jacob why he had decided to become a pilot.

"Well, I was like Dude. We both wanted to leave the farm. The harder our parents tried to get us to stay, the more we wanted to go. Dude found skiing. I found flying."

Dude laughed and shook his head. "Poor Joseph. He's our little brother. They'll probably chain him to the farm!" Jacob laughed too, but added, "With us gone, Dad needs his help more than ever."

"You guys are terrible!" Jennifer said. "I'll have to teach Joseph how to cope with you two." Dude was delighted by her remark. It meant Jennifer might want a relationship lasting beyond the Norway mission.

When they were finally seated, Jacob told them he felt lucky to have passed the eye exam and the strenuous physical test for Air Cadet training. The flight training would be at Randolph Field in Texas. He wanted to qualify for fighters, so he could take on the infamous Japanese Zero, but he would be happy to fly bombers if his first choice didn't pan out.

"Why did you become a nurse?" he asked Jennifer. "Doesn't the sight of blood bother you?"

"I like helping people," she said simply. "And, no, I'm not upset by the sight of blood. I'm still relatively new at nursing, but so far so good."

The conversation soon got around to how Dude and Jennifer had met. They, of course, had to mask the truth. "I was choking in a restaurant," Dude said. "Fortunately, Jennifer was there, and she saved me."

"Actually, Dude kept me from being run over by a car," Jennifer said. "We have been close friends ever since."

Jacob looked puzzled for a moment. Then he laughed. "You'd better think of something Mom will believe."

"All we can tell you is that we're going overseas together on a secret mission," Dude said turning serious. "We're allowed to tell our families not to expect to hear from us for a while, and that's all we can say."

"Are you sure that's all you can tell me?" Jacob asked.

"That's it, little brother."

"Okay, I get it. So, let's change the subject."

After a steak dinner and a final brandy to protect them against the night air, they all pledged to keep up with each other as best they could—and to meet again after the war to share one heck of a celebration. But where should they meet once it was all over?

"I've got it!" Jennifer said. "Let's meet under the clock at the St. Francis hotel in San Francisco! Party towns don't come any better, and the St. Francis would be perfect for a rendezvous. I've been there several times on vacation, so I know I'm right." Her eyes were sparkling.

"That's a wonderful suggestion," Dude said.

"I couldn't agree more," Jacob added.

With a triumphant smile, Jennifer said, "Good. It's settled."

With Jennifer snugly tucked between the brothers, the three walked back to their hotel. Their mood was light—almost euphoric. Conversation was not necessary. They simply enjoyed being together.

At breakfast the next morning, their mood was quite somber. Jacob would be leaving shortly, and Dude and Jennifer could not be certain that they would ever see him again. They sat silently, not knowing what to say.

Finally, Jennifer broke the ice. "Come on, you guys," she pleaded. "There must be something you want to say to each other. If it will help, just pretend I'm not here."

Dude thought for a moment. "Little brother," he said. "I'm very sorry for the times I thumped you on the head."

"And I'm sorry for giving you a reason to thump me."

"Well," Jennifer sighed. "I guess it's better than nothing." They finished their meal quietly.

Jacob went to his room to gather his belongings, and Jennifer and Dude waited for him in the lobby. When he reappeared, all three had trouble holding back their tears. "Come back safely," Dude said.

"You, too," Jacob replied. The three hugged, and soon Jacob was heading to Union Station and his own appointment with destiny.

The rest of the day was almost too busy for Jennifer and Dude, affording them little time to think of Jacob. Sergeant Johnson shuttled them from one place to another getting clothing, weapons, identification papers, and, most of all, briefings.

Their final briefing, this one on heavy water, took place in a top-secret area of the Army Headquarters building. Under tight security, Dude and Jennifer were ushered down the hall past General Marshall's office. They entered a briefing room with a big conference table, numerous chairs, and a viewgraph projector placed next to a lectern. Standing at the lectern was a tall, gangly second lieutenant with glasses. The lieutenant stepped forward to introduce himself.

"Hi, I'm Jack Dawkins, and I'm going to tell you everything you ever wanted to know about heavy water."

"That's what we're afraid of," Jennifer said, smiling. "Can you keep it as non-technical as possible?"

"I sure can, and don't hesitate to interrupt if you have any questions." *A nice guy for a technical type*, Dude thought.

Dude and Jennifer sat down, and Dawkins went back to the lectern. As he reached for the first briefing slide on a large stack of them, Dude raised his hand, feeling almost as though he were back at school. "I have an idea, Jack. Why don't you let us ask questions rather than go through all those slides?"

"Okay, shoot."

"I'll start," Jennifer said. "Why do they call it heavy water?"

"Well, because it's heavy."

"Okay, wise guy," Dude thundered. "Now give us the real answer!"

Dawkins snickered and used a handkerchief to wipe away a tear rolling down his cheek. "Sorry about that," he said. "But it was too good an opportunity to pass up. I promise to be serious from now on."

Regaining his composure, Dawkins continued. "A normal water molecule is composed of one atom of oxygen and two atoms of hydrogen. The atoms have negatively charged electrons orbiting positively charged nuclei, much like planets orbit the sun. The oxygen and hydrogen atoms are distinguished from each other by the number of electrons they have and the number of particles that make up their nuclei. Any questions so far?"

"No," Jennifer replied. "You're doing fine."

"How about you, Dude?"

"I'm good."

"Proceeding onward then, a hydrogen atom usually has a single proton at its center and a single electron spinning about that proton. But the hydrogen in heavy water also has a neutron—a particle with no electrical charge—in its nucleus. That neutron makes a dramatic difference. It means heavy water can be used to make a new kind of weapon, a bomb more destructive than anything the world has seen. Fortunately, heavy water is extremely rare. It must be concentrated, through a process such as electrolysis, from huge quantities of normal water."

"General Marshall said something about a new weapon the Germans might be developing," Jennifer said. "Are we working to build one, too?"

Dawkins shook his head. "No," he said.

"If we were, wouldn't we need heavy water?" Jennifer persisted.

"I don't think so. If we tried to build one—and I'm not saying we are—we'd probably listen to Leo Szilard, one of our scientists. Leo thinks that processed graphite—which is a lot easier to obtain than heavy water—would work just as well. Of course, we aren't telling the Germans that they might've made a major error by incorrectly assessing the potential of graphite."

Dawkins continued. "From here on," he said, "this briefing is going to get very technical in a hurry. Any more questions before we plunge ahead?"

"I guess not," Jennifer said.

I could ask one," Dude said, laughing. "But I'm sure I wouldn't understand the answer."

An hour later, after flipping through the slides and stopping regularly to inquire if there were questions, Dawkins concluded by saying, "I haven't been told what your mission is, but I can guess where you're going. Good luck!"

The last stop was the firing range, where both Dude and Jennifer blasted away until the instructor made them quit. By the end of the afternoon, Dude and Jennifer were exhausted.

After Sergeant Johnson returned them to the Mayflower, they had a quick dinner and then went to their rooms to attend to last-minute details, such as writing letters to their families. Jennifer wrote:

> *My Dearest, Darling Family:*
>
> *How I miss all of you! It seems as if we have been apart for an eternity. However, with the current world situation, I guess every American family will have to expect long separations.*
>
> *I am in Washington, D.C., waiting to start on a new assignment. Our nation's capital is absolutely beautiful. The Washington Monument, the Capital, and the White House are all gorgeous. I wish that I had time to visit some of them, but I don't think it will be possible. I will also have to pass on the Smithsonian Museum. However, I am now thinking that it may be for the best, as it would be a lot more fun to see these sites with all of you. You will definitely have to come here after the war is over!*
>
> *Daddy, I hope everything is okay with the farm. I worry about you having to work so hard. I hope that Billy and Buck are doing their fair share of the work. Buck, keep helping your brother with his math homework. It is important.*
>
> *Mama, I certainly miss your cooking! The thought of eating your fried chicken, mashed potatoes and gravy, and strawberry pie makes me drool! I hope someday that I will be as good a cook as you are and that my family will enjoy my cooking as much as I enjoy yours.*
>
> *Kristen and Kali, I can hardly wait to see you in your cheerleading uniforms. I'll bet you look adorable. I know you are good at it, having watched you practice in the backyard.*
>
> *My big news is that I might (just might!) have met Mr. Right. He is tall with brown hair and brown eyes,*

good-looking, well-educated, and very nice. He is athletic, and we have a number of interests in common. He also seems to like me! At this point, I am keeping my fingers crossed!

I mentioned earlier that I am in D.C. waiting on my next assignment. It will require that I don't contact you for a while. But I don't want you to worry! I will be fine and am very much looking forward to seeing you as soon as I can.

Well, I better close for now, as I have to get up early tomorrow.

Oodles and oodles of love always,
Jennifer

Dude wrote:

Dear Folks:

I am in Washington, D.C. I have a new assignment that will prevent me from contacting you for a while. But don't worry. I will be fine.

Jacob stopped by for a short visit, and it was great to see him. I hope all goes well for him in pilot training.

I have met a young lady who I think has all the qualities that I am looking for. She is smart, nice, and a very caring person. It certainly doesn't hurt that she is also very beautiful. I will keep you informed of progress in our relationship.

I miss you three very much and look forward to seeing you as soon as possible.

Love,
Dude

That night, in their separate rooms, Dude and Jennifer had trouble getting to sleep. Their great adventure was about to begin.

7

The Journey Begins

JENNIFER AND DUDE boarded a C-47 bound for Lakenheath Air Field in England. Jennifer plopped down onto a canvas seat. "I'm afraid these seats are anything but comfortable," she moaned.

"You're right. They're downright uncomfortable!" Dude replied. "By the way, do you remember our itinerary?"

"Yes. Our route takes us to Nova Scotia, Newfoundland, Greenland, Iceland, and then to Lakenheath."

"Some of those places I've never even heard of."

"Same here. It should be educational."

As the Army Air Force C-47 neared Halifax Nova Scotia, their first refueling stop on the flight to Lakenheath, Jennifer eagerly looked out a window. "What is so interesting out there?" Dude asked.

"*Anne of Green Gables* was my favorite book growing up, and the story takes place on Prince Edward Island. I think we may be able to see it from this altitude."

She turned to face Dude. "Have you read the book?"

"No, I haven't, but I guess I'd better. Tell me about it."

Jennifer was happy to oblige. "Anne is a very imaginative little girl who is an orphan and is desperately trying to find a home. She is headstrong and doesn't hesitate to speak her mind. I admired some of her traits and tried to be like her in certain respects."

Feigning shock, Dude said, "Well I can't ever imagine you being headstrong." She rewarded him for that remark with a playful poke in the ribs.

Soon, an island came into view that Jennifer thought must surely be her Island. The C-47's crew chief happened to be walking by her. She grabbed at his sleeve and asked.

"It certainly is, Lieutenant," he said. "You know your geography."

Looking out the window, Dude saw an island countryside of rolling hills, farmland, and pastures, and the island's tall cliffs dropping off into the ocean. Small ports notched the coastline.

"Well, now, I've seen something I always wanted to see," Jennifer said. "And just think, you've seen something you didn't even know you wanted to see."

Dude chuckled. "You're absolutely right, and I owe it all to you."

Airborne again after their stop at Halifax—next stop, Newfoundland—Jennifer dozed off with her head against Dude's shoulder. For him, the flight was long, but hardly boring. He was happy just to be with her.

When at last they arrived at Lakenheath, Major Francis Dunbar was there to greet them. "I am the British project officer assigned to your mission. I will see that you get to Norway and that you have transportation to return to England."

"Pleased to meet you, sir," Jennifer said.

"Same here, sir," Dude added.

"You must be very tired after your long trip. I'll take you to your quarters to get some rest. Then I'll be back to pick you up for dinner."

"What time will that be?" Dude asked.

"1800," Dunbar replied. "You will be meeting someone very special at dinner." Dude and Jennifer looked inquisitively at each other. "Tell us," Jennifer pleaded. The major just smiled and shook his head as the three got into the major's car.

After a few hours, Dude's alarm clock rang. Groggily, he turned it off and sat up in bed. "I wonder how Jennifer is feeling," he muttered to himself. He showered, dressed, and went outside. Looking at the next building, he saw the door open and Jennifer emerge. Suddenly, he felt better.

Dude walked over to where Jennifer was standing. "You're looking perky as ever," Dude said. "You must have gotten some sleep."

"Not really," Jennifer replied. "I was too excited about who we might see. I wonder if it will be the King of England."

"I don't know, but I'll bet it's someone really important."

Major Dunbar pulled up in front of Dude's building. Then he saw the two standing in front of Jennifer's quarters and drove over.

"Well, did you get some sleep?" he asked.

"I did," Dude replied. "But Jennifer didn't."

"Why not?"

"I was too excited about tonight," Jennifer said. "Can't you give us a hint about who we will be seeing?"

"I'm afraid not," Dunbar replied. "But I'm glad the accommodations didn't prevent you from sleeping. How were they?"

"Fine," both replied.

As Major Dunbar drove Dude and Jennifer into the heart of London, they were amazed at the damage done by the German *Luftwaffe*. Whistling softly, Dude said, "Major, will London ever be able to recover?"

"Absolutely. We Brits are tough! Bombs won't break our resolve. We'll stick it out here. Of course, we've evacuated a lot of our children to the countryside."

As the major swerved to avoid bricks, glass, and other rubble filling the streets, cleanup crews waved when they saw the American uniforms in the car.

Soon, Dude saw a famous landmark. Nudging Jennifer, he said, "There's Big Ben. We must be heading to the government complex." Was it possible that they would be dining with someone high up in the government? Finally, curiosity got the better of Jennifer, and she blurted out, "Please, Major, can't you tell us who we will be dining with?"

"Not yet, but you will find out very soon."

Dunbar parked in front of a brick building several stories high. As they approached the building, Dude noticed some stairs leading down that were surrounded by guards. "What's this?" he asked.

"These are stairs leading down to the prime minister's bunker."

"We're dining with the prime minister?" Jennifer said. "What a great honor!" she exclaimed. Dude made a feeble attempt to control his excitement.

"How did the prime minister even know we were coming?" Dude blurted out.

"In one of his encrypted messages," Dunbar said, "your President Roosevelt told Mr. Churchill that you were coming. Curiosity got the better of him, and he told us that he wanted to meet you. Obviously, you are very special, as someone at the very highest levels of your government selected you for this mission."

"Eating with him will be a tremendous honor for us," Jennifer said.

"As you'll see," Dunbar replied, "dinner is where the prime minister is at his best."

After descending the stairs, the three entered a passage lined with small rooms along one side. As they passed an open door, they saw a small bed and a beat-up desk with a microphone on it.

"This is where Churchill sleeps," Dunbar said. "And where he gives his radio broadcasts." Both Dude and Jennifer were impressed by the lack of amenities for such a great man.

They came to a room with maps attached to the walls. "Holy smoke!" Dude exclaimed. "Can we stop here a minute, Major?"

"Just for a minute."

"Look, Jennifer," Dude said. "These are maps of the Atlantic and Pacific Theaters. They show where all of the Allied forces are deployed and where the Axis units are located. Soon, there will be American troops included! Isn't that exciting?"

"Yes, it is," Jennifer replied. "But we can't keep the prime minister waiting."

The three continued down the hall. Finally, they entered a small chamber set up as a dining room. It couldn't be over fourteen feet by fourteen feet, Dude estimated. In the middle was a table with four chairs pulled up to it. *Even if leaves were added to the table*, Dude thought, *a maximum of eight people could be accommodated. Obviously, only select people ate here.*

At the far end of the room stood Churchill himself, alone, with his ever-present cigar in one hand and a drink in the other. The prime minister was wearing a zippered blue siren suit, a jumpsuit his staff called his "rompers." It gave him a whalelike appearance.

"Mr. Prime Minister," said the major, "I would like you to meet Lieutenants Jennifer Haraldsson and Jonathon Partude of the United States Army." With a twinkle in his eye, Churchill stuck out his hand. "Well," he said, "This is a real honor. My dinner these days is usually with a bunch of old fuddy-duddies. It will be a pleasure to host two young people who are starting on a magnificent journey. I only wish that I could go with you!"

"Thank you very much for inviting us, sir," Dude said.

"It is a real honor, Mr. Prime Minister," Jennifer added.

Churchill motioned for Dude, Jennifer, and the major to take their seats. During dinner, between bites of food, puffs on his cigar, and sips of wine, he spoke of the world situation. He expressed grief at America's loss at Pearl Harbor, asserted that Hitler's mistakes were piling up, and predicted that the Allies would be victorious.

"Sir, not to be argumentative, but could you give some examples of Hitler's mistakes?" Dude asked. "He seems to be doing pretty well so far."

"Ah, yes. Well, my boy, looks can be deceiving, and you are sitting in the middle of one of his biggest mistakes. He got bored with bombing our airfields, so he started bombing London. While it has been terribly hard on our citizenry, it allowed us to reconstitute our fighter force. And we are once again in control of our skies."

Taking a puff on his cigar, Churchill continued. "Looking to the east, Hitler undoubtedly attacked Russia with blinders on. The combination of weather and distance has brought his armies—for the first time, mind you—to a standstill. Will his armies regain their momentum when winter passes? I don't know. But I do know this: from a strategic standpoint, he should never have committed his armies to a two-front war. Fortunately for us, he did." The three guests nodded as a melancholy expression swept over the prime minister's face.

"The problem is," he added sadly, "there will be a terrible price to pay. Germany and her allies won't give up easily."

Changing the subject, Jennifer asked the prime minister how his visit with President Roosevelt in Washington. D.C. had been. His mood brightened instantly. "It was fantastic, my dear. Being with your President reminded me of opening a bottle of fine champagne. However, there was one small problem."

Looking around as if he didn't want the wrong people to hear, the prime minister said in a hushed voice, "He didn't have any ninety-year-old brandy!"

They all laughed.

"I am also happy to report that your President now knows that I have nothing to hide," Churchill added. "He came into my room one morning when I was stark naked!" They all laughed again, even harder. Dunbar nearly choked on his food.

Then Churchill turned serious. "I am afraid that FDR and I do have some serious disagreements. He agrees with your General Marshall, who wants our Allied nations to go straight for Hitler's throat by attacking Europe this year. However, I think it is too dangerous right now. I can't help but remember the fields of France running red with blood in the First World War. Many fine men lost their lives in that conflict. I think it would be much better for us to attack in other theaters, waiting until we are stronger before invading Europe. I only hope President Roosevelt will eventually agree with me."

He lost himself in his thoughts for a moment before continuing. "Your President is most gracious. It was his sad duty to inform me of our surrender at Tobruk. I could not fathom how thirty thousand British men could throw up their hands and surrender. Your President could have taken the opportunity to denigrate the British military, but he did not. He simply said, 'I'm sorry.'"

At the conclusion of dinner, Mr. Churchill told Jennifer and Dude that he wanted to show them his latest painting before they left. They followed him to another small room, where the painting still rested on its easel. It was a scene that he had painted at Chartwell, his country estate. It was a painting of the mansion and some of the grounds.

Churchill winked at Jennifer. "Not bad for an amateur, eh?"

"I'm no expert, Mr. Prime Minister," Jennifer replied, "but I think it's very good. I love your use of color, the details in the surrounding countryside, and the scaling of the objects."

"I have to agree," Dude added. "If it were for sale, I'd buy it!"

"Better be careful," the prime minister said with a laugh. "I just might sell it to you for a decent price."

He accompanied his American guests out to their car, then remarked that he wanted to feed the ducks in St. James Park. "Isn't it dangerous for you to be out? Jennifer asked.

"Even in London, there may be German assassins lurking," Churchill said. "But I like to dance with danger."

8

On to Norway

THE NEXT MORNING, Jennifer and Dude collected their belongings and waited for Major Dunbar to arrive. They had both eaten breakfast in the dining halls of their respective quarters.

Major Dunbar was right on time and whisked Jennifer and Dude to another nondescript building in a complex not far from Churchill's bunker. They walked up a short flight of stairs, entered the front door, and walked down a poorly lit hallway to a doorway on the left that admitted them into a conference room. A British officer was seated at the big, rectangular table that took up most of the space. He stood up and introduced himself as Navy Lieutenant Commander Tom Brookstone. After making introductions, Dunbar said, "You will see how Tom fits in when I start my briefing."

Motioning for Dude and Jennifer to have a seat, Major Dunbar began. "Tonight you will leave by submarine for the southeastern coast of Norway. The submarine is the *HMS Windstorm*, and Tom here is the skipper. Brookstone smiled and winked at Jennifer.

"You will travel submerged until you are near your destination," Dunbar continued. "After *Windstorm* surfaces, a small boat will take you to the coast where two members of the Norwegian Underground will meet you. They are Aksel Hansdtr and Lars Nefsteinn."

Dude could hardly believe it. "My gosh! Lars is my old college roommate!" Jennifer patted his arm. "Small world, isn't it?"

"Unfortunately," Dunbar said, "Aksel and Lars can only accompany you for a short way. The Germans have registered all Norwegian adults, and they do not allow people who might be in the Underground to travel far from home. However, Aksel and Lars will get you to a point where you can take a bus to Telemark. That is where Professor Flannigan is being hidden."

"What happens if we get stopped?" Jennifer asked.

"You will have papers identifying you as residents of Telemark." He gave them a map marked to show Flannigan's location. "Memorize that, then destroy it. You must not get caught with it."

"We know the Germans are looking for Flannigan," Dunbar continued, "so you won't be able to bring him straight back." He went to a map of Norway that was hanging on the wall and traced their escape route with his finger. "Instead, you will have to take a more circuitous route to meet the submarine here off the coast of the Vest-Agder area, which is farther to the southwest than where you will have landed. The Norwegian Underground has confirmed that this route will be your best hope of getting out undetected. The *Windstorm* will be surfacing off Vest-Agder at precisely 2100 hours every night for a week. A landing party will come ashore and wait for you. If you have not appeared by the end of the week, it will be assumed that you have not survived, and the submarine will not return again for you."

"That's a little extreme, isn't it?" Dude remarked. "If we don't make it to the coast on time, we're simply abandoned there?"

"The submarine will be needed elsewhere," Dunbar replied.

"Just try to get back in the allotted time," Brookstone said.

Dude wondered whether there was hidden meaning in Brookstone's response. Was the commander trying to tell them that he would wait for them if they were delayed? What about Dunbar? Could the major stand to sit idly by while they perished? After all, people at the highest levels knew of this mission, and Dunbar was more or less responsible for them. A lot of unanswered questions remained in Dude's mind.

Dunbar continued, explaining that Aksel and Lars would brief them on a series of cabins that they could use in making their way to the rendezvous point. The cabins, isolated and nearly undetectable from the air, would be stocked with supplies.

"I wish I were going inland with you," Dunbar said. "But if I did, I would blow your cover. So I will accompany you on the way over, and I will be on the *Windstorm* when you return."

"Where do we board the *Windstorm*?" Dude asked.

"Good question. You will be driven this afternoon to Portsmouth, which is a sixty- to ninety-minute drive from here. It is on the southern coast of England—actually on an island in the English Channel. The *Windstorm* is docked there."

"Any other questions?"

"No," Dude replied after looking at Jennifer.

"All right then. We'll get you some lunch and then head out." The three departed the building and got into Major Dunbar's staff car.

The drive through the countryside was peaceful, and the scenery was breathtaking. The landscape was a vivid green, and cottages with thatched roofs dotted the hillsides. Major Dunbar sat in the front with the driver, and the two Americans occupied the back.

As they dropped over a crest, Portsmouth Naval Base appeared. Even from a distance, Dude could tell that it was a beehive of activity.

"Aren't the British worried that this base provides an excellent target for German bombers?" Dude asked.

"Yes," Dunbar replied. "But as we get closer, you'll see all the anti-aircraft batteries. Anytime the Germans have made it this far, they've paid dearly."

"They've also had to take on your Spitfires and Hurricanes before they even get here," Jennifer added. "Isn't that correct?"

"Indeed it is," Dunbar said. "Our chaps rough them up pretty good while they're still out over the Channel."

Jennifer, Dude, and the major were driven to a terminal building. They got out of the car and got their gear. They entered the building. "Go ahead and change into your Norwegian clothing," Dunbar said. He pointed to their respective dressing rooms. "I'll go aboard the *Windstorm* to make sure they're ready for you. Then I'll come back."

After changing clothes, Dude and Jennifer came out to the lounge area and sat down. Dude noticed that Jennifer looked troubled. "You seem worried."

"I am a little. It concerns me that we may be stranded over there."

"I've been thinking about that, too. And it may not be as bleak as Dunbar tried to make us believe."

"Why?"

"Did you see the medals on his chest?"

"Yes. They're quite impressive."

"Exactly," Dude replied. "It doesn't make sense that they would have him simply ride back and forth on a submarine. There are a number of places where they desperately need a man with his credentials."

"You think he's coming along in case we get in trouble?"

Dude nodded. "I have a feeling that Churchill would lose face with Roosevelt if something happened to us."

"I hope you're right."

As evening approached, Major Dunbar came up beside them and said for them to follow him out a door and down a gangplank. At the bottom was a submarine with the markings *HMS Windstorm*. The three descended the narrow bridge and were piped aboard. The skipper, Tom Brookstone, greeted them.

Dude and Jennifer were shown to their quarters. After unpacking and settling in, they went up to the bridge to join Dunbar and Brookstone. Dude was enjoying being on the open water, and he could tell that Jennifer was too. About a half-hour out of port, however, the rollercoaster motion of the North Sea waves made both of them nauseous.

"Why don't you go to your quarters and lie down until the *Windstorm* submerges?" Dunbar said. "You'll be more comfortable." They took the advice and retired to the small rooms they'd been assigned. While Dude shared a cramped, reconfigured room with a junior officer, Jennifer had the luxury—if one could call it that—of private quarters.

As the *Windstorm* rocked from side to side, the drawers in the wall of Dude's room flew open with a bang and slammed shut with a bang.

Not feeling up to doing anything about it, he lay in his bunk listening to the mind-numbing noise for what seemed like an eternity.

The *Windstorm* finally submerged, and both Jennifer and Dude were very much relieved. Everything became calm, and the two Americans soon felt up to eating something. They joined Dunbar and Brookstone in the officers' mess. After they were seated, Dunbar passed a bowl to Jennifer. "What is this?" she asked.

"We'd like to know, too," Brookstone quipped. "No, you really wouldn't," Dunbar replied. "I spent time in Scotland, and people there call it *haggis*."

"Actually, it's pretty good," Dude said, taking a healthy bite. "It tastes meaty."

"Oh, it's got meat in it alright," said Dunbar, laughing.

Turning to Jennifer, Dude tried to get her to eat. "Come on, dig in. You'll need your strength." She tasted it, gingerly at first, but was bolder with her second bite.

As they ate, Brookstone told tales of the British Navy intercepting German shipping and how the Royal Navy had tracked down and sunk the mighty battleship *Bismarck*.

Dude asked, "Since Norway was neutral and still willing to trade with Germany, why did Germany feel the need to attack?"

"Well, for one thing," Brookstone replied, "it allowed the German Navy to establish bases in Norway. In just the past month or so, German subs stationed along the Norwegian coast have torpedoed three British ore ships."

"Have British subs been able to retaliate?" Jennifer asked.

"Actually, they have," Dunbar replied. "Tom was on the crew of the *Seawolf* when it bagged the German transports *Hamm* and *Bressheim*."

"We almost got the Battleship *Tirpitz*, too," Brookstone lamented. "We spotted it, but it was able to escape."

"Is the *Tirpitz* still in Norwegian waters?" Dude asked.

"Yes, it is," Brookstone said.

"Aha!" Jennifer said triumphantly. "There must be a lot of important German warships nearby."

"I think I get the point," Dunbar said, somewhat amused.

"What she's—what we're—hinting at," Dude added, "is that we hope you'll come to pick us up even if we don't make it back by the deadline."

Brookstone looked at Dunbar. "I can't answer that. Can you, Frank?"

"Let's leave it the way Tom put it on land. Do the best you can."

Not a big help, Dude thought, *but better than a total rejection.*

As they finished eating, Dude said, "I just have one more question. Major, what are your medals for?"

"Oh, he's too modest to tell you," Brookstone said, "so I will. The top ribbon—the crimson one—is the *Victoria Cross*. It's Britain's highest honor, like your Congressional medal. The old boy won it for great bravery at Dunkirk. He was one of the last to leave the beach."

"It's the lads who came to pick us up in all kinds of fishing vessels who deserve the credit," Dunbar replied.

Extending her hand, Jennifer said, "It's an honor to know you, Major."

"Ditto," Dude said with a respectful nod.

After their dinner with the skipper and Major Dunbar, Dude and Jennifer rested in their bunks until the *Windstorm* surfaced and it was time to board the dinghy that would take them to shore. As they exited their small quarters, they bumped into each other in the narrow passageway. The sight of Jennifer took Dude's breath away. She had very little makeup on but was still beautiful.

"Imagine!" he said. "Running into a beautiful young lady out here in the middle of nowhere."

"And my running into a handsome young man."

On deck, Brookstone and Dunbar were waiting for them. Breaking the ice, Dude said, "I guess we can be thankful for Norway's mountainous terrain. If you want to evade an enemy anywhere in the world, Norway is as good a place as any." All agreed.

Brookstone wished them Godspeed, and Jennifer and Dude saluted. The night was bitter cold as two men moved a small rubber boat out of a hatch in the *Windstorm's* side. Each man had an oar.

"My thoughts and prayers are with you," Dunbar said to the two Americans as they headed toward the dinghy. "The water looks calm," he added. "But it may get a little choppy before you reach land."

"Thanks, Major," Jennifer said. "You've made our journey a lot easier."

Dude jumped into the boat and turned around to extend a hand to Jennifer. After descending into the boat, she gave no indication that she wanted to let go. In fact, she grasped his hand even tighter. She sat as close to him as possible.

No one spoke as the rubber boat pushed off and fought through choppy waters toward the beach. "I'm beginning to feel nauseous again," Jennifer said. "So am I," Dude replied. "Thank goodness we don't have far to go."

Looking shoreward, Dude saw the dim glow of a flashlight pointed downward, a signal, he assumed, marking the spot where they were to land. As the dinghy drew nearer, he could see two shadowy figures within the pale circle of light. He felt a surge of excitement. One of them would be his friend Lars. The bottom of the dinghy scraped against sand. Dude clambered out of the boat, then helped Jennifer out. Holding hands, they waded into Norway.

9

Rendezvous

Dude and Lars hugged briefly, and introductions were made all around in hushed tones. "Let me look at you," Dude said. Lars appeared as Dude remembered him except for the scraggly beard and a somewhat thinner profile. "Are you getting enough to eat?" Dude asked. "Yes," Lars replied, "but as you Americans say, things haven't exactly been a piece of cake over here." Dude nodded sadly.

Holding out his arm, Lars said, "I'll walk with Jennifer, and Aksel can walk with you. Aksel just grunted, but Dude replied, "I see you haven't changed a bit. Always trying to steal the beautiful girls."

"Is there a more worthwhile undertaking?" Lars retorted. Jennifer smiled as the men bantered back and forth.

Lars turned serious. "We'll have to be as quiet as possible as we move inland. Aksel and I will use hand signals to let you know what we want you to do."

"Why?" Dude asked. "Are there German patrols out at night?"

"No," Lars replied. "But there are Quislings everywhere."

"What's a Quisling?" Jennifer inquired.

"I'll tell you later," Lars said. He put a finger to his lips.

They departed the beach and went up a rocky slope. At the top was a path that led through a heavily forested piece of land. Turning around, Lars signaled for them to walk single file. *Amazing*, Dude thought. It was nighttime, but the reflection off the snow was bright enough that they had no trouble seeing where they were going.

After what seemed to Dude to be about twenty minutes, they came to a small, unlit cottage with smoke coming out its chimney. Lars looked around briefly and motioned the others to follow him to the front door. He thrust a key into the lock, quickly turned it, and pushed the door open. The four hurried inside.

Aksel and Lars lit several candles that were dispersed around the room. After finishing, they collected coats and some light luggage that the Americans were carrying.

Dude looked around. *Not plush, but adequate*, he thought. Across the room, about fifteen feet away, was a big fireplace with an ample fire burning brightly inside. To the right was a small kitchen area. An iron pot hung over a hearth, and there was a crude wooden table with four chairs pulled up to it. To the back, behind the kitchen, there appeared to be a small room. Probably a bedroom, Dude guessed. There were three bearskin rugs scattered on the floor near the fireplace.

"Now we can talk, my friends," Lars said. He motioned for Jennifer and Dude to come over to the table and sit down. "I see that I have to bail you out once again, Roomie. Isn't it enough that I got you through your language requirement and taught you how to ski?"

"Maybe so, but you'd have flunked calculus without my help."

"Sounds pretty even to me," Jennifer said in her host's native tongue.

"Your Norwegian is excellent!" Lars said. "Far better than this oaf's."

Much to Dude's relief, Jennifer came to his aid. "Oh, I think he does pretty well."

Interrupting, Aksel asked Jennifer how her Norwegian had gotten so good. "My maternal grandparents are from Trondheim and spoke Norwegian in their home. It is very natural for me. I even came here with them for a couple of long visits."

"Ah, so you know your way around Norway," Lars said jokingly.

"No," she replied. "Dude and I will have to rely on you and Aksel. But, before you try to change the subject, what is a Quisling?"

"A Quisling is a traitor, to be blunt. Our—ha ha!—beloved leader's name is Vidkun Quisling. He is nothing but a puppet for the German government."

"Lars is absolutely right," Aksel said. "Norwegians who aid the Germans are called Quislings. You have to be very careful of them, as they will turn you in if they think you are doing anything to oppose the Germans."

"I'm glad you told us," Jennifer replied.

The conversation turned to lighter subjects. After Dude and Lars brought each other up to date on their families, Lars turned to Jennifer. "We want to hear all about you, and don't leave out any of the details!"

"I'll be short," Jennifer promised, as if anyone wanted her to be. As she talked, Dude watched Aksel and Lars. They were either totally wrapped up in what she was saying or hypnotized by her great beauty. He hoped it was the former. He felt a sense of relief when she finished.

Once again, Aksel spoke up. "It's time to brief you on your escape route from Telemark, once you have linked up with Professor Flannigan," he said. There was an old map of Norway on one of the cabin walls. Aksel stood in front of it, as if about to give a lecture. He traced with a finger the path they would take southwest through the mountains.

"Five cabins spaced at intervals of several kilometers have been stocked with supplies for you. We're certain the Germans have not yet discovered these cabins," he said. "But you should have no trouble finding them."

He described the landmarks they should look for on the approach to each cabin.

"What about skis and snowshoes?" Jennifer asked.

"You will be given footwear in Telemark," Lars said. "And there are skis in the cabins. But I don't know if the professor has ever used skis or even snowshoes."

"We'll soon find out," Dude sighed.

"Lars, is there anything else you want to tell us?" Jennifer asked. "I get the feeling you're hiding something."

"Well, there is one pass that could be a bit of a challenge. But I'm sure you can handle it."

"I'll bet," Dude said. "I remember when you told me something was a piece of cake. I was almost killed!"

"Oh, well," Jennifer sighed. "We'll have to accept whatever arises. If the professor can't ski or if there is a difficult hill to negotiate, there's nothing we can do about it."

"That's the spirit!" Lars said. "I think that fellow Norman Vincent Peale calls it thinking positive."

"We'd better move on," Aksel injected. "It's getting late."

The two Norwegians took turns peppering the Americans with questions to test how well they'd retained the instructions about the escape route and other matters. Finally, Lars turned to Aksel. "By golly, I think they've got it, don't you?"

"Yes, I do."

"I'm feeling a lot better about things," Dude said. "Somehow, we're going to make it."

"Especially if these guys are close by," Jennifer added. Both Aksel and Lars remained noncommittal.

"Who wants hot chocolate and cookies?" Lars asked. The unanimous response was "I do!" Lars lit the wood stove, and soon the aroma of chocolate filled the cabin. Meanwhile, Aksel retrieved some chocolate chip cookies that had been stored on a shelf outside. "These need to be warmed up, but I assure you they're delicious," he said.

After they'd consumed the treats, Lars said, "I think we should turn in for the night. You two have a long trip ahead of you. Jennifer, you can have the bedroom. We three will sleep here near the fireplace."

"Actually, I would prefer to be near the fire," she said.

"In that case," Lars said winking at his former roommate, "you and Dude can stay out here. Aksel and I will take the bedroom."

"Good!" Dude said. "I doubt she will snore as loudly as you two." Jennifer pounded him lightly on the shoulder.

After Lars and Aksel had retired to the bedroom, Dude and Jennifer placed their pallets close together near the fireplace and lay down, still fully clothed. Looking deeply into each other's eyes, they could no longer control their feelings. They were soon smothering each other with long, hard, desperate kisses, their hands trembling as each reached to unbutton the other's clothing.

At dawn, Lars opened the door of the bedroom and boomed, "Time to rise, sleepyheads." He added that they wouldn't peek while the Americans dressed.

"Is it that time already?" Dude moaned from deep under the covers.

Jennifer, her hair falling down over her eyes, raised her head and looked around. "It feels like I just got to sleep," she muttered.

Soon the two snapped out of their fog, then dressed themselves under the covers and rose from their pallets. Stretching, Jennifer smiled and said "Good morning, darling."

The two kissed briefly.

"Okay," Jennifer shouted towards the bedroom, "you two can come out now."

"*God morgen*," Lars said cheerfully, as he strolled out. Soon, Aksel appeared.

Lars set out breakfast. He'd brought fresh bread, fruit jams, and smoked sausages. He brewed a pot of strong coffee. "You must eat heartily," he said. "You will need lots of energy." But his encouragement was unnecessary, as Jennifer and Dude were famished.

Winking at Aksel, Lars said, "Aksel, did you hear any strange noises in the night? I thought I did, but I couldn't tell what they were."

"You know, I did hear something!" Aksel replied. "It sounded like squirrels falling from trees."

Jennifer merely blushed, but Dude said, "Talk about noise! You two snored so loudly I thought there were a couple of foghorns in that bedroom."

The four finished eating, and Jennifer and Dude got their belongings together. Each had a .38 caliber handgun with twelve rounds of ammunition. Soon, the foursome was ready to leave for the bus depot in the small town of Kristiansand.

As they departed the cabin, Dude saw that it was surrounded by mountains shrouded in clouds. *What a spectacular view,* he thought. Quickly the four donned the skis and goggles stashed in the cabin and started their downward trek, smoothly and effortlessly gliding over the powdery snow. Looking at Jennifer, Lars shouted, "You are a wonderful skier, Jennifer." She nodded but kept her eyes on the terrain ahead. She not only kept up with them but also moved a little out in front.

The terrain flattened after a half hour. At a convenient spot, they removed their skiing gear and placed it behind a clump of bushes. "Kristiansand is that way," Lars said pointing to the east.

They arrived at the edge of town after a ten-minute hike. They saw no German soldiers on the street as they walked toward the bus station, and there were none to be seen near the line of people waiting to board the bus.

The line moved rapidly. Jennifer was about to step aboard when two German soldiers came around the front of the bus. One of them commanded, "Halt!" and asked to see her papers. Lars stepped up to the soldier. "Hans, my friend, this is my sister," he said. "Isn't she beautiful? This ugly man behind her is her husband. I don't know how he was so lucky." Both Germans chuckled, and the one who had demanded Jennifer's identification waved her and Dude onto the bus. *Dodged a bullet there*, Dude thought. He guessed it was worth letting Lars get away with calling him ugly.

Part III

10

They Meet at Last

THE RIDE TO Telemark went without incident. When they arrived, they saw German soldiers everywhere. And not far from the bus station, as they walked rapidly toward the house where they expected to find Flannigan, they were stopped and told to produce their papers. Fortunately the soldiers found the papers to be in order, and the two were allowed to continue on their journey.

At the professor's hideout, Dude knocked for what seemed like an eternity before an elderly lady finally opened the door. She frowned at them. "What do you want?" she hissed.

"*Uavhengighet*," said Dude, using the Norwegian word for independence. The woman relaxed and smiled after hearing the correct password. "I'm Inger," she said. "The professor is being hidden in the attic. I can't climb stairs anymore, but you go to the second floor. You'll find a long pole leaning in a corner. Use it to knock rapidly four times on the attic door. Someone will drop a ladder from the attic for you to climb."

Dude and Jennifer went up together. They found the pole. Dude rapped it against the attic door, and it opened. A bearded man peered down. "We're here for the professor," they said

The man nodded, then disappeared. Soon, a ladder dropped down, and Jennifer began to climb up, giving Dude an unexpected view of her curvaceous figure. Momentarily, he forgot about the mission.

By the time Dude had reached the top of the ladder, Jennifer was already shaking hands with a short, bearded, rotund man he recognized instantly, from the photos he had seen, as James Flannigan.

"Professor," Jennifer announced, "we're here to take you home."

Looking stunned, the professor recovered quickly. "My dear," he said, "I was expecting a squad of commandos, not a beautiful young lady. Please forgive me if I seem somewhat surprised."

"I hope you aren't disappointed," Jennifer replied.

"Not at all. I would much rather be traveling with you!"

"By the way, I'm Jennifer, and this is Dude."

"I'm James, and the man who dropped the ladder is Anker," the professor said. "Anker brought me all the way from Vemork, risking his own life to save my neck."

"I glad to do it," Anker said in broken English. "I lead you out of Telemark tonight and start you to first cabin." Both Jennifer and Dude thanked him.

"I must admit," the professor said after Anker had left. "I'm curious as to why you two were selected."

"It's because Jennifer and I are advanced skiers," Dude replied, "and we both speak Norwegian."

"The fact that Dude and I could pose as man and wife didn't hurt either," Jennifer added. "General Marshall felt that we would attract less attention from the Germans."

"That all makes sense, but I hope the fact that you're both good skiers doesn't mean that we're going to do much skiing."

"No, not at all," Jennifer said. "Besides, I'm a nurse, and I'll take good care of you."

"My dear," Flannigan replied, "you may wish that you had an ambulance at your disposal before we're through!" All three laughed.

After a short rest, Dude and Jennifer briefed Flannigan on the escape plan. "How long do you think it will take to reach the coast?" he asked.

"We think it will take about five days," Dude said.

"What happens then?"

"A British submarine will be waiting for us."

"And if we don't get there in five days?"

"There's a backup plan," Dude said. "But I have to admit—we don't know exactly what it is." Jennifer nodded.

"I think I know," Flannigan quipped. "We become naturalized Norwegian citizens."

"Professor," Jennifer said laughing, "I can tell that you have a really good sense of humor." Flannigan smiled and winked.

As they rested in the attic through the afternoon, Jennifer found a quiet moment to speak privately to Dude. "He's overweight," she whispered. "And his reddish complexion means he might have high blood pressure. We'll have to keep a close eye on him."

Oh great, Dude thought. *As if we don't already have enough problems.*

That evening, before beginning their journey, they ate a hearty meal of lamb-and-potato stew. During dinner, Flannigan appeared very relaxed. "You said you'd met General George Marshall," he said, addressing Dude. "How is the old goat?"

Dude was shocked and at a loss for words. How could anyone refer to the great general as an old goat? Seeing his anguish, Jennifer reached over and patted his shoulder. "Calm down, dear. I think the professor is just having a little fun."

Flannigan laughed. "You're absolutely right, Jennifer. George and I grew up in the same hometown, and I hold him in the highest regard. I must admit, though, Dude's response was exactly what I was looking for. I thought we could all use a little levity."

"You're right, Professor," Dude replied. "Relaxation will do us all some good."

After dinner the professor sat in an upholstered chair and lit his pipe. Noticing something in his expression, Jennifer asked, "You seem sad, Professor? Is there anything I can do?"

"No, my dear. It's just that I fear my good friends Professor and Mrs. Jungstad, who were helping me monitor the heavy water plant, have been captured by the Germans. I got out of Vemork safely but had to leave them behind.

Jennifer nodded. "Professor, I'm sure there was nothing you could have done to help them."

"I could have avoided getting them involved."

"You did your duty, Professor," Jennifer said softly. "That's all any of us can do." Flannigan nodded.

Well after dark, Anker approached them and said it was time to go, and Dude, Jennifer, and the professor prepared to leave the attic. "I'll go down first," Dude said. "Jennifer, why don't you bring up the rear?"

"Sounds like a good plan," she replied.

By placing themselves above and below the elderly man, they were able to hang onto him just enough to insure that he got down safely. Inger was waiting when they reached the bottom. "Thank you for what you are doing for us," she said.

"No, my dear," Flannigan replied. "Thank you."

"Perfect response," Dude said. Jennifer agreed.

The travelers bundled themselves against the cold, shouldered their backpacks, and left the warm dwelling. They would wait until they were beyond the edge of town to put on the snowshoes. They wanted to avoid leaving conspicuous prints in the snow-dusted streets.

Part IV

11

Two-Front War

"GERMANY DECLARES WAR on the United States!" screamed the headlines of the local Norwegian paper. Walking by the newsstand on his way to work, Captain Otto Bruner of the German Schutzstaffel, or SS, was stunned. True, the United States had declared war on Germany's ally, Japan. *But there must be another way*, he thought. After all, Germany was presently taking on the Soviet Union as well as England. Must it also face the industrial might of America? While many in Germany believed Hitler's continual blustering—that America was soft, weak, and unprepared—Otto knew better. He was sure that a country with America's potential would quickly remedy any shortcomings.

Otto had to hide from his superiors that he was not a true believer. If they suspected that he had any doubts whatsoever, he would be removed from his posting in Oslo and sent to the Russian Front. The fact that he had distinguished himself as a staff officer on the battlefields of France would be of no consequence.

Bruner increased his gait, wanting to reach his office as quickly as possible. He was tall and thin, and his long legs moved him quickly through the Norwegian capital in great strides. He had dark brown hair and a kindly expression rather than the usual stern appearance of a German officer. As he passed Norwegians on this Oslo street, Otto nodded politely. Some nodded and smiled back.

Better get my mind back on the business at hand, Otto thought as he climbed the stairs in front of the SS headquarters. Word had come in from Gestapo agents that a famous American physicist, James Flannigan, was on a secret mission in Norway to check on Germany's development of heavy water. The task of bringing Flannigan into custody had been given to Otto, and he did not take the responsibility lightly.

As he reached the building entrance, he turned to gaze at the magnificent scenery circling the city, the sparkling waters of the Oslofjord, the majestic green hills, the towering mountains. *Can't spend much time daydreaming*, Otto told himself. If he did, the consequences could be severe.

A corporal waited at the door of Otto's small office. The corporal saluted smartly and handed Otto a folder marked "Secret." Otto returned the salute, tucked the folder under his arm, and entered his office. He dropped the folder on his desk and hung up his coat and hat on a rack in the corner of the room.

He ran a comb through his hair, then sat down at his desk and opened the classified folder. After reading its brief contents, he closed the folder, grabbed his coat and hat, and rushed out of his office, slamming the door behind him. "Time to see the major," he groaned.

12

Chain of Command

MAJOR PETER SCHMIDT was one of six thousand members of the German SS then stationed in Norway. The SS had been tasked by Adolph Hitler to take on the most important tasks as determined by the führer himself. Obviously, Norway was important to Hitler for a number of reasons. One of these was the availability of heavy water.

Schmidt was a favorite of Obergruppenfuhrer Wilhelm Rediess, the SS leader, who had given Schmidt the authority to handle tasks usually assigned to officers of much higher rank. One of these tasks was to stay abreast of any unusual activities in his sector and to take corrective action as necessary.

Although he was one of the youngest majors in the German Army, Schmidt was the consummate SS officer, with short, blond hair, steely blue eyes, and a total lack of sympathy for anyone other than himself. And he was ruthlessly efficient. He had unlimited potential for promotion.

He did appreciate the finer things in life. His cabinets were well stocked with the finest wines and champagnes. He'd brought his own personal chef from Germany, and he regularly kept an eye out for pretty young ladies who might be added to his substantial list of conquests. He also loved classical music, especially Mozart and Schubert.

The major had debated for only a short time about where to establish his headquarters. His choices included Trondheim on the west coast, Kristiansand on the south coast, and Oslo, the country's capital. Each had its advantages. Trondheim was close to Germany's archenemy England and would allow him to keep an eye on Norway's western approaches. Kristiansand was closest to his beloved Germany. Oslo had more creature comforts and was a hub of activity.

Being extremely ambitious, he based his decision—Oslo—on how he believed his superiors would view it. That was his modus operandi, and it had served him well in the past. His superiors, he knew, would applaud his locating in Norway's capital. Symbolism counted in the SS.

As soon as he arrived in Norway's capital, Schmidt confiscated a very comfortable residence in the city that was near to the center of government. It might not be the most luxurious, as there were German officials in the city who outranked him, but it was very nice. And it was spacious enough to provide both an office complex and his personal quarters.

Normally, Schmidt arrived at his office at about ten in the morning. This allowed him time to recover from the previous night's activities and to be at his sharpest when he settled behind his desk to get down to business.

In the rare event that someone important tried to contact him before ten o'clock, Schmidt had given his staff strict orders to put them right through to his apartment on the phone or have them wait momentarily in his outer office. Since he always shaved and showered at night, it was only a matter of minutes before he could dress, slip down the back stairs into his office, and be seated at his desk. The ruse had worked well in the past, and he was confident that it would keep working well in the future.

Outside his office was a parlor with two desks, one for an aide and the other for a secretary. It was his normal practice to have two armed guards with machine guns in the dwelling at all times. After all, one never knew if some malcontent might come storming in to do him bodily harm.

This day was starting as usual. His breakfast in bed included poached eggs, sausage, strudel, orange juice, and coffee. After dressing leisurely, he descended the stairs and entered his office. He had just lit a cigarette and sat down at his desk when he heard a rap on his door. "Come in!" he barked. "Oh, it's you, Bruner," he said upon seeing the young officer. "And here I was thinking it might be someone important!"

"I may not be important, sir, but I think the news that I bear is."

"I'll be the judge of that. Let's have it."

"Our agents have determined that Professor Flannigan is on his way to Telemark."

Schmidt thought for a moment. "Hmm. That is interesting. How sure are they?"

"Quite sure, I think. They didn't say 'could be' but said 'is.' You can read it yourself." Otto handed the folder to Schmidt, but the major brushed it away.

Schmidt leaned back in his chair, smiling. "Arresting a spy who is a world-famous physicist will be quite a feather in my cap. It should certainly help me get my next promotion."

"Will you be going to Telemark, sir?"

"Of course I will! You don't think I would leave it up to a *dumbkoff* like you, do you?"

"Of course not, Herr Major!" Otto said, clicking his heels.

"There is hope for you yet," Schmidt replied. The major was obviously pleased that his subordinate had shown complete subservience.

Turning serious, Schmidt continued. "Bruner, I want you to lead the house-to-house search for Flannigan. I expect you to be ruthless in tracking him down. If you fail, I will have you shot. Or I might do something worse. I might have you sent to the Russian Front. Do you understand?"

"I understand perfectly, Major."

Stories from the Russian Front had begun to trickle back. Severe shortages of winter clothing. Suicidal charges of the Russian masses. New Russian tanks more powerful than any the Germans had. *Maybe*

Schmidt was right, Otto thought. *Going to the Russian Front could be worse than the firing squad.*

"Make the preparations for us to leave in the morning," Schmidt said. "That is all."

"Sir, since we are now at war with the Americans, shouldn't we be concerned that they will send people to rescue the professor? If I were the American in charge, I would certainly want to get Flannigan out as soon as possible. After all, he has a great scientific mind."

"Nonsense! The Americans showed how inept they were at Pearl Harbor. If they do get some sense and send people, we shall simply dispose of them. Now go about your business."

Otto saluted and left. Hopefully, Schmidt was right. Otto did have to admit that he didn't understand the Americans. While he certainly understood why the Americans were interested in Germany's development of heavy water, how could they convince an elderly Nobel Laureate to take on such a dangerous assignment? Maybe most Americans lacked common sense and good judgment. He hoped so.

The next morning, Schmidt and his men set out for Telemark. Schmidt sat in the lead vehicle, a staff car used to transport members of the German high command. Two machine gunners accompanied him. The driver—considerably older than Schmidt—had been with Schmidt through the French Campaign. This man was one of the few people whom the major actually trusted, perhaps because Schmidt knew one of his sons quite well.

The soldiers followed Schmidt in a long convoy of trucks. While the major rode in a heated car, the ordinary soldier had no such luck. His only protection from the bitter cold was a thin piece of canvas. When reminded of this by the driver, Schmidt replied, "It's good for them. It will keep them tough."

The convoy roared into Telemark, insuring that the local populace was well aware of their arrival. Stopping in the town square, Schmidt got out of his car and motioned for Otto Bruner to come over.

"Bruner, while you are conducting the search, I am going to select my quarters. If there were time, I would show you how it's done. The conqueror should have the best of everything, and I know how to make sure that I get it."

"I'm positive you do, sir," Otto replied, trying not to sound facetious.

"Okay, Bruner, get to work." Schmidt said. "And let me know your progress." Otto saluted and went to rejoin his troops while the major started on a more casual chore.

Otto's search team consisted of over a hundred men. While Bruner and the squad leaders worked out a plan for the search, Schmidt, accompanied by three heavily armed soldiers, banged on the door of the best-looking house.

The house was a short distance from the town square. A stout man in an old black suit opened the door. Schmidt pushed passed him and walked into the parlor area. It was spacious, but the massive pieces of furniture were old and somewhat dilapidated, and the room had a dark, almost depressing, quality. *Oh well*, he thought when he saw a fairly expensive-looking phonograph at one end of the room, at *least I can listen to Mozart and Schubert*. There was also a wet bar positioned between the parlor and kitchen, so he could dull the impact of his substandard surroundings.

Knowing that there was probably nothing better in town, he turned to the man and proclaimed, "This is now SS headquarters in Telemark. Get out."

13

First Night Out

JUST BEYOND THE outskirts of Telemark, Anker told Dude, Jennifer, and the professor that it was time to put on their snowshoes. Then he departed. Slowly, the Americans bent over and donned the footwear. Dude noticed that Flannigan was having some trouble with the fittings. After quickly getting his own snowshoes on, Dude went to the professor's aid.

Looking at Flannigan, Dude said in a low tone, "Professor, those goggles on your hat make you look like a professional skier."

"That shows how deceiving looks can be." Flannigan replied.

Soon the three were ready to move out. Silently they started their trek. A full moon cast enough light for Dude to read his compass with ease. Majestic mountain ranges to both the left and the right constrained them to a fairly narrow route, guiding them toward the gorge in which the first cabin was nestled.

After a while, Jennifer dropped behind Dude to speak with Flannigan. Catching up again, she said, "He's puffing pretty hard, Dude. We'd better take a short break."

"You two can stop for a few minutes," he said. "I'll go on ahead. Just follow my tracks."

The professor found a big rock nearby and sighed as he sat on it. Dude saw him smile up at Jennifer. He marveled at the man who had yet to complain and always had that smile ready.

Dude walked rapidly ahead and was exhilarated by the beautiful mountain scenery and the snowy landscape. He came to a gorge where he thought the first cabin must be. But where was it? It certainly wasn't obvious.

Thinking back to Aksel's briefing, he recalled that the first cabin was hardest to find, as it was tucked in a branch of the gorge that angled to the northwest. Looking in that direction, he saw a likely passage and proceeded accordingly. It was not long before he spotted his objective. *No wonder the Germans hadn't found it*, he mused. It was really hidden in the trees.

He went back to tell his companions, who had ended their break and were not far behind. The stars twinkled brightly, the night was clear, and the outlook was good so far.

Approaching quietly, Dude and Jennifer drew their pistols and looked in a window to make sure the cabin was empty. Jennifer gave the all-clear signal to the professor, who had been instructed to wait in a nearby grove of trees.

Inside, the rustic little cabin looked like a five-star hotel to the weary travelers. It had one large room and a smaller one off to the side. The main room had a small bed against one wall and some bearskin rugs lying on the floor. *Perfect*, Dude thought. They would let the professor have the bed, and Jennifer and he could snuggle together on the bearskin rugs in front of the big stone fireplace that was built into the cabin's south wall. It would be just as it had been at Lars' hideaway—the best night of his life. They would, however, have to wait for the professor to fall asleep before starting the night's activities.

On the west side was a kitchen area that had a wood-burning stove with a large iron pot on top of it. A cabinet was mounted on the far wall above a counter that had drawers tucked underneath. Pushed against the northwest corner was a small wooden table with four chairs. *Quite satisfactory*, Dude thought.

Peering into the small room off the kitchen, Dude saw an old, beat-up metal bathtub. "Jennifer," he said. "Look at this." She walked over, gazed at the bathtub, giggled, and winked at Dude as she walked back.

There were windows on the north and south sides. The north-facing window was perfect for seeing anyone approaching, as the other three sides were protected by steeply rising ground. Noticing rifle shells on the counter, Dude said, "This place must be used by hunters. They forgot some ammunition."

"I remember Lars telling us that the five cabins are about the same," Jennifer replied. "If so, we're in good shape. We have everything we need." Dude nodded.

There was plenty of firewood, and as Dude started a fire, Jennifer examined a pantry to see what was available. "I can whip up dinner," she said.

"What can I do to help?" the professor asked.

"You should just rest," Jennifer replied. "You've done extremely well in traveling a good distance." Dude concurred.

Soon Dude had a roaring fire going, and the professor took off his outer garments. Eying Flannigan, Jennifer said, "Professor, you perspired quite a bit on the way here. Did we take enough breaks?"

"My dear, you and Dude did just fine. You needn't have changed a thing during the journey."

"Just to make sure, I'm going to take your temperature, pulse rate, and blood pressure before you go to sleep tonight."

"That's fine with me, but please don't go to any extra bother."

"No bother at all."

After eating—Jennifer had cooked a concoction of canned meat, potatoes, and onions in a big iron skillet—Dude exclaimed, "That's the best meal I've ever eaten!" Rubbing his stomach contentedly, the professor added, "I second that assessment."

"You two are certainly easy to please."

Flannigan asked if they minded if he smoked his pipe. "I love the aroma of pipe tobacco," Jennifer said. She and Dude moved from the table to be near the fireplace, where each selected a bearskin rug to stretch out on. The professor remained in his chair, puffing contentedly on his pipe.

"Professor," Jennifer said, "would you tell us how you won your Nobel Prize?"

"I'm afraid that it might bore you, since it was quite a tedious process. But if you insist."

"We do!" they replied.

Nodding, Flannigan pulled his chair overly close to them. He started by reviewing the work of others that had helped him unlock secrets of the atom. As he talked, years seemed to fade from his face. A twinkle came into his eyes, and he talked vigorously about concepts that were obviously at the very core of his being. It was as if he had lost track of time and space. Finally, he jerked slightly as if something had brought him back to the present.

"Well, that's it in a nutshell," he said. "I hope I didn't take too long."

"Not at all," Jennifer said. "And I think your students are mighty fortunate to have you," she added.

"I agree," Dude said. "But, Professor, if I see you on the street in twenty years, I hope you won't expect me to remember any of it!"

"Oh, no," the professor laughed. "You won't have to worry about that."

The professor started to get up and then sat back down. "Before we go to bed, though, I better tell you what I learned here. If I don't make it, you will be able to report it to your superiors."

"We'll all make it out," Jennifer assured him. Flannigan just nodded and continued.

"Professor Jungstad and I estimate that the heavy water plant is now producing about twenty kilograms of heavy water per month," he said. "Based on the expansion work going on at the plant, we estimate that in six months the output will be fifty kilograms per month. At that rate, the Germans will have enough heavy water to produce an atomic bomb in a year or so. Our recommendation, then—just to be on the safe side—is that the plant be eliminated within the next six months."

After a short pause, Flannigan chuckled.

"What's so funny, Professor?" Dude asked.

"A member of the Norwegian Underground told Jungstad and me that some of the workers were putting castor oil in the plant's converter units. For all we know, the Germans are getting more bubbles than heavy water!"

"That is funny," Jennifer said with a giggle. "And maybe it means that the Norwegians can take care of it without our help."

"That's a good point," Flannigan conceded. "But we have to assume that the Germans will weed out anyone who isn't helpful to their cause. They are very good at that sort of thing."

Dude and Jennifer parroted back to the professor the numbers they had memorized. "Good," he said. "I think you've got it."

"Professor, I have one more question," Dude said. "Why don't we go ahead and destroy the plant now?"

"Well, I can't speak for FDR or for George Marshall either," Flannigan replied, "but I suppose that our government has many high priorities right now. Anything that isn't urgent will probably be put off as long as possible."

"That makes sense," Jennifer said.

Flannigan tried, but failed, to suppress a yawn. As the professor finished with his pipe, Jennifer told him, "Before you go to bed, young man, I want to take your vital signs." Laughing, Flannigan replied, "Anyone who calls me a young man can get me to do just about anything!"

Jennifer took the professor's blood pressure and pulse rate. "Well, did I pass?" he asked.

Jennifer answered yes, but Dude could tell that there were problems. Jennifer's response had not been as enthusiastic as usual.

"Would you like to take a bath?" Jennifer asked.

"Not tonight," the professor replied. "I'm afraid it would make me too keyed up to sleep. But I'd love one in the morning."

"You got it," Dude said. "Morning it is. I'll melt some snow now." He winked at Jennifer.

Dude put on his coat and hat, then went to the open doorway and visually measured the tub. *Rather odd-looking*, he thought. *Oh well, it will certainly serve the purpose.* He picked up a bucket, walked to the front door, and exited into the cold, wintry night.

Flannigan, meanwhile, put out his pipe and got into bed. Soon, he was sound asleep.

It wasn't long before Dude returned with a bucket full of snow. He walked over and dumped it into a large cooking pot.

"You're mighty brave," Jennifer said. "It must be freezing out there."

"It is." Dude replied. "But it won't take me long, and then we'll have some just in case." By Jennifer's expression, Dude could tell that she knew exactly what he meant.

As Dude headed for the door, Jennifer motioned at the professor. "His blood pressure and pulse rate are both high," she whispered. "If we aren't careful, he could have a stroke or even a heart attack."

"I guess we'll have to take it very easy tomorrow," Dude said softly. "But tonight, I'd like a bath. Would you?"

"I think you know the answer to that."

"I'll be right back!"

Dude and Jennifer woke just before dawn. Dude quickly extinguished the fire so German reconnaissance aircraft and ground patrols would not see its smoke and call in a scouting party to investigate. Jennifer went to the small kitchen area to plan breakfast. It would have to be cold. Luckily, there was bread, jam, cold sausage, and dried fruit.

Soon, Flannigan stirred, sat up, and stretched.

"Good morning, Professor," Jennifer said. "How are you feeling?"

"Not bad for an old codger."

"That's good. Would you like to bathe or eat first?" Jennifer inquired.

"Let's eat. I'm famished."

They ate quickly, and Dude gathered more snow for the professor's bath. Soon, the professor was in the tub, lathering himself with a bar of coarse soap and using a scrub brush on his back.

"You don't mind if I sing, do you?"

"Not at all," Jennifer answered.

"This guy is sick?" Dude asked under his breath.

"He doesn't seem to be this morning," she replied in a hushed tone. "But that can be deceiving."

After Flannigan dressed, Jennifer told him that she would take his blood pressure one more time while Dude went outside to look around. As he rolled up his sleeve, Flannigan said, "Jennifer, I'm so fortunate that George Marshall had the good sense to send you and

Dude to rescue me. I had my doubts at first, but now I'm convinced that the old goat knew what he was doing."

When Dude came back inside, he saw Jennifer giving the professor a hug. Smiling, Dude asked, "What is this? A love fest? If so, can I get in on it?" Flannigan motioned him over to share the embrace.

Soon, they were ready to depart. The sky was still clear, and it was cold outside. The snow was piled about a foot high, but it didn't look like there would be any new snow that day. Donning their snowshoes, they headed off.

14

Day 1: Travel

DUDE SCANNED THE scenery, thinking how beautiful it was and how much he would enjoy it under different circumstances. Although jagged mountains glistening with snow rose on both sides, their path lay on fairly flat terrain.

They walked single file with Dude again leading the way and Jennifer now bringing up the rear. They'd agreed she would keep an eye on the professor and call for rest breaks as needed. After the first hour, they were forced to make frequent stops. It was obvious to Dude—and, he knew, to Jennifer as well—that the journey was taking a substantial toll on the professor. Flannigan's expression was now strained.

During one of the stops, under some juniper trees, Flannigan apologized for holding them back. "But I will make a Herculean effort to keep up with you," he promised. "I know I mustn't be a burden."

"You're no burden," Jennifer replied. "We enjoy your company."

"Professor, even if you are a burden," Dude joked, "you're a very pleasant one. And we're glad you came along!"

"I'll take that as a compliment," Flannigan responded. *He's obviously pleased*, Dude thought. *He's smiling!*

The three trudged onward. Suddenly, Dude heard an airplane approaching from the northeast. He turned, grabbed Flannigan, and pulled him under the cover of a cluster of pine trees. Jennifer quickly joined them. Looking up through a gap in the branches, they saw a plane with the markings of the German Luftwaffe making lazy zigzags in the sky.

"I wonder if the Germans have started a search for us," Dude said. "It's certainly possible that they've captured members of the Underground and forced them to talk."

"I don't think we've been spotted," Jennifer said.

"But the pilot might be able to see our snowshoe tracks," Dude replied. "If so, he could radio for a ground patrol."

Jennifer frowned at Dude, and he quickly got the point: Do *not* alarm the professor.

As the enemy plane moved out of sight, Dude said, "Okay, everyone, we can start walking again."

By sunset, as they were nearing the second cabin, Dude and Jennifer were walking alongside the professor, grasping his arms to help him along. Flannigan was beginning to gasp, but he uttered no complaint. With a sigh of relief, Dude pointed to the cabin. Taking no security precautions, they went right up to it and opened the door. Fortunately, no one was there.

Inside was a large fireplace in the main room and a kitchen area off to the side. Although the cabin had no plumbing, another small room contained a bathtub. "Nice," Jennifer said.

With the sun almost gone, they decided it would be safe to thaw out with a fire.

Dude built a roaring fire, and Jennifer soon had a very aromatic stew cooking in a big iron pot over the flames. When it was ready, she placed generous helpings on three plates. The three travelers sat down and dug in. "My dear," Flannigan said, "this is delicious. You are an absolute genius!" Dude seconded the professor's enthusiasm.

After filling up on the stew, Flannigan said he'd very much enjoy having a warm bath. Dude went outside to gather snow to heat. *First,* he thought, *I'll do it for the professor. Then I'll do it for Jennifer and me.*

After his bath, Flannigan went straight to bed and was soon snoring mightily. Dude heated water for another bath. When the tub was full,

Jennifer undressed and slid into its warmth. She smiled at Dude and wiggled her finger for him to join her. He stripped off his clothes and eased into the water. Soon they were lathering each other and engaging in horseplay, giggling softly and splashing each other with the warm bath water. Dude moved alongside Jennifer and put his arm around her. "This isn't so bad, is it?" he asked.

"I wouldn't have missed it for the world," she said. They kissed passionately.

Dude awakened just before daybreak. He quietly dressed and doused the fire so enemy patrols wouldn't see its smoke. Then he sat and looked at Jennifer until she awakened with a yawn, a stretch, a smile, and a kiss for him. She dressed quickly and went to the small kitchen to see what was available for breakfast. She brought back some cold cuts, cheese, bread, and jam.

"Let's eat here on our bearskin rugs," Jennifer said softly.

"Good idea! Anything to drink?"

"There are some bottles of juice." She nodded at a cabinet on the side wall.

"I'll get it," Dude replied. He walked over and poured the juice into two glasses. He carried them back and sat down next to her, his legs folded in front of him.

Dude and Jennifer ate quietly. He realized that he loved everything about her, even the way she chewed tiny bits of food. As they finished, Dude said softly "Darling, I'm going to scout the terrain up ahead."

"Don't you dare be gone too long!"

"I won't," he said with a smile. It was nice having her concerned about him.

Dude went over to the window and peered out. Turning to Jennifer, he said softly, "It's hillier out there than I remembered. Of course, I couldn't see very well last night."

"Would you rather use skis?" Jennifer asked quietly.

"Yes, but I didn't see any."

"They're over in the corner under that tarp. I spotted them last night."

Dude lifted the tarp and took one of the three pairs that had been left for them. He kissed Jennifer and quietly left the cabin while the professor slept.

Outside, he donned the skis and headed southwest. Before long, he saw that their route sloped downward at an angle that would challenge even advanced skiers. *This must be the pass Lars warned us about*, he thought. Shaking his head in disbelief, he wondered how they could possibly get Flannigan down in one piece. Had the professor ever even been on skis before? He wasn't sure. As he recalled, Flannigan had only made a vague comment about hoping that there wouldn't be much skiing.

Dude hurried back to the cabin and found the professor awake though still in bed. Jennifer, sitting on a chair beside the bed, was softly talking to him. The professor looked pale and feeble.

Dude tried to sound cheerful. "It's a magnificent day for skiing!" he said. "Do you feel well enough to ski, Professor?"

"I guess so. But the last time I was on skis was forty years ago, and I wasn't very good then."

"Maybe we can build a sled and pull you along."

"Oh, no—that's way too much trouble. You two should just go on without me. I'll rest today, then get myself back to Telemark. Maybe the Underground can find another way to get me out of the country."

"Now, Professor, you can't get rid of us that easily!" Dude protested. "You're stuck with us until we're safely back home."

"That's right, Professor," Jennifer added. "We're the three musketeers, remember? All for one and one for all."

"That's very kind of you, but first I'd like to get some more sleep. I'm feeling very weak."

"You can," Jennifer replied. "But you have to eat something first."

Sitting up, the professor ate some cheese and half a slice of bread. "That's all I can manage," he said as he lay back down.

Jennifer kissed him softly on the forehead and pulled the covers up around his shoulders. She moved with Dude to the far side of the cabin.

"How bad is it?" Jennifer asked softly.

"Terrible. Too difficult for the professor to make it on his own. There are jagged rocks sticking up through the snow. And we have to make sure that we don't go over the edge on the left side. We'd fall straight down hundreds of feet."

Jennifer shook her head. "That's worse than I imagined," she said. "But we can't let it stop us." Dude nodded.

"Your sled idea is a good one," she said. "Can I help you build it?"

"Sure," Dude replied. "Look for nails and something we can use for straps. I'll gather the wood we'll need."

Dude found an axe leaning against a corner of the cabin by the pantry. After giving Jennifer a kiss, he went outside to look for sturdy branches. He found some nearby and used the axe to cut and shape them so they could be assembled into a sled. Then he went inside to see what Jennifer had found.

"I have nails, leather pieces, and a hammer," she reported. "I also found some rope, which we can tie to the sled to guide it."

"That's good," Dude said softly with a chuckle. "We wouldn't want the professor to go sailing off into oblivion." Jennifer feigned displeasure.

They headed outside and went to work. Jennifer positioned the branches so that the sled had a rounded bottom in lieu of rails. Dude secured the branches with straps and nails.

After about thirty minutes, the sled was assembled, and the two stood back to admire their handiwork. It looked ragged, and both of them had trouble suppressing snickers.

"It reminds me of the stock car racer my little brother built when he was about five," Jennifer said.

"Well," Dude replied indignantly. "I'm no structures expert, but I think it'll suffice."

"I sure hope you're right," Jennifer said.

They went back into the cabin. It was cold inside, so Jennifer and Dude left their coats and hats on. Jennifer walked over to check on Flannigan.

"How is he?" Dude asked softly.

"He's still asleep," she whispered.

"Good. Would you like something to drink?"

"I sure would," Jennifer replied. "How about some of that juice we had earlier?"

"Coming right up." Dude poured a glass for each of them, and they sat down at the table.

"I could strangle Lars!" she said softly. "How could he think we could get the professor down that slope?"

"I doubt that he had a choice. This place is crawling with Germans, and he probably thought that this route would be the best for us."

"You may be right, but I still plan to give him a piece of my mind if I ever see him again."

"You'll undoubtedly have the opportunity."

They finished their drinks.

"I'm going outside," Dude said. "Those tracks we've made could alert the Germans. I'll sweep them away with a branch."

"Good idea," Jennifer replied. "But hurry. I already miss you." They kissed, and Dude went outside. Soon, he returned.

"That wasn't so bad, was it?" he asked.

"It seemed like an eternity," Jennifer replied. "Did you make the tracks disappear?"

"I certainly did."

They hugged, kissed, and then went over to the table and sat down. "He's still asleep," Jennifer said, looking over at Flannigan.

"Good," Dude said softly. "I hope you aren't overly concerned about anything."

"Well, there's nothing we can do about the route that was selected for us, so I'm not going to worry about it. But I hope Major Dunbar will have the *Windstorm* waiting for us if we're a bit late getting back."

"I do, too. And I think he will."

Jennifer went over to check on Flannigan and then walked back to the table. "He looks better," she reported. "His color is less flushed, and he doesn't appear as stressed."

"Good," Dude replied.

They huddled together, holding hands. "What is it, darling?" Jennifer asked. "You look as though you're miles away."

"Not really. I was just thinking how fortunate, how blessed I am, to be with you."

"So you would volunteer for this mission all over again, just to be with me?"

"Absolutely," Dude said softly. "No doubt about it."

"Does this mean what I think it means?"

Dude could tell that she sensed something. He knew her anticipation was peaking.

"Yes," he replied. "And if I don't pop the question, I'm going to burst."

Dude got down on one knee and grasped Jennifer's hands firmly in his. He cleared his throat. "I hope this doesn't sound corny."

"You don't ever have to worry about that," she assured him.

"Okay, here goes," he said softly, pausing momentarily.

"My darling, you are my one and only love. You are paradise on earth for me, and it will be my great honor to cherish you always, if only you will have me. Therefore, I am asking from the bottom of my heart: Will you marry me?"

"Beautiful!" Jennifer replied, tears welling up in her eyes. "The answer is *yes*, my dearest! *Yes!* A thousand times *yes!*"

The two embraced passionately and kissed. Time stood still for them. Time had no meaning. Danger lurked around the corner, at every bend in the road. It didn't matter. They had each other, a gift so rare that few would ever experience anything like it.

The professor raised his head. "What's all the commotion about?" he asked. Then he passed out again.

Dude and Jennifer giggled. "He'll just have to wait to find out our wonderful news," she said.

They decided to spend the remainder of the day in the comfort of the cabin. The rest would be good for the professor, and the two of them would spend the time just enjoying the other's company and their new status. If this meant that the *Windstorm* would be gone by the time they reached the coast, so be it. The thought of being Mr. and Mrs. Jonathan Partude relegated everything else to secondary importance.

15

The SS Responds

AFTER QUESTIONING DOZENS of Telemark residents, resorting to robust interrogation when necessary, Gestapo agents had gotten the information they wanted. The preeminent American physicist suspected of spying on the heavy water plant had indeed been there. But he had fled Telemark in the company of two other Americans—a young man and young woman. All three were fluent in Norwegian. They'd last been seen heading southwest, toward the coast. Destination: unknown.

"I want the physicist taken alive," Schmidt told Bruner. "Perhaps we can use him. As for the other two—kill them!"

What a waste, Bruner thought. They were only doing their duty and so should be taken prisoner and treated as specified by the Geneva Convention. Unless, of course, they resisted capture.

But first he would have to find them. Bruner called Captain Gerhard Heinkel, Operations officer for the air reconnaissance squadron stationed in Oslo.

"Gerd, I need your help."

"What?" Heinkel asked. "The mighty SS needs help from the lowly Luftwaffe?"

"Go ahead and have your fun. I suppose I deserve it after having made a big commotion over getting this assignment. Remember, though, I'm just regular Army on loan to the SS."

"Oh, that's a big distinction! But go ahead. I'm listening."

"There are three Americans heading southwest from Telemark. One of them is a famed physicist who could help Germany's war efforts. It's urgent that we find them."

"What do you want from me?"

"I'm requesting aerial reconnaissance. Look for tracks heading southwest from Telemark through mountain passages."

"There may be a lot of those," Heinkel replied. "How do you know they'll be the right ones?"

"I don't. But there's a chance that the recent snow has blanked out all but the most recent trails, the ones we're interested in."

"I suppose you're right. I can have a plane up first thing in the morning. Is that soon enough?"

"I guess it'll have to do."

Otto thanked the captain. With input from the Luftwaffe, he might be able to use his ground troops more efficiently.

At ten o'clock the next morning, Otto received a call from Heinkel.

"My pilot didn't spot any travelers," Heinkel said, "but he did see some interesting tracks along two routes that the Americans might use."

"Does he know what kind of tracks they are?" Otto asked.

"Snowshoe tracks, probably," Heinkel replied. "The pilot also saw cabins along both routes that are partially screened by forest."

Interesting, Otto thought. The screening could make the Americans think that it would be very difficult for the cabins to be seen from the air. It could give them a false sense of security and lead them to believe that the cabins are adequately camouflaged.

"Thank you very much, Gerd. You've been a big help."

"Let me know if I can do anything more."

Bruner went to Schmidt's quarters, only to be told the major had yet to arise. "Awaken the major," Bruner said to the valet. "This is urgent!"

"*Ja, Herr Kapitän.*"

Remnants of the delicacies and fine wine served the night before were still evident. Records—including one by Schubert—were on a counter. Obviously, the major had enjoyed himself.

"Bruner, this had better be good!" Schmidt said when he appeared in pajamas and a silk robe. A pretty young woman followed Schmidt into the room, but the major motioned her back. Obviously, Bruner mused, the major had been successful with his previous night's conquest.

Otto quickly passed on the information from Captain Heinkel.

"Good work!" Schmidt said.

Could it be? Otto wondered. *Have I actually done something to please the major?* He decided he'd better not get his hopes up too soon. He had done so in the past only to be disappointed.

Schmidt began pacing and barking orders. "Send a team along each of those routes. You will lead one of the teams. I will take personal command of the other. There are only mountains between here and the coast. Even now, the Americans can't have gone more than ten miles into them. We can overtake them by leaving early in the morning."

Early in the morning? Otto thought. *Why not leave today?* Could it be that the major had done too much partying the night before and would need time to recuperate? Better not press the point.

"I agree," Bruner said after a slight hesitation. "The elderly physicist will prevent the young man and woman from making good time. We can easily catch them by leaving in the morning."

"Did I ask for your opinion?"

"No, sir."

"Then don't bore me with it!" Schmidt said. "If I want your opinion, I'll provide it to you." The major cackled. *Some sense of humor,* Otto thought.

Schmidt directed Otto to plan for a four-day outing for both teams with a departure of four o'clock the next morning. "Before you go," Schmidt said, "I want to remind you that I like my comforts. Good food—make sure you give me someone who can cook. Also, good wine and plenty of clothes."

"Yes, sir. Anything else?"

The major paused for a moment. "Bruner," he finally said. "I have found you to be a fairly competent officer. But I question your toughness. Are you tough enough for this job?"

"Sir," Otto replied somewhat frustrated, "the only way we'll know is if I'm given the opportunity to find out."

"I suppose you're right. Consider this your chance. That is all."

Otto's sharp salute was returned nonchalantly as Schmidt turned to go back to his living quarters. *Perhaps*, Otto thought, *the major didn't do too much partying last night. Perhaps he wanted to party some more today!* That could also explain why they weren't leaving until the following morning.

As Otto headed back to his office, the snow came down in ever-thickening sheets. *Not a good sign*, he thought. Now they wouldn't be able to move as fast. Perhaps they wouldn't even overtake the enemy until the coast was reached. That is, if the coast was the Americans' objective. And what could be waiting at the coast—an enemy convoy? The British fleet had sailed into the fjords in the past and done substantial damage to German vessels. They certainly wouldn't hesitate to come into Norwegian waters and mix it up again, particularly if there was a good reason.

All things considered, it made sense to Otto that the Americans should be intercepted as soon as possible. But should he return to Schmidt's office and demand that they leave today? Probably not. While it would prove that he possessed toughness, there was no doubt in Otto's mind that the major valued blind obedience above anything else. Going back would be a losing proposition.

Otto trudged on somberly, realizing that he didn't control his own destiny. Schmidt would call the shots, but he, Otto, would get the blame if things went wrong. Didn't seem fair, but that's the way it was.

Back at his office, Otto dumped his coat, hat, and gloves on the edge of his desk. Noting the look on Otto's face, the first sergeant asked, "Bad meeting with the major, sir?"

"It was as usual."

Shaking his head, the sergeant replied, "Someday, sir, someone is going to put a bullet in the back of that man's head."

"You may be right, sergeant, but be careful about saying it. I can't afford to lose you."

"Yes, sir."

Otto selected the best men for the two teams and had the first sergeant call them together. He briefed them on the upcoming mission and then released them so that they could prepare for an early morning departure.

After eating a light dinner, Otto turned in early and tried to get some sleep. However, the uncertainties of the next day made it difficult. He got up and walked to the window. "Thank God," he said out loud. "The snow is letting up. Maybe everything will be all right."

16

Day 2: Travel

THE NEXT MORNING, Dude and Jennifer watched intently as Flannigan rose carefully up on his elbows. "Good morning, Professor," Dude said.

"Hi, Professor," Jennifer added. "How are you today?" Flannigan just nodded. *Maybe he isn't any better*, Dude thought.

Slowly Flannigan sat up, got out of bed, and walked to the table. Dude and Jennifer jumped up and helped him into a chair.

"Professor, I'll get your breakfast very shortly," Jennifer said cheerfully. "But first we have some wonderful news to tell you!"

"What's that?" Flannigan asked.

"We're going to get married!" Jennifer and Dude said almost simultaneously.

"That is wonderful news!" Flannigan replied with a burst of enthusiasm. "Am I invited?"

"Of course you are!" Dude said excitedly. "You'll probably be my best man!"

Tears welled in the professor's eyes. "That means a great deal to me," he said softly.

"Professor, please don't be sad," Jennifer said. "We want you to be happy."

"I am happy, my dear," Flannigan replied. "These are tears of great joy."

The three hugged, but Dude wondered if Flannigan was being candid with them. Perhaps the professor was truly sad, thinking he would not live long enough to see the wedding.

Jennifer brought for Flannigan the same things that she and Dude had eaten: cheese, smoked sausage, bread, and jam. "Aren't you two going to eat?" Flannigan asked. "We've already eaten," Jennifer replied.

Flannigan ate a good breakfast but at a much slower clip than his normal pace. And he was amused as Jennifer and Dude showed him, through the window, the sled that they had hurriedly put together. "I will be the Eskimo, and you will be the huskies?" he asked. They nodded, obviously relieved that the professor was perking up.

"If the terrain isn't really rugged," the professor continued, "I can negotiate it on my snowshoes or on the spare skis over there." He pointed to the wall where three sets of skis were leaning. "Of course, you may have to hold me up if I get on the skis."

Dude decided that he must alert the professor to what they faced but at the same time not cause him excessive anxiety. "The trail ahead is kind of steep in places," Dude said. "So, just as a precaution, we built the sled in case you want to ride."

"But whether or not you use it will be your decision," Jennifer added.

Flannigan nodded and finished eating. He walked over to the bed, took off the blanket that shrouded his body, and tried to dress. His hands trembled.

"Here, let me help you with that," Jennifer said. The professor gratefully let her take over, and Dude saw that a shocking change had taken place in Flannigan over the last couple of days. Was it normal for a fairly healthy individual to age so quickly? Could it be that the professor had an existing problem that no one knew about? Perhaps they would never know.

Finally, the professor was ready to go. They all strapped on skis and left the cabin, with Dude pulling the sled. Flannigan walked between his two young escorts, who were firmly holding his arms. For the first half mile, everything went smoothly.

Suddenly, the landscape changed dramatically. They stopped at the brink of the trail's downward slope. "Whoa!" Flannigan gasped. "I don't think I can do this, even in a sled."

Jennifer turned and looked at Dude with her eyebrows raised in surprise. "I told you, my dear," Dude said under his breath. Jennifer just nodded.

"It is a challenge," Jennifer said to the professor, "but I'm sure we can get you down okay. All you have to do is sit back and enjoy the ride."

"I trust both of you," Flannigan said, partially recovered from his initial shock.

He isn't very convincing, Dude thought. *But who can blame him?*

Dude and Jennifer, both accomplished skiers, could have negotiated the slope on their own without too much difficulty, but Dude knew it would be a challenge to get the professor down safely. In fact, it might take a miracle. The strategy was to use ropes that would allow Jennifer and Dude to each restrain one side of the sled.

After briefly discussing the situation, Dude and Jennifer tied the ropes to the sled and then around their waists. Dude removed Flannigan's skis and mounted them to the side of the sled. "Professor," Jennifer said, "are you ready to try out your new sled?" "Yes," he said. She helped him into the contraption, hoping the harness they had rigged for him would keep him from falling out.

"Professor, here's how we're going to proceed," Dude said. "We'll keep you and the sled between us, but you'll be out a little ahead of us. We'll keep the ropes as taught as we can going down so you don't swing back and forth or hit the rocks. We'll descend at a controlled speed. You just hang on."

"Professor, you better lower your goggles," Jennifer said. He complied.

Without further delay, Dude shouted, "Hang on, Prof!"

"Don't you think we should have practiced this first?" Flannigan yelled as they pushed off.

Dude felt his speed build as he started downward. Soon the landscape was a blur. Jagged rocks appeared, and he maneuvered hard and fortunately missed them, as the rocks could have smashed the sled to smithereens. Approaching a sharp curve, Dude made a hard turn. Out of the corner of his eye, he saw the sled tipped at a precarious angle. He hoped the professor was hanging on tightly. Apparently, he was. The sled righted itself with the professor still in it!

Glancing at Jennifer, Dude felt a sense of pride. She was handling her part beautifully. But he couldn't afford to be overconfident, as he was rudely reminded.

The sled skimmed a sizeable rock, and wood chips flew every which way. He prayed that the sled would hold together.

After what seemed like an eternity, they reached the slope's end, all in one piece. They each gave a big sigh of relief, and Jennifer and Dude sprawled out on the snow, seemingly oblivious to the cold. Flannigan stayed hunched down in the sled. "That wasn't so bad," he gasped.

Getting herself upright, Jennifer went to Flannigan, put a hand on his shoulder, and asked, "Professor, are you all right?" He looked dazed, but nodded his head. "Would you like to stand up?" He nodded again.

As she helped Flannigan stand, Dude inspected the sled. It had suffered extensive damage. Branches were severed, and the sled had buckled in the middle. But Dude thought it would hold up a while longer. He just hoped they wouldn't have to use it again.

After a brief rest, the threesome started out again, with Flannigan also on skis. Dude noticed that the professor needed more support than previously from both Jennifer and him to stay on his feet.

"Professor, why don't you ride?" Jennifer suggested. "We'll be glad to pull you."

"I know you would, my dear," he puffed. "But I have already been too much of a burden."

"You haven't been a burden!"

"Couldn't have done it without you," Dude said.

Dude glanced over his shoulder. Their skis and the towed sled were making a sizeable track in the snow, a track that could easily be seen from the air. It would not surprise Dude to have unwelcome company at any time.

Before too long, however, they sighted the next cabin. "Thank God," exclaimed Flannigan, who looked totally bushed.

"Why not let us pull you the rest of the way?" Dude suggested.

"I guess I have done a satisfactory amount of trekking for the day," Flannigan said. "I'm not rating myself an A, mind you, but surely I deserve a passing grade."

"At least an A-," Jennifer said.

"I like the way you grade," the professor replied, looking fondly at her.

"Here," she said. "Let me help you into the sled." Dude came over, and the two gently lowered the professor to a sitting position.

By the time they reached the cabin, it was obvious that the sled might soon fall apart. It was cracked in several places and no longer providing much in the way of support for Flannigan. Maybe they'd have to build a new one for him. Dude hoped not. He hoped the professor would be feeling up to proceeding without it. But that was a long shot.

Once inside the cabin, Dude ruled out a fire. Nazi aircraft might see the smoke. Jennifer shrugged and began to check the cabin's shelves for something she could prepare as a cold meal. Dude posted himself at a window to watch for intruders. The professor collapsed on the cabin's single narrow bed.

After they had finished eating—the evening's menu featured cold smoked herring, cheese, bread, and strawberry jam—the professor seemed quite melancholy and said that he wanted to tell them about his family. He pulled from his wallet pictures of his wife, children, and grandchildren. He had sparkling comments about all of them. His son, James, Jr., was a physicist also, and his wife, Virginia, was an excellent wife, mother, homemaker, and pillar of the church. "I don't think our church—Light's End Presbyterian—could make it without her," he said. "She volunteers for everything. Whenever they need someone to head a fundraiser, they know exactly where to come."

After Dude and Jennifer had passed the photos back to him, Flannigan fell silent for a moment. Then he said, "You two have become just like my own children, like my own flesh and blood. I want to tell you that while I still have the chance."

Dude saw tears in Jennifer's eyes as she replied, "Professor, we feel the very same way about you." Flannigan gently stroked Jennifer's cheek with one hand and reached out to touch Dude's arm with the other.

By the time Flannigan was tucked into bed, night had crept over the cabin. Using a flashlight while trying to shield its glow, Dude explored a closet at the rear of the cabin, hoping he'd find something useful. He soon had news for Jennifer. "I found two rifles and a couple of boxes of shells," he said quietly.

Awaking the next morning, Jennifer and Dude saw that a light snow had fallen overnight and discovered that Flannigan was burning with fever.

"You haven't told me, but I know you can't allow the Germans to take me alive," he said. "I would like to die with dignity. Leave one of your pistols. I'll hold off the Germans when they arrive and save the last bullet for myself."

"Don't talk so foolishly," Jennifer protested.

"You two are young, with your whole lives ahead of you. Please don't squander them on me. It would be senseless."

"New snow has covered our tracks," Dude said. "We're not giving up on you."

The professor sighed and fell back into a deep slumber.

"You would like to let him rest here as long as possible," Dude told Jennifer. "I know that. But the longer we stay here the more likely it is the Germans will find us. We've got to keep moving."

"I know, but couldn't we just stay here today? Build a new sled and then start pulling him again tomorrow? He's very sick."

Dude nodded. What could he say? He put on his coat and hat and went outside to look for sled-building wood.

As he intently went about picking up likely branches, he wondered if he could convince Jennifer to go on ahead alone. Probably not.

The cabin door opened, and Jennifer came out. "Is there something bothering you, darling," she asked, "other than the pickle we're in?"

He had to laugh. "Worst pickle ever," he said. Turning somber, he began, "I hope you will seriously consider what I am about to say."

"Uh-oh!"

"I want you to go ahead on your own. I'll stay here a while longer with the professor. Then I'll try to catch up, with the professor in tow."

Jennifer shook her head. "I won't leave you."

"I was afraid you'd say that."

From a selfish standpoint, Dude wanted to spend every moment that he could with her. However, the thought of seeing her hurt—or perhaps dying—was more than he could bear. *Focus*, he told himself. Otherwise, he would be useless in trying to outfox a cunning enemy.

After collecting the necessary material for the sled, the two went back inside. Silently, they watched out the window as the professor slept.

"It's so beautiful out there, isn't it?" Jennifer said softly.

"It sure is. Almost as beautiful as the person sitting next to me."

There was great comfort and joy just feeling her next to him. Even if death were nearby, the mission had allowed him to experience the greatest gift that life has to offer. He knew that Jennifer felt the same way.

As the two huddled together, storm clouds gathered once again on the horizon. Maybe a good snow would buy them time. Dude hoped that it would.

17

An Unexpected Arrival

AS THE END of the week approached, Dunbar became very uneasy as he stood in the conning tower of the *Windstorm*. "Tom, I should have gone with them," he said to Commander Brookstone. "You couldn't, Frank. You don't speak Norwegian that well, and the three of you would have made an odd lot going into Telemark. The Germans would have been suspicious right off."

"But the Americans should be showing up by now," Dunbar replied.

"Level with me, Frank. Are you responsible for their safety?"

"I haven't been told in so many words, but it's certainly implied. After all, I was *encouraged* to escort them on the *Windstorm*."

"So what do you want to do?"

"I want to go ashore."

"Okay, I'll put you on land tonight," Brookstone said shaking his head. "But I can't guarantee *Windstorm* will be here when you return."

"Understood."

At 2100, the major boarded the submarine's rubber raft. He carried a machine gun and a pistol. He turned and nodded to the crewmen as he set foot on land.

As Dunbar trudged through the falling snow, toward the last cabin on the Americans' escape route, the wind rose quickly—perhaps, he feared, blowing in a blizzard from the North Sea. He pushed onward, not letting the bad weather stop him.

On and on he went, half-frozen. Finally, he stumbled into a cabin. *This has to be it*, he told himself. He peered in the window. The cabin was empty.

He entered quickly and went straight to the fireplace. There was plenty of firewood bundled on the floor and some matches on the mantle. With numb hands he started a fire. His next priority was food. Once again, luck was with him. A small pantry was stocked with canned meats and vegetables. He opened a few cans and ate as he warmed himself at the fire. Then, exhausted, he drifted to sleep.

It was still dark when Dunbar awoke, but the wind had died down, and the snow had stopped. He didn't know whether the clearing would turn out to be good or bad for the Americans. They might be able to travel faster, but the Germans might be able to find them more easily. He wolfed down some more food and headed out for the next cabin along the escape route.

The sky began to brighten. He heard, far off, the faint drone of an aircraft engine. He stopped and tried to find it. There! A plane making lazy circles in the sky, like a vulture waiting for something to die. He waited under some trees until it was out of sight, resuming his trek when it was safe.

As he reached a bend in the trail, Dunbar noticed a glint out of the corner of his eye. He immediately ducked behind some bushes and drew his revolver. Looking back, he saw a lone traveler. He was certain that it wasn't the enemy, as it was common knowledge that the Germans only traveled in substantial numbers so that they could readily subdue any opposition. *If not a German, who?* Was it a hunter or someone willing to risk imprisonment to get to a desired location? Dunbar would soon find out.

As the traveler got closer, there was something about him that Dunbar recognized. The man was tall and lanky with an athletic gait. Dunbar finally recognized that it was Lars. Breathing a sigh of relief, Dunbar called out his name and hoped for the best.

Hearing the call, Lars fell to the ground and pulled the rifle from around his shoulder. "Who is it?" he asked. The major stood up with a big grin on his face, and the two comrades approached each other, meeting with a bear hug.

"I'm surprised you remembered what I look like," Lars said. "We've only met once, and that was about a year ago."

"You're pretty hard to forget," Dunbar said with a wink. "Where do you think they are?"

"I don't know," Lars replied. "I've been watching cabin five on and off, but they never arrived, so I thought I'd come up to check cabin four."

"The same with me. I slept a few hours there last night, and I ate some of the food."

"I wondered who had been there," Lars said with a grin.

Well," Dunbar said, "we had best press on."

They were now close to cabin four, so they hurried to reach it. Soon, the cabin was in sight. Peering from bushes near the cabin, they agreed that it looked unoccupied. The major told Lars to cover him. He stealthily approached a window, peeked inside, then motioned to Lars that all was clear.

Inside the cabin the two rested and ate some cheese, bread, and jam for nourishment. "It's only about two miles to the next cabin," Lars said.

Peering out the window, the major replied, "I don't see anyone out there. Since we'll be running out of daylight soon, they probably won't come any further than cabin three today."

"Provided they get that far," Lars said with a worried look on his face.

The major nodded. Hurriedly they gathered their gear and started out once more. It didn't take them long to get to the next cabin, with Dunbar matching Lars stride for stride. They stopped short of their destination and observed it carefully from some thick brush. Dunbar saw a flicker of movement at the window. "There's someone inside," he whispered.

"I don't think it's Germans," Lars said softly. "They'd have a guard posted."

"I'll sneak up to the window. Cover me."

It was dusk as Dunbar peered into the cabin. Jennifer screamed as she saw a face looking in, and Dude picked up a gun and dashed for the window.

"Don't shoot!" Dunbar yelled. "It's me—Dunbar!"

Jennifer ran to the door, threw it open, and greeted Dunbar with a big hug. "Thank God you're here," she said. Dude came over and grabbed Dunbar in a bear hug. *Nice to be wanted*, the major thought.

"What's going on up there?" Lars called out with a smile. "Isn't anyone happy to see me?"

"Not particularly, you big oaf," Dude yelled back. "We have some bones to pick with you."

"Don't let him kid you," Jennifer said. "We've prayed that you would show up."

"Now that's better!" Lars replied. "Hearing it from Jennifer makes it worthwhile to risk my precious hide."

The major motioned for Lars to come up, and joyful greetings were exchanged.

The celebration didn't last long. Once inside the cabin, Major Dunbar saw the gravity of the situation. The old man was drenched in sweat and looked very feeble. He realized that they had their work cut out for them.

While aboard the *Windstorm* and on his way inland, Major Dunbar had pondered why the Americans were late. Maybe one of them had fallen and broken a bone, or had gotten sick, or maybe one or all of them had been captured or killed. But now he knew. It was due to the professor's failing health. For a moment, he didn't know what to say.

"What's wrong with him?" he asked Jennifer in a muted tone.

"He has high blood pressure—and even worse—I think he's got pneumonia."

"What can we do?" Dunbar asked.

"Two things," she said. "We need to get some nourishment in him. Probably warm broth. And then we can try and get his temperature down by bathing him in lukewarm water."

Lars and Dude had come over and were listening intently. "I'll start a fire shortly," Lars said. "It's getting dark, and the Germans don't usually move around after the sun goes down."

"We thought as much," Dude replied. "We've lit a fire every night, and there hasn't been any unwelcome company. Just to make sure, though, I'll keep an eye out."

"It's good to be cautious," Dunbar said to Dude. "I saw a reconnaissance plane making circles in the sky earlier today. The pilot was obviously looking for something important—probably the three of you. And the Germans might want to take one last look before it's totally dark."

"True," Dude replied.

After a few minutes, Jennifer spoke. "I can't wait any longer. I need to prepare some broth for the professor."

"I'll get the fire started," Lars replied. Soon, a roaring blaze was warming the cabin, and Jennifer heated some vegetable broth to give the professor. She sat down on his bed and gently shook him.

"Would you like some broth?" she asked. The professor shook his head.

"Okay. I'll let you sleep for now," Jennifer said. But I'll be back soon, and you'll have to eat something then." Flannigan nodded, and then he dozed off again.

"I'll prepare something for the rest of us," she told the others. Lars was already opening some cans.

"It looks like we can have some sausage and cabbage," Lars said.

"And there are jams and bread on the top shelf." Jennifer said.

"Good," Dude said walking up. "We sure won't starve."

The sausage and cabbage were dumped into a big iron pot hanging over the fire. Soon the pleasant aroma of the food cooking filled the small cabin.

"Let's eat as soon as it's done," Dude said. "I'm famished."

Jennifer opened a drawer. "There isn't much in the way of silverware. Just some big spoons that we've been getting by with." She held up one of the spoons.

"That's okay," Dunbar replied. "We can pile the cabbage and sausage on bread and pick it up with our fingers. It'll taste every bit as good."

Jennifer took out four plates and dished up the concoction. The four sat at the table and started eating. Dude and Jennifer smiled at each other as they ate.

"Okay, you two," Lars said as he looked at them. "Something must be up, or you wouldn't be smiling at each other like lovesick puppies."

"Well, you're right," Dude said. "Jennifer and I are getting married!"

"Congratulations!" Dunbar roared. "Break out the champagne!" Then he looked sheepishly at the professor to make sure he had not awoken him.

"*Gratulerer!*" Lars added. "I don't have champagne, but maybe I can dig up something." He walked over to a loose board, lifted it, and pulled out a dusty bottle. He blew the dust off and grinned. "We keep these bottles well hidden," he said. "Otherwise, they might be empty when we need them the most."

"What is it?" Jennifer asked.

"You'd probably call it rot-gut," Lars replied. "But it's not so bad once you get used to it."

"For this special occasion," Jennifer said looking at Dude, "I'll have some." Dude winked at her.

The couple was toasted, and everyone had refills. Lars, having had more than one refill, rose and spoke. "I know our situation's bad, but we have a lot to be thankful for. The professor is still alive, we're all together, and soon Jennifer and Dude will be living in wedded bliss."

"Lars is right," Dunbar added. "If we stay positive, I think things will work out."

Dude laughed. "What's so funny?" Jennifer asked.

"It reminds me of something I was told once. This friend of mine told me to cheer up, that things could be worse. So I cheered up, and things got worse!"

"Oh you!" Jennifer said, punching him softly on the shoulder.

"No more of that kind of talk," Dunbar added. "Jennifer, why don't you check on the professor? After that, we'll decide how to proceed."

Dude stood up. "Before she goes, I have something to say. Jennifer and I will always appreciate what you two are doing for us. You're risking life and limb when you don't have to."

"Maybe we do have to," Lars replied. "After all, we have to look at ourselves in the mirror when we shave."

"No, Lars. Dude is right," Jennifer said. "And we will always be grateful to you and the major."

She went to check on Flannigan. "He's about the same," she said as she returned to the table. "I'll try and get a little nourishment in him." She went to the iron pot and spooned some broth into a bowl. She took another spoon and carefully tasted the broth. "Just about the right temperature," she said to no one in particular.

Back at the professor's side, Jennifer nudged him gently until he awoke. "Professor, I'm going to give you a little broth." He nodded.

Balancing the bowl on her lap, she placed her hand under his head and gently lifted it up. He wheezed and coughed.

"Are you all right?" Jennifer asked. Flannigan nodded.

She filled the spoon with broth and carefully brought it to his lips. Feebly, he sucked the soup in and swallowed. "You're doing great," Jennifer said reassuringly. "Just a couple more swallows and I'll let you rest."

As Flannigan finished, he asked for some water. Dude, standing nearby, heard the request. "I'll get it," he said. He filled a glass from a pitcher containing melted snow. Quickly, he walked over and handed the glass to Jennifer.

"Here you are, Professor." She lifted his head as he took the glass from her. After a couple of sips, he handed it back to her. He thanked her and slipped back into a deep slumber.

As the evening went on, the professor didn't seem to be improving. His breathing became even more labored, and he developed a hacking cough.

Sitting around the table, the four discussed what they were facing. "I'm more certain than ever," Jennifer said, "that he has pneumonia. His temperature and lung congestion are sure signs."

"It's obvious the professor won't be able to do any walking," Lars said. "I see you've started collecting material for a sled. Good!"

Looking at the professor, Dunbar said, "Even on a sled he might not make it, considering his condition. It will be a hard ride for him."

Flannigan moved and opened his eyes. He motioned for the others to come over. "I can't continue," he said. "Even if the Germans take me alive, what use can I be to them? I'm a goner. Please go on without me and give yourselves a chance to live!"

Jennifer began to sob. "We won't leave you, Professor. Ever!"

Dude reinforced Jennifer's position. "Remember, Professor, it's all for one and one for all. Besides, you're going to be a key player at our wedding." Flannigan smiled weakly.

Well, that's that, Dunbar thought. Dude and Jennifer were clearly determined to get Flannigan to the coast even if he died before they got him there.

The professor went back to sleep.

"Sorry I lost control," Jennifer told the others. "It won't happen again."

"You needn't apologize," Dunbar said. "The professor is a fine man, and your dedication to duty is admirable."

Dude gave her a hug and a kiss on the cheek.

While the professor was able to sit up during his first sled ride, he would no longer be able to travel upright. "I'll start building a sled that will allow the professor to travel lying down," Lars said. "I'll have it finished tonight, and we can start early in the morning."

"Have you ever built a sled?" Dude inquired.

"Absolutely!" Lars replied. "And we'll need a lot more material than what you've collected."

Lars quickly sketched the sled and said that he would start gathering wood and cutting it to the right length.

"Can I help you gather it?" Dunbar asked.

"Yes," Lars replied. "Let's take these kerosene lanterns so we can see what we're doing. It's dark out there." They put on their coats and hats and walked out, quickly closing the door behind them.

Soon, Dude and Jennifer heard a thump on the door. "They must be back already," Dude said. He was right. Lars and Dunbar entered, their arms full of branches of varying thickness. They dropped their cache on the floor and took off their outer garments.

"I'll have to build it inside to have enough light," Lars said. "If I remember correctly, everything we need is in that cabinet." He pointed to a floor-length piece of furniture in the southeast corner of the room. He was right. Rope, nails, a hammer, and a saw were neatly stowed inside. Soon, the sled started taking shape.

Jennifer was the first to pay him a compliment. "Lars, I must say that your sled is looking a lot better than the one we built earlier. You can see its remnants over in the corner."

"If that sled held up coming down Heartbreak Pass, then you two are the ones who deserve a compliment."

"You call it Heartbreak Pass?" Dude asked facetiously. "I wonder why!" Even the major laughed.

"I warned you about it," Lars replied defensively.

"But we were too naïve to ask if there wasn't a less stressful route!" Jennifer retorted.

"I can assure you there wasn't," Lars said emphatically, shaking his head.

"Okay," Dunbar snapped, "let's forget the past. We still have plenty to worry about."

After a pause, Dunbar continued. "In the morning, we'll bundle up the professor, load him onto the sled, and proceed onward. For now, we'd better get some rest."

Jennifer agreed. "It will be hard on him. But our only hope is to get him better medical care than I can give him. And I know that the *Windstorm* has medical facilities and a medical officer."

Well put, Dunbar thought. *If only the Windstorm will be there when we arrive.*

18

Hot Pursuit

THE GERMANS WERE now in hot pursuit, with Major Schmidt heading squad number one and Captain Bruner heading the second squad. *What a pain*, Otto thought, as Schmidt contacted him every few seconds by radio. Well, it seemed like every few seconds, anyway. Obviously, Schmidt didn't want Otto to reap the glory of capturing the professor. Schmidt would think of something, Otto feared, that would let him swoop in and snatch the professor out from under Otto if need be. While Schmidt appeared to be a loyal German officer, Otto believed that the major's primary allegiance was to himself.

"*Damit kannst du dich begraben lasse,*" Schmidt raged into his radio. Otto had to snicker to himself. So Major Schmidt's route wasn't worth a tinker's damn. *Served the SOB right! Better try and calm him down, though*, Otto thought.

"Sir, I doubt that my route is any better. It's treacherous to say the least."

"It better be, Bruner! If I was misled by my intelligence staff, someone is going to pay for it."

"Yes, sir," Otto replied.

"Let me know at once if you see the Americans. I may come join you before their capture is attempted. After all, you may not have the skill to extract the professor safely while disposing of the others."

"Signing off," Otto replied tersely. He didn't try to be polite or respectful as he normally was. Perhaps Schmidt would get the point. Everyone had feelings. Was his response too curt? Probably, but the major had it coming.

Otto and his men trudged on. *What a terrible journey for an old man*, Otto thought. It was cold, the snow was deep, and the trail was anything but level. The data they had received showed the professor to be sixty-eight, the age of Otto's grandfather. Could his grandfather make this trip? Not a chance. Who knew whether or not the professor would even be healthy when they caught up to him?

Otto heard an excited buzz from his men up ahead. There it was—a cabin! Otto moved to the head of the column and motioned for his men to hold back. His first sergeant, Gustav Kleiner, approached.

"What would you like us to do, sir?"

"Approach very carefully. Don't startle anyone who may be inside. Report back to me at once if the cabin is occupied." The sergeant saluted and moved forward.

Word came back that the cabin was unoccupied. With long graceful strides, Otto reached the cabin door. He took off his snowshoes and entered. Looking around, he found signs that the cabin had been occupied not too long ago. There were fresh embers—a couple of days old at the most—in the fireplace. Residue in food cans that had been dumped in a trash container appeared fairly fresh. Looking around, Otto noted that whoever had been here had tidied up before leaving. A woman, perhaps? He walked out and put on his snowshoes.

Otto went over to his first sergeant. "There are still several hours of daylight left," he said. "Assemble the men and prepare to move out."

"Yes, sir," Kleiner replied. "But, first, may I show you something?"

"Certainly."

"If you look over there, you can see three sets of faint tracks heading in a southwest direction. They brushed out their tracks near the cabin but didn't bother once they moved away."

"Very good, Kleiner," Otto said. "I think you're on to something. Now, let's get going."

Everything was adding up to the fact that they were on the trail of the Americans. Who but a woman would have left the cabin so neat? How many people traveled in parties of three? It must be the Americans! What luck it would be for him to capture the world-famous physicist.

But what about Schmidt? Must he contact the major now? *No!* he decided. It only made sense to be certain before notifying Schmidt. After all, if he called him now, it would just be offering the major a premature invitation to meddle.

At sunset, as his squad rounded a bend, Bruner saw another cabin beside the trail. A quick reconnoiter revealed the cabin to be empty. Bruner decided to share the cabin with his men, as the tents they had brought would provide little shelter against the frigid night.

"Sir, you are very kind," Sergeant Kleiner said. "But do you think it is proper for an officer to share quarters with enlisted men?"

"Kleiner, I appreciate your concern, but it won't do me any good if my men are frozen, will it?"

"No, sir." The sergeant saluted and ordered one of the men to build a fire in the hearth to warm the cabin.

Looking at his men, Otto could tell they were pleased to be staying inside. Two of the younger ones even mouthed *Danke schön. Better treat them right out of combat*, he thought. After all, they might be expected to die for *der Fatherland* sometime in the future.

Even in the relative comfort of the cabin, Bruner had trouble falling asleep. It wasn't just the snoring, which had reached a crescendo level. So far, he'd managed to avoid killing. Although he was eager to capture Flannigan, he hoped he wouldn't have to kill the other two Americans. *Was this a sign of weakness?* Perhaps it was. More and more, he was learning that a conscience was a liability in war. Only cruelty earned rewards. Just look at Schmidt!

The lessons he had learned as a church-going child could not help him now. *Oh, Lord*, he prayed, *give me strength! Forgive me for what I might have to do to please that evil man!*

He opened his eyes. The fire cast its flickering red glow on the walls of the cabin. *I am already in hell*, he thought. He closed his eyes and tried to calm himself.

At first light, one of the men reported to Bruner something new. Although the tracks they'd followed to the cabin had been made by three people on skis, the tracks leading away included a wider trace that looked like it had been made by something being dragged, perhaps a sled of some sort. Bruner knew that Flannigan was an old man, almost seventy. Perhaps he had grown weak or been injured. But the trace left by the sled wasn't deep enough to have been made by a load as heavy as a person. And there were still the three sets of ski tracks that were visible under the fresh snow.

"Why would the Americans be pulling an empty sled?" Bruner asked Kleiner.

"I don't know, sir," the sergeant replied. "Perhaps they are taking it along in case the old man falters."

"You could be right," Otto said. "Let's prepare to head out."

Soon, the squad was heading southwest at a brisk pace. Bruner remained puzzled until they came to the brink of a long, steep, and rock-strewn drop in the trail from which only two sets of ski tracks and the now-deeper imprint of the sled led downward.

"Sergeant, this answers our question," Otto said in a relieved tone. "Obviously, the physicist is not a good enough skier—or in good enough health—to remain upright on this slope, so they're letting him ride."

"I think you're right, sir," Kleiner replied. "But I hope the old man remains healthy until we capture him."

"I do, too," Otto said with a sigh. "Schmidt will have my neck if anything happens to him."

As he skied quickly but carefully downward, Bruner saw chunks of wood scattered on both sides of the sled's tracks, especially just beyond jagged rocks it must have hit. Whoever had been aboard would have had a wild ride.

At the bottom, Bruner was happy just to have made it down in one piece. Quickly recovering, Otto looked around to survey the evidence. Since there were no dead bodies or other signs of catastrophe, it was assumed that the Americans had made it and were pressing onward.

Looking ahead, Otto noticed that there were three sets of skis plus the trail of the sled, which must have been badly damaged. More importantly, it looked as if two members of the party were half-carrying and half-dragging the third one. Under different circumstances, Otto mused, he would have thought the wobbling and weaving were the result of too much Oktoberfest!

Within a few hours, Bruner and his squad came upon the third cabin. Before they approached it, Bruner used his binoculars to scan for any signs of life. He noticed movement at a window. *Success!* He called his radioman to his side. It was time to contact Schmidt.

Noticing the frantic activity inside the cabin, Otto knew they had been spotted. *Routine mission so far*, he thought, *but that is all about to change.*

19

Their Luck Runs Out

"WE HAVE COMPANY," Lars said. The others joined him at the window and cautiously peered out. "Six that I can see," Dunbar said. "There may be more hidden by the brush or trees."

"I'll see if there are any out back," Lars added. He quickly moved to the rear window. "None," he reported.

Dunbar turned and saw the professor spring out of bed and pick up a revolver on the table. "No, Professor!" Dunbar shouted. "Stop him!"

Jennifer screamed and ran toward him, but it was too late. The professor flung the door open and emptied his gun at the figures lurking a short distance away. Automatically, two of the Germans fired back, and the professor slumped to the ground.

"Wait!" Dunbar ordered as Dude and Jennifer raced to the door. "It won't do any good to get yourselves killed." The Americans stopped and crouched down by the open door. "Damn!" Dude said. "I wish I had my rifle."

"Just stay there," Dunbar commanded. "I'll get the weapons." He crawled over to the corner where the machine gun and rifles were standing. Carefully, he picked them up and crawled back to the window. He nodded at Jennifer and Dude, then slid two rifles toward them.

Jennifer and Dude picked up their rifles as Lars bellied up next to the major. "What do we do now?" Lars asked.

"Let's see what they do," Dunbar replied. He handed Lars a rifle.

"Americans!" Bruner yelled through a bullhorn. "Go to your comrade. See if you can help him. We will not shoot."

Soon, all four of the professor's companions were at his side. Lars and Dunbar carried the professor back into the cabin, and Jennifer frantically tried to resuscitate him as he lay on the bed. It was to no avail. Blood gushed from two holes in his chest. Looking up at his companions, the professor smiled and said, "Thank you." He took his last breath.

Putting his arms around Jennifer, Dude said softly, "The professor is now at peace, darling. You don't have to worry about him suffering any more." With tears slowly trickling down her cheeks, she nodded and clutched Dude tightly.

Waving a white flag, Captain Bruner approached the cabin. Major Dunbar and Lars went out to meet with him, and Otto saluted crisply.

"I see I was mistaken," Bruner said. "I thought there were only Americans, but you are British, and you are Norwegian."

"That is correct," the major said.

"I'm very sorry for your loss," Bruner added. "But all I can do is give you an hour to make preparations and bury the professor. As of now, you are my prisoners, so please hand over your weapons."

"Not a chance," Dunbar replied. "A large group of resistance fighters is on its way. Soon these hills will be swarming with them, so I suggest you give us your weapons." Lars nodded supportively.

As he studied the captain, Dunbar noticed the flustered look in Bruner's eyes. Obviously, the captain hadn't faced this situation before, nor was it spelled out in the German field manual.

It was several seconds before Bruner responded. "Have it your way," he said. "I will still give you the hour, but after that I will take you by force if necessary."

"Maybe," Dunbar said defiantly. The major and Lars went back into the cabin, and Otto rejoined his troops.

Back inside, Dunbar motioned for Dude and Jennifer to come over. "The captain is inexperienced," Dunbar said. "And I think I was able to bluff him. He wanted us to turn over our weapons, but I said he should turn over his—that resistance fighters were on their way. He looked puzzled, so I assume he will call his superiors to receive his orders."

"By the way," Dunbar added. "I couldn't have done it without Lars' support." Lars grinned as Dude patted his Norwegian friend on the back.

"So what do we do now?" Jennifer asked.

"Let's bury the professor, get something to eat, and head out," Dunbar replied. "The German captain is giving us an hour before he attacks."

"Right generous of him," Dude muttered.

"By the way," Dunbar continued, "Lars, you said the Germans hadn't moved in back of the cabin, correct? Well, that's the direction we want to go."

"Yes," Lars said. "We may be able to catch them by surprise. We are all good skiers, so who knows? We may win out!"

They carried the professor out of the cabin and placed him on the frozen ground at the edge of the woods. Loose material was piled on top of him. "I'll come back in the spring after the ground has thawed," Lars said. "I'll give him a proper burial." The others nodded.

Dunbar looked at the two Americans and said, "If either of you wants to say a few words, we have time."

"I'll start," Jennifer said softly. "Oh, Father, please take the professor into your heavenly arms," she prayed. "He has lived a kind, generous, and Christian life. Please help him to find peace and happiness in your kingdom as he awaits the arrival of loved ones. Amen."

"Father," Dude added, "I agree that the professor was a wonderful man. Please take good care of him. Amen."

The four stood in silence for a moment and then went back into the cabin. Moving to the table, they peeled off their hats and gloves and unbuttoned their coats. They got out the food and started to eat.

"It's all my fault," Lars said dejectedly as he ate his bread and sausage. "I put my pistol on the table last night while I built the sled. If I hadn't done that, the professor would still be alive."

"Don't blame yourself," Jennifer said reassuringly. "You couldn't have known what the professor would do."

As Otto waited to hear Schmidt's voice over his radio, he looked at the two men who had shot the professor. They looked fearful, Otto thought, and rightfully so. Anyone who had incurred the major's wrath knew that it was a very unpleasant experience. "I'm not going to report you," Otto said, "so relax."

Dejectedly, Otto gave the major the bad news. As expected, Schmidt flew into a rage. When Otto tried to explain, Schmidt cut him off. "Bruner, do you realize that you have ruined my chance for a spot promotion? I assure you that you will pay and pay dearly!"

"I expected as much, sir."

"Shut up and listen. I'm going to make the others in the professor's party pay with their lives, and I don't want you screwing it up!"

"Yes, sir."

"Have you disarmed them?" Schmidt asked.

"No, sir."

"Why not?"

"This British major refused my order to surrender their weapons. He says that there are a large number of resistance fighters on the way. He was bold enough to say that I should turn over my weapons to him!"

"A British major?" Schmidt demanded. "Who else is there that I should know about?"

"To the best of my knowledge," Otto replied, "there are four that are still alive. Besides the major, there are the two Americans that we knew about and a man that I suspect to be in the Norwegian Underground."

"Hmm. Maybe I can still turn things to my advantage," the major said, obviously not paying much attention to Otto's reply. "After all, I wouldn't be one of the youngest majors in the German Army without being clever."

What arrogance, Otto thought.

"Bruner," Schmidt snapped. "Here is what you are to do. Let the four escape. Given the chance, they will continue heading for the coast, where I will be waiting to execute them. I will show the world what happens to anyone who messes with Peter Schmidt!"

Has he gone mad? Otto wondered. Wouldn't it be better to engage the enemy now while his squad was in contact with them? After all, as the Americans say, "A bird in the hand is worth two in the bush."

"Next," Schmidt continued, "bring the professor's body with you. This will prove that we do have him."

"Isn't our word good enough?" Bruner asked.

"No!" Schmidt barked. "The Allies will deny, deny, deny unless we can show them Flannigan's pudgy, lifeless body."

Oh, well, Otto thought, *there's no use arguing with him*. Besides, if the British major was being honest, there would be enemy reinforcements on the way. So it would be just as well to get the heck out of there.

"Bruner," Schmidt concluded, "you may fire at them to make them think that they are being engaged, but you are not to hit any of them. Do you understand?"

"Absolutely, sir," Otto replied.

The four Allies finished eating, mainly just picking at their food. "We still have a little time before the hour is up," Dunbar said. "But we should leave in the next five or ten minutes." The others nodded.

"What does the German captain look like?" Jennifer asked. "I didn't get a good look at him."

"He doesn't have fangs or a long, crooked nose if that's what you mean," Lars replied. "I thought he might resemble the devil, too, but he doesn't."

"Just a regular-looking chap, I guess," Dunbar added. "It's pretty difficult to tell about a man's appearance when he has on a ski cap. But why do you ask?"

"I want to remember any distinguishing features of the man responsible for the professor's death," Jennifer said.

"I don't think you can blame him for the professor's death," Dude countered. "After all, he does what his country tells him to do just like we do."

"I suppose you're right," Jennifer replied. "But his country is telling him to do some pretty rotten things."

Dunbar changed the subject. "I know things look bleak," the major said. "But we have a chance, and maybe a good one. Lars did a great job of helping me convince the German captain that help was on the way. This may cause the Gerries to hesitate in firing at us, thinking it will expedite the arrival of overwhelming force."

"I don't mind fighting to the death, anyway," Dude replied. "My concern is for Jennifer. I want her to get out safely if at all possible." Jennifer smiled and gently stroked Dude's shoulder.

"You don't have to worry about that," she said. "I don't want to live if something happens to you."

"Oh, please!" Lars moaned. "That's enough of that kind of talk."

"Lars is right," Dunbar urged. "We don't want to talk about dying but about living. We have a chance, so let's take it." Everyone nodded.

"What's the plan, Major?" Dude asked.

"We're all good skiers, so we'll start skiing toward the coast as if we're in a cross-country meet. We'll move in a rapid, systematic fashion. The Germans are obviously good skiers, too. If they get too close, we'll have to take them out. If not, we'll let them be."

Turning to Lars, Dude said, "This is right up your alley, isn't it, good buddy?"

Smiling, Lars poked him on the shoulder.

"We have a machine gun, three rifles, and some pistols," the major continued. "We may be outgunned, but our arsenal is still something to be reckoned with. Let's go!"

They got up, put on their outer garments, and quietly slipped out the back door. Their dash for the coast had begun.

20

The Chase Begins

D UNBAR FOLLOWED THE three out the door. "I'm glad you're
in top physical shape," he said under his breath and to no one in
particular. "We can give them a run for their money."

As his men waited impatiently, Bruner motioned for his first
sergeant. "Kleiner, Major Schmidt has ordered us not to engage the
enemy. He wants to kill them himself."

"What should I tell the men?" Kleiner asked.

"Two things," Bruner replied. "We're to keep them in sight if they
run. And we're to bring the body of the old man as proof that we didn't
let him escape."

"Yes, sir. We'll fetch him now."

"Not now," Bruner instructed. "Wait until they leave. Let's not do
anything to agitate them unnecessarily."

"Yes, sir," Kleiner replied. He left to brief the team members.

Otto marveled at Kleiner's loyalty and efficiency. *They don't come
any better*, he thought.

Suddenly, Otto heard a squad member yell "*Ausstiegsklausel!*" as
Dunbar and the others raced out of the cabin's back door. Otto looked

around and saw the four heading in a southwesterly direction. *Time to take over*, he told himself.

"Kleiner, go ahead and get the old man," Otto said as he raced over. "But treat his body with respect. I don't feel comfortable digging up the dead."

"Yes, sir!" Kleiner replied. The sergeant barked orders, and soon the professor's covered body was brought forward on a sled-like device that had been used to haul provisions.

Otto went over to the sled and stood next to Kleiner. He pulled back the tarp and momentarily peered at Flannigan's face. *A lot of character*, he thought.

"Kleiner, it's a shame this great man died in such a fashion. In the end, though, I guess death treats us all the same. Perhaps that's a good thing."

"Yes, sir."

"Cover him up again. I don't want any of him exposed."

Otto motioned for the men to gather around him. "Men," Bruner said, "our orders are to keep the enemy in sight. They are obviously headed southwest to the coast. I think there will be an enemy vessel waiting to transport them."

Pausing for a second, Otto continued. "We are not—I repeat, *not*—to wound or kill any of them. If you fire at them for some reason, make sure you miss. Major Schmidt is reserving the role of executioner for himself. Are there any questions?"

"Sir, has our Navy been alerted so that they can intercept the enemy ship?" Sergeant Kleiner asked.

"No, they haven't," Bruner replied. "The major doesn't want anyone else receiving any glory. Any other questions?"

"No, sir."

"Okay, let's move out."

As they pursued the enemy, some of the better German skiers moved out in front. Bruner called to them to hold back, but one ignored Bruner's shouts and raced onward, closing quickly on the group ahead.

Bruner saw the British major kneel down and take aim. *Crack! Crack!* Two shots were fired, and the German skier went down. Bruner raced to his side, took off his glove, and felt the soldier's neck for any sign of a pulse. There wasn't any. "Is he alive, sir?" Sergeant Kleiner asked as he rushed over. Bruner sadly shook his head.

Bruner was momentarily stunned. How could this young man have been so careless, particularly after the warnings that had been issued? He pulled off the young man's identification tags and gently closed his eyes. "Cover him with a blanket," he said softly to his sergeant. "We'll come back and bury him later." Kleiner nodded and pulled a blanket from the dead soldier's backpack.

Bruner glared at the enemy major who was now standing and looking in his direction. More than anything, Otto was livid that his squad couldn't fight back. For the first time, he was feeling the sting of battle. He had been in support units during the battles in France and the Low Countries and not on the front lines. *How easy it was to stay on the moral high ground back then*, he thought. Now, as he kneeled over his dead soldier, it was a different matter. Was he becoming another Schmidt? He hoped not, but he wasn't sure.

Bruner stood and motioned for his soldiers to press on. By now, the enemy major and his companions had headed out. In front, the terrain was flat and open. *Better be extra careful*, Bruner thought, *or the British major will pick off some more of my men.* Perhaps a half-mile back would be about right. Not too close but not far enough to risk losing them.

The men in Bruner's squad had learned their lesson, so Otto didn't have to remind anyone to be careful. They stayed close to him, but he could tell what was on their minds. They wanted to avenge their fallen mate, and the sooner the better. Unfortunately, his hands were tied, and they would have to wait.

Dude approached Dunbar and said, "Good shooting, Major!"

"I didn't want to do it," Dunbar replied. "I'm sure that lad was young enough to be my son."

Looking over at Jennifer, Dunbar noticed that her gaze was fixed on the Germans who were pulling a sled. "What's wrong?" he asked.

"Isn't that the professor's body on that sled?" she replied.

My God!" Dude gasped. "I think it is! It sure looks like his profile."

"But you can't be sure," Lars said. "They've covered him well with that tarp."

"I'd swear it is," Dude replied. "After all, Jennifer and I spent enough time with him to recognize his outline."

"What are they doing with him?" Jennifer asked stormily. "Don't they have any respect for the dead?"

"I don't know, but we don't have time to find out!" Dunbar growled. "Let's go!" With Dude nudging her forward, Jennifer reluctantly turned around and began skiing. *If we reach the* Windstorm *in one piece*, Dunbar thought, *it will be a miracle.*

Dunbar noted that Lars and Dude were alert, but Jennifer seemed to be preoccupied. He skied over to her.

"Jennifer, I know the professor's loss is overwhelming to you. But you must concentrate on what's happening now. Otherwise, we won't make it."

"You're right, Major. But now Lars won't be able to give the professor a proper burial. It bothers me."

"I know it does. But if you don't snap out of it, none of us will get a proper burial."

"You're right," Jennifer replied. "I'll do better."

The major nodded. Underneath, though, he wondered if he had been too hard on her. "Perhaps something can be done," he said. "We'll discuss it on the *Windstorm*." He was pleased to see that she seemed relieved.

As sunset approached, the foursome came to a good, long downward slope. As they sped down on their skis, Dude pointed to a cabin off to the side and yelled to Jennifer, "That must be cabin four." She nodded.

Hoping that the downward slope would last all the way to the coast, Dunbar was soon disappointed. The terrain became flat once more, and their pace slowed considerably. He called to the others, "It's flat as far as I can see." If they want to engage us, this is their best opportunity so far. Everybody stay alert."

"How much further, Lars?" Dude asked.

"It's a ways. Probably another two miles to cabin five," Lars replied.

"Then how far?" Jennifer inquired.

"Not far at all."

The others seem more invigorated, Dunbar thought. Good! They would need to be.

21

Ultimate Sacrifice

MAJOR DUNBAR KNEW they were getting close to the coast, and he was certain the enemy knew it too. So wouldn't the Germans have the presence of mind to figure that help was on the way from the British Navy? They must! Using this line of reasoning, Dunbar figured that now would be a perfect time for the enemy to attack.

Looking over at his companions, Dunbar saw that Lars was alert, but Jennifer had lapsed back into an inattentive state and Dude seemed to have drifted off. Perhaps they were preoccupied with the professor's death, as Jennifer had been before. Or maybe they were wondering if they would make it to their wedding. Whatever the reason, neither of them was paying much attention to the nearby threat. *Time to motivate once more,* Dunbar decided.

"Hey, you two," the major bellowed. "Wake up!" He pointed to the threat behind them. "Look toward them regularly. If someone's aiming at you, be ready to duck and fire. Don't make me tell you again!"

Dude was outwardly embarrassed. "Sorry, sir."

Jennifer was, too. "We'll stay alert, Major."

As they passed a cabin nestled in the trees, Lars called out, "That's cabin five. We're getting close."

Dude said softly to Jennifer, "The *Windstorm* will be a beautiful sight for these tired eyes.

"I hope we make it," she said.

Dunbar had his own doubts. Why did the enemy follow and not engage? They appeared to be first-rate troops, yet they were holding back. *Better alert the others to the possibilities*, he thought, motioning them to come closer.

"For some reason, the Germans don't want to engage us," Dunbar said. "And it doesn't make sense. They have more weapons than we do. Either there's a trap up ahead, or they're waiting to engage us on the beach where they think we'll be pinned against the water."

We could stand and fight now," Lars replied.

"I'm not for that," Dude said. "If we make it to the beach, the *Windstorm* can help us."

"*If* the *Windstorm* is there," the major replied. "Remember, we are past the appointed hour."

"What do you think, Major?" Jennifer asked. "Should we count on the sub?"

"It's our best hope, and I know Tom Brookstone will do everything he can to keep it there."

"Then let's get to the beach as soon as possible," Jennifer said.

"That's the spirit," Dunbar said. "Now let's spread out."

The four picked up the pace, and the enemy did the same. *When would the Germans show their hand*, Dunbar wondered? The beach couldn't be far away.

Pointing to a ridge up ahead, Lars said, "We can see the beach from there."

"Great," Dude and Jennifer replied almost simultaneously. Dunbar, however, eyed the woods to their right suspiciously. *Great place for an ambush*, he thought. *Dude is closest to the woods, and Jennifer is next to him. Better change that now.*

Too late. "Something to our right!" Dunbar shouted as he motioned at the woods.

"I see them!" Dude yelled. "Head for the ridge! I'll cover you!" He yanked his rifle down and crouched in a firing position. Jennifer raced toward him, dropping her ski poles.

"I'm not leaving you!"

"You have to!" Dude ordered. "Major! Lars! Get her!"

The two dashed to her side and started dragging her toward the ridge. "No!" she screamed. "You go—I have to stay!" It did no good. Her pleas went unanswered as she dug her skis into the snow. Half-carrying her and half-sliding her along, the two men headed for cover.

Machine-gun fire broke out. Looking back, the three saw Dude fall forward. "No!" Jennifer yelled. She broke free and skied frantically toward him.

Dunbar and Lars fired their weapons and sped after her. In a frenzy, Jennifer pulled Dude to her bosom and rocked him. Instinctively, she tried to hold in the life-sustaining blood that poured from his chest. Soon, her hand and wrist were covered.

"Hold on, darling," she sobbed. "We'll get you out of here. Please don't leave me."

"You must go," Dude said softly. "Live for both of us."

Mustering all of the strength that he had left, Dude began moving his shoulders. With a mighty effort, he rolled over, cocked the bolt action, and fired the rifle. He repeated the process in rapid succession. Moans were heard from the woods, verifying that his fleeting moments were not wasted.

Dunbar and Lars raced up and pulled Jennifer away. They fired their guns awkwardly as they headed for the ridge with Jennifer in tow. *With any luck, we might make it,* Dunbar thought. After all, he had witnessed the miracle of Dunkirk. Maybe one more miracle was in the works.

Bullets danced around them in the snow. The two men weaved frantically.

Struggling mightily, Jennifer tried to free herself from her friends' grips. She dug one ski deeper into the snow, then the other. "I can't leave him," she wailed.

"You must!" Dunbar ordered. All the while, her anguished gaze was focused on the young man firing valiantly as he lay in the blood-soaked snow.

Dude's head started bobbing. His grip on the gun loosened. He looked back at Jennifer one last time as his head slowly dropped into the snow.

Jennifer struggled even harder. "My God, she's strong," Lars muttered. "It's all I can do to hang onto her." He dropped his rifle and tugged on her arm with both hands.

"Jennifer!" Dunbar bellowed, "Get ahold of yourself! Don't throw your life away—Dude wouldn't want that!" Suddenly, her resistance softened. Maybe he'd reached her.

"You two get to the ridge," Dunbar said. "I'll cover you." He kneeled down and fired his machine gun in the automatic mode. This time, he was more effective, as firing from the woods momentarily ceased. Looking over his shoulder, he saw Lars and Jennifer disappear. Now was his chance. He wheeled around and shot forward from a crouching position, skiing toward safety with long, powerful strides. He zigzagged frantically. Maybe he'd get there in one piece.

Otto watched sadly from below. He couldn't help but feel compassion for the foursome as he watched what was happening up ahead. His men were not taking part in the firefight, leaving it up to Schmidt and the other squad. This suited Otto, as the fight was very much one-sided.

Otto imagined that Schmidt was very much enjoying his revenge. If it weren't for this group, the world-famous physicist would be in the major's hands, and Schmidt would be enjoying the greatest triumph of his career. Did it matter to Schmidt that German soldiers were being lost in the process? Probably not.

Bullets from Dunbar's machine gun were forcing Schmidt's soldiers to keep their heads down, and Schmidt shouted to his troops to keep firing. Otto was sure that the major wanted to report that the enemy had paid dearly for keeping Professor Flannigan from being captured.

Jennifer now worked with Dunbar and Lars in the struggle for survival. Schmidt and his men had emerged from the woods and were in hot pursuit. There wasn't a moment to spare. Lars motioned in the direction that they should go as the three sprinted on their skis, each having abandoned their ski poles. Soon they came to a gradual rise in the trail.

At the top they were able to see the water and the small rubber raft from the *Windstorm*. *Thank God*, Dunbar thought, *Brookstone came back.*

The three tumbled downward as the trail dropped abruptly. At the bottom, they ripped off their skis. Lars and Dunbar, holding Jennifer firmly, got up and rushed toward the raft. They plunged into the shallow water—Jennifer matching them stride for stride—and were soon scrambling to get aboard the dinghy. Pulling the three into the craft, the two crewmen began rowing mightily.

"I see you're in a spot of trouble," one yelled to Dunbar.

"That's putting it mildly," the major replied. "Anything we can do to help?"

The crewman nodded at the two oars lying on the raft's floor. "Pick those up and start rowing."

Dunbar and Lars complied. "Anything I can do?" Jennifer asked.

"Just stay down," Dunbar ordered.

It was getting dark. Suddenly lights beamed down on them from the top of the rise. Major Schmidt motioned for one of his men to hand him a machine gun. He opened fire and hit the launch attendants and Lars with the first burst. All dove into the frigid water. For the raft attendants, it was too late. Dunbar quickly checked them and then looked for the others.

"Jennifer? Lars? Where are you?" Dunbar barked, spitting out water.

"Over here," Jennifer yelled. "I'm with Lars. He's badly hurt."

"Hang on. I'm coming."

As he reached them, Dunbar saw that Jennifer was towing Lars with her hand under his chin and supporting his back on her body. Lars was objecting. "Go! Leave me! I'm finished."

"Nonsense," Jennifer replied. Dunbar grabbed one of Lars' arms and started swimming along with Jennifer.

Jennifer gasped. "Can we make it to the *Windstorm*?"

"There's a second raft on board," Dunbar replied, sucking air. "I'm sure Tom will send it for us."

While Schmidt fired from the top of the ridge, German troops slid down the embankment and prepared to fire at the three in the water.

Viewing the danger from the *Windstorm's* bridge, Commander Brookstone turned to his executive officer, John Whitcomb. "John, have our main gun fire at the ridge and our machine gun fire at the Germans on the beach."

"Yes, sir!"

Whitcomb barked the orders. Soon, the lights on the ridge went out. "I'm not sure whether we hit the lights or whether the Germans turned them off," Brookstone said. "Cease firing at the ridge for now, but keep peppering the beach."

"Aye, aye, sir."

After several minutes, the gunfire from the beach stopped. "Good," Brookstone said. "Let's turn on our searchlight and see if there are survivors in the water."

"Isn't that dangerous, sir?" Whitcomb said. "The Germans may still have some working guns on the ridge."

Brookstone smiled slightly. "Maybe. But if they start firing, we'll make them wish they hadn't."

Soon, the searchlight was on. As the light passed over them, Jennifer and Dunbar used their free hands to wave frantically. Dunbar yelled "Mayday!" Jennifer followed suit.

"There they are, Tom!" Whitcomb said.

"Thank God," Brookstone replied. "Blink the search light so they know we see them. And get that other raft into the water."

"Aye, aye, sir."

The second raft was soon on the way. The big uncertainty was the status of those in the water. Would they be healthy enough to fight the strong current and icy water until the raft reached them?

A full moon appeared overhead. Brookstone watched intently as the raft moved through the choppy waters. Minutes seemed like hours, and Brookstone found himself rocking back and forth in rhythm with the rowers' strokes.

"Do you think Major Dunbar made it?" Whitcomb asked.

"I have no idea, John. I heard a man and a woman calling, but I don't know if the man was Dunbar. And I couldn't tell how many went into the water."

Sporadic firing came from the beach, but it was inaccurate. Still, Brookstone was in no mood to take chances. "Keep firing," he shouted to his machine-gun crew. "We don't want them to get lucky and hit one of our people."

The raft reached the survivors as Brookstone and Whitcomb watched. "Keep that spotlight on them," Brookstone directed.

One was pulled aboard. Then a second. Finally, a third.

"John, I counted three," Brookstone said. "How many did you see?"

"Three, also. But one of them seemed to be in pretty bad shape."

Brookstone nodded.

Did Dunbar make it? Who among the Americans did? The woman obviously made it, but what about the other two? It wouldn't be long now. The raft was rapidly approaching.

Suddenly, the lights on the ridge came back on, and heavy gunfire started pouring in. Brookstone shouted to his gun crew to commence firing at the ridge. Shortly they made a direct hit, and men and equipment went flying in all directions. Brookstone sighed in relief.

Gunfire from the beach suddenly stopped. *Why not?* Brookstone thought. The *Windstorm's* main gun had probably taken out the German brass. And the troops on the beach were more than likely leaderless.

Standing on the bridge, Brookstone said, "You stay here, John. I'm going down on deck to meet them." Whitcomb nodded as Brookstone descended using the hand and foot rails.

As the raft arrived, Brookstone recognized Jennifer and Dunbar. But who was the third? And what had happened to Partude and the elderly physicist? He would have to wait to find out.

Jennifer and Major Dunbar were both shivering badly, but Lars was unconscious.

"Welcome back," Brookstone yelled.

"Thanks," Dunbar said looking up, his teeth chattering. "And thanks for waiting for us."

A hatch opened in the *Windstorm's* side, and the raft disappeared from view, along with its passengers. The hatch closed, and Brookstone scrambled up to the conning tower. "After you," he said to Whitcomb, pointing to the ladder that descended into the submarine's interior. The executive officer started down. The captain followed, slamming the hatch after him.

At the base of the ladder, they entered the control room. "Mr. Whitcomb," Brookstone bellowed, "take her down! The commotion may bring some unwelcome company."

"Aye, aye, sir," Whitcomb replied. Hurrying over to the sub's intercom system, he picked up a microphone and flipped a switch. "Dive! Dive!" he shouted into the mike. Levers were pulled, water rushed into the boat's ballast tanks, and the *Windstorm* creaked and groaned as it began its rapid downward trajectory. Passengers and crewmen alike were thrown about, and people remained upright any way they could.

Jennifer and Dunbar trailed the crewmen who were carrying Lars on a stretcher. The crewmen turned into an area no bigger than a cubbyhole and placed Lars on what appeared to be an operating table. There were cabinets along the walls that contained medicines and sterilizing equipment.

Lieutenant Sam Johnston introduced himself. "I'm Sam, the ship's medical officer. We met on the way over."

"I remember," Jennifer replied. Dunbar stood in the background.

"You two had better change before you get hypothermia," Johnston said. "I'll do everything I can for him." Jennifer and Dunbar nodded and hurried off.

"It won't take me long," Jennifer replied over her shoulder.

She rushed to her assigned quarters, quickly dried off, and changed into clothes furnished by the ship's crew. She weaved from side to side in the narrow corridor as she raced to return to Lars' side. She was too late.

"Isn't there something more we can do for him?" she asked grief-stricken.

"I'm afraid not," the medical officer replied sadly. He gently pulled a sheet over Lars' face.

Dunbar stopped in the doorway. Slowly, he walked over to Jennifer. He knew words wouldn't be adequate right now, so he simply put his hand on her shoulder. She momentarily put her hand on his.

In a stupor, Jennifer slowly walked back to her small compartment. She was only vaguely aware of Brookstone's frenzied chatter up ahead: "Fire one! Fire two!" Even the *Windstorm* lurching backwards and the explosions that followed weren't enough to pull her out of her daze.

With Lars' death, Jennifer knew that a significant part of Dude's life was being erased. Dude and Lars were the closest of companions, and they would have carried each other's memories for as long as they lived.

Back on land, as Otto Bruner regained consciousness, he was suddenly aware of two things: he'd been wounded in the right shoulder, and the shooting had stopped. But he could hear moans and cries for help all around him. He pulled himself to his feet and surveyed the damage that had been inflicted by the *Windstorm*'s guns. Even in darkness, he could see bodies strewn on the bright snow. The *Windstorm* gunners had been effective.

Looking out to sea, Otto saw the raft arriving at the submarine. Dutifully, he looked around to see if there were any guns with which he could engage the enemy one last time. Not seeing any, he moved to his second task, assessing the condition of his men.

In spite of his own substantial wounds, Otto jogged to the top of the ridge where he'd last seen Schmidt. The major, who was bleeding profusely from his chest, struggled mightily to prop himself up. Looking at Otto, he asked for a status report.

"We have a lot of casualties, sir."

"I don't mean them, you idiot! I want to know if any of the enemy reached the submarine!"

"A couple of them did."

For a moment, Otto marveled at the major. Here was a man, obviously dying, who was being the consummate soldier to the end. Whereas Schmidt was thinking of the mission, Otto suspected he would spend his own last moments praying to God for forgiveness.

Looking up once again, Schmidt gasped and said, "Bruner, I'm finished, so here is what you're to do. First, report the position of the enemy submarine. Next, request that our Navy send a vessel to evacuate any of our troops who are still alive. Finally, save as much of our equipment as you can."

Schmidt's breathing became much more ragged. He coughed, and Bruner saw dark blood splash from his mouth onto the snow. "Long live the fatherland!" Schmidt sighed with his last breath.

To Bruner's surprise, he found himself choking up at Schmidt's death. He gently closed the major's eyes and momentarily contemplated why he was saddened. The major was utterly ruthless, but Bruner knew Germany would need as many Peter Schmidts as it could get if the war was to be won. Fortunately or unfortunately—however one looked at it—Bruner doubted that he could ever be one of them.

With moaning and confusion all around him, Otto was quickly brought back to reality. Looking around, he spotted a radioman who appeared to be okay. Going over to him, Otto asked the man if his radio was operational.

"I believe that it is, sir. Should I put out an emergency call?"

"Yes, but first report that an enemy submarine is departing this area."

When Otto counted casualties, he found that only ten out of the twenty-four men in the two squads were still alive. *What a terrible price to pay for a failed mission*, he thought. What if he had engaged the enemy party at the cabin when the professor had died? Maybe it would have turned out better for them. But it had been the major's decision—not his.

By now, Otto was feeling woozy from the loss of blood. He looked around for a second in command. Spotting his first sergeant, Otto sat down and called the man to his side.

"Sergeant, you'll have to take over, as I'm fading fast," he said. "Keep the ones who are alive as comfortable as possible and collect as much of our usable equipment as you can. The Navy should have a vessel here shortly." Then Bruner's consciousness faded. He felt his cheek hit the snow before he passed out.

The losses on both sides were substantial. Those that had made it would return to fight another day.

22

Huge Void

IN A DAZE, Jennifer sat in her cramped quarters aboard the *Windstorm*. She got up and went to the small basin which had been partially filled with water. She took off her shirt and washed off the blood that had caked on her neck, hands, and arms. What was Dude's and what was Lars'? She wasn't sure, although she thought most of Dude's must have washed off when she jumped into the water. In a trance, she dried off and put back on the dry shirt that had been loaned to her by a crewman. She walked over to her tiny bunk and curled up on it as best she could.

Soon there was a soft knock at her door. It was Major Dunbar. "I'm so sorry for your loss," he said. "Is there anything I can do?"

"Would you stay with me for a while?"

"Certainly."

Dunbar pulled a chair out from the small desk and turned it so he could sit facing her.

"I wasn't sure you or anyone else knew how much Dude and I loved each other."

"I could tell," Dunbar interrupted, "even before the two of you said that you were getting married."

"It may not have been love at first sight," she continued, "but it was very close."

Her gaze was distant. "The first time I saw him," she said, "was in General Marshall's outer office. He looked so handsome, so confident, so full of life that I asked myself, *Is he the one?* After we had dinner together that night, I knew he had everything I was looking for. He was warm, intelligent, and sensitive. But what really clinched it was when we went to the firing range and he put his arms around me to help steady my aim. In his arms I could barely concentrate on shooting. I just wanted to make love."

She put her hand to her mouth. "Oh, sorry, Major. I didn't mean to be so graphic."

"That's quite all right. For what it's worth, it seems you two did more and felt more in a few weeks than most people do in a lifetime." Jennifer nodded.

"I keep thinking about how the professor didn't want us to sacrifice our lives for him. Maybe I shouldn't have been so stubborn and should have listened to him. It's possible that Dude would be alive right now."

"I think you know better than that. Anything less than what you did wouldn't have met the intent of your mission."

"I suppose you're right."

"You should try to get some sleep now," Dunbar said. He stood and pushed the chair back under the desk. As he turned towards the door, Jennifer said, "Dude and his brother and I all agreed we'd meet under the clock at the St. Francis Hotel in San Francisco to celebrate the end of the war. For Dude, the war is over now."

Dunbar hesitated, pulled out the chair, and sat down again.

"Jennifer, I'm telling you this, not for any sympathy, but because it might help you. In 1940, my wife and five-year-old son were killed in the London Blitz. I was devastated. How could I go on? Finally, I was able to convince myself that I must go on living for all three of us. That gave me the strength to survive my grief. And you must be strong, so Dude—and the professor and Lars, too—can continue to live through you. It takes time, but the pain will eventually start to fade."

Jennifer managed to smile at him. "Thank you, Major," she said. "I'm so sorry about your wife and your son. You must have loved them very much."

"I love them still," Dunbar said. "In our hearts, the ones we love never die."

She reached out to touch his cheek, now damp with tears. "Thank you," she said again.

The next morning, Jennifer went to the officers' mess. Major Dunbar was already there, and he stood up as she entered. "I can recommend the *Windstorm's* special breakfast," he said. "Eggs and pork bangers."

"Just coffee will be fine," she replied. "I'm not sure I could eat anything."

"By the way, I was so distraught last night that I didn't ask what the excitement was about. I did hear some explosions."

"Oh, you mean the destroyer we sunk," Brookstone said as he approached. "We think it was the *Bruno Heinemann*, but we didn't stick around to find out." He slid into the chair next to Jennifer.

"I must have really been out of it," Jennifer said softly as if still in a mild state of shock.

"No one can blame you for that," Brookstone replied. "Incidentally, we'll be docking in short order. We're on the surface in Portsmouth harbor."

"Jennifer," Dunbar said, "I know you must be eager to return to the States, but if you're up to it, the prime minister would like to see you before you go."

"I would look forward to seeing him again," she replied.

"By the way," Brookstone said. "I suggest you two gather your things and meet me topside. A band will be playing for us as we dock. I expect it will be quite impressive!"

"Won't some admirals be there, too?" Dunbar asked.

"One or two," Brookstone replied. "Maybe more. It depends on whether a high ranking admiral comes." Smiling at Jennifer, he added, "With our American guest, I wouldn't be surprised to see someone really important."

"Sounds exciting," Dunbar said. "Jennifer, I'll meet you outside your room in about fifteen minutes. Is that enough time for you?"

"Yes, plenty."

Brookstone took a last sip of coffee and stood up. "I'll see you on the bridge." Jennifer and Dunbar nodded.

Soon, Jennifer and Dunbar had gathered their baggage and headed to the bridge. Dunbar opened a watertight door, and the crisp morning air stung Jennifer's face. Directly in front, sailors formed a single line and stood at attention. Jennifer and Dunbar saluted Brookstone as they approached his side.

"It won't be long now," the ship's captain said. "You can hear the band."

Jennifer recognized "Onward Christian Soldiers," but, she wondered, why they weren't they playing "God Save the Queen"? Perhaps because she was American.

"My God!" Brookstone said. "That's the old boy himself—Andrew Cunningham."

"Pardon my ignorance," Jennifer said. "But who is Andrew Cunningham?"

"He's the admiral who led our Navy to a great victory at Cape Matapan off the coast of Greece. The Italians lost three heavy cruisers and two destroyers, while we lost only one torpedo plane. That knocked the Italian Navy out of the war."

"That's very impressive," Jennifer said. "Will there be some kind of ceremony once we dock?"

"Yes," Brookstone replied. "Cunningham and the others will come aboard and congratulate us. All we'll do is salute and answer their questions."

Brookstone was right. After being piped aboard and returning Brookstone's and Dunbar's salutes, Cunningham came right over and introduced himself to Jennifer. "I want to express my great sadness for your loss," he said as the two exchanged salutes.

"Thank you very much," Jennifer replied. "Sir, I also want to say that the crew of the *Windstorm* has been wonderful. And, of course, Commander Brookstone and Major Dunbar have been magnificent. Words aren't enough to express how much they've done for me."

"Always glad to hear good things about our lads. By the way, are you all set with transportation and accommodations?"

"Yes, sir. Major Dunbar has made the arrangements." Jennifer decided not to tell the admiral she would be dining with the prime minister. After all, it was possible that he hadn't had that pleasure yet.

After the admiral and his staff departed, Commander Brookstone walked Major Dunbar and Jennifer to a waiting staff car. Turning to Jennifer, he said that he wished they could have met under more pleasant circumstances.

"I wish we could have, too," Jennifer replied. "But I do appreciate all you did for me and what you tried to do for Dude."

"My pleasure," Brookstone said as Jennifer and Dunbar got into the back seat of the staff car.

That evening at 1800 sharp, Major Dunbar arrived at Jennifer's door to take her to what he described as an "informal dinner" with the prime minister and Lady Churchill. They rode in silence through London's battered streets until the car stopped at the entrance to the bunker where she and Dude had last seen Churchill. But instead of descending into the tunnel, they were escorted to the upstairs living quarters, near 10 Downing Street.

Churchill and his wife were waiting in the foyer. Lady Churchill hugged Jennifer and kept an arm around her waist as they walked into a sitting parlor. The prime minister was his effervescent self, thanking Jennifer and her companions for what they had done for the Allied cause.

"My dear," Mr. Churchill added, "We decided that tonight we would eat upstairs using the fine china. After all, with what you've been through, the thought of a German bomb or two probably isn't very scary." More somberly, he said, "Mrs. Churchill and I extend our deepest sympathy for your terrible loss."

But then Churchill brightened and launched into a treatise on champagne, concluding with the brand and year of champagne that would be served that evening. At one point, Jennifer glanced over at the major, who had an amused look on his face. Obviously, he had heard the champagne review before—perhaps many times before!

As the evening drew to a close, Jennifer said, "Mr. Prime Minister, if it weren't for Major Dunbar, I wouldn't be here tonight. I owe him my life."

"Yes, the old boy is pretty good, isn't he?" Churchill said. "However, I'm plenty mad at him for being the one to rescue a pretty young damsel instead of me!" Everyone laughed, but Jennifer noticed a blush on Dunbar's face.

"Tonight, I will be visiting some of the areas of London hardest hit by German bombing," Churchill said. "Perhaps you would like to accompany me, Jennifer? You will meet people who have had their lives shattered, people like millions of others in this terrible war who haven't done one thing to deserve it but have simply stood in the way of tyranny."

The prime minister stood up, then began to pace and puff mightily on his cigar. "It will remind you that your Lieutenant Partude and the others who were with you gave their lives for a very noble cause—the cause of freedom."

"Thank you, sir. I'd very much like to go with you."

"Give me a minute to hop into my 'rompers,' and we'll be off."

While the prime minister changed, Jennifer and Major Dunbar chatted with Lady Churchill. Jennifer asked how many children they had. The answer was five, but Lady Churchill said sadly, "Unfortunately, our beloved Marigold died as an infant."

Looking pained for an instant, Lady Churchill soon cheered up as a young lady in an Army uniform entered. "Mary, my dear, you have met Major Dunbar, but please come and meet our other guest. Jennifer Haraldsson, this is Mary, our youngest child."

The two shook hands. "I'm very pleased to meet you," Jennifer said. "I can tell that you have a very loving family." Laughing, Mary replied, "Well, we have our moments just like every other family, I suppose. While I'm sure that my father and brother love each other very much, there's an eruption every time the two of them are in the same room!" Jennifer and Major Dunbar laughed, but Jennifer thought that Lady Churchill seemed a little embarrassed.

Soon, the prime minister returned, beaming when he saw his daughter. Hugging her, he said, "Mary, I'm so glad to see you. Will you come with us while I show our American friend the damage that the incessant bombing has done?" His daughter nodded, and the dinner guests bade Lady Churchill goodbye.

As Jennifer and Dunbar rode with Churchill and his daughter in the center of a line of cars that Churchill explained was a Scotland Yard security escort, Jennifer could scarcely believe her eyes. Thousands of buildings had been destroyed or severely damaged by the bombing. People everywhere were sifting through rubble, looking for something—anything—to salvage. As the motorcade passed one such group of people, Churchill told his driver to stop, then got out and walked over to them. Their spirits were lifted simply by the presence of this great man.

What a man, Jennifer thought. He must have been put on Earth specifically for the job of rallying the British. There was no doubt in Jennifer's mind that, much like President Roosevelt, Mr. Churchill was the right man in the right place at the right time.

As the group grew into a crowd, at this and other stops, people tried to touch the prime minister and to shake his hand. Churchill's security men attempted to keep the people back, but Churchill simply ignored their concern and waded into the crowds, shaking as many hands as he could. It seemed to be something he loved to do.

Back in the car after what seemed to Jennifer like dozens of such stops, Churchill told her, "My dear, I have one more place to show you, and then I will let you go. I know you have to catch a plane home early tomorrow."

Just then they were passing St. Paul's Cathedral. Mr. Churchill had the driver stop, and he and Jennifer got out. After talking with some of the people who were relaying buckets of sand hand-to-hand up the cathedral's steep front steps to dampen fires from the bombing, Churchill told Jennifer, "St. Paul's would be in ruins today if not for these wonderful Britons."

Jennifer saw that many of those hoisting the heavy buckets were beyond middle age and struggling to keep up with the pace of the work. She marveled at their determination and said to one of the oldest of them, "You must be exhausted!"

"Oh, it's nothing much, Miss," the man said, panting but not breaking the rhythm of his movements. "Just doing what must be done, you might say."

The next morning, Dunbar drove up in a staff car to take Jennifer to the airplane waiting at R.A.F. Mildenhall. Neither spoke much during the hour-long trip.

At the air terminal, Dunbar helped Jennifer with her baggage. On the ramp, an American C-47 airplane warmed up its engines, and military passengers walked up the gangway steps into the rear of the plane. Dunbar and Jennifer hurried over and set her baggage down at the base of the steps.

"Well," Dunbar said, "I suppose this is it."

"I guess it is," Jennifer replied. She started to salute, then hesitated and said, "What the heck? Come here." She hugged the major, and he enthusiastically reciprocated.

"Major," she said, "at the end of the war, please celebrate with us in San Francisco, under the clock at the St. Francis Hotel."

"You can bet I will be there!" he said. As the plane taxied down the runway, Jennifer waved from a window. Dunbar stayed until the plane was out of sight.

Days later, Otto Bruner awoke in a hospital. He vaguely remembered being loaded onto a stretcher and taken aboard a ship. He also recalled hearing explosions on the water. German vessels must have engaged the enemy sub.

As he lay recuperating, Bruner was haunted over and over by scenes from the ridge. He did not know if he could forgive himself for the loss of the young Germans. If only he had not been so generous and given the Americans time to bury the elderly professor, perhaps he could have ended the engagement at less cost in lives. In any event, he would have needed Major Schmidt's permission, so it was useless to keep wondering about it. Even so, he was not sure that he had the mental toughness to put it out of his mind.

Strangely, Otto was equally torn by the image of the young American woman disregarding her own safety to run to the fallen American on the ridge. Even in death, Otto thought, the young American man was very fortunate to have the love of such a woman. Otto hoped that some day he would be lucky enough to find a woman who would love him as passionately.

As hours turned into days, Otto found himself fantasizing about the young American woman. What kind of a personality did she have? If he could see her face, would she be as beautiful as she was graceful? What would it be like to hold her and make love to her? He suspected that it would be heavenly.

Reminiscing, Otto felt that perhaps he had become somewhat bonded to the Americans as he followed them on the long trek to the coast. He hadn't been able to take his eyes off the young woman. She'd had amazing stamina as well as grace, as she matched the others in her party stride for stride.

Otto remembered being mesmerized by the feminine sway of her hips and the general aura that surrounded her. While not a big believer in the supernatural, Otto could not help but think that this special encounter might mean that they would meet sometime in the future. If they weren't predestined to meet again, wouldn't it be easier to take his mind off her? He certainly hoped that this was the case, and he desperately wanted to come in contact with her again. Of course, he would want it to be under entirely different circumstances!

In the hospital, Bruner's first visitor was Obergruppenführer Wilhelm Rediess, head of the SS. Rediess asked how Otto was doing, but he didn't really seem to care, as evidenced by the fact that he immediately began to lament about his own problems.

"Bruner, this assignment has been nothing but trouble for me. First, we let the Norwegian parliament and the royal family escape to England. Since then, they have done everything they can to stir up unrest. They send broadcasts from England, publish through an underground press, and even have the audacity to sponsor commando raids! Don't think for one second that my head isn't on the chopping block. Heinrich Himmler and even the führer himself are furious at me for letting them escape. Then, as if my situation weren't bad enough, you and Schmidt can't even capture an old man alive. I tell you, Bruner, everything is working against me. I am certain that I will pay dearly."

He ranted on like that for a while before mumbling, just before departing, that he hoped Otto would keep mending and soon be back on active duty.

Bruner was left to consider how strange it was that Rediess hadn't mentioned whether he, Bruner, would be moving up to Schmidt's position or even be staying in Norway! Perhaps the leader of the SS in Norway was being stripped of his authority. From Otto's vantage point, it didn't appear that things were any better at the top than they were for a lowly captain. In fact, they could be a lot worse!

As the weeks passed, Bruner slowly regained his strength. Wandering the halls of the hospital, he worried about his next assignment. Would he be allowed to stay in Norway, or would his superiors send him elsewhere? He assumed that it would depend on how Major Schmidt had rated him. He very much hoped that he would be allowed to remain.

The Nazi propaganda machine was continually putting out stories of favorable conditions in all theaters of operation, but Bruner had heard otherwise through the grapevine. There were horror stories circulating about just how bad conditions were on the Eastern Front. While the mighty German Army rolled easily during the warm summer months, winter had brought the troops to a standstill. Warm clothing was not reaching the front in sufficient quantities, and German soldiers were foraging for just enough food and clothing to survive.

France or one of the Low Countries, Holland or Belgium, would be acceptable to Bruner, even North Africa, where Rommel was driving back the British. Anywhere would be better than the Eastern Front! When would he learn his fate? Soon, as it turned out.

Colonel Hans Meier came into his room.

"How are you doing, Bruner?"

"Much better. Thank you, sir."

"Good," Meier replied. "I'll bet you're anxious to know about your next assignment, aren't you?"

"Yes, sir!" *What a dumb question*, Otto thought.

"Well, your orders have arrived."

Bruner felt a sudden chill.

"Major Schmidt had doubts about you. Seems he thought you were competent but lacked the skills to handle difficult situations.

Obviously, that opinion was confirmed by your fiasco on the beach. Do you have anything to say for yourself?"

Oh, so now it's my fault, Otto thought, *not 'our' fault*. Wasn't Schmidt blamed at all? Apparently not. With resignation, Otto replied "No, sir." He held his breath.

"I commend you for your objective response. You will be reporting to the Sixth Army on the Russian front. *Heil Hitler.*"

"Yes, sir." Bruner wanted to scream. "*Heil Hitler!*"

After the officer left, Otto felt like giving himself a good, swift kick. Once again, he had short-changed himself. It was quite possible that, had he taken a different approach, he could have convinced the officer that he was fully capable of taking over for Schmidt.

Having failed to look out for himself, Otto was going to the worst place imaginable. Were there any advantages to going to the Russian front? He couldn't think of any. He hoped his commanding officer would be someone he liked. But was there such a thing as a likeable senior officer in the German Army? He was beginning to doubt it, but he could still hope. After all, a good commander could make up for a number of other shortcomings.

Now that he had his assignment, Otto's thoughts were taken off Jennifer and shifted to the Russian front. Instinctively, he knew that he would have to stay focused on his upcoming assignment in order to do his best for the men serving under him and for his country. Regardless of how well he performed, though, would he still be going from the frying pan into the fire? Only time would tell.

23

A Sad Return

THE LONG FLIGHT back only intensified Jennifer's grief over losing Dude. As her plane touched down at Andrews Field, Jennifer wondered if the pain would ever subside.

Stepping off the plane, she saw that General Marshall was waiting on the tarmac. She was shocked. How could someone so important find time to meet her? But then she recalled that the general was known for stopping his car to give a ride to enlisted personnel. He obviously cared very much for the people under him.

Jennifer walked over, and the two returned salutes. "I'm so terribly sorry," Marshall said softly. Perhaps the British had informed him of her feelings for Dude.

Trying very hard not to lose control, Jennifer said, "Thank you very much, sir. I'm sorry that we couldn't get Professor Flannigan home safely. He was one of the finest people that I have ever known."

"You did everything humanly possible to complete an extremely difficult mission. War is a dreadful business, and there are going to be tragic losses along the way."

Pausing, the general continued. "All of us have loved ones who are at risk. None of us are exempt, not even the president. His four sons

169

are entering the services, and my stepson was recently commissioned as an infantry officer in the Army."

Jennifer was shocked. People at the top had many of the same problems that others experienced.

Jennifer collected her luggage, and they got into Marshall's 1941 Ford. "I've arranged transportation for you to see your family," the general said. "You have two weeks' leave coming up."

"Thank you, sir," Jennifer replied. "What about the Flannigans and Partudes?"

"The families have been notified, of course, and I arranged for Jonathon's brother to come here to see you. I think it will do you both good. He'll be here tonight."

"Thank you, sir. I do need to talk to him." Marshall nodded.

"I also intend to write the Flannigans and Partudes," Jennifer sighed.

"I'm sure it won't be easy for you," Marshall replied. "As you know, President Roosevelt was extremely interested in your mission. He's planning to host a small get-together for those involved and for their families. When it will occur, I don't know. The president is very busy. In the meantime, he wanted me to give you this." The general handed her an envelope with the presidential seal!

"I'm overwhelmed!" Jennifer said.

"Read it at your leisure. If you're up to it, I would like you to give a short debriefing to my staff. It can be tomorrow if you prefer."

"I can do it now, sir. Professor Flannigan told us the results of his calculations, and I'm eager to share them before I forget something."

"Good. The appropriate person has been told to meet us."

General Marshall pulled up to the entrance of the Army Headquarters building. Waiting there was the tall and gangly Jack Dawkins, the man who had initially briefed Dude and Jennifer on heavy water. The lieutenant walked over to the car, saluted Marshall, and opened the door for Jennifer. She got out, shut the door, and watched as Marshall pulled into his prime parking spot.

"Should we wait for him?" Jennifer asked.

"No," Dawkins replied. "He has his agenda, and we have ours."

Hasn't lost any of his cockiness, Jennifer thought.

The two lieutenants entered the building and walked to the conference room where they had met previously. This time, Dawkins was very serious. "I'm so sorry for your loss. I could tell that there was something special between you and Partude."

"Thank you," Jennifer said somewhat impatiently. "Can we get on with it?"

"Certainly."

Jennifer relayed the results of Flannigan's findings, and Dawkins wrote everything on a page marked "Top Secret." Whistling softly, he said that the Germans were ahead of predictions.

As they walked to the building exit, Jennifer said, "I'm sorry I was short with you back there. I'm very tired."

"I understand. After what you've been through, I couldn't have complained if you had taken my head off!"

As they stepped outside, Marshall's aide, Sergeant Johnson, pulled up in a staff car. He quickly saluted and opened the door for Jennifer.

"I have your baggage, Lieutenant," he said. "You're staying at the Mayflower Hotel again."

When they pulled up in front of the hotel, fresh memories of Dude flooded Jennifer.

Maybe Major Dunbar had been right, maybe Dude was looking down on her and would always be with her. True or not, that thought felt very comforting and reassuring.

For a few moments Jennifer stood looking at the beautiful exterior of the hotel, remembering how excited she had been the last time she was here. How things had changed since she last stood in this exact spot! She had gone from being on top of the world to being at the very bottom. *If life held these kinds of ups and downs, she wondered, how did people survive into their sixties and seventies? They must be quite resilient, or they would never make it.*

After ducking into the ladies' room to regain her composure, she went to the check-in desk. A message from Jacob was waiting, saying that he would arrive at 9 p.m. and asking if she would meet him. *Certainly,* she thought. She looked forward to seeing him again.

The desk clerk remembered her and asked if she wanted the same room. Jennifer nodded. She went to her room and took out the letter from the president. She opened the envelope carefully, not wanting to damage the seal:

> *Dear Jennifer:*
>
> *Congratulations on a job well done. I know how difficult it was, and I want to say that you and the others did this country a tremendous service. You, Lieutenant Jonathon Partude, and Professor James Flannigan are the very essence of why I am confident that we will win this war. Patriots such as yourselves make and will keep this country great.*
>
> *I am only sorry that victory will also require terrible pain and sacrifice.*
>
>
>
> *In sincere appreciation,*
> *Franklin Delano Roosevelt*
>
>

What a wonderful letter, Jennifer thought. She knew she would treasure it forever.

At nine o'clock, Jennifer was already in the Mayflower hotel lobby when Jacob strode in carrying a duffel bag. He looked very distinguished in his Army Air Force uniform. Although Jennifer had noticed the family resemblance before, now she thought he looked almost uncannily like Dude.

When he saw her, Jacob rushed over, dropped his bag, and embraced her. They held each other in silence until Jennifer finally asked, "Would you like to check in?"

"I would rather talk first," Jacob replied. They went to a sofa and sat down.

"Are you up to telling me what happened to Dude?"

Jennifer hesitated and then nodded. General Marshall had warned her and Dude about the importance of secrecy. Maybe it still held and maybe it didn't. She could at least tell some of the story, she thought. After all, the Flannigans knew that the professor was dead.

"We went to Norway to try and get a professor, James Flannigan, out safely."

"Is this the famous Professor Flannigan? The one who was a Nobel Prize winner?"

"Yes. I can't tell you what the professor was doing there, but unfortunately we were unable to get him out alive. He died as we were trying to reach the coast, where a submarine was waiting to take us to England."

After pausing, Jennifer continued. "We buried the professor in a shallow grave. Lars, Dude's old college roommate, was with us. He promised to go back in the spring, after the ground thawed, and give the professor a proper burial."

"I met Lars and liked him very much." Jacob said. "I'm sure he'll be true to his word."

Jennifer shook her head.

"Why not?" Jacob asked.

"He didn't make it, either," Jennifer replied.

Jacob whistled softly. Stunned, he said, "I hope the mission was worth it."

Jennifer didn't respond.

They sat in silence for a few minutes. Believing that the time was as right as it ever would be, Jennifer said, "Your brother and I had fallen in love. We were planning to get married."

Jacob looked painfully at her and grasped her hands tightly. "After seeing you two earlier, I suspected you would. I can't begin to tell you how sorry I am." Jennifer nodded, losing her composure momentarily.

"I know it's very painful for you, too." But, if it's any help, Dude died very bravely. He died providing cover for the rest of us."

"I knew the big lug was brave," Jacob replied, trying mightily to suppress tears. "I'm very proud of him."

"I would never have left Dude, but Lars and this British major dragged me away. I wish that I had died and Dude had lived."

"Dude certainly wouldn't have wanted that outcome."

"That's what Major Dunbar said."

"Is he the British major?"

"Yes, he was wonderful to both Dude and me. If it weren't for him, I wouldn't be here now. He came back on land to help us after our original evacuation window had closed. I can't say enough good things about him."

"I hope to meet him someday."

"You will. I invited him to attend our celebration at the St. Francis at the end of the war."

"That's right! We do have a reunion planned." Jacob's enthusiasm cheered the mood slightly, but he soon slumped down in his seat.

"Anything else you want to know?" Jennifer asked.

"Well," Jacob replied, "how did Lars die? I know I shouldn't ask, but—"

"That's okay," Jennifer said, cutting him off. "We were in the dinghy heading out to the submarine. The Germans opened fire, and Lars and the two crewmen were hit. We were able to get Lars to the sub, but his wounds were too extensive." Jacob shook his head.

By now, it was getting quite late. Jennifer waited as Jacob checked in, and then the two departed for their rooms.

"Call me if you need anything," Jacob said.

"And you do the same," Jennifer replied.

24

Sharing the Grief

THE NEXT MORNING, Jennifer awoke early and decided to write the families of Dude and the professor. She got up and went to the small desk. She started with the Flannigans:

Dear Mrs. Flannigan,

I can't begin to tell you how sorry I am about your husband's death. Lieutenant Jonathon Partude and I were with him at the end. He was one of the finest people I have ever known, and I will cherish his memory always.

The professor was very brave clear up until his death. He died rushing the enemy with his revolver blazing. I know that he was trying to save Lieutenant Partude and me. He was such a kind, gentle, caring person that I will always remember him in this light.

Professor Flannigan mentioned his good friends the Jungstads to me. You might know them also. While I don't know what happened to them, I will try to find out if you would like. Please let me know.

I hope to meet you someday, as I now consider you family. Please let me know if there is anything I can ever do for you.

Love always,
Jennifer

Jennifer reread the letter. *No use telling Mrs. Flannigan how sick the professor was*, she decided. That would serve no purpose. Now for the letter she dreaded—the one to the Partudes.

Dear Mr. and Mrs. Partude and Joseph:
I have never met you, but I feel like I know you. I was with your son Jonathon when he died. He and I had fallen in love and were going to get married. His death has left a void in me that can never be filled. I will love him always.
I'm sure you know all of Dude's virtues, so there is no need for me to repeat them here. I do want to tell you how brave he was. He gave his life providing cover for the rest of us. While I wish I had died instead, his sacrifice only reinforces that I had selected the right one.
I have met Jacob, and I look forward to meeting the rest of you. Dude kidded that I would be the daughter that you never had, and I would consider it a great honor. You will always be part of my family.

Until we meet,
Love forever,
Jennifer

Jennifer showered, dressed, and packed. She then went to the restaurant in the Mayflower lobby to meet Jacob for breakfast. On the way, she put the letters in the drop box.

They met at the entrance to the dining room and hugged briefly. A maitre d' led them to a table and helped seat Jennifer. He handed them each a menu.

"You look better this morning," Jacob said. "You must've gotten some sleep."

"I had to force myself," Jennifer replied. "I knew I would be writing letters to the Flannigans and your family this morning, and I knew it would be difficult."

"How did it turn out?"

"Not too bad, actually. It wasn't as hard as I thought it would be."

"But you look perplexed," Jacob noted. "Why?"

"Well," Jennifer replied. "I wasn't totally honest with the professor's wife. I didn't tell her how sick the professor was when he died?"

"What would that have accomplished?" Jacob asked.

"Nothing," Jennifer acknowledged. "But the professor did suffer those last few days as he struggled mightily to keep up with us. Maybe she should know what he went through."

"I don't think so," Jacob said. "But you can always tell her later if it is still bothering you. And by then, she should be over the shock of the professor's death."

"Good advice," Jennifer replied. "I guess we better decide what we're going to eat."

They studied the menus and then closed them.

As they waited for their orders to be taken, Jennifer asked, "How is your flight training going?"

"It's going very well, but I won't know for a while yet if I'll make fighter pilot."

"That's what you want to be?"

"Yes. I dream of flying free as a bird. Being a fighter pilot is as close to that as I'm likely to get."

"I remember now," Jennifer replied. "I hope you get your wish."

The waiter approached, and Jennifer ordered toast and coffee. "I'll have two eggs over easy, bacon, and hash browns," Jacob said, "with orange juice and coffee." *Nothing wrong with his appetite*, Jennifer thought.

As the waiter turned to leave, Jacob called after him. "Please bring me an apple Danish also." The waiter nodded.

The two sat peacefully, just looking at each other. Finally, Jacob broke the silence. "I can see why my brother fell in love with you," he said. "You're not only physically beautiful, but you also have a beautiful soul."

Jennifer wasn't sure how to respond. Was this a romantic overture? Surely not. Jacob wouldn't dishonor the memory of his dead brother by making a play so soon. She knew she'd have to be careful with her answer. It might be a long time before she was ready to think of finding someone new.

"Thanks," she said. "I can see you're a charmer just like Dude."

The waiter returned with their orders, and Jacob dug in with enthusiasm. Jennifer ate much more slowly. Even the strawberry jam that she put on her toast didn't seem to have much flavor.

As they finished breakfast, Jennifer looked up to see Sergeant Johnson approaching their table. "When you're ready to head to Andrews, let me know," Johnson said. "I'll be in the lobby."

"Thanks, Sergeant Johnson," Jennifer replied. "We'll be there shortly."

Jennifer and Jacob finished breakfast and went to get their bags. They got on the elevator and pushed the buttons for floors four and six. Jennifer got off on the fourth floor and called over her shoulder, "I'll meet you at the checkout desk in about fifteen minutes."

"Roger that," Jacob replied. The elevator door closed, and the motor whirred as it carried Jacob up to his floor.

By the time Jennifer returned to the lobby, Jacob was at the front desk handing money to the checkout clerk. She got in line behind him. Turning around, Jacob beamed and said, "Fancy meeting you here." She smiled.

"Would you like a receipt?" the clerk asked as she moved to the front.

"Yes, please," Jennifer replied. She put her change and receipt in her purse, and the two headed over to where Sergeant Johnson was sitting.

"We have a little extra time," the sergeant said as he stood up. "Would you like to see some of D.C.?"

"I'd love to," they said almost simultaneously. They went out to a parking space marked "Government Parking Only" and got into the staff car. Soon they were viewing the Washington skyline.

How beautiful it all is, Jennifer thought. The dome of the Capitol Building appeared majestic as it towered over the city. Soon, the different buildings of the Smithsonian Museum came into view. Old architecture was mixed with new in an impressive fashion. Colors ranged from red to sandstone grey.

Nearby was the Washington monument knifing 550 feet into the sky and undoubtedly making George proud. Over to the side, and barely visible through the trees, the semicircular columns of the White House could be seen. Someday, if the president followed through on his offer, she would be seeing the magnificent building from the inside! Finally, there was Abraham Lincoln, sitting in stately fashion as if presiding over the nation from his perch at the edge of the Potomac River. *What a tour*, Jennifer thought, as the car swung south toward its destination.

After a short ride through the Maryland countryside, they arrived at Andrews Field. Sergeant Johnson let his passengers off at base operations. They carried their bags to a counter that was manned by a very youthful-looking corporal.

"Ma'am, sir, do you have your orders?" he asked.

"Yes," they replied.

The two officers supplied the appropriate paperwork to the corporal, and soon they were heading to the air strip where parked C-47s would take them to their respective destinations.

"How long will you be in Idaho?" Jacob asked.

"Two weeks," she replied. "I feel guilty for not going to see your family and the Flannigans, but I think it's best to have some correspondence with them first."

"I think you're right," Jacob replied. "You'll feel like you know each other by the time you meet."

"And what about you?" Jennifer asked. "How long will it be before you leave Randolph Field?"

"If all goes well, I'll leave in about six months."

Jennifer nodded. She was developing a sinking, empty feeling at the thought of having to part company with Jacob. She could tell that he had similar feelings. She tried to think of something comforting to say, but it was not easy.

Finally Jacob broke the ice. "Jennifer, you do know that Dude would want you to live your life to the fullest, don't you? He wouldn't want you to waste your life feeling sad about him."

"I know," Jennifer replied. "I also know that he would want me to help you if you ever needed it." She continued, "I expect you to write often. If you don't, you're in big trouble!"

Jacob nodded appreciatively.

Jacob's plane was soon ready for boarding. The two embraced, each not wanting to let the other go. Finally they kissed softly on the cheek, and Jacob made his way to the plane. Jennifer kept the plane in view as long as possible as it began taxiing down the runway.

It was now approximately six weeks after she and Dude had first met at General Marshall's office on that fateful day. How the world had changed! In the Pacific, American and Allied troops in the Philippines had retreated to the Bataan Peninsula and the island fortress Corregidor. Since Jennifer knew many of the nurses who were serving in the Philippines, she could not help but think of them. She knew that they were undoubtedly serving with distinction to support the fine troops who now had their backs to the wall.

The road ahead would be long and difficult, she thought. There would be many battles to be fought, and, as an Army nurse, Jennifer would have an important role to play. She didn't know where she would be going, but she did know that she would always carry Dude with her. His soul and hers had become one.

The past month had been difficult, even devastating. Had it been worth it? Would she do it again if she had the chance? Jennifer closed her eyes, thought for a moment, and reacted with a painful, melancholy smile. The answer was a resounding "Yes!"

25

A Brief Recess

OTTO BRUNER'S TRAIN pulled into the Berlin train station on March 28, 1942. A wave of excitement came over him as he peered out the window. Soon, he would see his parents and probably his sisters, Liesl and Gretchen. It was too much to hope that he would see his brother, Klaus. After all, Klaus was the watch officer on the submarine U-126 and was probably off sailing in some distant waters.

Everywhere he looked, huge flags with the Nazi swastika draped downward. Otherwise, the old Grunewald station was pretty much as it used to be.

There they were—his parents, Herr and Frau Bruner, and his two sisters. *What a sight for sore eyes!* How long had it been? Fourteen months? Time flew even when he wasn't having fun!

He caught their attention, and they waved excitedly. The train came to a stop, and Otto eagerly went to the exit. He bounded down the stairs and out into the station. So much for military bearing. He wasn't going to try to hide his enthusiasm.

"Mama! Papa!" he said. "It's so good to see you. And I've missed you girls, too!" They hugged so tightly that Otto had trouble getting his breath.

"Are you all right?" his mother asked, holding his head in her hands and gazing deeply into his eyes.

"Yes, I'm fine. Everything has healed nicely."

"How long will you be with us?" his father asked.

"I have to leave the day after tomorrow."

"Not very long," Herr Bruner replied under his breath.

After gathering Otto's luggage, they piled into the Bruner's car, and off they went.

"What have you girls been up to?" Otto asked.

"Nothing much," Liesl, who was seventeen, replied.

"Any boyfriends?"

"Well," she answered somewhat sheepishly, "there is this one."

"Oh, he's not good enough for you," Herr Bruner injected. "You can do much better!" *Some things never change*, Otto mused, *even in the midst of a World War.*

"What about you, Gretchen?"

"I want to become a famous pianist. I'm working very hard at my lessons."

"Good! I encourage you to continue."

Soon, they came to the big apartment building where the family had lived since Otto was born.

"How does it look to you?" Frau Bruner inquired.

"Wonderful!" Otto replied. "Home sweet home."

"What about Berlin?" his father asked. "Does it look the same to you?"

"It hasn't changed much at all," Otto replied. "The only difference I've noticed is the big anti-aircraft guns on the outskirts of town. Has there been any damage?"

"Some, but not very much," Herr Bruner said.

"But they have these air raid warnings in the middle of the night," Gretchen moaned. "So we have to get up and go to shelters. I feel tired all the time."

"It's better to be safe than sorry," Otto said, rubbing his hand over her cheek.

Herr Bruner parked the car, and they got Otto's luggage out of the trunk. "Here, let me help you," Liesl said to Otto, struggling to pick up the largest. Gretchen also took a bag, and Otto was left with only a briefcase to carry. "I don't remember you girls being so helpful in the past," he teased.

Fortunately for the two girls, the Bruner apartment was on the first floor. Huffing and puffing, they managed to get the bags inside the building and to the door marked 1. Frau Bruner put her key in the lock, turned it, and pushed the door open.

"Surprise!" shouted a bearded young man jumping into the open doorway.

"Klaus, is that you behind all that facial hair?" Otto yelped as the two embraced.

"Yes, it most certainly is!"

"We wanted to tell you that Klaus was here, but Mama wouldn't let us," Gretchen said somewhat indignantly.

"Doesn't matter," Otto beamed. "I'm just happy to see the old *witzbold.*"

"And I'm very happy to see you, too," Klaus replied. "Here, let me give you a hand with your bags." The two carried the luggage to the middle bedroom, between the one the girls shared and their parents' bedroom, which was at the end of the hall.

Klaus' luggage was still piled on one of the twin beds, so they dumped Otto's bag on the other. "This room sure brings back memories, doesn't it?" Otto asked.

"It sure does. Remember when we carved our initials in the headboards so we would never get our beds mixed up?"

"I sure do. I can still see mine," Otto said as he rubbed his forearm over some scratch marks. "I thought the folks would skin us alive after they found out what we'd done."

"Luckily for us and the führer they didn't," Klaus said laughingly. Looking around, he continued, "Everything seems to be exactly as we left it." He pointed in a sweeping fashion at the overstuffed chair, the four-drawer chest, and the small desk that the two had fought over when it came time to do homework.

"Doesn't the room seem smaller than you remember?" Otto asked.

"It sure does. I don't remember things being as squeezed in as they are."

"Probably because you're now used to the openness of the high seas," Otto joked.

"And you?" Klaus countered. "You've been gallivanting over the vast Norwegian landscape!"

"True, but not for long."

"Oh? Where are you headed?"

"The Russian Front."

Stunned, Klaus seemed momentarily at a loss for words. "Does the rest of the family know?"

"Not yet," Otto replied. "But I'll have to tell them." His brother nodded solemnly.

Seeing that Klaus was quite upset, Otto decided to change the subject. "Let's get back to you," he said. "I never in a million years expected you to be here. How did you manage it?"

"It just worked out that way. We'd been on patrol for a number of months—mainly in African and Caribbean waters—when we were ordered to go up the east coast of the United States. Picking off merchant ships there was absurdly simple."

"Why?"

"Because ships come out of the ports without any naval escorts. It's like shooting ducks on a pond."

"Hmm. I wouldn't count on that continuing. The Americans aren't dumb."

"That's your trouble, little brother. You worry too much. I predict we'll continue sinking ships faster than the Americans can build them! And by the way, I do think the Americans are dumb!"

Otto shook his head. "So you are here because you sunk all of the American ships and there is nothing else left to do?"

"No," Klaus laughed. "We came home so that we could get some rest and get decorated. None other than Admiral Roeder himself presented the awards. All of this just happened to occur when you were coming home."

"I'm glad it did. I guess we better hang up some clothes and join the others."

The two quickly unpacked their suitcases and stuffed the empty bags under their beds. They went out to the living room where the others had assembled. As they entered the room and Otto saw the family members sitting there, he couldn't help but be elated. How good it was to be home.

"Mama, you can't imagine how much Klaus and I are looking forward to your cooking, particularly some schnitzel and noodles. Oh, and don't forget your delicious apple strudel!" Klaus nodded enthusiastically.

"I won't!" Frau Bruner was obviously pleased.

What a comfortable, secure feeling, Otto thought. If only he didn't have to go back to the miserable war. Nothing he could do about that, though, so he might as well enjoy the moment.

Soon, dinner was on, and they were seated around the table in their customary places. They joined hands, and Herr Bruner said a prayer: "Heavenly Father, thank you for this bounty and the safe return of our sons, Klaus and Otto. Please protect them and all of us in this time of great danger."

"Beautiful, Papa," Otto said. "It's wonderful hearing words of praise to God rather than Adolph Hitler."

"Otto, shhh," Frau Bruner said sternly. "If anyone outside of the family hears you, we could all be in big trouble."

"If you weren't my brother," Klaus interjected, "I'd turn you in myself!"

Am I dreaming? Otto wondered. He'd never seen such a menacing look on his brother's face. Oh, well. He'd better apologize.

"Sorry, Mama. Sorry, Klaus. Sorry, everyone. It won't happen again."

"That's better," Klaus snarled.

Soon, everyone relaxed, and the atmosphere was again pleasant. "Where will you be going from here?" Herr Bruner inquired.

Oh-oh, Otto thought. Oh well, he'd have to get it out of the way sooner or later. "To the Russian Front," he said. "My unit is presently near a place called Karkov."

Silence. As he suspected, even civilians knew things were not good on the Eastern Front.

"Klaus is the one you should really worry about," Otto said as he clumsily tried to change the subject. "Going down to the ocean depths in that hunk of metal is far more dangerous than what I will be doing."

"Not so, little brother," Klaus replied. "With a skipper like mine, Captain Ernst Bauer, I will be as safe as sitting here on the living room couch."

"I'm afraid both of you will be in great danger," Frau Bruner said as she brushed away a tear. "But I'm afraid there's nothing I can do about it."

"You're right, Mama," Herr Bruner replied. "Are either of you going to see your old friends while you're here?"

"No," the two sons replied looking at each other.

"Our old girlfriends are married," Klaus said. "And our male friends are in the Army or Navy and stationed all over. I think you're stuck with us."

"That's fine with us," Herr Bruner replied. Frau Bruner and the girls agreed.

The next day, Herr Bruner went to his job at the bank, the girls went to school, and Otto and Klaus relaxed around the apartment. Their mother continued fixing wonderful meals for them, saying they were too thin and needed to put on some weight.

In what seemed like a heartbeat, it was time for Otto and Klaus to leave. Not wanting to be emotional at the train station with their family, the young officers ordered a staff car to take them.

Saying goodbye at the apartment was every bit as difficult as Otto thought it would be. Words were few but tears were plentiful.

As he waited with his brother for the staff car, Otto couldn't help but be concerned. Bombing raids on Berlin would only get worse, and life on the Eastern Front was already beginning to have all the earmarks of a disaster. Would being a submariner prove to be as safe as Klaus speculated? *Doubtful*, Otto thought. Klaus' brainwashing was probably evident to even the most ignorant of the family members.

As they rode in the staff car, Otto turned to Klaus and said quietly, "Please big brother, don't be over-confident. That can get you killed." Klaus sneered and looked away. *My God,* Otto thought, *there is no reasoning with him.*

The two brothers were of equal rank, although Klaus was the senior of the two. Klaus exited the car first, turned, saluted his brother, and walked off. *Is Nazism stronger than blood? Perhaps it is!* The only thing he could do now was to pray for Klaus.

As he walked down the long, narrow corridor of the Grunewald train station, Otto felt totally alone and empty inside. Not even the magnificent brick archway and the windowed cathedral ceiling, which he loved to look at not too long ago, could brighten his spirits. His brother, whom he had looked up to all of his life, had walked off without even saying goodbye. The last vision he had of his parents and sisters was sad if not pitiful. It was as if they were wondering if they would ever see him again. What did life have in store for him? What had it dealt the young American woman who had lost her loved one on the coast of Norway?

26

Assignment

JENNIFER RETURNED TO Washington after her two-week furlough. She hailed a cab and went directly to the Mayflower Hotel, where she was once again quartered. As she approached the check-in counter, she recognized the clerk as the one who had signed her in on her previous two stays. He looked up and smiled. "Good afternoon," he said. "I have a message for you."

The message had the Army chief of staff's seal on the envelope. Quickly, she opened it. "Report to my office 0800 tomorrow," the message read. "Johnson will assist you." *Just like the chief,* Jennifer thought, *short and to the point.*

"Would you like your same room?" the clerk asked.

"Yes, please," she replied. Why not? It was becoming a second home to her.

At 0730 the next morning, Sergeant Johnson was waiting in front of the hotel with the staff car. He saluted smartly and opened the door for her. After the short drive, she was whisked into the general's office. Looking up, the general returned her salute and motioned for her to have a seat.

"You won't be doing any nursing for a while," he said.

"I won't?"

"No. I need anyone who has had experience with the British to be on a coordinating committee."

"I would like that very much," Jennifer said enthusiastically.

"Before you get too excited," Marshall warned, "I have to tell you that it will be difficult. The American-British coalition that we're trying to put together will be the greatest that the world has ever seen. Naturally, there are suspicions on both sides. So we need people who are diplomatic as well as capable. That is where you fit in."

"I'm honored, sir," Jennifer said.

"Results are all that count, Haraldsson, so don't get ahead of yourself."

"I won't, sir. Thank you."

"By the way," Marshall continued, "these are now yours." He reached into a desk drawer and pulled out a pair of silver captain's bars. Jennifer was being spot-promoted from second lieutenant!

"I don't know what to say, sir."

"You don't have to say anything. You earned them. Congratulations."

Marshall told her she would once again be working with Major Dunbar.

"I couldn't ask for anyone better, sir. The major is a great officer and a fine person."

In what seemed like no time at all, Jennifer was boarding a plane for England. She took plenty of reading material, including Dostoyevsky's *War and Peace,* to help her keep from dwelling on Dude. She couldn't afford to sink into depression pining for him.

The flight was as long and tiring as the first time. When the plane touched down in England, she looked out the window and saw Major Dunbar waiting for her. But there was something different about him. *Aha!* It was his shoulder boards. He had been promoted to lieutenant colonel! She eagerly waited for the door to open.

As she descended the steps of the plane, Colonel Dunbar looked elated. "I knew it," he said. "You are too good not to promote. Congratulations!"

"My congratulations to you, too!" Jennifer replied. They hugged briefly.

As the colonel drove Jennifer to her quarters, he told her that they would once again dine with the prime minister, this time in his underground working bunker.

"I'm surprised the prime minister takes the time to meet with us," Jennifer said.

"He likes you very much," Dunbar replied. "But I think that he will have less and less time as the war goes on. The demands on his time seem to be increasing daily."

That evening when they entered Churchill's cramped office in the bunker, they found him pacing back and forth with a frown. He smiled only slightly when he saw Jennifer.

My dear, I'm happy for your promotion," he said. "However, you Americans are not among my favorite people right now. Your General Marshall insists that we should invade Europe next spring or in 1943 at the latest. But we will not yet be strong enough!"

What an understatement Marshall's comment about "suspicions" had been! *Friction and disagreement* more accurately described the situation. But perhaps the general had not wanted her to know just how strong the feelings were. In any event, she would have to be at her diplomatic best.

"But I have forgotten my manners!" Churchill said. "I don't mean to upset you. I am grateful to the Americans. If it weren't for your lend-lease program, England would probably be under Hitler's boot by now. But we lack sufficient men, arms, and landing boats to make a successful landing on the continent. I shudder to think of the flower of American and British youth lying dead on the beaches of France because we've rushed to invade without any hope of being successful."

"Mr. Prime Minister, I don't know enough about the situation to offer intelligent advice. I will have to leave it up to people with more experience than I have."

"My dear, that is an absolutely perfect response. It makes me all the more pleased that I requested you to work with us."

Who thought of it first? Churchill or Marshall? Jennifer would probably never know.

Turning to a map on the wall, Churchill pointed to the French coastal town of Dieppe. "What I am about to tell you is top secret," he said. Jennifer nodded.

"The Americans aren't the only ones itching for battle on the continent. Some Canadians are, too." He relit his cigar and tapped the map. "So I intend to let them test the German defenses by attacking Dieppe."

"If the Canadians can establish a beachhead," Churchill continued, "I will bow to your General Marshall and let him press on with Operation Bolero, the buildup for the invasion of the European continent. If a beachhead cannot be established, I will remain adamant that the Americans should first help us conquer the Germans in North Africa."

"Your plan sounds reasonable to me, sir," Jennifer replied. "What will I be doing?"

"You will work in an office next to him," Churchill said pointing at Dunbar. "He will furnish the communications coding gear that you will use to contact General Marshall's staff."

Hesitating for a moment, Churchill continued, "I want you to keep Marshall informed of the progress in our planning. I want you to be perfectly candid about your perceptions of our planning. He trusts you, and we will not hide anything from you. Now, let's eat!"

Churchill pushed a button on his desk and almost immediately a steward brought in a cart with dishes of roast beef, steamed potatoes, Yorkshire pudding, and boiled cabbage.

"Wait a minute," Churchill told the steward as he swept the papers on his desk into a pile and dropped them into a drawer. "Okay. Now just pile the food here." The steward complied.

Churchill motioned for Jennifer and Dunbar to pull up chairs. "You may wonder why we're eating in here," he said. "Well, one time I saw President Roosevelt and an aide eating at the president's desk. They had lobster shells spread all over, but it looked like such fun that I thought we'd try it tonight!"

Looking around the prime minister's desk, it didn't appear to Jennifer that there was one inch of open space. When the champagne bottle and glasses came, the arrangement grew even more precarious.

"I can balance my plate on my lap," Jennifer said.

"Not necessary, my dear," Churchill replied. "Plenty of room."

Food was passed and plates were filled. Obviously, the crowded conditions didn't bother the prime minister one bit. As he dug in, Jennifer marveled at the way he attacked his food. *Certainly a world-class appetite*, she thought.

During dinner, the prime minister was the perfect host, making sure that everyone was getting enough to eat and drink. Feeling no pain after a refill of her glass, Jennifer asked, "Mr. Prime Minister, do you ever drink plain water?"

"Heavens, no! I use water for baths!"

Jennifer laughed. "I have just one more question for you."

"What is it?" he asked as he chewed on a generous chunk of roast beef.

"How did you and Colonel Dunbar become such good friends?"

The prime minister stopped chewing and thought for a moment. He swallowed and began to talk. "It was after Dunkirk," he said. "I heard of this fellow Francis Dunbar who waited until everyone was off the beach before leaving himself. That impressed me so much that I wanted to meet him."

The prime minister took another bite and continued. "After I met him, I found that I really enjoyed our conversations. Ever since, we have been the best of friends."

Really enjoyed their conversations? Jennifer thought. What the prime minister really meant was that he enjoyed the fact that Colonel Dunbar was such a good listener! Looking over at the colonel, Jennifer noted that Dunbar had an amused look on his face. He must have been thinking the same thing.

The evening came to an end all too soon. Jennifer bade farewell to the great man once again. Would she see him in the future? She hoped so.

The next few months were very dark for both the Americans and the British. German submarines took a terrible toll on Allied shipping. Bataan and Corregidor fell to the Japanese. The British lost Singapore and Tobruk, and the mighty warships *Prince of Wales* and *Repulse* were now at the bottom of the Pacific. Nonetheless, the Allies fought on valiantly.

Jennifer threw herself into her work. She attended daily staff meetings of the Dieppe Task Force and went to the training sites where British and Canadian troops were practicing beach landings and town seizure. She made an occasional suggestion, and much to her surprise, the task force personnel considered each one very carefully.

She had to keep reminding herself that many of the men would probably not make it back. She would have to be prepared for more loss in her life.

Part V

27

Training Ends

JACOB'S DAYS WERE filled with flying, so he didn't have a lot of time to think of Dude or Jennifer. With the war in full swing, the instructors were cramming in a lot of material in a very short amount of time. Much to his surprise, Jacob found that he took the heavy load easily in stride. While others were being washed out at a substantial rate, Jacob was actually excelling.

By now, Jacob had mastered the art of employing ailerons, elevators, and rudders to control the plane's roll, pitch, and yaw. He found that he could maneuver with the best of the trainees and was looking forward to moving to the next phase, aerial gunnery. The man who would be instructing this phase was Major Tex Whittaker. As his name suggested, Whittaker was a Texan, lean and tall and tougher than hardtack.

Jacob knew that he had a chance to finish at or near the top of his class. He'd heard scuttlebutt that the top graduates of his class would have the opportunity to fly the new Lockheed P-38 Lightning, a dream of an airplane with a top speed of 420 miles per hour and real no-nonsense armament: four .50-caliber machine guns and a 20-millimeter cannon, all nose-mounted. *Any fighter pilot would give his eye teeth to fly such a magnificent machine,* Jacob thought. So he would have to do something spectacular to get the instructor's attention and cement his spot in the class standings.

At 0600 on a clear Monday morning, Jacob and the other trainees assembled in a classroom for the first day of gunnery practice. When Whittaker strode in, they snapped to attention.

"As you were," he said. "Men, those of you who master aerial gunnery will probably live. Those of you who don't probably will not. The procedure is straightforward in theory. You simply get the target in your gun sight and squeeze the trigger. In practice, however, aerial gunnery is much more difficult and complex. Elements such as anticipation and hand-eye coordination become paramount."

Whittaker went on to explain that the trainer planes would go up in flights of five, with each plane having a chance to fire at a towed target. "You must not—repeat, *must not*—hit the tow plane. That's an automatic washout. And that would be just the start of your troubles."

Should be a lot of fun, Jacob thought. *This is what it's all about— firing and hitting something!*

He was in the first flight of five, so he was soon airborne. But much to his dismay, he would be the fifth to fire at the target. As he watched the others blow holes in the target, he realized he would have to do something really special if he hoped to stand out. What if, instead of shooting at the target, he shot at the towline? It would be pretty darned spectacular if he could sever that towline! He could approach from the side, commence firing slightly above the line, and then inch his aim downward.

When his turn came, Jacob did a hard roll and broke to the side. Turning sharply in a 180-degree arc, he made his run at the target. He let out a burst of gunfire, and nothing seemed to happen. Uncertainty racked him as he peeled off. Had he cut the line or not? Only time would tell.

Unable to control themselves, several pilots snickered into their radio mikes. *I've done it this time,* Jacob thought. He circled to rejoin the flight. Suddenly, he heard a gasp. "My God," one of the pilots shouted. "He cut the tow line!"

Jacob smiled to himself. *Mission accomplished.*

As Jacob landed and taxied to a stop, Whittaker marched up to the plane. Jacob thought that the major was probably so pleased with him that he wanted to offer personal congratulations.

"Come to my office now!" Whittaker barked. *Oh-oh*, Jacob thought, *maybe the major is not pleased?*

Inside his office, Major Whittaker backed Jacob against a wall and growled, "If you ever grandstand again, it will be the last time you ever fly an Army Air Force plane. Do you understand?"

"Yes, sir!"

"Good. Now get out of here!"

Crushed, Jacob staggered out. It was early afternoon, but not too early to have a drink at the Officers' Club. By happy hour Jacob was feeling no pain, and he was able to laugh at the ribbing heaped on him by his fellow pilots. Underneath, though, Whittaker's chewing out still hurt a lot. There was nothing to do but drink some more.

As he sat dejectedly, a pretty young lady in a flight uniform approached.

"You look like you just lost your last friend," she said.

"Maybe I did."

"Want to tell me about it?"

"No, but I will."

That's how he met Sandy Higgins, a pilot in the Women's Auxiliary Ferrying Squadron, which was created to deliver aircraft to overseas bases and to perform other flying functions.

"I think what you did was very clever," she told him as she helped him to a table.

"You really think so?" He felt a little better already.

At 1700 hours, Whittaker entered the office of Colonel Shack Slater. The colonel smiled and pulled a bottle of Scotch from a drawer. He poured two glasses and said, "Well, how did it go today, Tex?" It was the usual ritual.

"Actually, not too bad, sir. I had to ream out one of our pilots, but I didn't ground him."

"What'd he do?"

"He shot off the tow line! Can you believe that?"

Laughing, the colonel replied, "He reminds me of myself at that age. Did I ever tell you about the time I flew under the Golden Gate Bridge? I thought I would never live that down. Who is the pilot?"

"Partude, sir. Jacob Partude."

"Oh, yes. He seems to have real potential as a fighter pilot. Send him to see me first thing in the morning. I'd like to have a chat with him."

"Will do, sir."

With that, the conversation turned to lighter subjects. The men finished their drinks and then departed for the evening.

Meanwhile, Jacob sobered up over a good steak dinner with Sandy. Looking at her, he asked "What brings you to Randolph Field?"

"I'm serving in the Women's Auxiliary Ferrying Squadron. Our Squadron frees up men like you to go to combat assignments."

"Oh, so you ferry planes to different places?"

"Exactly. We also fly mundane sorties that don't receive much enthusiasm from you guys."

"How did you qualify for the job?"

"I received my commercial pilot's license about three years ago, and I had over 500 hours of flying time when I applied," Sandy said. "I love flying even more than teaching, which I did previously. I have a bachelor's degree in Elementary Education."

"Impressive."

After a cup of coffee, Jacob asked if he could walk Sandy to her barracks. She nodded, and the two departed into the moonlit evening. Reaching her quarters, Jacob asked if he could see her the next evening.

"Yes," she replied with a smile. Maybe, Jacob thought, the day had finally turned for the better.

The next morning Jacob was sporting a real hangover when he reported to Colonel Slater's office.

"Have a seat," Slater told him.

"Yes, sir."

"Partude, I am not condoning your silly stunt. You're to do nothing like that again. However, I've studied your record, and I think you could be a fine pilot. I'm even thinking of keeping you here for awhile as an instructor after you complete training. How does that sound to you?"

"I would be honored to be an instructor, sir, but I would rather be assigned to combat."

"I'm sure you would, but you could be of more value here. What type of airplane do you most want to fly?"

"Sir, the P-38. That is one sweet fighter!"

The P-38s are now coming to Randolph Field in substantial numbers," Slater replied. "So that won't be a problem."

He thought for a few moments, then continued, "Partude, I'll tell Whittaker to have you cross-trained in the P-38 as soon as you finish basic flight training." Looking at the calendar, he added, "That will be in three weeks. Any questions?"

"Just one, sir. How long will I be assigned here?"

"Consider your instructor assignment to be for one year. After that, we'll see."

Jacob was dismissed, and he rejoined his classmates and Major Whittaker. His hangover had vanished, erased by the thought that he would soon be flying a P-38.

When the class went back up for target practice, Jacob was a model student, following all directions to the letter and not showing off in any way. At the end of the day, he showered quickly and put on an immaculately clean uniform before going to get Sandy. He wanted to be at his best so that she would be duly impressed.

When he arrived at her quarters, Sandy was waiting for him in the lobby.

"Wow, you certainly look different than you did last night," she said. "Better day today?"

Jacob smiled.

They strolled to the Officers' Club and had a drink in the bar while Jacob told her about his conversation with Colonel Slater. Jacob decided to join Sandy and just have a glass of wine, as he wanted to make sure that he didn't overdo it as he had done the night before. They emptied their glasses and moved to the club's dining room.

During a lull in the conversation between the entrée and dessert, Sandy looked at Jacob with a big smile on her face. Noticing, Jacob asked with mock disgust, "Okay, what's so funny?"

"I have a confession to make," Sandy said. "I was pulling that tow plane yesterday, and I wondered who the wise guy was that shot out my tow line!"

"Oh my God! What if I had hit you instead of the tow line?"

"Well, you didn't. Lucky for both of us."

"Why do they let women fly such dangerous missions?"

"It's because they can't get you brave men to volunteer!"

"Oh," Jacob replied meekly.

They finished eating, and Jacob walked Sandy back to her quarters.

Where is this relationship going? he wondered. *What about Jennifer?*

Life was complicated, he had to admit. But, in this case, it was complicated in a good way.

28

The Russian Front

IT WAS LATE May 1942, and Otto Bruner was on Russian soil. How quickly the time with his family had passed, he thought. The wounds he had suffered in Norway had healed just in time for him to be part of the massive push by the German Wehrmacht to force the Soviet Union to capitulate. Would they be successful? He wasn't sure.

When their drive had bogged down the previous fall due to the onset of winter, the German Army was at Moscow's doorstep but couldn't quite get in. Now it would be even more difficult, as the harsh winter had extracted a substantial toll on the Wehrmacht. The continuing guerilla warfare conducted by the Russians was also proving to be a significant source of attrition in the German Army. As the train rolled over the vast expanses of the Soviet Union, Otto felt only one emotion—sadness.

Otto disembarked from the train about twenty miles from the headquarters of his new boss, Lieutenant Colonel Wilhelm von Schlechten. Word was that the rails up ahead had been cut by saboteurs, so the train couldn't continue. As he stepped off the train, a messenger approached. "I see by your nametag that you are Captain Bruner, sir. This message is for you."

Otto tore the envelope open. It read: "Staff car will be there for you. Be patient." It was signed "von Schlechten, Commander, 12th Battalion." *Oh, great*, Otto thought. *It's hurry up and wait once again.* He pulled out a cigarette and lit it. Though not much of a smoker, he found that a cigarette helped in times like these.

Much to his surprise, a staff car arrived shortly. Otto watched as a corporal got out and scanned the men who were milling around the train platform. Seeing Otto, he hesitated briefly and then approached. Otto cut him off. "Yes, I'm Captain Bruner. Can we go?"

"I'm here for a Captain Fritz Hauser also, sir."

"Hauser? I've heard that name before. I didn't know he was on the train."

The two men started searching through the crowd. Soon, Otto spotted a tall, thin, blond German with a captain's insignia. *That might be him*, Otto thought. He glanced at the nametag. Sure enough, it was.

Otto introduced himself and extended his hand. "I understand you also have the honor of being one of von Schlechten's new company commanders.

"That's right," Hauser replied, releasing his grip. "But how did you know?"

"Your name was on the orders along with mine, and the corporal here said he was here to pick you up as well as me." Bruner and Hauser picked up their bags and headed to the car.

"Sirs, please let me carry your bags," the corporal pleaded. The two officers complied. Soon, the three were at the car. The corporal placed their bags in the trunk, and the two officers got into the back seat.

Bruner was amazed at the destruction all along the route. Buildings and homes were flattened, and fields of wheat had been burned. This must be the scorched Earth policy that he had heard about. The enemy was leaving absolutely nothing for them to use as it retreated. *No wonder Napoleon had had to withdraw in defeat a century and a half earlier*, Otto mused. Any invader would have a hard time maintaining adequate supply lines over these vast distances.

"Are you returning to the Russian Front or coming for the first time?" Hauser asked.

"I'm new," Otto replied. "How about you?"

"I've been here from the beginning," Hauser said. "About six months ago, I was wounded and sent back to Germany. I'm still not 100 percent—you may have noticed that I walk with a limp—but there's a shortage of manpower. So here I am."

They rode in silence for a while. "Have you met von Schlechten?" Otto asked.

"Oh yes. I used to work for him. You'll find he's a decent fellow."

Otto noted that the driver was intent on watching the road ahead, so he leaned toward Hauser. "What's it really like here?" he asked quietly.

"Not good," Hauser replied in a muffled tone. "Everything was fine at first. Then our supply lines became too long. Now we need more of everything."

"Do we still have weapon superiority?"

"No. The Russian T-34 tank is superior in almost every respect to our tanks. They say we'll soon have the new Tiger tank and regain superiority. But they also told us that we would have warm clothing before winter came last year. That never happened, and my men had to wear whatever they could find, including red coats taken from Russian peasants! You should have seen the look on the senior officers' faces when they visited the Front."

Otto glanced at the driver. The young corporal didn't appear to be eavesdropping, but Bruner couldn't be sure. They rode the rest of the way in silence.

At their destination, Bruner and Hauser shook hands. "I'm going to my quarters first," Hauser said. "I'm sure they're in that building." He pointed to his left.

"Are my quarters near yours?" Otto asked.

"Most definitely," Hauser replied. "Junior officers bunk together."

"I think I'll go meet my new boss first," Otto said. "Which way?"

Hauser looked around and pointed directly ahead to a dugout. "That has to be it. Headquarters is always the one with the most beams."

Otto told the corporal to take his bag to his quarters. He started walking. *Not a very pleasant picture*, he thought. Everyone seemed to have the old siege mentality, probably no longer feeling invincible. After all, who could be sure that their mighty tank arm, the Panzer units, would still lead them to victory? He returned salutes and nodded as he passed soldiers. He was sure that his new boss would tell him that building morale would be a top priority.

Looking out in front, he was in awe of the vast expanses. Build morale with all of this facing them? How could they possibly take all of this territory with the men and equipment that they had? Why should they take it, anyway? It certainly didn't belong to them.

Otto knew he had better change his thinking, or he would be in hot water right away. He struggled to put on a positive air as he went to meet with his new boss, Lieutenant Colonel von Schlechten.

As he neared the dugout, he noted that it was made of heavy timbers with thick patches of straw and mud in between. The dugout was sunk into the ground, with barely three feet of it above ground level. He went down a ramp and ducked as he went through the doorway. Inside, there were some rickety tables and chairs. A lieutenant and sergeant popped to attention. Otto motioned for them to be seated. Pouring over a map was his new boss, Wilhelm von Schlechten.

The colonel looked around, got up, and shook his hand. *This was a good sign*, Otto thought, as it indicated that his new boss was quite different from Peter Schmidt. When he met Schmidt, all he had received was an icy stare. Von Schlechten actually seemed pleased to have him there!

"Ah, Bruner, I'm glad that you are here. Please, sit!"

"Thank you, sir."

"Bruner, we have our work cut out for us. You can't begin to imagine how hard the winter was on us. Many of our troops froze, because they had no winter clothing. The Russian devils continually harass us, at all hours of the night and day. It has been a nightmare. And now we are expected to resume the offensive as if none of this had happened?"

Sir, I had heard rumors of our difficulties, but most Germans think that fighting on this front is proceeding as planned."

"Yes, I'm sure that the propaganda ministry is hiding the truth. However, we must be careful not to express that thought in public, as Secret Service and Gestapo people are everywhere. Also, we must appear upbeat to our men."

The colonel went on to explain that there were severe shortages of men, so company strength was being fixed at less than half of the standard number. Otto would be a company commander, and the number of soldiers in his unit would be eighty rather than the standard number of more than 170. Otto shook his head and whistled softly. The major concurred with his obvious dismay, noting that the German Army was expected to move forward across the whole front, irrespective of the fact that it was in such poor shape.

"Bruner, our ultimate objective in this campaign is Stalingrad. God help us if we haven't taken Stalingrad by the onset of cold weather."

"How far away is it, sir?"

"It's over 250 miles."

Wow, Otto thought, *that's a long way to go.*

"Bruner, I'm going to have to depend on you mightily. I'm giving you these two gentlemen to help." The major motioned for Lieutenant Hans Kruger and Sergeant Johann Bergmeister to approach. The three shook hands.

"Kruger will fill you in and introduce you to the men in your company," von Schlechten said. "By the way, I sleep under a tank at night. It's the only place I feel safe. Feel free to pick one out for yourself." Bruner nodded.

Von Schlechten turned his attention back to the map and pointed out the area in which Otto's company would advance. "Bruner," he said, "I expect you to gain at least five miles a day. There will be no excuses. Understood?"

"Yes, sir."

Otto saluted and departed with Kruger and Bergmeister. He was eager to meet his men and get started. It wasn't a task he relished, but he didn't have a choice.

Outside battalion headquarters, Otto asked, "Kruger, where are our men?"

"Sir, they are spread out about five miles up ahead."

"Good. Let me clean up, and I'll meet you back here in about twenty minutes. I'm anxious to meet them." Salutes were exchanged, and Bruner headed to his quarters.

In the coming days, Otto's company was often given the most difficult tasks and stayed in the thick of the fighting. Otto even surprised himself with his own capabilities. Under Major Schmidt, he'd been put down most of the time and never given the opportunity to excel, but von Schlechten seemed to consider him one of his best company commanders.

On numerous occasions Otto demonstrated bravery above and beyond the call of duty. When enemy fire was greatest, he moved up and down the lines offering encouragement and help to anyone who needed it. More than once he risked his own life to pull a wounded man to safety. His actions did not go unnoticed by his superiors or the by troops under him.

The German Army continued moving briskly forward as August approached, even though the Russian Army continued to throw waves of soldiers at it. Was there no end to the Russian supply of manpower? Were there enough German soldiers to see the war through to the end? As long as the Russians outnumbered them by only ten to one, the Germans were able to prevail through better training and superior tactics and strategy. Now, however, it appeared that Russian troops outnumbered the Germans by more than twenty to one, and Otto began to think that the German advance might soon falter.

When the Germans first moved into new towns, the residents seemed to be glad to see them. Bruner could almost believe that the townspeople looked upon the Germans as liberators! Soon, however, the Gestapo and SS moved into the towns and began treating the Russian people with typical brutality, turning potentially friendly populaces into incensed enemies.

One evening, weary from the day's battle, Otto joined von Schlechten and Captain Hauser for dinner. "What a waste," he said. "If we treated the Russians right, they would probably come over to our side."

"I agree," Hauser replied. "Have you noticed how ruthless the Russian high command is? If their soldiers start to retreat, their own people mow them down."

"Can't argue with either of you," von Schlechten said. "But I must caution you. In the first place, there's nothing you can do about it.

Secondly, there are German agents and SS officers all over the place who are on the watch for 'incorrect thinking' among German officers."

"I know, sir," Otto replied. "But what are we going to do? The Russians burn everything useable as they retreat, leaving nothing for us to scavenge. They poison wells and kill any livestock that has survived. I think malnutrition, dehydration, and disease will become serious problems as we approach Stalingrad."

"There is only one thing to do," the colonel replied. "And that is to enjoy a good glass of schnapps." He went over and poured three glasses. Returning, he handed a glass to Otto and one to Hauser and raised his in a toast, "To my two friends." The three clinked glasses.

How good the schnapps tasted, Otto thought. It was his first taste of alcohol in months, and it relaxed him almost immediately. He would try to be less negative, as none of this was von Schlechten's fault.

But the colonel wasn't ready to drop the subject. "Otto, you're correct. No one up the chain of command, including the führer, truly understands the importance of logistics. Before coming here, I fought in North Africa. I saw Rommel outrun his supply lines on more than one occasion, resulting in disaster. How anyone in Berlin thinks we can keep moving forward without adequate supplies is more than I will ever know."

Both captains shook their heads.

Otto continued to take care of his men as best he could. However, it became more difficult with each passing day. Whereas Russian soldiers could get by with a knapsack of vegetable greens, German soldiers were used to a full diet including hearty portions of meat. As supply lines stretched longer and longer, adequate food supplies became even scarcer.

"Herman Goering boasts that the German air force can keep us adequately supplied, but that is a myth," Bruner told his second in command, Lieutenant Kruger. "How in the world we are able to keep gaining territory is beyond me."

"Maybe," Kruger replied, "it is because of your sparkling leadership."

"Now that really is a myth!" Otto said. *But maybe—just maybe—it did have something to do with him. Anyway, it was nice to think so.*

The Germans pressed on toward Stalingrad. During a lull in the fighting at the end of August, Otto was called to von Schlechten's dugout. As he entered, he noticed a tall, lean man standing next to the colonel. It was none other than General von Paulus, commander of the Sixth Army!

"Bruner, I am hearing good things about you," von Paulus said. "I have decided to make you a major, and you are being awarded the Iron Cross."

Otto was stunned. He hadn't been aware he was being considered for either of these honors. "Thank you very much, sir. I owe my success to my men and to Colonel von Schlechten."

General von Paulus pinned the Iron Cross on Otto and handed him his new rank insignia. After the exchange of salutes, the general called for an aide to break out a bottle of his finest champagne. This was a reason for celebration, and Otto had heard that the general never missed such an opportunity.

The champagne was far better than any Otto had ever tasted. He had heard that General von Paulus was a connoisseur of fine wines and champagne, but he had no idea that the *really* good stuff was so much better than what ordinary folks were used to. He thought how easy it would be to become spoiled and no longer enjoy the common varieties.

Then von Paulus had another pleasant surprise for the new major. "Bruner, I am sending you to the battalion commander's course in France. I believe that I can spare you now more than I will be able to later. I commend you for your exceptional work," he said.

Salutes were once again exchanged, and the general departed. *What a day this has been*, Otto thought. While he owed a lot to General von Paulus and even more to Colonel von Schlechten, it did cross his mind that maybe he should try to stay in France once he got there. After all, he did not believe that things would improve here on the Eastern Front, and they could get a lot worse. In any event, the future looked very uncertain, fraught with danger wherever he went.

Once they were alone again, von Schlechten stepped forward and clasped both of Bruner's shoulders. "I am very happy for you, Otto," he said. "And I have one suggestion: Try to stay in France. Your chances of survival will be much better there."

"Sir, the only thing that may keep me from taking your advice is that I would like to serve with you again."

"I'm very happy that you feel that way. However, if Germany loses this war, we'll need young men with high principles to rebuild the country. I can think of no one finer than you."

"Thank you very much, sir."

Would they both survive the war and see each other again? Otto knew that it was very doubtful. In spite of the dire situation, though, he was thrilled at his success. He hurried out of von Schlechten's quarters to return to his tent and write a long overdue letter to his family. Arriving at his makeshift facility, he went to a wobbly table, pulled up a chair, and took out a pen and a sheet of paper to write his parents and two younger sisters, Liesl and Gretchen.

> *Dear Folks,*
>
> *I think of you often and apologize for taking so long to write. I pray for you nightly and hope everything is okay with you. In these difficult times, I know that I can't hope for things to be any better than just okay.*
>
> *We continue to move forward here. The fighting is difficult, though, and enemy resistance is fierce. In spite of everything, I try to remember my Christian upbringing and not do anything that would make you ashamed of me.*
>
> *Papa, I hope all is well at the bank. Mama, I miss your cooking and your caring more than you will ever know! I am thankful every day that I have such wonderful parents. Oh–I almost forgot—my sisters aren't so bad either, and they both better still be in school!*
>
> *I had some good news today. I received the Iron Cross and am being promoted to major. The award was presented by none other than General von Paulus himself, the commander of the Sixth Army. The general is sending me to Battalion Officers' School, so there is*

*a chance that I might get some leave time! If so, I will
come to Berlin and see you. I would like nothing better,
and I will keep you informed.*

*If there is anything you need, please let me know.
While I can't be certain that there is anything I can do
about it, I will try my best.*

*Love always,
Otto*

Bruner only had a few days to prepare Lieutenant Kruger to take over the company. The two of them were working in Otto's tent when Colonel von Schlechten appeared.

"Otto, you're supposed to see a Colonel Fischer in my quarters," the colonel said.

"What about?"

"I don't know, but it can't be good. Fischer is SS."

Otto hurried over to the command post.

Colonel Fischer was seated at a table and was staring at a map. As Bruner entered, he looked up. His eyepiece dropped on its cord, and he gave Otto an icy stare. Salutes were exchanged.

"Bruner, as you know, letters from the front are censored. Quite frankly, I didn't like yours."

"May I ask why?"

This was all it took. In a rage, Fischer leapt to his feet, with maps flying in one direction and the table in another.

"Fierce fighting?" he shrieked. "Absolutely not! The swine are collapsing under the might of our Wehrmacht. As for your remark about Christianity," he sneered, "I can't begin to tell you how much that upsets me. We only acknowledge our great leader, Adolph Hitler! Do I make myself clear?"

"Yes, sir!" Otto replied. And he'd thought Schmidt was bad.

"I'm warning you, Bruner," Fischer continued. "You are being watched. Your Iron Cross won't keep you from being severely punished if you exhibit any more incorrect thinking. That is all."

The colonel motioned for an aide to clean up the mess. Otto saluted, but the colonel was staring off into space. It was as if Otto were no longer present.

Glory is a funny thing, Bruner thought. *One minute you have it, the next you don't. Perhaps it's the same for everyone.*

29

Testing the Waters

B Y AUGUST, JENNIFER was finding her involvement with the powers-that-be decreasing. Churchill no longer had time to host her and Dunbar at informal meetings in his bunker. American generals, including Dwight Eisenhower and Mark Clark, were now in London, but Jennifer was not even sure they knew of her existence. All this was fine with her, because she could devote even more time and effort to interfacing with the Dieppe mission planning staff without having to worry about pleasing superior officers.

At her last meeting with the prime minister, Mr. Churchill did concede that the Dieppe raid would not only prove to the Americans that an invasion of the continent would be difficult but would also take some of the pressure off Stalin. Attacking Dieppe would keep the Germans honest. They would have to keep substantial numbers in the west rather than maintaining only a skeletal force and sending everyone else to the Eastern Front.

The prime minister's admission made Jennifer feel better. She had become attached to many of the men who would be going to Dieppe, and she did not want to feel that loss of life would be the sole responsibility of the Americans.

She wrote Jacob regularly, sending at least two letters per month. Her tone was upbeat and for the most part she didn't mention Dude.

> *Dear Jacob,*
>
> *Hope everything is well with you. I'm still enjoying London and working with Lt. Col. Dunbar. I must say that the Brits and Canadians have been wonderful to me. They actually listen to what I have to say!*
>
> *I haven't seen Mr. Churchill in some time. The arrival of Ike and others has pushed me pretty far down the totem pole. Oh, well. It was great while it lasted.*
>
> *I have been working closely with our Allies on an upcoming mission. They let me practice with them on their training exercises. I get up early in the morning for the five-mile run and then participate in obstacle course drills. Needless to say, I am in the best shape of my life.*
>
> *Working closely with these men makes me feel that women should take the same risk as men. It's unfair to expect the men to take all of the risks. I'm planning to state my objection to a Canadian major general very soon. Hopefully, he will take me with him when he goes into battle. After all, the Norway mission already exposed me to combat.*
>
> *I think of you and pray for you every day.*
>
> > *Love to you and your family,*
> > *Jennifer*

Jacob's letters to Jennifer were more infrequent, coming at a rate of about one per month. Still, Jennifer thought that was pretty good for a man!

> *Dear Jennifer,*
>
> *I am alarmed that you want to go into combat. I'm not trying to tell you what to do, but I certainly hope you will reconsider.*
>
> *I'm glad that the Allies have the good sense to appreciate you. If they didn't, I would seriously consider*

coming over and punching someone in the nose! You are far too good to ignore.

Things for me have really straightened out and gone well after a rough patch. I have to admit that I did try and show off a while back. Thankfully, I wasn't grounded, and I have been on my best behavior ever since. It has really paid off, as I have been asked to be an instructor pilot. While I will miss going into combat, I have to admit that it is a great honor to be selected for an instructor slot.

I have met a young lady named Sandy whom I really like. She is a pilot in the Women's Auxiliary Corps and ferries planes to different locations. She also tows aerial targets that we practice on. Her job led to an interesting encounter that I will tell you about someday. It is too early to know if something serious will develop between us.

Well, duty calls, and I had better sign off for now. I also think about you and pray for you daily.

Love,
Jacob

Interesting, Jennifer thought. Jacob may have found a romantic flame. It was still too early for her to think of anyone but Dude. Besides, she was thousands of miles away, so there wasn't much she could do about it anyway.

"A schilling for your thoughts," Colonel Dunbar said as he dined with Jennifer.

After a moment, she replied. "The more I think about it, the more I want to participate in General Roberts' upcoming mission. Do you have any suggestions?"

"Only one," he said. "And that is that you forget about it."

"But what if you wanted to go?" Jennifer asked. "How would you approach it?"

The colonel put down his knife and fork and sat back in his chair. "Well," he said. "There's always the tactic that your General Patton used when he wanted to go into Mexico with General Pershing to hunt for Pancho Villa."

"Oh? What was that? I'm not familiar with it."

"As I recall, the year was 1913," Dunbar said. "Patton was a young lieutenant on General Pershing's staff in the state of New Mexico. Villa had been making raids across the border into the U. S., and Pershing was tasked with tracking him down. Patton wanted to go on the raid so badly that he sat at attention outside of Pershing's door for three days. Finally, as Pershing was coming out of his office, he looked down and asked, 'What the hell do you want?' Patton told him, and, as they say, the rest is history."

"It's worth a try!" Jennifer said excitedly. "Thank you!"

Dunbar nodded, and the two finished their meal talking about lighter subjects.

Early the next morning, Jennifer went to the office of Major-General J. H. Roberts, commander of the Canadian 2nd Infantry Division. Plans called for Roberts to lead the landing force at Dieppe. His door was closed. "Is he in yet?" she asked the sergeant at the beat-up desk guarding the entrance.

"No, ma'am," the sergeant replied. "Is there something I can do for you?"

"Sergeant, if it's okay with you, I'm going to pull this chair over and wait to see the general. I don't have an appointment, but maybe he can spare a few minutes."

"It's fine by me," the sergeant said with a grin. "I would enjoy your company."

Jennifer positioned the chair beside the general's door and sat down. Her posture was ramrod straight.

In the past, she had been in meetings with Roberts, sitting at the back of the room and not saying anything. So she was sure that he didn't know her. But she felt that she knew him, and her assessment of Roberts was that he was tough but fair.

Soon, the major general walked up, carrying a briefcase. His brow had deep ridges in it, and he was obviously consumed by thoughts of his upcoming mission.

"Sergeant, who is my first meeting with?" Roberts asked.

"Colonel Stanhope, sir," the sergeant replied. "He should be here shortly."

"Good. Send him in as soon as he arrives." Roberts walked into his office and slammed the door. *Didn't even notice me*, Jennifer thought.

Over the next few hours, Roberts exited and reentered his office several times. Finally, he said, "Captain, do you want to see me?"

Sitting at attention with eyes straight forward, Jennifer replied, "Yes, sir."

"Well, why didn't you say so?" he growled. "Come on in." He motioned for her to sit down in one of the two leather chairs in front of his desk. He plopped down into his own chair.

"What is it you want?" he asked.

"First, let me introduce myself." He waved her off. "I know who you are. Just tell me what you want."

"Sir, I want to be in the Dieppe landing party."

Roberts made a dismissive motion with his hand. "Preposterous!" he said. "Why in the world would you want to do that?"

"Sir, I fully realize how dangerous this mission is. But I have become very attached to the men. As a nurse, I believe that I might be a big help to them. My life is no more valuable than theirs. I should be willing to take the same risks they do."

Roberts shook his head. "I admire your enthusiasm, Captain, but I wouldn't dare authorize you to go, definitely not without the approval of the American Government."

Would you try to get that approval, sir?"

Roberts thought for a minute. "All right," he said. "But I'm sure permission won't be granted, so don't get your hopes up."

"Thank you, sir!" she said almost gleefully. She saluted and left the general's office. Now to tell Colonel Dunbar.

Jennifer's request went up the British chain of command and over to U.S. Army Chief of Staff General Marshall. When he saw it, he realized that it had implications that were legal and political as well as military. He immediately made an appointment to see President Roosevelt.

FDR responded pretty much as Marshall had expected: "By golly, I knew that young lady had spunk! It is this kind of dedication that will allow us to win the war. Tell the British that it is okay with me for her to go along to Dieppe. But not in the first wave, of course. And only as a nurse, wearing the Red Cross emblem. And tell them they'd better not let anything happen to her."

When word came back, General Roberts was dismayed. He'd hoped Jennifer's request would be denied. Now on top of all of his other headaches, he had to be responsible for the safety of this brash—though quite charming—young lady. He decided to request that Colonel Dunbar be assigned to the Dieppe invasion force, with the sole responsibility of safeguarding Jennifer. Of course, she was not to be told that. This was, after all, a woman who had distinguished herself under enemy fire.

Dunbar was pleased. He'd become restless just doing staff work. When General Roberts told him his primary—and secret—duty would be to protect Jennifer, he was even more pleased. He'd always enjoyed her company.

Jennifer was equally happy. Dunbar had seen her through the darkest moments of her life. Having him nearby on this very dangerous mission would be a comfort.

Early on the morning of August 19, 1942, the invasion fleet sailed for the seaport of Dieppe. It carried about five thousand Canadian troops, a thousand British troops, fifty U.S. Rangers, and a few Frenchmen. While it was known that Dieppe was well fortified, both Canadian and British strategists thought—perhaps blindly—that the attack would be successful. If so, the Allies would have a beachhead for the later invasion of Europe.

As the first wave of landing craft neared the beach, the Germans raked them with machine-gun and mortar fire. Watching through binoculars in the predawn light, Jennifer was horrified. Boats and men were blown apart, and she could do nothing to help from such a great distance. And to make matters much worse, a dozen German naval ships had suddenly appeared to attack the left flank of the landing craft. The fierce fighting on the water made it questionable as to whether there would be any protection on the left at all.

Some of the troops and tanks on the landing craft managed to reach the beach, but the tanks were unable to move beyond the beach, because they could not gain traction on the loose pebbles. Without tank support, the troops were finding it more difficult than anticipated to move past the seawall and into the city.

Sporadic good news did arrive. On the right flank, a British commando unit managed to climb a steep cliff and neutralize some large guns. But other units that were supposed to hook up with the commandos were unable to do so, and the commandos soon withdrew. The few Allied units that were somehow able to move inland were soon cut off and forced to retreat.

By now more medics were climbing into boats to head for shore. General Roberts said that Jennifer could go in with them. As she climbed down the netting that was draped over the side of the ship, Dunbar stayed right beside her and made sure she got into the Higgins boat safely.

By the time they got ashore, the wounded were being evacuated from further inland to the beach. Jennifer and Dunbar saw that an overwhelming number of wounded were being attended by short-handed medics. As Jennifer rushed to help, she heard the whistle of an incoming mortar round. Before she could move, Dunbar pushed her to the ground and threw himself on top of her. The round exploded. She felt his body jerk and then go limp. Jennifer could tell even without moving that he had been hit by shrapnel. She rolled him off her. He lay splayed on his back, with blood soaking through his shirt.

She put some compresses on his wounds to try to stop the bleeding. He was staring at her, grimacing with pain, trying to speak. "Hurt," he said. "Go. Leave me."

"No, sir! You and I are in this together."

Jennifer had once read about how Soviet women saved the wounded by dragging them to a safe place before lifting them up and carrying them back to friendly lines. Was she strong enough to drag the colonel? Well, she could try. She raised herself to a crouching posture, positioned herself at his head, hooked her arms under his armpits and tugged with all her might. Slowly, slowly she dragged him back to the base of the seawall, the closest approximation of shelter she could see.

A sergeant passing by offered to help. "No!" she snapped. "Find someone who needs help." She was surprised—and somewhat embarrassed—by the terseness of her response.

She propped Dunbar up against the seawall and asked, "Colonel, can you hear me?"

Dunbar nodded.

"I'm going to rock you forward and try to pick you up. I'll carry you across the beach to the boat. I'm getting you back to the ship."

Dunbar nodded again. *Now or never*, she thought. She rocked him forward to get a shoulder under him and then stood up. She barely noticed his weight—he was thin but quite tall—and guessed she owed her sudden strength to a surge of adrenaline. She staggered across the beach toward a boat that was just landing. A dozen soldiers rushed out and ran for the seawall. Two sailors on the boat splashed ashore, grabbed Dunbar from her, waded back to the boat, and laid him gently on its deck. Jennifer followed them and collapsed to her knees beside the now-unconscious colonel.

It was only after she was back in London that Jennifer learned the landing at Dieppe had quickly become a complete disaster. By 1300 that day, it was all over. Less than half of the six thousand men who'd stormed ashore were rescued from the beach. The rest were left behind, either dead or soon to be taken prisoner.

Doctors were able to remove some of the shrapnel from Dunbar's body, but other pieces remained embedded in him, because they were deemed too close to critical organs or arteries. As he lay unconscious, Jennifer maintained a vigil at his bedside. Luckily, she was left alone by her superiors. She couldn't help but wonder whether it was because they thought she would be most valuable at Dunbar's side or because they didn't know what to do with her. Either way, she was happy that she was getting to stay.

Jennifer coasted in and out of sleep as she remained with Dunbar in his cramped, tiny room. Periodically, she would look over at him to see if there was any change. So far, there hadn't been. He was still comatose.

In a sleepy haze on the second morning after the operation, Jennifer was vaguely aware of someone standing in the doorway. As her senses returned, she recognized the prime minister. "Mr. Prime Minister," she squealed in a low voice, "I'm so happy to see you, but I must look a mess!"

"Nonsense," Churchill replied softly. "You look absolutely ravishing." The two embraced near the doorway, and Jennifer briefly disappeared. When she returned, she had a folding chair.

"You take that chair," Jennifer said motioning at the one she had been lounging on. "And I'll take this one." Eyeing the folding chair that Jennifer was setting up, the prime minister didn't object.

Pulling their chairs close together, the two talked in muted tones. "How is he?" Churchill asked.

"The doctors tell me that he should be all right. His vital signs are good. But, as you can see, he's still unconscious." Churchill nodded sadly.

"My dear," Churchill said after a few moments, "I've heard from the generals. Now I would like your view of what happened."

"The men hitting the beaches didn't have a chance. The German fire was well coordinated, and our armored vehicles couldn't get any traction in the sand. But it certainly wasn't the fault of our troops. We just have to be better prepared next time."

Churchill nodded. "As you know, I tried to prevent that invasion, thinking it was premature. But I must admit that we've learned important lessons for when the time is right. This makes me feel better, knowing that those brave soldiers didn't die in vain. Let's just make sure that the gallantry of all who fought and died at Dieppe is never forgotten."

"I wholeheartedly agree, Mr. Prime Minister."

"Well, I must be going," Churchill said as he stood up. "Incidentally, I have informed President Roosevelt and General Marshall of your great bravery. Undoubtedly, you'll be hearing from them." Pausing, Churchill looked at Jennifer admiringly and shook his head.

"Imagine! You hoisting Dunbar on your shoulder and carrying him to safety under withering fire. I'm very proud of you."

"He would have done the same thing for me if the situation had been reversed. But thank you very much, sir."

"No—I should thank you. And please tell the old boy 'hello' for me when he wakes up."

"I certainly will." The two embraced once again, and the prime minister was off.

After Churchill had gone, Jennifer sat in silence broken only by Dunbar's still-ragged breathing. In the dimly lighted room, she felt Dude's presence very strongly. The time was not yet right to let him go. Perhaps it would never be right.

30

On With the War

AS JENNIFER KEPT her vigil with Dunbar, she couldn't help but wonder where she would be going and what she would be doing as the war progressed. For now, everyone was leaving her alone.

She was deep in thought when Dunbar began to stir. She hurried to his side and asked, "Colonel, can you hear me?" She placed her hand on his shoulder as his eyes began to flicker.

"Where am I?" he asked.

"You're in a hospital in Portsmouth. You were seriously wounded at Dieppe. Do you remember any of it?"

"I think I do," he replied as his focus sharpened. "I seem to remember you carrying me across the beach. After that, everything is a blank."

"That's because you blacked out once we got in the landing craft," she said. "I'll go for the doctor. You just rest."

"Before you go…" Dunbar said weakly, "…thank you."

Jennifer smiled and headed off. *Good news,* she thought. It appeared that the colonel would be all right.

Jennifer spotted Dunbar's surgeon at the nurses' station. "Dr. Nelson, Colonel Dunbar has regained consciousness."

"Great! I'll be right along."

Jennifer hurried back to the colonel's side. Soon, Dr. Nelson appeared.

"Well," Nelson said, "I see my miracle surgery saved another patient."

"Indeed it did," Dunbar replied. His responses were still quite weak, but his mind was sharpening. "What do you pill pushers have in store for me now?"

Nelson laughed. "You'll have to remain here until you get stronger," he said. "Then we'll ship you to London for a convalescence period."

The doctor took Dunbar's vital signs and then left.

"Jennifer, will you be able to stay with me until I'm ready to go to London?"

"As far as I know, I will," Jennifer said. "Nobody has told me that I'm to do anything other than to watch over you."

"Good! If anyone does, just let me know." The colonel slipped into a peaceful slumber. *Much better than before,* Jennifer thought.

On October 10, 1942, the train carrying Colonel Dunbar and Jennifer pulled into London's Paddington Station. Dunbar was walking now with the aid of a cane and seemed nearly back to his old self. There would be no need for him to be in a rehabilitation center. Rather, he could continue his recovery in his own quarters.

As they got off the train, an attractive redheaded woman in a driver's uniform approached. "By your nametag," she said to Jennifer, "I see that you're the one I'm looking for. I'm Kay Summersby, General Eisenhower's driver."

"What could you possibly want with me?" Jennifer asked curiously.

"General Eisenhower wants a meeting with you. It's set for 1500 hours tomorrow, and I'm to pick you up at 1430 at your quarters."

"Where is the meeting going to be held?"

"At General Eisenhower's office at Number 20 Grosvenor Square."

"Can I bring someone?"

"No, ma'am," Kay replied sheepishly. "I think the general wants to talk with you privately."

Kay nodded politely to both Jennifer and Colonel Dunbar, and then turned and walked away.

"I wonder what I could have done to bring on this meeting," Jennifer wondered aloud.

"I certainly wouldn't worry about it," Dunbar said with an amused look. "Your performance has been flawless, and, of course, if Eisenhower doesn't like it, I can always get you a position in the British Army!" Jennifer laughed.

The two picked up their baggage. "I know this great little pub," Dunbar said. "They serve excellent corned beef and cabbage, and we can get a pint of brew. Care to join me?"

"Lead on."

The two hailed a taxi, and off they went. Suddenly, the next day's meeting didn't seem nearly as important.

At precisely 1430, Kay Summersby arrived at Jennifer's quarters. Jennifer was waiting outside. When the car pulled to a stop, Jennifer opened the back door and got in. Greetings were exchanged, and off they went.

"Can you tell me something about General Eisenhower?"

"Well," Kay said. "The general—or Ike, as they call him—has a wonderful smile and appears very mellow to the uninformed. However, he is tough as nails and doesn't hesitate to show it if someone doesn't live up to expectations. But as long as a person does their job, they'll be fine."

"Anyone else I should know about?" Jennifer inquired.

"Oh, yes. Major General Walter Bedell Smith. General Smith is Eisenhower's chief of staff. People liken him to a bulldog. He growls at everyone and does Ike's dirty work. My best advice to you is to try and stay on his good side."

"I will."

Soon they were at Eisenhower's office. Kay stopped in front. "Go on in," she said. "I'll park the car and be in shortly."

The two sentries at the front entry saluted smartly as Jennifer approached. They asked to see some identification. After making sure that she was the one who was expected, the guards opened the door and directed her to Sergeant Mickey McKeogh, Eisenhower's aide. On her way, a little black Scottie puppy ran up to greet her.

"Well, who are you?" Jennifer asked as she bent down to pet the dog.

"You've just met General Eisenhower's dog," a man said as he approached. "His name is Telek."

"Well, my word," Jennifer said to the puppy as she cupped his ears in her hands. "I guess that I had better salute you!"

Looking up, Jennifer saw a master sergeant smiling down at her.

"Hi. I'm Sergeant Mickey McKeogh, the general's aide."

"I'm happy to meet you, Sergeant."

"Please follow me. The general is expecting you."

As they walked down the corridor, Telek jumped up and down at Jennifer's feet, trying to get her attention. Finally, she reached down and picked him up. "Oh, all right," she said. "I'll carry you for a little ways."

They reached a posh, spacious office in which there were three big, wooden desks. On each side of the office was a closed door. "That's General Smith's office," McKeogh said pointing to the door on the left. "He's the chief of staff. Over here is General Eisenhower's office." He slowly opened the door on the right. Jennifer put Telek down and followed the sergeant in.

Hard at work at a massive desk in the room was a bald man with three stars on his shoulders. The man had a cigarette in his hand, and, from the looks of it, had forgotten several cigarettes still smoldering in ash trays on a long conference table. *All this smoke can't be good for him,* Jennifer thought.

Telek, obviously right at home, went over and jumped up on the general. "Hello, boy," the general said. "How are you?"

"General Eisenhower," Sergeant McKeogh said, "I'd like to introduce Captain Jennifer Haraldsson." Salutes were exchanged, and the general walked over to shake her hand.

"Captain, I've heard some very good things about you. It's a pleasure to meet you."

"Likewise, sir."

"Please have a seat." The general pointed to a leather-upholstered chair. He sat down in an identical chair that was close to hers.

"I want to first commend you for your bravery at Dieppe. As you can probably guess, the raid was a shocker for General Marshall and me. We had planned to launch an attack on the European continent by the end of this year, but Dieppe proved we aren't ready. It's possible that we won't be ready even by the end of 1943."

The general, appearing deep in thought, lit another cigarette. He didn't bother to get an ashtray, instead flicking the ashes onto the carpet. *When you have all of his responsibilities,* Jennifer thought, *why worry about a carpet?*

"Will we wait to do any fighting until we're ready to attack the continent?" she asked.

"No. But what I'm about to tell you is top secret. I'm leaving in a few days for my new command post at Gibraltar on the Mediterranean Sea. I will be commanding a joint force of American and British troops that will land in North Africa. The decision has been made by President Roosevelt and Prime Minister Churchill that we will gradually work our way to the continent by first knocking the Germans and Italians out of Africa. After Africa, Sicily perhaps."

Kay Summersby was right. Ike, on the surface, appeared mild-mannered. Underneath was a man consumed with the need for victory. Just the right man for the job!

By now, Ike was in a cloud of cigarette smoke. "What I need you to do, Captain, is to continue interfacing with the Brits. They like you a great deal, and I need to take advantage of the trust you have built up with them. If we are to succeed, relations—all up and down the chain—have to get a lot better than they are now."

"I understand, sir. Will I still report to General Marshall's staff?"

"Good question, and the answer is no. You are now part of my 'American Observer' staff, and you will report to Colonel Andrew Dickens. You will still interface with the same Brits and in particular that fellow you rescued. What's his name?"

"Lieutenant Colonel Francis Dunbar, sir."

Ike nodded. "Mickey, go get Beetle so we can start this ceremony." The sergeant scurried out.

"Beetle," Ike explained to Jennifer, "is what we call my chief of staff, General Smith. As you'll see shortly, it really doesn't fit him, but we like it anyway."

"Did you say ceremony, sir?"

"Yes, Captain," Ike said. "You are being decorated."

General Bedell Smith entered the room, with Mickey McKeogh and Kay Summersby following. As usual, Bedell Smith was wearing a scowl. Jennifer saluted the chief of staff smartly as Ike whispered to her "See what I mean?" She knew better than to say anything.

"Captain," Ike said. "Is it okay with you if we keep everything informal?"

"Absolutely, sir."

"Good, just the way I like it," Ike replied as he lit another cigarette. "Mickey, go ahead and read the award citation." Jennifer was receiving the Bronze Star for gallantry at Dieppe!

After Ike pinned the medal on her uniform, cake and punch were served. The atmosphere was very relaxed, and Jennifer could tell that it was doing Ike a lot of good just to have this break. As for pure enjoyment, Telek's was unmatched. The puppy was getting ample dessert from everyone, even the stoic Bedell Smith.

The activities drew to a close. "You will eventually get back to nursing," Ike told Jennifer as he walked her to the door of his office. "For now, maintaining good relations and coordination with the Brits is paramount."

"I understand, sir." Jennifer thanked everyone and then headed for the staff car with Kay Summersby.

That evening, Jennifer joined Dunbar for dinner. "Well," he said. "Was it as bad as you feared that it might be?"

"Absolutely not." She pointed to the new bronze star ribbon that she was proudly wearing on her uniform.

"Congratulations! I had a feeling that it might be an award ceremony of some sort."

"Not only that," Jennifer replied. "But the general said that I would continue working with you. That pleased me most of all."

"I'm very happy to hear you say that, but I received some news of my own today."

"Oh?" Jennifer said with a concerned look. "I have a feeling that I won't like it."

"You may not. I'm shipping out the day after tomorrow."

"But you're still walking with a cane," Jennifer blustered. "Why can't they let you stay here until you're fully recovered?"

"I appreciate your concern. I really do. But the war waits for no one. And I'm more fit now than many of the poor chaps who have to stay on the front lines."

A member of her shrinking inner circle was departing for a fate unknown, and she couldn't help but feel a sense of loss. The exuberance that she had felt earlier in the day was giving way to a sobering dose of reality. The world was at war, and she was not immune to the sacrifices that still had to be made.

31

A Wish Is Granted

BY THE END of 1942, Jacob had become a captain and a distinguished instructor pilot. He had trained scores of P-38 pilots, but he yearned for actual battle. He envied pilots who had combat ribbons on their chest. And it didn't help when he received a letter from Jennifer describing how she had won the Bronze star for rescuing Colonel Dunbar at Dieppe. While she tried to downplay it, her description of carrying Colonel Dunbar to a landing craft was impressive. It served to fan the fires that were already burning in him.

Sandy and Jacob—now in love—met that evening at the Officers' Club for dinner. "What's up, darling?" she asked. "You look like you have the weight of the world on your shoulders."

"I guess several things are bothering me," he moaned. "I got a letter from Jennifer today, and she won the Bronze Star for bravery. She has a combat medal, and I don't have any! I'm both happy for her and envious."

"That's understandable," Sandy replied. "But you shouldn't forget how important your work is here. I don't think there is anything more important than training pilots for combat."

"Thanks," Jacob said. "I need the reinforcement."

"You're welcome. Now how did she get her medal?"

"She rescued Colonel Dunbar—the British Officer I told you about—at Dieppe."

"Go on," Sandy urged. "I read a little about the raid and how it failed, but I didn't know that an American nurse was there."

"I didn't either until her letter arrived. Apparently, Jennifer had volunteered to be an American observer during the landing and to accompany Colonel Dunbar ashore. Once the landing started, everything apparently fell apart. Dunbar was wounded shortly after they crossed the beach, and—get this—Jennifer hoisted him on her shoulder and carried him to a rescue craft."

"I'm impressed. She must be strong as well as brave."

"She is. I also think that she should have gotten the Silver Star instead of the Bronze Star."

"I agree," Sandy replied. "Carrying someone over open ground while you're being shot at certainly defines gallantry." Jacob nodded.

They sat quietly for a few moments before Sandy spoke again. "I can tell that something is still bothering you."

"I might have a problem—I'm not sure. I told you about Dude and Jennifer being in love. Well, I thought at one time that something might develop between Jennifer and me."

"You needn't worry about that," Sandy interrupted. "I figured you did."

"But now I'm concerned that she may have feelings for me."

"In that case, you should write her. You'll feel better when you're sure that there are no misunderstandings."

"Good advice," Jacob replied. "I'll write her tonight. But would you read the letter before I send it?"

"Sorry, flyboy. With this one, you're on your own."

After returning to his quarters, Jacob sat down to write.

> *Dear Jennifer,*
> *First of all, I want to congratulate you on the medal you received. For what you did, you deserve that medal and more. I am very proud of you.*

There is no easy way to say the following, as I think the world of you. Therefore, I am just going to blurt it out. I have fallen in love with Sandy, the young lady I told you about who ferries planes. We are getting engaged and plan to marry after the war is over.

I know that you and I never had any romantic discussions, and you may feel that I am very arrogant for thinking that you may have feelings for me. If so, I apologize. However, I wanted to be perfectly honest with you so that there wouldn't be any misunderstandings. The thing I would hate most of all is if I caused you any unnecessary pain.

I hope you will be a part of my life forever. I have told Sandy all about you, and she is very eager to meet you. I have a feeling that the two of you will be the best of friends.

In the meantime, please don't hesitate to contact me if there is anything I can do for you.

Love always,
Jacob

Days turned into weeks as Jacob waited for Jennifer's response. He checked his mail daily, trying to anticipate her response. Would she be amused or devastated? He hoped neither! The wait was agonizing. Finally, it was over, as a letter from the European Theater arrived.

Quickly, he tore the envelope open.

Dear Jacob,

I must admit that I was shocked reading your letter. I by no means had ruled out becoming romantically involved with you. In fact, I had even given it serious thought. My first impulse was to come and fight to win your love from her.

In all honesty, though, I can't say that my feelings for you weren't a carryover from my love for Dude. You remind me a great deal of him. Therefore, I would always wonder, as I'm sure you would, if I were recreating Dude through you. It wouldn't be a healthy situation.

After thinking it through, I want you to know that you have my blessing and my best wishes. I hope that you and Sandy will be very happy, and I look forward to meeting her.

Love,
Jennifer

Jacob was relieved and rushed to call Sandy. "Darling, you were right," he said. "I had nothing to worry about. She gives us her blessing and is eager to meet you!"

"I'll write and invite her to be a bridesmaid. "She sounds like someone I really want to know."

In December, word came back to Jacob about the success that several of his P-38 pilots were having in the Southwest Pacific. In one of their engagements, eleven Japanese fighters were shot down with only one American casualty.

"That's wonderful," Sandy exclaimed, when he passed the news on to her.

"That it is," Jacob replied. They were dining again at the Officers' Club. He lifted his glass, swirled the wine around in it, and set the glass back on the table.

"Sandy," he began, but she shushed him.

"I know you have to go, and I won't try and hold you back. But please promise me you'll be careful."

"You bet I will! I just have to get in on it!"

The next day, Jacob went to see his former instructor, Major Whittaker, who was the assistant wing operations officer.

"Major, did you hear how many Zeros were shot down by our guys in New Guinea?" he asked. "Pretty soon there won't be any left for me!"

The major grinned. "Partude, here's news for you. I'm going to New Guinea to take over a P-38 Squadron. I could use a good second in command. Would you be interested?"

"Sir, give me an hour to pack, and I'll be ready!"

"So, get started."

When he told Sandy that night, she smiled bravely. "I'm very happy for you."

"Darling, there's nothing in the world like the P-38," he said. "It can go from sea level to twenty thousand feet in less than six minutes. It has a top speed of 420 miles per hour and has wonderful armament. And it has a thick hide, so it won't go down easily."

"I know all that," she said softly.

"I'll be fine. Just wait and see!"

"Overconfidence can get you killed," she replied. "When I've ferried P-38s, I noticed that the plane can feel sluggish in a turn. You must constantly keep that in mind. The Zeroes are much lighter. They probably don't slow down as quickly in a maneuver."

Jacob shook his head. "You worry too much. But I'll be careful."

"Good!"

They finished their meal in near silence, barely taking their gazes off each other. Sandy stood up, took Jacob's hand, and pulled him up from his chair. "Come on, flyboy. Let's go to my room and loop the loop again."

32

The Atlantic Wall

A ND THE WAR raged on. Major Otto Bruner remained in France, while outside Stalingrad the German Sixth Army starved and died under the recently promoted Field Marshall von Paulus, who finally had no choice but to surrender. Some ninety-five thousand German soldiers were rounded up, shipped to Moscow, and paraded through the streets, utterly humiliated.

Because of his high finish in Battalion Officers' School, Bruner had caught the eye of several high-ranking German officers from the Atlantic Wall, Hitler's answer to the large pre-invasion buildup of men and material in Great Britain. Reduced manning was planned for the almost-impregnable wall so that more troops could be sent to the Eastern Front, which was now in desperate shape and almost at the point of collapse.

As 1944 began, Bruner was told that he would stay in France and work on the Wall. The part of the Wall that he would man was still to be determined. But he would know shortly. In the meantime, he was given a small office in a Parisian building that had been confiscated by the German Wehrmacht. His living quarters were in a nearby hotel.

Otto waited impatiently for his orders. Sitting in his office on a cold January morning, he looked up as a gaunt-looking colonel walked in. Otto snapped to attention.

"Sit down, Bruner," the visitor commanded. He dumped his coat and hat on Otto's desk and sat down in the only other chair in the little room. "You may not remember me, but we met in Norway."

"Yes, Colonel Meier," Otto replied. "I remember you. You're the one who gave me my orders to the Sixth Army."

"That is correct. And I see by your records that Major Schmidt was wrong. You are an exceptional officer. I extend my congratulations."

"Thank you, sir."

"Once again, I am here to give you orders," Meier said as he passed a sealed envelope to Otto. "You will work on the western part of the Atlantic Wall. The details are in your orders. You may take a look at them."

Meier paused while Otto thumbed through the rather lengthy document.

"Before you leave Paris," Meier continued, "you are to attend a briefing by Field Marshal Irwin Rommel. The führer has given Rommel responsibility for the Wall's defenses, all the way from Belgium down to Normandy in France."

"When is the field marshal's briefing?" Otto asked.

"Look at the last page of the document," Meier replied pointing to Otto's orders. "It will tell you everything you need to know."

The colonel stood and picked up his coat and hat. "Bruner, I'm proud of you. Keep up the good work." Meier extended his hand.

What a difference from the last time we were together, Otto thought.

By the time Otto arrived, there were a hundred or more officers in the auditorium where the field marshal was to speak. When Rommel strode in, everyone shot up and stood at attention. As Otto stood stiffly, he noted that the field marshal was very serious. Did Rommel's demeanor validate the rumors that were floating around—that the job at hand would be difficult, perhaps impossible?

"Gentlemen," Rommel said. "Please be seated." The field marshal shuffled some cards and placed them on the podium.

He waited a moment before beginning, looking over his audience. Finally, he began.

"Members of the Wehrmacht, it is up to us to fortify the continent against invasion by the so-called Allies. Our prospects are not bright. As you know, Germany has sustained huge losses in men and equipment on the Eastern Front. This means that we will have to defend the Western Front with fewer troops then we would like. Some are not fully trained. Others are not combat-hardened. So we must build a wall that is physically impenetrable. We will have to lay millions of mines, install huge numbers of obstacles, and build bunkers and dig tunnels on a scale that has never been attempted before. But if we do not destroy the Allies on the beaches, all could be lost."

The field marshal frowned.

"My position," he continued in halting fashion, "has been that we should have enough armored divisions close to the beaches so that we can make an immediate counterattack. However, Field Marshal von Rundstedt has overruled me. He insists that our Panzer divisions be concentrated further inland, waiting to stop our enemies once their line of advance can be determined."

The field marshal paused to take a drink of water.

"Are there any questions? Please identify yourself when you stand."

Otto stood up.

"Yes," Rommel said, nodding at Otto.

"Sir, I'm Major Otto Bruner. Do we know the approximate date of the invasion, and do we have any information to help pinpoint its location?"

"Good questions," Rommel replied. "I think the landing will begin at the Pas de Calais, perhaps as early as May, so we don't have much time. The Pas de Calais is best for them, since it is the shortest route from Great Britain to the Continent. However, the attack may come at some other point since we have our Fifteenth Army at Calais. Therefore, we have to be prepared all along the coast."

Others stood up, but Rommel appeared deep in thought.

"Let me add something," he said. "We know that Patton is in England, putting together an Army group, and that Bradley, whom newspapers say will lead the ground invasion for the Americans, is building another Army group in a different part of England. We also think the first invasion may be a fake and that a second, even larger, invasion is a possibility. Thus, we have to maintain constant vigilance."

Rommel nodded for the next question at a major with a patch over one eye.

"Sir, I am Major Dirk Fischer. I served with you in North Africa."

Rommel smiled. "I remember you," he said.

Fischer continued. "My experience there convinces me that you are correct, and that we should have most of our tanks at the beaches. How can Field Marshal von Rundstedt possibly believe otherwise?"

"Because he has not seen what we have seen," Rommel replied. "His only command experience came when our Air Force controlled the skies. Now that Allied airpower is in control, it is a dramatically different situation. We can no longer expect our Panzers to move around at will. They will be harassed every inch of the way by Allied aircraft."

Murmurs arose from the audience. Those who were standing sat down. *If ever there was a need for a pep talk,* Otto thought, *now was the time.* Apparently, the field marshal agreed.

"Gentlemen, I certainly don't mean to discourage you. Even though you will have fewer troops than you want, and many of them will be inexperienced, I assure you that they will fight fanatically when the time comes. And some of your troops are among the best, brightest, and most capable fighting men anywhere. You must do your very best. If you do, I am sure we will be successful, and our beloved fatherland will survive all of the challenges that it now faces."

The field marshal took one last look around. "That is all," he said. The audience stood, and the field marshal departed the chambers.

Otto looked forward to one last night in Paris, but first he had to go back to his office and thoroughly read his orders. After all, he couldn't afford to start a new assignment on the wrong foot.

Back at his office, Otto pulled his orders out of the middle drawer. Carefully reading them, he found that he would be going to a small village on the French Normandy Coast named Colleville-sur-Mer. He looked it up on a map. The village was about 170 miles west of Paris.

He could think of much worse places to be assigned and felt a sense of relief. He was to be a battalion commander for coastal defenses.

His new boss was Colonel Heinrich Dietz, whom he had met—and not been overly impressed with—at a recent social function. Dietz had obtained his rank by being a member of the old aristocracy and serving in World War I. Otto figured that picking Dietz for a job as important as coastal defense meant that Germany was indeed hard up for manpower.

After taking care of some action items, Otto left to enjoy his last night in Paris. The one-eyed major, Dirk Fischer, was right down the hall. Otto had nodded to Fischer on several occasions but had never introduced himself. *Now is as a good time as any*, Otto thought. Fischer might want to go out on the town with him.

Otto knocked on Fischer's half-open door. The major looked up and motioned for Otto to come in.

"Hi. I'm Otto Bruner. We'll be working on the Wall together." The two shook hands.

"Yes," Fischer replied. "I remember you from today's meeting with the field marshal. What can I do for you?"

"I was wondering if you would like to go out on the town tonight. Perhaps to a good dinner and then to the opera."

Fischer thought for a minute. "You know, that sounds good to me. Tomorrow I leave for my new assignment, so who knows when I will have a night off again?"

"It's the same with me," Otto replied. "Can we meet at La Parisienne at 1830?"

"I'll be there."

Otto arrived at the restaurant at 1815. *No need to wait until the last minute*, he thought. Looking around, he saw people mainly in German uniforms at the tables. Earlier that day he had seen Parisians gathering hickory nuts and leaves from the streets. The leaves, someone had told him, would be burned for heat. Evidently, shortages of just about everything were making it very difficult for the average resident.

At 1830, Major Dirk Fischer walked in. "Hi Dirk," Otto said. "I'll get the maitre d'." Otto motioned to a man in a tuxedo, and soon the two were seated at a very nice table.

"I hear the *coq au vin* is delicious," Fischer said.

"In that case," Otto replied, "I'll try it."

Soon, dinner was served, and neither man was disappointed. "Whatever else one thinks about the French," Fischer said, "one has to admit that they are culinary geniuses."

"I agree with that," Otto replied. Underneath, he was feeling somewhat guilty about eating so lavishly when the ordinary person was having a hard time. No use mentioning that to Fischer, though, as he would probably feel differently.

How did you acquire a taste for the opera?" Fischer asked.

"It was through my association with a Major Peter Schmidt in Norway," Otto replied.

"I've heard of him," Fischer said. "Wasn't he kind of a devil to work with?"

"You have that right," Otto responded. *Perhaps Fischer was a decent type. Anyone who didn't sing Schmidt's praises couldn't be all bad.*

After several glasses of wine, Otto no longer felt any guilt. Life was good in the German Army, as long as one was far from the Russian Front. He would get as much enjoyment as he could from this night, as he did not know what—if any– the amenities at Colleville-sur-Mer would be.

As Otto stood up to depart for the opera, he was unsteady on his feet. Noticing, Fischer quickly came to his aid. "Here," he said. "Let me help you." Otto liked his newfound friend better all the time.

Once at the opera it didn't take Otto long to sober up. *The music was beautiful and at the same time tragic, much like his own situation,* Otto thought. By the time it ended, Otto was depressed. Noting this change, Fischer suggested that they go to the Moulin Rouge or to Maxim's for a nightcap and some cheery entertainment.

"Which do you prefer?" Fischer asked.

"I'd prefer Maxim's," Otto replied, "because Maurice Chevalier is performing there. Is that okay with you?"

"It sure is. Let's go."

The two departed Maxim's after watching the show twice. They headed for their quarters.

"Maurice Chevalier was sure good, wasn't he?" Otto asked.

"Yes, he was," Fischer replied. "And the girls dancing in short skirts weren't bad either!" Otto laughed and nodded.

In the lobby of their hotel, they bade each other farewell.

"Well, comrade," Fischer said. "It has been a great evening. Thank you for inviting me out."

"It was my pleasure," Otto replied. "I wish you the best in your new assignment."

"And the same to you."

They shook hands and headed for their rooms. In a few scant hours, it would be time for Otto and Fischer to once again face the monumental challenges of the times.

The next morning, Otto had more than a slight hangover as he reported for duty. Fortunately, he found that he would not be leaving for the coast until nightfall. Allied aircraft were patrolling the roads and shooting at anything that moved during daylight hours. This timetable suited Otto fine, as it would give him one last chance to look around the beautiful city of Paris.

At dusk, a staff car was waiting outside Bruner's building. The driver introduced himself as Sergeant Gerhard Schmidt. "I am to be your orderly," he said.

"Are you any relation to a Major Peter Schmidt who served in Norway?"

"No, sir."

"Good!"

As they drove to the coast, the only light they could see came from their own dimmed beams, cast downward on the cratered road. From time to time, Otto could make out, on either side of the road, the dark silhouettes of Tiger tanks. They had been carefully camouflaged so that they would not be seen from the air. *What an eerie scene*, Otto thought.

They arrived in Colleville-sur-Mer well before dawn. Bruner's quarters were spare but adequate. Bruner tried to get a couple hours' sleep, but he was too excited about beginning his new duties to drift off quickly. It seemed that that he'd only just closed his eyes when his orderly banged on his door to awaken him. He quickly shaved, showered, dressed, and stepped outside into the brisk early-morning air, where Schmidt was waiting with the car.

Schmidt drove Otto to the Officers' Mess. As Otto entered the building, he was met by the aroma of Bavarian sausages frying on a grill and, underneath that, an appetizing waft of fresh-baked strudel. After finishing a big breakfast and three cups of strong coffee, Otto was fully awake and ready to report to Colonel Dietz for his first day's duties.

"Your job is straightforward," Dietz told him. "You are responsible for a twenty-mile stretch of coastal defenses and also the bluffs of Pointe du Hoc, just a little south and west of here. We had some large guns on top of those bluffs, but we had to move them due to Allied bombing."

"Sir, where are the guns now?"

"They are hidden in some trees behind the bluffs."

"Shouldn't we try to reposition them on top of the bluffs? From there, wouldn't they be able to fire at any approaching ships?"

The colonel glared at Otto. Apparently, he didn't like anyone challenging his decisions and was trying to think of reasons why his approach was best.

"Bruner, you are new here. You should wait until you have at least inspected the defenses before you start throwing out hare-brained ideas. The bunkers at Pointe du Hoc are not strong enough to adequately protect those large guns. Reinforcing those bunkers would take an unreasonable amount of effort and distract us from the immediate need to improve our defenses on the beach. You are dismissed, Bruner."

The colonel returned his attention to the paperwork on his desk, neglecting to respond to Bruner's parting salute.

This chewing-out, on top of very little sleep the night before, left Otto bewildered. He did have to admit that the colonel could be right. As the colonel said, he really should wait until he had a better grasp of the situation before he started giving input. He would not make that mistake again.

Sergeant Schmidt drove Otto to his headquarters, located in the center of a series of bunkers connected to each other by concrete tunnels. Bruner was impressed by the entire complex. From his vantage point, he could look down on a long stretch of beach. From up here, machine guns and mortars could sweep the beach with deadly crossfire. If the attacking force was not too large and more impediments and mines were placed on the beach and in the water, he just might be able to repel the invaders.

As Otto stepped into his office, a young-looking captain waiting inside snapped to attention.

"At ease, Captain. What is your name?"

"Ernst Peiper, sir, your second in command."

"How long have you been here?"

"About six weeks."

"Acting as Officer in Charge?"

"Yes, sir."

Otto shook his hand and said, "Tell me about the projects that are underway and the people in this unit I can really depend on."

Over the next hour, Captain Peiper gave a very thorough briefing. When the captain finished, Otto complimented him and asked, "Are you any relation to Lieutenant Colonel Joachim Peiper, the tank commander?"

"Yes, sir. He is my brother."

"You come from very good military stock!"

The two departed for a tour of the working sites. As they viewed the ongoing work, Otto was alarmed at how many of the workers looked emaciated. He asked Captain Peiper about their food rations.

"Sir, these are mainly prisoners, so no one has worried about their diet very much."

"That is not only immoral, but it prevents us from accomplishing as much as we could. Your primary duty as of now is to find more food for our workers. Immediately! Go!"

"Yes, sir!" The captain took off at an enthusiastic clip, which pleased Otto.

The days turned into weeks, and the weeks into months. Otto was satisfied as work continued on the defenses: more mines emplaced, more barricades installed in the water and all along the sandy beaches, new bunkers built, and older ones reinforced with more concrete. The question that worried Bruner: How much is enough? It was a question that could only be answered correctly in hindsight.

Bruner hoped that Field Marshal Rommel would soon make an inspection. Rommel, he respected; Dietz, he didn't. Dietz, in Otto's opinion, was incapable of grasping the magnitude of the potential danger. Other than making the required reports and attending the mandatory meetings, Otto avoided contact with the colonel.

One morning in mid-May, as Otto was pouring over schematics and diagrams, Rommel came by his office.

"Let's go take a look," Rommel said. After several hours of careful inspection, the general was satisfied, "Bruner, you have done an excellent job. I am proud of you."

"Thank you, sir. I only wish I knew how much it would take to be sure we throw any invaders back into the sea."

"We will never have enough to be sure of success," Rommel said. "With what you have had to work with, you have done amazingly well."

Rommel made a few suggestions and then departed to inspect other sections of the Atlantic Wall further west along the coast. *The first inspection*, Otto thought, *had been a success.*

As the sun descended over the Atlantic, the beauty and peacefulness of what lay before him struck Otto. What a pity, he thought, if this scene were to erupt into a firestorm in which the two sides frantically fought for their very survival. *If this firestorm did occur*, Otto wondered, *whose side would God be on?* He desperately hoped that it would be his, but he was certainly not sure. He had witnessed too many excesses committed by German troops as they went forward. Otto decided that the only thing to do was to drop to his knees and pray. He prayed with a passion that he had never felt before.

33

Surprise Meeting

THE DATE WAS June 1, 1944, and Otto Bruner and Ernst Peiper continued placing land mines, obstacles, and barbed wire along their section of the Normandy coast.

"Is it enough?" Ernst asked.

"Probably not if the Allies decide to come here," Otto replied. "But don't say that to our troops. We have to remain very positive."

"Yes, sir."

Too many miles to protect, Otto thought. All the way from the German-Dutch border in the north to the Italian border in the south. That was one problem. Another was that the limited manpower available wasn't being deployed in accordance with sound military doctrine. *Probably the result of the führer's meddling*. Otto would of course keep this thought to himself.

As they viewed the construction from their vantage point on the Atlantic Wall, Otto saw a man in a naval uniform approaching. There was something familiar about the way he walked. Could it be? Yes, it was! It was his brother, Klaus.

"Ernst! That's my brother, Klaus. Come meet him!"

The two hurried over to greet Otto's sibling. After the two brothers exchanged bear hugs, Otto introduced Klaus to his second in command. "Sir, I'm very happy to meet you," Ernst said. "Major Bruner has told me a great deal about you."

"Well, I hope at least some of it was good."

"It was all good, but I better get back to work and let you two talk." Ernst saluted and went back to overlooking the construction efforts.

"Otto, is there somewhere we can go to talk in private?"

"Yes. My office is empty right now. Let's go there."

The two trudged up the hill. Once inside the building, Otto unlocked the door to his office and pushed it open. The two walked in, and Otto motioned for Klaus to have a seat. "Coffee?" he asked.

"Yes. Black," Klaus replied.

"When did you give up sugar in your coffee?" Otto asked with a puzzled look.

"During those long nights of being the watch officer on a submarine. I was getting too much sugar in my system." Otto nodded.

Klaus looked around the small, sparsely furnished office. "I would expect you to have more luxurious accommodations. After all, you're a Wehrmacht major now."

"I could have them if I wanted them," Otto replied. "But I certainly don't need them, and I don't want to take labor away from the job at hand. Colonel Dietz, however, views everything differently and lives in the lap of luxury."

"Who's he?" Klaus asked.

"He's my boss," Otto replied in a whisper. "And about as worthless as they come."

Klaus laughed. "There are a few of those in the Navy."

Otto finished making the coffee and poured two cups. He walked over to the table where his brother was seated and set the cups down.

Pulling up a chair, he studied his brother for a few moments. *Certainly thinner and more drawn than I remembered,* Otto thought. After taking a sip, he said, "Okay, big brother, what is it you wanted to talk to me about in private?"

Rather sheepishly, Klaus said, "First, I want to apologize for being an ass the last time I saw you. I was way off base."

"You have nothing to apologize for. You were simply being loyal to the cause you believed in. If anyone should apologize, it should be me. I got Mama upset as well as you."

"I appreciate your generosity," Klaus said in a subdued fashion.

"But surely," Otto said inquisitively, "You have more on your mind than just that."

"You're right," Klaus replied. After a pause, he continued in a hushed tone. "For the first time, I am admitting to myself that the war is going badly for our submarine fleet."

Otto was shocked. While he knew the Army had severe problems, he thought the Navy was holding its own.

"How can that be?" he blustered. "From what I read, our submarines just sank a number of Allied vessels off the coast of England. I also read that the Allies try to bomb our submarine pens, but they haven't done any damage at all."

"All true, but the ships we sank are nothing compared to the buildup of Allied ships. I tell you that they are assembling the mightiest armada the world has ever seen. Right off the coast of Britain! And we have nothing near capable of stopping them."

"But what about our U-boats?" Otto moaned. "Aren't they free to come and go as they please from their invincible pens?"

"There are hardly any U-boats left. The Allies have placed radar on picket ships that are all over. When our subs surface at night to recharge batteries, ships and planes from all around converge. I would bet that three out of four submariners that I started out with are now dead."

I told him the last time I saw him that the Allies weren't dumb, Otto thought. But he saw no need to rub it in.

"How are things along the Atlantic Wall?" Klaus asked, wanting to change the subject. "Is it as impregnable as Hitler would have us believe?"

"If the armada we will face is as great as you say, I'm skeptical. A point in our favor is that General Rommel himself is in charge of coastal defenses, but how much can one man do? In any event, Rommel says that we will have to defeat them on the beaches. Otherwise, all will be lost."

Klaus nodded somberly. "I can believe that," he said.

Otto looked around to make sure no one was in earshot. "Have you wondered why Germany doesn't try and negotiate an armistice?" he asked. "After all, with things as bad as they seem, that would appear to be the right thing to do."

"I know the führer would never consider that," Klaus replied. "And the Allies might not agree to anything less than unconditional surrender. But we better quit talking like this. Otherwise, we could find ourselves swinging from a rope."

"You're right," Otto said. "What do you hear from the family?"

"Mama wrote that they are well but that they are practically living in air raid shelters. And food and staples are getting harder to come by."

"She wrote me the same thing, which reminds me…while you are here, where should we try to meet if things don't go well?"

"You mean if we lose the war?" Klaus asked in a whisper. Otto nodded.

Thinking for a moment, Klaus said, "Well, I hate to admit it, but you're right. We have to think of the safety of our parents and sisters and do some planning."

As they sat thinking about it, Otto mused that there wasn't much planning that could be done. If Germany lost, the continent would be in chaos. All they could do would be to try and reach the rest of the family. He said as much to Klaus, who agreed.

"We've settled that," Otto stated. "Now, big brother, what does the Navy have in store for you?"

"I'm finally getting my own vessel."

"A submarine?"

"Yes."

"That's wonderful," Otto said as he gave his brother a congratulatory hug.

"Yes," Klaus groaned. "Just in time to take a crew to the bottom of the ocean!"

"Maybe not," Otto replied. "Anyway, it's lunchtime, so let's get some food and celebrate. And you will get to meet my hero, Colonel Dietz."

The two brothers laughed and headed off. "Any chance Field Marshal Rommel will come by today?" Klaus asked.

I'm afraid you're out of luck," Otto replied. "Bad weather is predicted, so the Allies aren't expected to attack for the next few days." Otto puffed as they walked up the steep incline.

"So, let me guess," Klaus said. "The field marshal is taking advantage of the situation by going home."

"Yes. It's his wife's birthday."

"Well," Klaus sighed, "I hope the weather forecasters are right."

"You and me, both," Otto replied.

Would the two brothers see each other after this day? They could only hope so.

34

The Calm before the Storm

EVERYONE IN LONDON awaited the Allied invasion of northern Europe. Nobody knew exactly when it would be, but there was no doubt that it would be soon. Great Britain was about to sink under the weight of all the Allied troops and equipment that had arrived. It was the greatest military buildup the world had ever seen.

By May of 1944, Jennifer was getting antsy. What role would she play? She welcomed being told to report to Major General Albert C. Kenner, Chief Medical Officer for the Supreme Headquarters Allied Expeditionary Forces, or SHAEF.

Jennifer waited in General Kenner's outer office. Soon, General Kenner's orderly announced that the general was ready to see her. As she entered the general's office, he walked over to meet her.

"Captain Haraldsson, it's a real pleasure meeting you," General Kenner said. I have heard many outstanding things about you. Please have a seat."

"Thank you, sir."

"Let me get right to the point, Captain. Shortly after the invasion, you will be sent, as chief nurse, to one of our field hospitals in France. You will supervise twenty-four nurses, and you will report to Major

Brad Taylor, the head surgeon. I can't tell you exactly when the invasion will be. All I can say is that once a beachhead is established and we are there to stay, you will be on your way."

He handed her a sheet of paper. "That's Major Taylor's address here in London. Meet with him as soon as possible. Do you have any questions?"

"No, sir." She had too many questions to pick just one.

Wow, Jennifer thought, *twenty-four nurses under my command. It's a big honor and a big responsibility.* She thanked the general, saluted, and departed.

When she returned to her office, there was a note from 'Colonel' Francis Dunbar. *Promoted to full colonel. Fantastic! He must have some exciting things to tell me.* The note read:

Just returned to London. Would love to see you. If you can, please meet me at the Brown Hotel for dinner tonight at 1800.

What a break, she thought. *Now I have someone to celebrate my good news with, and I can catch up on what's been happening with him.*

As her cab pulled up to the entrance of the Brown Hotel, she saw a tall, lanky figure in a British Army uniform standing out front. No doubt about it. It was the colonel. She quickly paid the driver and got out.

"Colonel, it's so good to see you!" she said. "How long has it been?"

"Too long, I'm afraid," the colonel replied. After a friendly embrace, the two entered the hotel and went to the dining room. The maitre d' took them to a table, where the colonel pulled out a chair for Jennifer.

"Congratulations on your promotion," Jennifer said. "You're a colonel now! And you've selected a really nice place for dinner so you must have some very good news to tell me."

"I do, but first I want to hear all about you."

"Well, I've finally gotten a command of my own. I will be head nurse at a field hospital after the continent is invaded."

"That's wonderful news!" Dunbar said. "I have no doubt you will do splendidly."

"Thank you," she replied. "How long—*Oops!* I shouldn't ask that."

"It's okay, because I don't know. But I hope it's soon. If it isn't, I fear that England will sink to the bottom of the ocean, with all the humanity and material that has collected here." Jennifer smiled and nodded.

"Now," she said. "Where all have you been and what are you up to?"

"After North Africa," Dunbar replied, "I went into Sicily with Montgomery."

"Oh," Jennifer said. "I've read in the papers about the 'disagreements' between Montgomery and Patton. Off the record, who do you think was right?"

"This is strictly off the record, mind you, but I do believe Patton was given a bum deal. He was supposed to serve in a support role to Montgomery, guarding Monty's flank. And Patton was denied use of roads, meaning he had to inch his way over the mountains."

"So you don't think he was wrong for making an end run by way of Palermo?"

"No, I don't. And I doubt that Monty would either if Patton hadn't beaten him to Messina."

"By the way, Jennifer," Dunbar continued, "I'm impressed by your interest in tactics."

"Thank you, sir," Jennifer replied. "But now that Sicily is liberated and an invasion of Northern Europe appears eminent, what will you be doing?"

"Well, I've been given a regiment, and I think that I will be working night and day to get the seven hundred lads properly trained."

"That's wonderful! I'm very happy for you."

Soon, they ordered their meals, and Jennifer's thoughts strayed back to earlier times.

"I was just wondering. Whatever happened to the hydroelectric facility in Norway and the Germans' heavy water production?"

"A lot, and I guess I can tell you now," Dunbar replied. "The Allies started making serious raids back in mid-'42. The earliest was a glider operation—the first of the war, I might add—and a complete disaster. After that, the U.S. started bombing the area quite heavily.

The bombing, coupled with commando raids, forced the Nazis to move their accumulated heavy water supply to Germany. As they were moving it across a lake, the ferry carrying it was bombed, so the Germans lost most of it."

"Did the Germans quit trying to produce heavy water?" Jennifer asked.

"No," Dunbar responded. "They moved the electrolytic cells from Norway to Germany and tried to develop an alternative heavy water plant inside their country. But American bombers destroyed the plant. So now, as far as I know, they have given up."

"That's a relief," Jennifer sighed.

As the evening progressed, Dunbar noticed that Jennifer was drinking more heavily than usual. "Is anything wrong?" he asked. "You're throwing those highballs down at a pretty good clip."

Slightly embarrassed, she pushed her drink glass away.

"No, not really. Well, I did receive a letter this week from Jacob, Dude's brother. Jacob informed me that he has met the love of his life. I don't know why this bothers me, but it does. I suppose it's because Jacob reminds me so much of Dude that I'm jealous of this new woman. It's like losing Dude all over again. I know it's silly; Jacob and I were never involved that way."

"Letting go of memories and people is never easy," Dunbar said sadly. Jennifer suddenly realized that the conversation had reminded him of his own lost wife and son.

They gazed quietly at each other before Jennifer chuckled and said, "We should start a mutual admiration society."

"I agree wholeheartedly!"

They clinked their glasses and toasted each other's health. Dunbar paid the bill, and, as they prepared to depart, Jennifer noticed that the colonel had a slight limp. *Probably the result of shrapnel at Dieppe*, she thought.

"Is your limp due to your wounds at Dieppe?"

"Yes. It really isn't that bad, though. It's just that my leg gets stiff and achy after I've been sitting for a while." *That can't be pleasant,* Jennifer thought. She gave the colonel a sympathetic nod.

"Can I give you a lift to your quarters?" Dunbar asked.

"No, thank you. I can easily get a cab."

"I insist. My car is right around the corner."

"Well, if you put it that way." The two headed for the colonel's car.

At her quarters, Jennifer got out of the car, and the two reconfirmed their desire to stay in close touch.

Early the next morning, Jennifer went to see Major Brad Taylor. He was seated at a desk in a small office with no windows and very little furniture. Besides his desk setting, there was only a small filing cabinet and one chair. *Couldn't hold a very big meeting in here,* she concluded.

After completing her quick gaze, Jennifer knocked on the open door, and the major looked up. "You must be my new head nurse," he said with a smile.

"Yes, I am," she replied. Brad walked over and they shook hands. He motioned for her to have a seat.

The major was tall and thin with dark brown hair. He appeared to be in his early thirties and had the mannerisms of a professional. "We can dispense with formalities," he said. "You can call me Brad, and I will call you Jennifer."

"That's fine with me."

Looking around the office, Jennifer saw a picture of a woman and two children on his desk.

"Is that your family, Brad?"

"Yes."

"You have a beautiful family."

"Thank you very much."

Brad walked to a map of France that was hanging on the wall. With a sweep of his hand along the French coast, he turned the conversation to the business at hand.

"We don't know where the invasion will occur. The shortest distance would be here." He pointed to the Pas de Calais, perhaps a distance of fifteen miles across the English Channel. "However," he continued, "the Germans are anticipating that the invasion will be here. They have stationed a whole Army—the Fifteenth, I believe—in this area."

"So where do you think it will be?"

"God only knows. But from our standpoint, the casualties are expected to be large—perhaps as high as 20 percent—so we will have our work cut out for us. We will probably be short on space and supplies. Most definitely, we will be short on sleep."

Jennifer was impressed with Brad's apparent grasp of the situation that would be confronting them when they got to France. He asked if Jennifer had met any of her nurses. She said she had not.

"Some of them served with me in Sicily, and I found them to be capable and dedicated. I suggest that you appoint Molly Davis as your second in command. She is very reliable. The decision, of course, is entirely yours."

"Brad, if I may be candid, I'm surprised that I've been chosen to be your head nurse, since some of the other nurses have already served with you."

Brad thought for a moment before responding.

"As you probably know, people at very high levels have been quite impressed by you. I was told that you would be my head nurse. I thought of fighting it, but then I decided that you deserved a chance. Now seeing you in person, I'm glad that I made that decision."

"Thank you. I will try and live up to your expectations."

Brad said that they should meet at 9:00 a.m. the next day and Jennifer should have her gear with her. They would be transferring to Portsmouth, where the nurses and doctors of their field hospital were stationed. That location would be their jumping-off place for the continent.

"One last point, Jennifer, is that you shouldn't judge Molly by first impressions. She comes across as fun-loving and a free spirit. In reality, she is just the opposite. She outworks just about everybody and is as dependable as anyone that I have ever met."

Jennifer smiled and asked, "Are you trying to warn me that Molly is a character?"

"I guess I am."

They both laughed, and Jennifer said that Molly sounded like the ideal type of person for a field hospital.

"I'm really looking forward to meeting her."

"You will meet her very shortly, and I think the two of you will make a great team."

Later that day, as she was packing, Jennifer called Dunbar to tell him that she would be transferring, with Brad Taylor, to Portsmouth to join the rest of the hospital staff and prepare to move to France.

"My regiment is now based in the Portsmouth area," Dunbar said. "I only come into London to meet with the brass, so we can have dinner in Portsmouth, too, as often as you'd like."

"Wonderful! I'm sure you'll know just the right places for us to go."

Jennifer arrived early the next morning at Major Taylor's office with her duffel bag and briefcase. They rode to Portsmouth in an old bus that was showing significant wear and tear. The sides were scratched and dented, the tires were almost bald, and Jennifer thought she noticed steam coming out of the radiator. She was glad when the trip was finally over.

First Lieutenant Molly Davis was at the Portsmouth depot to meet them. She had flaming red hair slightly in disarray and a mischievous grin. When Brad pointed her out, Jennifer was highly amused. Based on Brad's description, Jennifer thought she could have picked Molly out anywhere.

"She looks almost exactly the way I had her pictured."

"That is because you were reading between the lines!"

Both of them had to suppress chuckles, as Molly had spotted them and was making her way over.

"Hi Brad," Molly said. She shook hands with Jennifer. "I suppose you're my other fearless leader."

"It's a pleasure meeting you, Molly. I've heard wonderful things about you."

"Well, you shouldn't believe all of what he's told you."

Molly had come in a staff car and drove them to their quarters.

"I'll give you two forty-five minutes to settle in," she said. "Then I expect you to be out front waiting for me. We'll be late for the start of happy hour as it is." Brad and Jennifer nodded.

"By the way, Jennifer," Molly said after a pause. "The other doctors and nurses are anxious to meet you."

I'm glad to hear that," Jennifer replied.

The captain and major were quartered in adjoining buildings. Molly stopped in front and helped them get their bags. After everything was out, Molly saluted, got back in the car, and sped away.

"And that was Hurricane Molly," Brad said.

"I'm not sure," Jennifer replied, "whether I'll be giving her orders or she'll be giving them to me!" The two laughed.

"I often wonder the same thing," Brad said momentarily.

They went to their rooms, dropped their bags, and freshened up. Well before the allotted time was up, they were both outside again.

"I was afraid that if I were even one minute late, Molly wouldn't wait," Jennifer said.

"Me, too," Brad admitted.

As soon as Molly screeched to a stop in front of them, they jumped into the car. Before they were even securely seated, Molly hit the gas pedal, and away they went. After recovering, Jennifer and Brad exchanged amused glances. Jennifer was discovering that riding with Molly was a true adventure.

It was a comfort to set foot on solid ground when they arrived at the Officers' Club. Jennifer and Brad watched as Molly drove off to park the car.

"I don't know about you," Jennifer said. "But I'm ready for a drink."

"Yes," Brad replied. "That's at the top of my priority list, also."

"Should we wait for Molly?" Jennifer asked. "Or go on in?"

"Let's go on in. Molly won't have any trouble finding us."

As soon as they entered the lounge, other staff members of the field hospital began coming over to say hello to Brad and to meet Jennifer. All of the doctors and nurses seemed very pleasant to Jennifer. She was sure she'd enjoy working with them.

By eight o'clock, the club was really rocking. A band was playing the latest swing tunes, and the liquor was flowing freely. Jennifer had danced with several of the doctors and was laughing with several of her nurses when someone tugged on her arm. It was Molly.

"Let's find a quiet place to talk," Molly said.

"Sure. What about?"

Molly led her to a table in a far corner and told a waiter to bring them each another drink. Molly was very serious although slightly tipsy.

"I'll level with you," she said. "I wanted your job. I feel I deserve it. I know for a fact that Brad does too. Since I don't have it, however, I intend to do everything I can to support you and to keep you out of trouble."

"I appreciate that."

"Just shut up and listen. I saw it all in Sicily. Taking care of the wounded is only part of the problem you will have to deal with. Some men will threaten you if you don't take care of their buddy first. You may have a goddamn Patton come in and slap a soldier he believes doesn't belong there. You will become attached to a soldier and feel terrible when you can't save him. You will have to cope with all of this and more. I know it's difficult to do the right thing at all times, but I will be there to help you. It will be up to you to let me."

Jennifer looked at Molly in stunned silence. Then she reached over and hugged her tightly. Here was a new friend for life!

The next day, on the morning of June 1, everyone got down to business. There were inventories to be checked, shifts to be assigned, and plans to be made. All the while, Molly stayed at Jennifer's side, agreeing to take on anything asked of her. *I will have to tell Brad just how good she is,* Jennifer thought.

The next two days flew by. Excitement reached a crescendo, as there was no doubt that the invasion was imminent. The biggest armada the world had ever seen was anchored off the British coast, and planes droned overhead continuously. On visits to the center of Portsmouth, it appeared to Jennifer that there were more Americans than Brits presently occupying this small island nation.

On June 3, Jennifer got a call from Dunbar. "Are you free for dinner tonight?" he asked.

"I certainly am, and I would be delighted to join you."

"Good. I'll have a staff car pick you up at 1800. See you then."

Jennifer was waiting outside when Colonel Dunbar's driver pulled up. Quickly, the driver got out, saluted Jennifer, and opened a rear door for her. Jennifer returned his salute and thanked him.

Dunbar's regimental headquarters was a tent. As Jennifer walked toward it from the staff car, she noticed more armed guards than she had expected. Just before entering she caught a familiar whiff of cigar smoke. Odd. Dunbar wasn't a cigar smoker. But whose was it? She entered the tent and immediately recognized the famous profile. "Mr. Prime Minister," she squealed. "I'm so happy you're here! I wasn't sure we'd meet again."

"If that is the case, my dear, you don't know me very well!" he exclaimed as he hugged her.

"Instead of going to a restaurant, I thought you might enjoy dining here with us," Dunbar said to Jennifer. "This establishment does have a certain rough ambience." He gestured at the canvas walls and offered her a camp stool at the makeshift table.

As soon as she sat down, a parade of regimental mess men brought in bowls of steaming food. There were lamb shanks, roasted potatoes, boiled turnips—and two bottles of champagne that Churchill had brought along, which were cooling in buckets of ice.

The prime minister winked at Jennifer and said, "My dear, I predict that one of these days we will be addressing this man as Sir Francis Dunbar!" Jennifer turned to Dunbar and said, "Colonel, I'm very proud of you." Dunbar thanked them both for their kind words.

As they ate, Jennifer told them about her new job and the new people in her life. Dunbar reported that his "lads" were coming along nicely in preparation for a "tour" of the continent.

For once, Jennifer thought, the prime minister seemed willing to let others do most of the talking. Perhaps it was due to the burdens arising from the upcoming invasion. Finally, Churchill chimed in.

"I was so hoping that President Roosevelt would be coming over to be with me at the time of the invasion," he said. "But the president is in ill health. He's unable to make the trip."

Alarmed, Jennifer said, "I hope it isn't anything serious."

"No. As I understand it, the president is battling some bronchitis. I don't believe it is anything to worry about."

"I hope, Mr. Prime Minister, that you're guarding your own health," Jennifer said, "given the pressure you must be under now."

"Oh, I take good care of myself," Churchill replied. He took a sip of champagne and relit his cigar. "All I can do now, you see, is sit back and wait for the invasion to begin."

"Will it be soon?"

"Mustn't be impatient, my dear."

35

A Herculean Struggle

A T 5:00 A.M. on June 6, 1944, a siren blast pulled Otto Bruner out of a deep sleep. He wasn't groggy for long, as the first barrage of explosions jolted him wide awake. "Must be the beginning of Rommel's Longest Day," he muttered. *Bet I don't find any sleepy sentries when I get there,* he mused.

Bruner dressed quickly and headed for an observation post. When he got there and looked out to sea, he gasped. Allied ships stretched for miles. He had never seen anything like it.

He began to bark orders, relayed by his non-commissioned officers, as troops rushed to their positions along the forward walls. Was Field Marshal Rommel correct? Would the war be won or lost right here at the beach? He hoped the question would be nullified by the German Army repelling the invaders before they established a foothold.

A phone next to Otto started ringing. It was Colonel Dietz.

"Bruner, I am moving my command post inland," Dietz said. "You are in command here. I will be out of contact for some time. If you need anything in the interim, call Division Headquarters."

"Very well, sir."

So, the rats are abandoning the sinking ship. Otto was not surprised; he had half expected it of Dietz anyway. But he couldn't worry about Dietz now. He saw waves of landing craft heading for the beach. Soon the fronts of these ships would open, and enemy troops would be running ashore.

Bruner grabbed a machine gun from a rack and raced to an open position along the Wall, yelling encouragement to his men. Zero hour was now at hand. As the first of the landing craft hit the sand, ramps at their bows dropped down to disgorge streams of enemy soldiers.

Bruner and his men fired furiously, mowing down the advancing enemy. *The intruders were brave,* Otto thought, *very brave.* Hitler's propaganda had portrayed Allied soldiers as soft and weak, but these men were nothing of the sort. They were as courageous as any that Otto had ever seen.

Scanning the Wall, Otto noted that his men were holding all along the line. The murderous machine gun and mortar fire seemed to plunge the Allies into disarray. So far, the Allies were unable to make any coordinated push to reach the base of the Wall. *If this condition held,* Otto thought, *the day would be saved.*

Lifting his gaze from the carnage on the beach, Bruner saw Allied destroyers steaming toward the beach. *What were they doing? Didn't they realize that they would soon run aground in shallow water? Maybe their captains had been ordered to risk everything if necessary.*

Otto was getting a sinking feeling in the pit of his stomach. Those warship guns could wreak havoc with his bunkers and the very integrity of the Atlantic Wall if they got close enough. The warships kept on coming. Some were now close enough to fire at the German positions at almost point-blank range. Cursing under his breath, Otto lamented that the German big guns were not in firing position on Pointe du Hoc! The six 155- millimeter weapons could have done extensive damage to the Allies. But would Dietz listen to him? No! Even Rommel's off-handed comment that the Allies wouldn't attempt to scale the cliffs hadn't swayed Dietz.

As Otto scanned the Wall with his binoculars, something in the direction of Pointe du Hoc caught his eye. Ladders were being fired upward. The Allies were attempting the impossible! They were going to try to scale the cliffs. *The fools,* Bruner thought, as the first soldiers trying to climb the ladders were shot off of them by German soldiers at the top. Who knew, though? The Allies might eventually be successful. Perhaps even Pointe du Hoc wouldn't be a safe haven, but Otto couldn't dwell on that. He had problems of a more pressing nature.

Hours passed, and the German line held. But the enemy kept coming, inch by inch and foot by foot. On the beach, Allied soldiers were organizing themselves into groups. Bruner watched their officers directing them with hand motions, as the groups coalesced and began to take on tasks beyond sheer survival. The warships poured in even more covering fire as the allied soldiers tried to breach the Wall.

What are they doing now? Otto wondered. They were hauling a long tube forward. Suddenly it dawned on him. They're going to put a torpedo through the base of the wall! "Sergeant," Otto shouted. "Don't let them bring that tube forward!" The sergeant nodded, barking orders to a nearby machine gun crew.

Several attempts to bring the tube forward were repulsed. But, finally, the Allies succeeded. With an enormous explosion, the Wall ruptured in a narrow slit, and the Allies began moving forward.

Frantically, Otto ran to a nearby message center and telephoned Division headquarters.

"This is Major Otto Bruner at the Front, and I need to talk to your commanding general. It is urgent!"

"This is General Graetzer. What do you want?"

"Sir, the enemy has breached the Atlantic Wall at Colleville-sur-Mer. We need tanks up here immediately."

"Impossible, Major. There is no one here who can authorize release of the Panzers. You will have to make do with what you have."

"Look, General, I don't care if you have to call Hitler himself. Just tell him to get off of his fat rear end and get me those tanks! *I need them now!*"

"How dare you, Major! I will have you strung up by your thumbs for insubordination!"

"That is fine by me, General, but you'd better do it quickly. Otherwise, the Allies will do it for you!"

Otto slammed down the phone and ran back to monitor the Wall, where Allied and German soldiers were now engaged in chaotic hand-to-hand combat. Bruner realized that what was left of his regiment would have to fall back to a new defensive position to the east.

Quickly Otto rounded up Captain Peiper and sketched out a rear-guard action on a piece of paper. At the point of the breach, they would allow the Allies to move inward to a point at which the Germans could establish a new defensive line. They would then slowly retreat at other points along the wall to keep the Allies contained. He hoped the German Army could counterattack when the tanks became available and throw the Allies into the sea. In the meantime they must depend on rear-guard action to keep the Allies in check. Otherwise, everything would be lost.

"Major, I volunteer to lead the rear-guard action."

"I appreciate that, Ernst, but my goose is cooked in the German Army. There is a general that wants my hide. My only option is to remain here and fight. You'll have to lead the retreat."

Ernst nodded sadly that he understood, and Otto named the units that would be held for rearguard action. The two shook hands, and Ernst moved out to head up the retreat.

Otto wished that they had been able to practice what to do in the event that retreat became necessary. However, Colonel Dietz would not hear of such negative thinking. The colonel would simply say "Oh, no!" anytime Otto suggested that they set up the appropriate procedures. *Where was Colonel Dietz now that retreat had become a necessity?* Probably hiding in some hole farther inland!

Otto and his compatriots fought desperately, giving ground ever so slowly. Otto hoped they were giving enough time for Ernst and the main body to escape. Even if they weren't, there was nothing they could do about it. Their ranks were down to a very few.

Suddenly Otto felt a sharp pain in his left shoulder. He struggled to continue fighting but found that it was a lost cause. He slumped to the ground, dropping his machine gun in the process. He was now totally at the mercy of the oncoming enemy. Would they treat him humanely, or would they let him die? The answer would soon come, as an American corpsman was approaching. The medic dropped to one knee beside him.

"Major, I am going to try to stop your bleeding. Do you understand?"

Otto nodded. He could barely get out a word of thanks only partly due to the wound. He was moved by the kindness being afforded him. If he lived, he told himself, he would spend the rest of his life being kind and generous to others. What wonderful things kindness and generosity were!

The corpsman jabbed Bruner with a needle to pump morphine into him. Soon, Otto found himself about to doze off. He wasn't sure he would ever regain consciousness if he passed out. It would be up to God and the American medical staff.

36

A Meeting to Remember

EARLY JULY 1944 was a difficult period for the Allies. Britain's Field Marshal Montgomery had failed to take Caen, and the Americans had failed to break out of the Cotentin Peninsula. But there was no doubt that the Allies were on the continent to stay. For this reason, medical units with nurses attached began arriving in France. Jennifer's unit was among them.

When they landed on Omaha Beach, Jennifer, Brad, Molly, and the others were shocked at its chaotic appearance. Evidence of the bloody fighting was everywhere. The beach was strewn with all sorts of debris, which men were combing through to find any much-needed material that could be moved inland.

Moving off the beach, the nurses and doctors arrived at a temporary hospital consisting of tents that had been set up not far from the front lines. Here an exhausted staff of doctors and corpsmen were continuing to attend to the wounded.

"Am I glad to see you beautiful people!" Lieutenant Colonel John Harris, the head surgeon, told his replacements. "Casualties have been heavy, and we have worked almost around the clock since D-Day. I don't expect the situation to get better."

271

"Incidentally," he continued, "we do have some German wounded." He pointed to a tent off by itself, surrounded by guards. "The highest-ranking German is a Major Otto Bruner. He's been in a coma since arriving. He may not make it."

After relaying more details about the wounded, Colonel Harris and his exhausted staff packed up and headed back to the beach. Soon the new crew was working at full speed, and it was as if the transition had never taken place, except that some of the conscious Americans began flirting with the nurses.

It was twenty-four hours before Jennifer or any of the others finally managed to get some rest. In the nurses' quarters, Jennifer and Molly collapsed onto adjacent cots. They talked briefly about the day's events and upcoming priorities.

"Jennifer," Molly said, "I know how you feel about the Germans. They killed your fiancé. But we do have to see about them soon."

"I know. Let's talk about it in the morning."

They slept for four hours and then went for chow.

As they finished, Jennifer looked at her companion. "Okay, we'll check on the Germans first." Molly nodded.

The first patient that Jennifer saw was the still-unconscious Otto Bruner. Out of uniform he could have been a typical young college fraternity man, she thought. Could she stand to touch someone she thought of as her mortal enemy? She would have to try.

With some hesitance she reached down and felt his forehead. He felt rather hot. She would get him some antibiotics. She checked his intravenous tube, and it seemed to be okay.

As Jennifer made notes on Otto's condition, she realized that there was something about him that haunted her. His profile looked vaguely familiar, something to do with his nose and chin. Had she seen him sometime in the past? Probably not, but she would try and find out who he was and where he came from.

Even more oddly, Jennifer felt a strange sensation. Was it Dude trying to communicate with her from the hereafter? What could he want? Did he want her nursing the enemy, or did he want her to stay completely away from those he considered responsible for his premature death?

Get over it, she told herself. It was probably nothing more than her imagination spinning out of control. After all, she had never been a big believer in psychic phenomena. Still...

Suddenly Molly was at her side, and Jennifer saw a mischievous little gleam in Molly's eye. *Uh-oh! What would be coming now?*

"Gee, I saw you actually touch a German soldier!" Molly said. "Are you okay? Did some Nazism rub off on you? Will you have to go to sick call?"

Jennifer laughed. "Contact wasn't so bad. Thank you."

"Thank you? For what?" Molly asked.

"For bringing me back to reality."

"If you say so," Molly said, shaking her head.

At a break, Jennifer went to see Lieutenant Leo Cardoni, the officer in charge of prisoner interrogation. "What can I do for you?" Cardoni queried.

"I was wondering if you know anything about our comatose prisoner, Major Bruner." Jennifer replied.

"Let's see. He has the Iron Cross, so I know he's brave. Oh! And I found out from one of the other prisoners that Bruner had been on the Russian Front. Other than that, I know nothing. But why do you ask?"

"I have this strange feeling that I've seen him before, but I don't know where. It bothers me."

"Spooky! I'll see if I can find anything else out about him. I'll let you know if I do."

Jennifer thanked Cardoni and returned to her station. The days and nights that followed were so busy that Jennifer didn't have much time to think about anything but caring for the sick and wounded. Each day, though, she would find a little time to sit by Bruner's side. He looked very peaceful. It almost seemed a shame to wake him. However, she had to try. Would holding his hand be enough stimulus to help him come around? It certainly couldn't hurt.

The first time she tried, she felt no response. But after several days she thought she could feel him attempting to grip her hand. She decided to continue with the daily hand-holding sessions.

After one especially frantic day of tending to other wounded, he moaned when she grasped his hand. Was he coming around? She tried talking to him.

"Hi, Otto. *Sprechen sie English*, Otto? Hello, Otto."

Otto opened his eyes. Looking at her, he said weakly, "I must have died and gone to heaven. I have an angel watching over me."

Jennifer smiled. "I guess you do speak English, and very well, too," she said. "Just rest and I'll get the doctor."

Late that night, after finishing her other duties, Jennifer went to the prisoner's ward and quietly approached Otto's bed. He had been gazing blankly at the ceiling, but when he saw her, he beamed. Obviously he'd been waiting for her.

"Hello, Otto. Would you like a little soup?"

"Yes, please."

Seated at Otto's side, Jennifer slowly began feeding him beef broth. After taking a couple of sips, Otto looked at Jennifer with a pained expression.

"What's wrong?"

"You are so kind to me, and our countries are at war. It makes me very sad."

"Don't think of anything but getting well. That's the only thing that counts."

"I will try to take your advice."

After a few more sips of soup, Otto fell asleep, and Jennifer left. Her day had been grueling—more of the Allied wounded had died—but her contact with Bruner made her think that he was out of danger. This success invigorated her.

With each passing day, Otto gained strength. Soon, with the aid of a cane, he was able to walk around. Although she was very busy with other duties, Jennifer looked forward to seeing him whenever she could. By now, it was obvious to almost everyone but Jennifer that their relationship was more than that of nurse and patient.

Pulling her aside, Molly said, "Jennifer, he is the enemy, you know. You better be careful. You're raising eyebrows around here. Some of the other nurses resent the attention you're giving him."

"How ridiculous! I'm simply carrying out my professional duties. Besides, what I do on my own time is my business. It isn't as if Otto is a threat to anyone."

"Okay, but don't say that I didn't warn you."

Molly started to walk away. Then she turned around and came back.

"I'm sorry. Here I've always been one to throw caution to the wind, and I'm telling you to be cautious. Forget everything I just said. I'll support you in whatever you decide to do."

"Thank you," Jennifer replied softly.

The more Jennifer talked to Otto, the closer she felt to him. They had a great deal in common. Both enjoyed skiing, the opera, and fine dining.

"Otto, were you disappointed to find that you had been captured?"

"No. I'm just glad to be alive. During the battle, I insulted my general, because he refused to send up tanks he was holding in reserve. If the general could have reached me, he would have hung me for insubordination."

"What did you say to him?"

"I told him to tell Hitler to get off his fat rear end and get those tanks over to me!"

Jennifer laughed. "Would a general dare say something like that to Hitler?"

"Absolutely not. They are all afraid of him, which is why we will lose this war."

I'm glad about that, but no use rubbing it in, Jennifer thought.

The next morning, Jennifer received a note from Lieutenant Cardosi telling her to come see him, as he had new information on Major Bruner. Hurriedly, she went to his office.

"Come in," he said, looking up. "One of the other prisoners recalled hearing Bruner say that he had been stationed in Norway."

"Oh my God!" Jennifer shrieked. "That's it! I was in Norway on a special mission. I lost the man I loved there."

"Did Bruner have anything to do with it?" Cardosi asked.

"I'm sure he did. I only saw him from a distance, but I know it was Otto."

Jennifer thanked Cardosi and left his office in a daze. She looked for Molly and found her attending an American patient in one of the hospital tents. Grabbing her by the arm, Jennifer said, "I need to talk to you. Let's go outside."

"What's up?" Molly asked. Jennifer, still holding her arm, pointed to some empty chairs where they could sit.

"I've just received a terrible shock. Cardosi told me that Otto had been stationed in Norway. Then I remembered. It was he and his men who were following us to the coast and pushing us into the trap that got Dude killed."

"What are you going to do?"

"I have to ask Brad for a transfer. I don't think I can ever stand to see Otto again."

"I'll hate to see you go," Molly said, "but I certainly understand how you feel."

That afternoon, as Brad was making his rounds, Jennifer approached him. "Brad, can I talk to you?"

"Sure," he replied. "Let's go to my office."

Jennifer related her experiences and said that she was requesting a transfer. Reluctantly, Brad picked up a field telephone and called the head surgeon at a nearby unit to arrange for her immediate reassignment.

"I'm really going to miss you," he said.

"I'll miss you, also."

The two hugged, and Jennifer went to pack. Back at her quarters, Jennifer found Molly sitting on her cot.

"Did Brad release you?" Jennifer nodded.

"What do you want me to do?"

"Tell Otto why I'm leaving," Jennifer replied.

"Okay. If that's what you want." Molly got up and started to walk out.

"Come here, you." Jennifer said.

She gave Molly a big hug and a kiss on the cheek and said softly, "You're the best."

Molly, for once, was speechless.

Jennifer finished packing, said her goodbyes, and headed for a staff car that Taylor had ordered. As she approached the staff car, she saw Otto standing outside his tent. Guards were stationed nearby, so he had obviously gotten permission to do so. He looked very sad, she thought, leaning on his cane.

"I'm terribly sorry," he shouted. "I wish I had died instead of him." Jennifer could only nod.

37

The Other Side of the Earth

IN 1943 AND 1944, through brilliant maneuvering, General MacArthur's forces moved up the coast of New Guinea to the northern tip with dramatic success. In accomplishing his objectives, MacArthur used Army, Navy, and Air Force units in a coordinated fashion never before achieved. The coordination allowed Air Force and Naval units to hold large concentrations of Japanese troops in check in order to outflank them. Army elements assigned to MacArthur could then storm key strategic positions without the worry of large groups of enemy reserves being brought in from surrounding areas. Employing Allied forces in this manner resulted in the minimization of Allied casualties.

Jacob and his former teacher—Tex Whittaker—were stationed in New Guinea to provide air support. Tex was squadron commander of a lead fighter squadron, the *Fighting Fifth*, and Jacob was his executive officer. Both were now air aces: Tex had shot down six Japanese Zekes, and Jacob had destroyed five. They were also best friends.

As they were standing at the squadron coffee bar one afternoon, they were notified to see the wing commander, Colonel Jeff Smalley.

"It must be important," Whittaker said to Jacob. "Smalley doesn't have impromptu meetings unless something big is up." Jacob nodded as they headed to the colonel's office.

"Come in." Smalley barked in response to the knock on his door. After returning salutes, the colonel told Whittaker and Jacob to have a seat.

"Gentlemen, I have some interesting—and what I think is good—news for you. Charles Lindbergh will be coming to fly with us. He has an idea on how to save fuel and to extend the range of our P-38s."

Looking impressed, Tex Whittaker replied, "This will be a real honor. I have always wanted to meet Lindbergh. He can get airplanes to do things that others can't."

"Larger range would be a real plus for us," Jacob said. "Right now, there are too many good targets just beyond our reach."

The Colonel smiled. "Gentleman, I know that I can depend on you two in what I believe will be a very important project. Lindbergh will be arriving this evening, and I want you to fly with him. Any questions?"

Jacob shook his head, but Whittaker had one. "Sir, will he be flying with us as a military officer or as a civilian?"

"He'll have civilian status. When he was doing some field testing for the United Aircraft Company in its F4F Corsair, he found a way to dramatically reduce fuel usage. So he's out here—as a civilian—to see if his theory will reduce fuel usage in our Lightnings. And I think it will work."

Jacob and Tex departed the Colonel's office.

"What's the matter?" Whittaker asked Jacob. "You don't look happy."

"I can't help but remember how Lindbergh said we shouldn't get in a war with Germany," Jacob replied. "He thought they were too powerful for us. That really tarnished his reputation with me."

"I'm sure Lindbergh realizes now that he made a big blunder," Tex said. "Don't let your grudge interfere with your performance."

"I won't."

Suddenly, Jacob looked shocked. "What if we run into enemy planes while Lindbergh is with us?" he asked.

Tex laughed. "I suspect he can take care of himself. Before this is over, we'll probably find out."

The next morning, Smalley introduced Tex and Jacob to Lindbergh, wildly famous as the first flier to cross the Atlantic Ocean solo. Lindbergh had an air of quiet competence about him and seemed genuinely happy to meet them.

Tex asked Lindbergh if it was okay if they called him Charles.

"Absolutely. You can even call me Lindy if you want."

"Agreed," Tex replied. "We'll call you Lindy."

Jacob, Tex, and Lindy walked to a revetment in which a P-38 was parked. Jacob noted that the plane was leaking hydraulic fluid. He'd tell the crew chief after the meeting, just to make sure the problem was fixed.

Lindbergh leaned against the plane. "When I was flight testing the F4F, I did some experimentation with manifold pressure and rpm," he said. "I found that I could improve range—reducing fuel usage in the process—by trading one for the other."

Jacob whistled softly. "Lindy, I don't think you will win any friends among crew chiefs with this idea. They'll say it will cause too much wear and tear on the engines."

"That is exactly what the Corsair crew chiefs thought. But I showed them they were wrong."

"Well, gentlemen," Tex said. "Let's give it a try. The three of us will go up this afternoon. We'll test the concept in an area where we won't be bothered by enemy planes."

Tex looked at Lindbergh. "What are your instructions?"

"They're quite simple," Lindy replied. "I'll tell you how to vary your settings as we proceed."

"Fair enough," Tex said. "If the test looks good, we'll try it in a combat mission. Lindy, if you want to go with us, we'll have to get permission. After all, you are a civilian."

The three laughed.

Soon, they were in the air. Using Lindbergh's method, the P-38s flew smoothly and without any problems.

After two weeks of flying in the way Lindbergh suggested, the engines were taken apart and inspected for any excessive damage or wear and tear. Much to the surprise of the crew chiefs, the engines showed nothing out of the ordinary.

By now, Tex and Jacob were convinced that Lindy had a brilliant concept. Stopping by Colonel Smalley's office after a mission, Tex didn't try to hide his enthusiasm.

"Sir, I think that Lindbergh's idea will reduce our fuel usage dramatically. We can probably increase our range by up to 900 miles."

"That is impressive! By the way, what kind of pilot is Lindbergh? Is he good enough to take into battle?"

"He certainly is. He can fly with the best of us."

"All right, then, take him on an actual mission. If his concept holds up in battle, we'll add it to our operating procedures."

The next morning, Tex and Jacob rounded up Lindbergh and one other pilot, Lieutenant Jack Miller. Jacob would be Tex's wing man, and Miller would be Lindbergh's. The mission would involve six planes from another squadron, and Whittaker was to be the mission commander.

As the pilots were about to begin their run to strafe an enemy air base, six Zeroes zoomed in from the horizon. In seconds, all-out aerial combat erupted, and it was every man for himself.

Jacob tried to stay at Tex's side, but it was impossible. Clouds enshrouded the battle area, and Jacob lost sight of all the other planes. As he broke through a cloud bank, he saw Lindbergh fire at a Japanese Zero. The enemy plane smoked as it went out of control. Soon the Zero was hurtling right at Lindbergh. Jacob depressed his radio transmitter button.

"Pull up, Lindy," he shouted. "Pull up!"

Fortunately, the Zero missed Lindbergh's plane—but not by more than ten feet.

After destroying the attackers or driving them off, the P-38s strafed the airfield and knocked out as many anti-aircraft batteries as possible before getting out of the way to let the arriving heavy bombers do their work. As the P-38s headed home, their pilots could look back and see the damage being done by the heavy bombers. Clouds of black smoke billowed up from an oil depot at one end of the air base. Fortunately, none of the P-38s were lost that day. And Lindbergh had suffered no harm.

After landing, Lindbergh went over to talk with Tex and Jacob. "That was most exciting," he said. "I wish I could go on more missions with you."

"I wish you could, too!" Whittaker replied.

"But I did what I came to do," Lindbergh said. "I showed you guys how to reduce your fuel usage in the P-38s. So now I'll go home and encourage people to buy victory bonds!"

38

The Return of the General

"JACOB, WAKE UP!" Lieutenant Sam McCall said as he roughly shook Partude awake. "MacArthur has landed the U.S. Sixth and Eighth Armies on Leyte Island. I heard it on the short wave radio."

"What day is it?" Jacob asked sleepily.

"October 20, 1944—all day long!"

Jacob sat up on his cot, now wide awake. "So the general kept his pledge to return to the Philippines."

"Yes," McCall replied. "His speech from Leyte was on the radio. He kept saying 'I' instead of 'we.' No wonder a lot of guys don't like him. He takes the glory while they do the grunt work."

"True," Jacob said. "But what they don't realize is that his casualties are a lot lower than Eisenhower's. The guy has smarts."

"I grant you that," McCall replied as he hurried off.

Jacob quickly shaved, showered, dressed, and departed his quarters to find his boss, Tex Whittaker. Hopefully, Tex would know what was in store for the "Fighting Fifth."

As he'd expected, Jacob found Tex sitting in the mess hall. Whittaker had finished breakfast and was reading the paper.

Jacob's first stop was the cafeteria line. He picked up a tray and pushed it along the rails. He was hungry as usual. He placed Wheaties, milk, a banana, sausage, hash browns, and chipped beef on toast—affectionately nicknamed "SOS"—on his tray. He added orange juice and coffee and then went to join Whittaker.

"Have a seat," Whittaker said, sliding a chair out from the table.

"Thanks, boss."

Whittaker lit a Chesterfield as Jacob sat down and dug in. "Not much of an appetite, I see," Whittaker said.

Jacob grinned.

"Let's see," Tex said. "I suppose you heard of the invasion and want to know what we'll be doing now."

Jacob nodded.

"It's going to be hurry up and wait for a while, I'm afraid. There's nothing much we can do from here. Biak Island is too far away from MacArthur's landing zone."

"So we'll just go on supporting the Navy's Marianas Campaign?"

"Yes, until MacArthur is successful in Leyte Gulf and we can build airstrips on Philippine soil."

"That's no fun," Jacob said. "Most of the Zeroes around here have been shot down. We need a new challenge."

"I know, but you'll have to be patient," Whittaker said as Jacob finished the last of the chipped beef. He poked Jacob on the arm. "I hope you won't starve before lunch."

Over the next several days, Jacob spent considerable time at his desk in squadron headquarters, reading status reports about the ongoing skirmishes in Leyte Gulf. The Japanese, it seemed, were throwing everything they had at the Allies. After reading one such account, Jacob hurried into Whittaker's office.

"Tex," Jacob said, "did you see where the Japanese duped Halsey into chasing a fake Japanese Armada? That leaves MacArthur with no air cover and very few naval ships to cover his rear. I'll bet he'll really want us up there now!"

"I don't know," Tex replied. "The sailors who are left at Leyte have fought magnificently. They're holding a much bigger enemy force at bay."

"That's true," Jacob groaned. "Maybe we'll spend the rest of the war on this desolate island."

Tex smiled. "Oh, I wouldn't go that far."

The next few weeks went by slowly. One cloudy afternoon, Tex and Jacob were called into Colonel Smalley's office.

"Please take a seat," Smalley said. "Gentlemen, MacArthur's main Philippine objective is the capture of Luzon, the island where the capital, Manila, is located. To support this objective, he needs air support, and lots of it." Whittaker looked at Jacob and winked.

Smalley went to a map and pointed to the island of Mindoro. "MacArthur," he said, "has selected Mindoro as the site for an advanced air base. He thinks this is close enough to Luzon to provide adequate support."

After lighting a cigarette, Smalley continued. "Mindoro has the potential to supply adequate airfields so that we can bring in a lot of P-38s. The planes will be needed to fend off the suicide planes—*kamikazes* as they are called—and any remaining naval vessels that the Japanese might throw at us. An added bonus is that our aircraft will be close enough to attack the Japanese that are entrenched on Luzon."

"Where do we fit in?" Whittaker asked.

"I'm just getting to that, Tex," Smalley replied. "General Kenney himself has selected you to head up the task of getting the airfields on Mindoro ready to use. You have carte blanche authority to decide where they should be located and to do whatever it takes to get them operational as soon as possible."

"That is a big honor, sir," Tex said.

"It may be, but it could also be hazardous to your career. Kenney isn't the most patient of people. He won't hesitate to relieve you if you aren't making adequate progress."

"I understand," Whittaker said. He pointed at Jacob. "I assume it's okay to take this guy with me."

"Absolutely," Smalley replied. "Turn your squadron over to Jack Miller if you think he can handle it. Otherwise, I'll put your squadron in with the Fourth."

"No doubt in my mind," Whittaker said. "Miller can handle it."

Jacob wasn't so sure, but he said nothing. He knew that the last thing Tex would do was to hand his men to another squadron commander.

The two saluted the wing commander and walked to the door. Whittaker stopped and turned around. "Colonel, you realize, don't you, that Mindoro is still in Japanese hands?"

"Certainly," Smalley said with a smile. "So General Kenney can't be accused of not planning ahead." Whittaker and Partude nodded as they departed.

As they worked over maps late into the night, Tex asked his deputy, "Where do you think we should locate the airfields?"

"Well, it would certainly be best to put them nearest Luzon, in the northeastern part of the island. The weather up there is bad a lot of the time, but if there are any Japanese bombers or fighters left on Luzon, we would be within easy striking distance."

Whittaker thought for a moment before responding. "I see your point. But with our new longer range, we could even locate in the southwest corner and still reach nearly all parts of Luzon."

"That's right," Jacob replied. "And there would be advantages to locating in the south. We would be close to Mangarin Bay, which is Mindoro's best anchorage. Resupply by boat would be a lot easier."

"What about the soil content?" Tex asked. "Is it adequate to support the airfields? We don't want another disaster like what happened on Leyte."

"I checked with the engineers on my way back from chow, and they don't foresee any problems."

"How sure are they?"

"Very sure. They were able to analyze soil samples that were smuggled out of Mindoro as well as other islands. The Mindoro samples come from various parts of the island, and they didn't find soil issues anywhere. "

"Okay!" Tex said. "The southwest corner it is. Let's make some charts and prepare to tell the colonel."

"I know that the Japanese still control Mindoro. But don't you think that we should sneak in to Mindoro and look the situation over before making the decision?" Jacob asked.

Tex pondered the question. "No, I don't think so. We have to trust the engineers. They know more about it than we do. So, since time is of the essence, we might as well make our decision now and be ready to start as soon as it is in our hands. "

"Can't argue with that," Jacob replied, shrugging his shoulders.

By 0300, they were finished with the briefing slides. They returned to their quarters to get a few hours of shuteye.

At 0800, they reported to Colonel Smalley's office. Whittaker briefed Smalley on the plan.

"I like it very much, Tex. It's clear enough that I will send it to Kenney. If he has any questions, he will contact you."

"Thank you, sir. Partude was a huge help on this project."

"I'm sure he was. Congratulations, Jacob."

"Thank you, sir."

The next day, word came down that Kenney had signed off on the plan.

Jacob waited impatiently for Lieutenant General Walter Krueger's Sixth Army to take Mindoro. Since they would be working with the engineers on construction of the airfields, he and Tex were temporarily taken off flying status and assigned to ground duties. Jacob didn't like being grounded, but he was glad to have input on the planning and building of the airfields. The sorry state of the airfields on Leyte was proof enough that pilots using the fields should have more of a say.

Krueger's forces invaded Mindoro on December 15, 1944. There was very little resistance, and soon the defenders were overwhelmed. By the end of the first day of the invasion, Army engineers, with Tex and Jacob looking over their shoulders, were hard at work building the airfields that would be used to support the invasion of Luzon. One airfield was ready in five days, and a second airfield was ready in thirteen days. Soon after, Colonel Smalley moved his entire wing to Mindoro.

The wing was now operational, and, though Jacob was eager to get back in the air, he wasn't feeling very well. Mindoro had numerous mountains and only a few narrow plains—along the coast—which could be used for the airstrips. The mountains induced daily rains, high humidity, mosquitoes, and malaria. Although quinine kept the disease under control, Jacob was feeling malaria's effects. He had a low-grade fever and constantly felt tired.

Despite his ailments, Jacob refused to be taken off flying status. After all, none of the pilots felt very well. He would tough it out, just like everyone else did.

Tex and Jacob shared a room on Mindoro. They lay in their bunks waiting for their first sortie.

"I think the rest of the war will be a piece of cake for us," Jacob said. "I don't see either of us getting shot down with what the Japanese have left."

To Jacob's surprise, Tex's response was stinging. "Thinking like that is what will get you killed! Overconfidence is the worst thing in the world for a fighter pilot. The unexpected is our worst enemy."

"Gee, boss. I didn't think of that. I apologize!"

"I didn't mean to be so sharp," Whittaker said. "But intelligence says the Japanese are still turning out about two thousand planes per month. And their pilots, though short on training, have shown that they're willing to die for the emperor."

On January 9, 1945, all pilots of Colonel Smalley's wing were told to report to the briefing room at 1400. Once they were assembled, Colonel Smalley came to the lectern.

"At ease, men. Today, General Krueger's Sixth Army landed 175,000 men on the Luzon beachhead. Initial resistance was light, as General Yamashita, commander of the Japanese troops in the Philippines, had moved his troops into the mountains. Yamashita took this precaution knowing that there would be no replacements or resupply coming in, since the Japanese navy transports are now essentially nonexistent. Yamashita's plan is to fight a war of attrition, holding out as long as possible in the mountains."

The colonel took a sip of water.

"While the initial ground resistance was minimal, Japanese kamikazes are a continual menace to the Navy ships in the area. They come night and day. By now, some of our fighters are equipped with radar and can patrol at night. Therefore, we will launch sorties around the clock. Our sole mission will be to intercept as many kamikazes as possible. Your assignments are listed on the bulletin board in base ops. I wish you good luck and good hunting. That's all." The men stood as the commander departed.

Jacob's squadron was detailed to daylight duty against the *divine wind* defenders. As deputy squadron commander, he called the squadron members together and briefed them on their upcoming mission, detailing the area that they would patrol.

Whittaker provided the pep talk.

"Men, I know that you think that these kamikaze pilots are fearless, that they won't be deterred from attacking their targets. However, you're wrong! They have feelings and families to think about just like everyone else. They want to prolong their lives as long as possible, even if it means just a few more minutes before they ram a ship. So I want to instill fear in them! I want you to be so bold that they start worrying about you rather than thinking about hitting one of our ships. I want them to be so busy trying to avoid us that they won't even be able to find their targets. Now go get 'em!"

Wow, Jacob thought, *what a great pep talk!*

On this mission, too, Jacob would be flying as Tex's wingman. However, if they did encounter only kamikazes, Jacob would break off and go after his own targets.

Once airborne, it didn't take the squadron long to reach Lingayen Gulf on the northwestern coast of Luzon. Krueger's Sixth Army soldiers had landed on the sheltered beaches along the gulf and were now moving inland. Looking down at the vast armada of U.S. ships anchored in the area, Jacob saw them as tempting targets for kamikazes.

And soon the unwanted company began to arrive from all different directions. Jacob saw that it would be difficult if not impossible for all of its attackers to be neutralized. Frantically, members of the squadron broke off and went after targets of opportunity.

Between their own shooting and that of the ship's gunners, few kamikazes were getting through. But Jacob knew even one was too many. In a momentary lull, Jacob looked around for Tex. He spotted him going after a plane at very low altitude. Tex's target broke into flames as Tex attempted to pull out of a very steep dive.

"Pull up! Pull up!" Jacob shouted into his radio.

Horrified, he watched his best friend's plane hit the water. Frantically, Jacob radioed *Mayday*, describing Tex's position in the water. Circling back, Jacob could see a small Navy boat heading for Tex's limp, floating body. He prayed with all his might that Tex would somehow be okay.

Since he was now in charge of the squadron, Jacob knew he had to pull himself together to lead effectively. Wiping tears from his cheeks, he cleared his throat and called the other P-38s to form up and head for home.

Colonel Smalley met them when they reached the Mindoro air strip. "Did he make it, sir?" Jacob asked.

"No, son, he didn't," the colonel said sadly. Smalley handed Jacob a set of major's oak leaves, patted him on the shoulder, and walked off.

Jacob had never known the grief that he was now feeling. Not even Dude's death had caused him so much pain. Becoming squadron commander was no consolation. The only way to get some relief was to write Sandy. She was the only one who could truly share his agony. He took out pen and paper.

39

Chance Meeting

JENNIFER WANTED TO get as far away from Otto Bruner and Normandy as she possibly could. Because the war in Europe was proceeding rapidly, anyone volunteering for the Pacific had a decent chance of going. She was no exception. She landed on Leyte Island in the Philippines on December 2, 1944.

Bad things happen in threes, she told herself. Hers were Dude's death, losing Jacob to Sandy without even knowing if she loved him, and starting to fall for Otto before learning that he was the scoundrel from Norway. If there was any justice, things should start going her way.

Wanting to make a break from the past, Jennifer did not write Jacob to tell him she was coming to the Pacific, although she intended to, eventually. For now, she just wanted a fresh start. If their paths crossed, fine; she would be glad to see him. Otherwise, she would let well enough alone.

Upon arriving at the nurses' quarters in hot, muggy Leyte, she found a note waiting. It was from Major Bill Thomas of Special Operations. The note was short: "Please see me at your earliest convenience." What could he want? It was her understanding that she would be assigned to nursing duties. Her orders even said so. She decided to first check in with the head nurse and then look up this fellow Thomas.

After unpacking and settling in, Jennifer went to the Quonset hut that housed the head nurse. She walked in and saw a middle-aged lady sitting at the second of two desks in the room. Both desks were piled high with papers.

Looking up, the lady said, "Hi, I'm Linda Thornton. May I help you?"

"Yes, I'm Jennifer Haraldsson, and I recognize your name. You're the head nurse, aren't you?"

"That's correct. And you're the new nurse that I need so desperately. However, since Bill Thomas wants to see you, I know better than to count my chickens before they're hatched. You'd better talk to him before I make any plans for you."

"How do I find him?"

"He's in the hut two down on the left." Pointing the way, Thornton said, "You can't miss him."

"I hope I'll be back soon," Jennifer said.

"Don't count on it," Thornton said. "Thomas can be a real thorn in the side. No pun intended."

Jennifer thanked her and left.

Following Thornton's instructions, Jennifer walked to the second hut. She pushed the door open and saw a dark-haired man in his early thirties sitting at a desk. The man was wiry and appeared to be in top physical condition. Looking up, he smiled and returned her salute.

"You must be Jennifer."

"You must be Bill. It's all right if I call you Bill, isn't it?"

"Certainly."

Thomas stood, shook her hand, and motioned for her to have a seat.

"How was your trip over?" he asked.

"Long and tiring," Jennifer replied. "And I feel that I lost touch with what was happening. Can you give me a quick update?"

Thomas shrugged. "Outside of this theater, I can only give you generalities. But from what I read, the war in Europe is going pretty well. Germany's air force has been destroyed, and the Allies are making good progress across France and Belgium."

"Then you think the war is over?"

Thomas shook his head. "I didn't say that. The Germans will fight savagely as we cross into Germany. And who knows what they have in the way of new and terrible weapons? Those rockets that they're firing at London are nothing to be sneered at."

"You're right," Jennifer said. "But I've taken enough of your time getting caught up. What can I do for you?"

"I've been reviewing your record, and it's very impressive—Norway, Dieppe, Normandy. I think you're just what I'm looking for."

"And what is that?"

"I'm looking for a nurse who doesn't hesitate to volunteer for dangerous missions."

"I don't know, Major. I may have had my fill of volunteering."

"I understand how you could get burned out, but this mission may be of special interest to you."

"How so?"

"Do the names Jean Simpson and Ellie Goldberg mean anything to you?"

"Sure. They're two of the nurses that were captured on Bataan."

"Would you like to be in on their rescue?"

Thinking for a moment, Jennifer smiled and replied, "You knew I couldn't refuse this mission, didn't you?"

"Guilty as charged," Thomas said. "And since you've so graciously accepted, let me first give you the standard rhetoric. You can't talk to anyone about this mission who isn't part of it. If you do, you'll be declared a naughty girl, and very bad things will happen to you. Understood?"

"Yes, sir."

"Good. Now let's get down to business."

Thomas went to a map of the Philippines and pointed to the main island of Luzon. "The nurses, along with some others, are being held prisoner at Santo Tomas Internment Camp in Manila. We will rescue them with a small, mobile force using tactics that would make Jeb Stuart proud."

"The Confederate general?" Jennifer asked.

"One and the same," Thomas replied. "The success of our mission will depend on secrecy, coordination, and physical conditioning. As for conditioning, I'm encouraging the men to get in the best condition of their lives. I want them to bench press 50 pounds more than they could previously, and I want them to run farther and faster than ever before."

"Can I participate in the physical conditioning program?"

"Yes, and I encourage you to do so." He paused as he looked her over. "On second thought, though, I don't want you showing me up!" Both laughed.

"I can't promise, Major. I'm very competitive."

"I'll bet you are."

"Seriously, though, what is the condition of the nurses in the prison camp, or do we know?" Jennifer asked.

"Based on the spotty data we've received, they're generally in better shape than you might think. However, we know that some of the internees will have to be brought out on stretchers. That's one reason I asked for you."

Thomas hesitated. "I know that nurses here are in short supply, but since you haven't started work yet, you won't be missed that much. At least I hope not."

"I hope you're right," Jennifer replied. "When do I learn about the mission specifics?"

"If you're up to it," Thomas said, "I can go over them right now." Jennifer nodded.

"Our nickname is the Flying Wedge. We'll be moving rapidly, and we'll have tanks so that we can crash through the gates once we get there. My orders from MacArthur himself are to go around the enemy, bounce off the enemy, blow past the enemy—but do whatever it takes to get to Manila quickly."

"Can I ride in a tank?" Jennifer asked. "I want to be up front."

He gave her a steady look. "Sure, if you want to," he said.

"Well, those are the highlights," Thomas said in conclusion. "I'll brief you on the camp layout when I brief the others. Anything you want to ask now?"

"Nothing that I can think of, Major. But I do want to thank you for this opportunity."

Thomas smiled. "Let's walk over to the training area. I'll hook you up with Staff Sergeant Sam Kilpatrick. He's the commander and driver of tank 605, the one you'll be riding in."

As they approached the training site, the profile of a Sherman tank loomed directly ahead. *What a monster*, Jennifer thought. The treaded vehicle had a huge gun pointing out the front of the turret and a machine gun mounted on top.

"I'd sure hate to have that thing coming at me," Jennifer said, somewhat in awe.

"I can't argue with that," Thomas replied.

Reaching the tank, Jennifer knocked on the hull. "Ouch," she yelped. "This thing feels like it's made out of solid iron!"

"It is."

Kilpatrick was stretched out under the tank, both feet kicking in the air. The sergeant cursed as he struggled to loosen something.

"Careful, Sam," Thomas cautioned with a grin. "There's a lady present."

Kilpatrick wheeled out from under the tank, wiping his hands with a greasy rag.

"Sergeant Sam Kilpatrick," Thomas said with an introductory flair. "I'd like you to meet Captain Jennifer Haraldsson. She's a nurse, and she'll be riding with you into Santo Tomas."

Kilpatrick's mouth hung open as he stood up. *He's obviously at a loss for words*, Jennifer mused. She seized the opportunity to right the situation.

"Don't worry, Sergeant," she said. "I know that you're the tank commander, and I'll follow your direction to the letter." All Kilpatrick could do was nod.

"By the way," Jennifer added as she stuck out her hand. "I don't mind a little grease."

Finally, Kilpatrick relaxed. "Major," he said. "I think the captain and I will get along just fine!" He heartily shook Jennifer's hand.

"Would you like to sit in Old Betsy?" the sergeant asked.

"Sure," Jennifer replied. "What do I do?"

"You can go in through that hatch," Kilpatrick said as he pointed to the one on the left near the front of the tank. "Or you can go in through the turret."

"What do you normally do?"

"I usually go in through that one." He nodded at the hatch on the right.

"That's good enough for me," Jennifer replied. She walked over to the tank, hoisted herself up, and scooted over to the hatch. From a sitting position, she twirled around and dropped her legs through the opening. Luckily, she was wearing slacks. She lowered herself easily into the hatch until she got to her mid-section.

"Obviously," she groaned. "These weren't made for people with broad hips." But through athleticism, twisting, and determination, she made it. Both men were relieved.

Peering through the hatch, Thomas asked, "Are you comfy?"

"Well," she replied with a sigh, "it could be worse." She peered around at the dials and gauges that littered the front panel.

"Sergeant, just let me know what I can do to help as we go in."

Winking at the major, Kilpatrick said, "I thought I would have you fire the machine gun."

"Fine with me," Jennifer replied.

Kilpatrick was surprised by the casualness of her answer. He turned serious and gave a half-hearted shrug. "Who knows? Maybe I will."

Thomas smiled. "I think you could make a worse decision."

In the following weeks, Jennifer threw herself into the mission. She learned the Santo Tomas camp layout by heart, and her physical fitness improved significantly as she went through the strenuous exercises with other members of the raiding party. She was also a huge help to Major Thomas in planning for the medical supplies that should be brought with them.

The days dragged on. Jennifer began to wonder whether the mission would really take place, and she finally confronted Thomas. "What's the holdup?" she asked with more than a tinge of frustration in her voice.

"I'm as irritated about it as you are," Thomas replied. "All I can tell you is that General Eichelberger hasn't reached some necessary objectives as quickly as hoped. But I can guarantee this: The mission will proceed, and sooner rather than later."

"I'm sorry, Bill," Jennifer said. "I know you have enough worries without me adding to them."

"You have nothing to apologize for," Thomas replied. "I'm just happy to know you're eager and ready."

No sooner had he said that than the radio operator came running up. "Sir, I have an urgent message for you."

Thomas tore the envelope open and scanned the contents. Smiling, he said, "This is it. We leave tonight."

The next few hours were filled with frantic activity. As they prepared to depart, Major Thomas climbed up on a tank and addressed his warriors.

"You are embarking on a mission of the greatest importance. You will be rescuing people who have endured suffering beyond what we thought was humanly possible. Remember this date: February 3, 1945. It is a day that should never—and will never—be forgotten. It is the day that the heroes of Bataan are finally freed, and, in turn, it is the day that you will earn your honored place in history. Go forth, now, and let nothing stop you from achieving total success."

A huge cheer erupted, and the members of the raid party dashed to their assigned vehicles. The convoy formed up and headed out.

The night of February 3 was pitch-black. Jennifer sat in tank 605 next to Kilpatrick. The tank was stopped a fair distance from Santo Tomas so that those on foot could quietly move up and get in place. Jennifer yearned for the order to attack.

They waited for what seemed like an eternity. "Sam, how do you do it?" Jennifer asked as she squirmed in her seat.

"Do what?" he replied.

"Sit in these contraptions for hours!"

Kilpatrick grinned. "Captain, this 'contraption' is going to keep us nice and safe. I bet by the time this night is over, you'll have come to appreciate Old Betsy as much as I do."

"I guess you're right," Jennifer said with a sigh.

Suddenly, the command "Go! Go! Go!" came screaming through their headsets. Kilpatrick turned on his lights and gunned the tank. Jennifer felt a shudder as the tank lunged forward.

Soon the iron gate of the prison camp appeared directly ahead of them. Jennifer heard a crunching, grinding noise as the tank flattened the obstacle. They were now inside the compound and getting their bearings.

Kilpatrick stopped at the first building. He threw open his hatch, stood in plain view, and waved at faces peering out from the building's barred windows. "Hello, folks," he said.

His Midwestern twang sent the prisoners wild. Screaming and shouting, they poured out the door. Climbing out of the tank, Jennifer ran to embrace them. Some of those liberated sobbed, and someone started singing "God Bless America."

As more of them came out of the building, they picked up their liberators and carried them on their shoulders, shouting and crying. It was a miracle, Jennifer thought, that these sick, emaciated people were able to muster enough combined strength to respond in this fashion.

Better go inside, Jennifer thought, *and help the needy*. She entered the first building and inched past people trying to exit. Soon, she spotted her friend Jean Simpson. "Jean, it's me, Jennifer!" Shrieking, the two hugged.

Stepping back, Jean said, "You look so big."

"I'm about the same size, but you're a lot smaller," Jennifer replied. Jean nodded sadly.

"Where can I be of most use?" Jennifer asked.

"Just follow me," Jean said. They walked down the hall, and Jean gave Jennifer a rundown on the conditions of the others still inside. They entered a room in which the occupants were barely clinging to life.

"Haven't the Japanese provided medical assistance?" Jennifer inquired.

"Not much," Jean replied. "If it weren't for the Red Cross packages that were finally coming in, I doubt if any of us would still be here. So, what do you want me to do to help?" Jean asked.

"We have to prepare these people as best we can to be evacuated," Jennifer said. "Where are the other nurses?"

"Scattered about. Would you like me to get them?"

"Are there immobile people in other areas?"

"Yes," Jean replied.

"In that case, I'd prefer that you have the nurses disperse and get all of the people who can't move themselves ready to leave."

"Will do," Jean replied. Jennifer marveled at the stamina that Jean showed.

As Jennifer worked on the patients, she was aware of fighting still continuing in parts of the camp. Taking a break near dawn, she walked outside. Descending the steps, she saw a familiar figure leaning against the wall and smoking a cigarette. It was Sergeant Kilpatrick. As she approached, he dropped the cigarette, came to attention, and saluted.

She returned his salute. "I didn't mean to interrupt your cigarette," she said. "But why are the Japanese still here?"

"We came through the gates so fast that they didn't have a chance to leave," the sergeant replied. Now they've decided to fight to the death. They're holed up in three fortified emplacements and fighting ferociously." The sergeant pointed to the three locations.

"Do you think the camp internees can be evacuated while the fighting continues?" Jennifer asked.

"Oh, sure," Kilpatrick replied. "The Japanese are well-enough contained that they won't be a problem. And if I were to bet on it, I would say that the Japanese won't last another hour."

The sergeant was right on both counts. The shooting stopped, and soon afterward, amtracs arrived. The nurses from Bataan and the other internees were loaded and evacuated. They were finally free after almost three years in captivity.

Jennifer remained in the Philippines as the fight for Manila progressed. On July 5, 1945, the last of the Japanese resistance in the Philippine capital succumbed, and MacArthur declared the Philippines entirely liberated. However, Jennifer couldn't go home just yet, as the Allies were preparing for a massive attack on the Japanese mainland. Luckily, the attack never took place. In early August 1945, two American B-29s, the *Enola Gay* and the *Bockscar*, dropped atomic bombs on Hiroshima and Nagasaki. On August 14, 1945, Japan surrendered, and the terrible war ended.

40

Joy, Sorrow, and Hope

O N October 10, 1945, Jennifer waited anxiously under the clock at the St. Francis Hotel in San Francisco.

At precisely five o'clock, a tall, thin gentleman in civilian clothes entered the front of the hotel. It was Colonel Dunbar. Jennifer ran over to hug him.

"Colonel, it's so good to see you! How are you?"

"I'm fine, but please call me Frank."

"Of course, Colonel!"

"By the way, the prime minister—former prime minister, that is— sends his regards. He thinks the world of you."

"I feel the same way about him. How is he doing?"

"Not too good, I'm afraid. He seems rather lost now that he doesn't have a war to run. The fact that he was pushed out of office doesn't help matters either."

"People are so ungrateful! After all that Mr. Churchill did for them, you'd think that they'd keep him in office forever."

The colonel nodded. As the two waited for the others to arrive, they brought each other up to speed on what had happened in their lives.

"In Normandy," Jennifer said, "we had a number of German patients to care for. One of them was an Otto Bruner. He was the officer who led the squad that chased us a good distance in Norway! Small world, isn't it?"

"Well, I'll be! Did you wring his neck?"

"No, but I wanted to. Instead, I transferred to the Pacific, so I'd be as far away from him as possible."

"Actually, Bruner wasn't such a bad chap, I suppose. He did give us time to bury the professor." Jennifer nodded.

"That reminds me," Dunbar added. "I thought you'd be interested, so I researched the couple that Professor Flannigan had stayed with in Vemork, Norway. Does the name Jungstad ring a bell with you?"

"It sure does," Jennifer replied. "The professor talked about them often."

"Well," Dunbar proceeded, "they were placed in a prison camp after the SS found that they had housed Flannigan. But they survived the war. Now they're back home."

"I write Mrs. Flannigan often, and I'll be sure and tell her. As I recall, the professor said that his wife knew the Jungstads, too."

She looks sad, Dunbar thought. *Better try and control the damage.*

"I'm afraid I reminded you of Dude," he said. "I shouldn't have mentioned the Jungstads."

"Nonsense!" Jennifer said. "I'm very happy to know they're alive. Now I want to hear all about you!"

"Well, after Normandy, I participated in the biggest fiasco of the European Theater. It was called Operation Market Garden. Have you heard of it?"

"No," Jennifer replied.

Dunbar continued, "It was Monty's—Field Marshall Bernard Montgomery's—brain child. Or should I say pipe dream? We dropped troops well behind enemy lines at Antwerp, Belgium. They were to hold a bridge for forty-eight hours until we broke through and relieved them. In theory, it was a good idea. In practice, it didn't work. The Germans were much stronger there than Intelligence predicted, and we lost a lot of fine men."

"Unfortunately, there was a lot of that during the war," Jennifer said.

"Yes, I suppose so," Dunbar replied. "And I think it was perhaps more so in Europe than it was in the Pacific, at least with MacArthur. From what I've heard and read, MacArthur was a genius at using the Army, Navy, and Air Force in coordinated fashion to minimize his losses."

Jennifer nodded. "I never understood why the enlisted men called him Dugout Doug. I don't think they ever realized how fortunate they were to have him looking out for them."

"Probably not," Dunbar mused. "But old reputations are hard to shake. The fact that his B-17s were destroyed on the ground at Clark Field a full day after Pearl Harbor is inexcusable. And don't forget, his men on Bataan weren't defeated by the Japanese. They were defeated because they ran out of food, ammunition, and medical supplies. Then, when he was rescued and they went on the death march—oh, well, I won't go into that."

"Frank," Jennifer said, "you know more American history than most Americans!"

Dunbar laughed. "You're right. I have a real affection for you people."

Jennifer looked at her watch. "Since the others are late," she said, "I'll buy you a drink at that bar over there. We can carry them back here so we won't miss anyone."

"Great idea," Dunbar replied. "But I'll buy the next round." Jennifer nodded.

They walked to a staircase and up the half dozen stairs to a mahogany paneled bar. Jennifer ordered a red cabernet wine for herself and a scotch for Dunbar.

"Did you know that Admirals King and Nimitz met at this hotel all through the war to plot strategy in the Pacific?" Jennifer asked.

"No, I sure didn't."

"A nice lady who permanently rents a suite on the top floor loaned it to them for their use."

"I can't think of a nicer place than this," Dunbar said as he looked around.

As they walked back to the famous clock, Jennifer could tell that there was something that the colonel wanted to say to her.

"Okay, Frank," she said. "Let's have it. What aren't you telling me?"

"Well, I *have* met someone."

Without waiting to hear more, Jennifer threw her arms around him, spilling some of her wine on the floor.

"That is absolutely wonderful! I'm so happy for you! Tell me all about her."

"She reminds me a great deal of you, actually. She's a nurse whom I met in a field hospital in France. Her name is Ann, and she is very compassionate and caring. We found that we had a lot in common, and it wasn't long before we were in love. The rest, as they say, is history."

"Have you set a date?"

"Yes, we have. February 4, and you are on the guest list. I have told Ann so much about you that she wants you to be a bridesmaid!"

"I am honored to accept. I wouldn't miss your wedding for the world!"

"Great!" Dunbar replied.

"Well, that's enough about me," he said. "How about you? Any romantic interests on the horizon?"

"No. I guess I'll end up an old maid."

"Rubbish! The right man is out there, and I'm confident you'll find him."

Feeling a poke on her shoulder, Jennifer turned around to see Molly beaming up at her. With shrieks of joy, the two embraced. When Jennifer introduced Dunbar to Molly, he put out his hand, but she pushed it aside.

"Give me a hug, big guy," she said. "I'm not much for formalities."

The three laughed and the evening was off to a great start. Dunbar was still in the military, but Jennifer and Molly had been discharged. Looking at Molly, Jennifer asked, "How are you finding civilian life?"

"Rather dull, to be honest."

Dunbar interrupted. "Where are you working and what are you doing?"

"Oh, I'm sorry, Frank," Jennifer said. "I should have brought you up to speed."

"Now, Jennifer," Molly interjected. "I'm perfectly capable of telling him what I'm doing."

"You're absolutely right," Jennifer replied, somewhat embarrassed. "Please continue."

"Well, Frank, I'm working in a small hospital in southeast Kansas. Do you know where Kansas is?"

"Center of the country, isn't it?"

"Yes! Give that man a cigar!" Molly responded. "And to be truthful, I find that most of the time the pace is excruciatingly slow. I miss the excitement and camaraderie of military life."

"I do, too," Jennifer said. "And unfortunately, I'm not sure what I want to do."

Jennifer noticed that Molly had that familiar mischievous look on her face. "Okay, what is it?" she asked.

"I know what's holding you back," Molly retorted. "You still have feelings for Otto! Incidentally, the last time I saw him, he said to thank you for everything that you did for him."

Jennifer was stunned. "Feelings for him?" she replied defensively. "I never, ever think of him!" But she felt herself blushing.

"Are you talking about that German fellow?" Dunbar asked Molly.

"That's the one."

Suddenly, Jennifer's feet were off the ground, and she was swinging in the air. She felt two muscular forearms holding her tightly. She looked around. Sure enough, it was Jacob.

"Jacob! It's so good to see you. How have you been?"

"I'm fine," he replied as he put her down. "But I'm mad at you for not contacting me when you were in the Philippines."

"I'm sorry about that."

Jacob, still in uniform, looked much more mature than Jennifer remembered, and he had a chestful of ribbons. Turning to the young lady with him, Jennifer said, "You must be Sandy." Smiling, Sandy nodded, and the two hugged.

Introductions were made, and Jacob said that he was famished. "When do we eat?" he groaned. Jennifer assured him that it would be soon.

They went out onto Powell Street and caught a trolley for a ride through San Francisco's cool evening air to Fisherman's Wharf. They would eat dinner there.

They got off at the end of Powell street. The wharf was full of people. As they walked along, venders were steaming crab, shrimp, and other delicacies from the sea.

"Shall we go into Fisherman's Grotto #9?" Jennifer asked. "It's a wonderful place, and it's only a short walk straight ahead."

"We're with you," Jacob said. "Lead on."

They walked down the pier and into a building. After walking up a flight of stairs, they were at the famed Grotto. The maitre d' came over. "How many?" he asked.

"Five," Jennifer replied. "And could you put us at a window table, please?" The maitre d' nodded.

Jennifer arranged the seating: Dunbar, herself, Sandy, Jacob, and Molly. She thought it seemed to be a comfortable arrangement.

A waiter came over and took the drink orders: red wine for the ladies and scotch for the men. He returned shortly with the libations. "Well," he said smiling. "Not much of a problem to know which goes where."

"I propose a toast," Dunbar said. "To the King and to the president of the United States."

"Hear! Hear!" the others said as they rose. "I also propose a toast to Dude, the professor, and Lars."

Jennifer tried not to cry, but her attempt was futile. It didn't matter, though, as the others were just as shaken.

Soon Jacob stood up as well. "I have someone to toast. His name is Tex Whittaker. Every day I thank the good Lord that I knew him. God rest his soul." Sandy gently patted his arm.

Finally, Jennifer got up, too. "I want to toast all of those who gave their life for freedom."

"Hear! Hear!" was the universal emotional response.

The waiter returned for the dinner orders.

"What do you suggest?" Molly asked, turning to Jennifer.

"I suggest the Fisherman's Platter. You can't go wrong with it."

"Shall we all get it?" Dunbar asked. The response was unanimous.

Soon, they were eating shrimp, scallops, clams, crab, french fries, and cole slaw. Jennifer could tell that they were all enjoying the fare.

"It doesn't get any better than this," Molly said. There were some corroborating grunts.

Eventually, the conversation got around to what Sandy and Jacob intended for the future. "We're getting tugs from both families," Jacob said. "Sandy's wants us to go to Louisiana, while mine wants us to spend the rest of our lives on the farm. A slight smile came over Jacob's face. "Jennifer, you probably remember how Dude and I kidded about escaping from the farm and dumping it on poor Joseph.

"I certainly do," she chided. "I also remember saying that I was going to work with Joseph to show him how to stand up to you two."

Jacob started to respond, but Jennifer cut him off. "Are you sure you're getting out of the military?"

"Yes," Jacob said. "I don't have a choice. I'm getting the ax along with millions of others. When you see me after the next month or so, I will no longer be in uniform."

"That's too bad," Dunbar lamented. "It's the same way in Britain, though. The military is being cut way back, just like it was after the First World War. If countries such as the U.S. and Britain had stayed strong militarily, Hitler might not have wreaked the havoc that he did."

Molly clapped. "Well said, big guy."

"Thanks, Molly," Dunbar said. "But I'm curious. What do you plan to do, Jacob, given that you don't want to go back to the farm?"

"I would like to fly for an airline," Jacob said. "And Sandy wants to teach, at least until we start our family. Naturally, she will always want to fly, so we will join a flying club and maybe buy our own airplane. Right, Sandy?"

Sandy smiled and nodded. "If we can afford it."

Molly, with a devilish twinkle in her eye, turned to Dunbar. "Okay, big fellow, what will you be doing?"

Dunbar was both amused and somewhat taken aback by Molly's lack of protocol. He quickly recovered. "Well, I guess I will be the only one still stuck with the military. I am scheduled to report to the Defense Ministry in London next month."

"Wow, maybe the prime minister was right and we will be calling you Sir Francis Dunbar in the not-so-distant future," Jennifer teased.

"Oh, I doubt that. Those lofty titles will probably be reserved for someone like Monty."

"Okay, everyone," Molly said, obviously thinking that the time was right. "Let's take care of a problem that we have."

"Problem?" Jacob retorted. "What problem? All I see are people thoroughly enjoying themselves."

Pointing at Jennifer, Molly continued, "This good friend of ours found the perfect man, a German prisoner of war, while we were in France together. However, she left him in the lurch when she found that he was part of the group chasing them in Norway. Help me convince her that simply because he was on the wrong side and doing his job is not a valid reason for leaving him."

Jacob looked totally stunned. "How can you encourage her to fall for a German?" he blurted out. "They killed my brother and a lot of other good Americans!"

Looking as if she wanted to strangle him, Molly shook her finger. "Don't you dare insinuate that I don't feel deeply about the Americans that were killed or wounded by the Germans. I do, and so does Jennifer! In fact, it was a long time before Jennifer would even treat the wounded prisoners."

After taking several breaths and trying to calm down, Molly continued. "Jennifer got to know this man Otto Bruner as a person rather than a soldier. It is the person that she fell in love with. Then she had the bad luck of finding out that he had been in Norway in pursuit of them."

"Who said I was in love with him?" Jennifer shrieked.

"Now hold on a minute," Dunbar said looking at Jennifer. "I don't know whether you love him or not. But after thinking on it, my dear, I have to agree with Molly. He was merely doing his duty." Jennifer just shook her head, sobbing.

Dunbar put his hand on her shoulder and gently rubbed it. "I remember him, of course. He seemed like an honorable chap, disregarding the fact that he was an enemy soldier. I must say that it was most kind of him to give us that hour to bury the professor. It may have ended up saving our lives."

"I don't believe any of this," Jacob blurted out.

"If she truly loves the German," Sandy said, "I think Dude would want her to be with him."

Jacob shook his head. "That's totally outrageous!"

Jacob," Molly interjected, "if you don't start helping, you and I will be stepping outside!" Jacob glared at her momentarily and then chuckled. "You are a feisty one, aren't you?"

"You bet I am!"

The tension subsided, and everyone but Jennifer laughed. Her thoughts were now elsewhere.

"Do you think that I could find him in Germany?" she asked Dunbar. "Given the state it's in?"

"Europe is a mess, all right. But I would say that you could find him if anybody can. Of course, I will be more than willing to provide what limited assistance I can."

Jennifer thanked him, remembering the anguished look in Otto's eyes as she'd stormed off the last time she saw him. What if her rejection had caused him to give up? What if he truly had nothing to live for back in Germany? What if he hadn't survived?

Soon, they were saying their farewells. Almost choking on the words, Jacob told Jennifer that he wanted her to be happy, and if it meant spending her life with Otto, he would approve. That earned him an extra hug.

"Where are you two staying?" Jennifer asked.

"We're staying in Sausalito," Sandy replied. "We thought it would be romantic to take a moonlight cruise over there."

Looking up at the somewhat shrouded stars, Dunbar said, "You've picked a perfect night for it." Perhaps that was a bit of an exaggeration, but no one took exception to it. The three waived as Jacob and Sandy disappeared into the foggy San Francisco evening.

That left only Dunbar and Molly with Jennifer.

"Where are you staying, Frank?" Jennifer asked.

"I'm out at Travis Air Field. That's where I'll be leaving from in the morning."

"Thanks for coming all this way, especially for such a short time."

"I wouldn't have missed it for anything," Dunbar said. Taking Jennifer's hands in his, he continued. "I wish you the best, and I look forward to seeing you at the wedding."

The two embraced, looking at each other with an intensity that reflected all that they had been through together.

"Please tell Mr. Churchill hello for me."

"I certainly will," Dunbar replied. "Oh, by the way, Molly, you're invited, too!"

"Thanks, big guy. I'll be delighted to come."

The colonel waved down a cab, and soon he was gone. Jennifer looked at Molly with mock anger. "I should be mad at you for stirring up a hornet's nest!" she said. "But you may have saved me from the biggest mistake of my life."

"That's what best friends are for. And I want you to know that I'll go to Europe with you to find lover boy."

"Thank you," Jennifer replied. "Your company will be most welcome."

"By the way," she added. "where are you staying?"

"Wherever you are," Molly replied. "Why do you think I've been lugging this suitcase with me?"

"I should have known," Jennifer said giggling. "You're lucky there's a spare bed in my room."

"Well, am I welcome to it or not?"

"You certainly are, and I'll even carry your bag!"

As the two walked to the cable car, Jennifer promised herself that she would not let anything keep her from finding Otto and determining if he was the right man for her. She knew that Dude would approve and that he'd want her to be happy. While she'd previously thought that her greatest adventure was behind her, now it appeared as if it was just beginning!

Acknowledgements

For those of you who haven't yet published, I can assure you that those famous words, "It's a Long Way to Tipperary," are totally applicable to writing a novel. I started on this magnificent journey about five years ago, and I had no idea that it would take so long to get the book into print. But the wait was well worth it, and I am delighted that the story is now ready to be shared with you.

I owe a great deal to family, friends, and colleagues.

First of all I want to thank my wife, Linda, for her continued encouragement, support, and suggestions. But most of all I want to thank her for always stopping to listen when I wanted to talk about my latest thoughts on the book.

I want to thank Sally Wood for her early encouragement and editorial suggestions. Fellow author Dick Peck deserves my thanks for his encouragement and many suggestions, including the one that I contact Frank Zoretich. I fondly nicknamed Frank the "Red Quill." Frank taught me about SDT and POV.

Patti Dammier, the wife of a colleague, made the suggestion that I contact iUniverse. Patti published with them in the past and was pleased. I was assigned to Rosalie White, who has done a tremendous job of helping me, and, as they say, the rest is history.

Others who deserve my thanks for their encouragement, comments, and interest are: Andrea Aiello, Mr. and Mrs. Francis D. Baty, Patricia and Russ Bearly, Mary and Walt Bishop, Jane and Don Bonnell, Phyllis and Robert Boverie, Sharon and Ray Bruce, Carolyn Calloway and Bill Schuler, Becky Cavallo, Barb Chase, Michelle Crowe, Sue and Bill Fickel, Lois and Marty Fleck, Marion Fleck, Dorothea and Ed Fortier, Rosemary Gregory, Gretchen Jones, Lores Klingbeil, Sara Livingston, Clara Lou Nanninga, Paula G. Paul, Karen and Jim Phippard, Nita Pileckas, Mary and Ray Reed, Ann Rehovec, Bernadette Salcido, Barb Scott, Helen Shuster, Joyce Smith, Barbara Vanderpool, Shirley Kay Wolfersperger, and Hannah Wood.